My Best Friend's Girl

DOROTHY KOOMSON

sphere

SPHERE

First published in paperback in Great Britain in 2006 by
Time Warner Books
Reprinted 2006 (seventeen times)
Reprinted by Sphere in 2006
Reprinted 2006 (three times), 2007 (three times), 2008 (three times)

A CIP catalogue record for this book
is available from the British Library.

ISBN 978-0-7515-3707-9

Typeset in Bembo by M Rules
Printed and bound in Great Britain by Clays Ltd, St Ives plc

Papers used by Sphere are natural, renewable and recyclable
products made from wood grown in sustainable forests and certified
in accordance with the rules of the Forest Stewardship Council.

Sphere
An imprint of
Little, Brown Book Group
100 Victoria Embankment
London EC4Y 0DY

An Hachette Livre UK Company
www.hachettelivre.co.uk

www.littlebrown.co.uk

For

Sam, Kathleen and David – you're three of
the most courageous, loving and interesting people
I've ever known.

I just want to say: 'I'm smiling because you're my
siblings, I'm laughing because there's nothing you
can do about it.'

thank you

Emily Partridge, Richard Atkinson and Alix Johnson for taking the time to read the early versions of this book and being an incredible trio of cheerleaders.

Maryam, Dawood, Maraam, Muneerah, Yusuf, Ahmad and Ameerah; Lyiah, Sky, Aasia and Joshua; Luc; Jonathan and Rachel; Ellie and Sam, and Georgia for letting me into your worlds and being, in your own ways, the inspiration for this story.

Agnes and Samuel Koomson, my wonderful parents, for all your support and love over the years.

Habibah, David and Jade, for making honest people of my siblings.

Sharon Wright and David Jacobson, Stella Eleftheriades, Emma Hibbs, Rhian Clugston, Christian Lewis, Janet Cunniff, Andy Baker, Adam Gold, Bibi Lynch, Graeme Delap, Jean Jollands, Marian and Gordon Ndumbe, Martin and Sachiko O'Neill, Sarah Berger, Jo Thorne and Matthew Keenan, Emma Frost, Margi Conklin, Shona Abhyankar, Rose Obianwu, Stuart Smith, and Ginny and Paul Baillie, for being there. Always. I couldn't have done it without you.

Sarah Ball, Denise Ryan and Natasha Harrison, my novel-ist buddies, for the pep talks, plot analysis and phone calls in the middle of the night.

Rebecca Buttrose, Rebecca Carman and Lucy Tumanow-West, for all your help Down Under.

Antony Harwood and James Macdonald Lockhart for being the first to believe in the book and for being the best agents in the world – and I say that having lived on different sides of the globe.

Joanne Dickinson for your honest editing, belief in my book and the brilliant chats. You're a star!

Jennifer Richards and Louise Davies for the beautiful cover and eagle-eyed editing.

To you, for buying this book. I hope you enjoy it.

prologue

To be honest, I'd been tired for so long I don't remember, not accurately, when I realised something serious was wrong with me. I put up with it, though. Told myself I needed more rest and that it'd pass. But it didn't.

No matter how much I slept I was always tired. Proper, bone tired. It wasn't until Tegan asked me to go to the doctor that I realised. My four-year-old actually voiced what I couldn't – wouldn't – face, the simple fact that I wasn't myself any more. She'd gotten tired of me being too exhausted to play with her. Of me having nosebleeds. Of me being breathless after even the smallest amount of exertion. 'Mummy, if you go to the doctor she can make you better,' she said one day out of the blue. Just said it, and I did it.

I sat in the doctor's, told her what was wrong, and she did a blood test. Then called me in for more tests. More tests with names and words I'd heard on the medical shows on telly, then words that never had a happy ending on TV were being bandied around. But they couldn't truly have anything to do with me. Not really. They were eliminating possibilities.

Then, I got the call. The call saying I had to go see my doctor straight away. Even then . . . And even when she told me . . . When she said she was sorry and then started talking about treatments and prognosis, I didn't believe it. No, that's not right. I did believe it. I just didn't understand. Not why. Not how. Not me.

It took a good few days for what I'd been told to sink in. Maybe even a week. Every second counted, they said, but I still couldn't comprehend. I didn't look that ill. A little paler, a little slower, but not really and truly ill. I kept thinking they were wrong. You hear about it all the time, the wrong diagnosis, people defying the doctors' theories, people finding out they had glandular fever instead of . . .

About a week later, on my way to work, I got to the train station early, mega early, as usual. You see, I'd built lots of compensators — things that made normal activities easier — into my life to accommodate the disease invading my body: I left for the station early so I wouldn't ever have to run for the train; I brought food to work so I wouldn't have to walk to the sandwich shop at lunchtime; I cut the childminder's hours so I wouldn't be tempted to go for a drink after work.

Anyway, on this particular day I sat at the station and a woman came and stood beside me. She got her mobile out of her bag and made a call. When the person on the other end picked up she said, 'Hello, it's Felicity Halliday's mother here. I'm calling because she's not very well and she won't be coming to school today.' I fell apart. Just broke down in tears. It hit me then, right then, that I would never get the chance to make a call like that. I would not get to do a simple mum thing like call my daughter's school. There were a million things I would never get to do again and that was one of them.

Everyone was terribly British about it all and ignored me as I cried and sobbed and wailed. Yes, wailed. I made a hideous noise as I broke into a million, trillion pieces.

Then this man, this angel, came to me, sat down, put his arm around me and held me while I cried. The train came, the train left. As did the next one and the next one. But this man stayed with me. Stayed with me as I cried and cried. I totally soaked and snotted up the shoulder of his nice suit jacket but he didn't seem to mind, he waited and held me until I stopped wailing. Then he gently asked me what was wrong.

Through my sobs, all I could say was, 'I've got to tell my little girl I'm going to die.'

'mummy?'

chapter one

The postman jumped as I snatched open the front door to my block of flats and eagerly greeted him.

Usually when we came face to face, he'd have buzzed up to my first floor flat and I'd come shuffling down, pulling on my dressing gown as I tried to rub dried sleep drizzle off my face. Today, though, I'd been hanging out of my window waiting for him. I was still in my usual post-receiving attire of dressing gown and had sleep-sculpted hair, but this time my eyes weren't barely open slits, I'd washed my face and I was smiling.

'Special day, is it?' he said without humour.

He clearly didn't like this reversal of roles. He wanted me to be sedate and disorientated when he handed over my post. It was probably the only power trip he got of a day. Ahhh, that's not fair. He was lovely, my postman. Most postmen are nice, aren't they?

In fact, everyone in the world was lovely today.

'It's my birthday,' I grinned, showing off my freshly cleaned teeth.

'Happy birthday,' he commented, dour as a priest at prayer time, and handed over the post for the four flats in our block. I keenly took the bundle that was bound up by a brown elastic band, noting that almost all of the envelopes were red or purple or blue. Basically, card coloured. 'Twenty-one again, eh?' the postie said, still unwilling to be infected by my good humour.

'Nope, I'm thirty-two and proud,' I replied. 'Every birthday is a bonus! And anyway, today I get to wear gold sequins and high heels and brush gold dust all over my cleavage.'

The postie's small brown eyes flicked down to my chest area. Even though it was the height of a long, hot, humid summer, I was wearing pyjamas and a big towelling dressing gown, so he didn't see anything suggestive – he was lucky to get even a glimpse of my throat skin. That seemed to startle him, that the chest of which I spoke was highly covered, and he immediately snatched his eyes away again. It'd probably occurred to him that he shouldn't be eyeing up the women on his delivery route – especially when said lady wasn't even undressed enough to make it worth his while.

He started backing away. 'Have a good day, love,' he said. 'I mean, dear. I mean, bye.' And then he legged it down the garden path far quicker than a man of his girth and age should be able to.

The postman moved so fast he probably didn't even hear me call 'You too' after him as I shut the door. I slung the letters that weren't for me, but had the audacity to arrive at this address today, on the floor of the hallway. They landed unceremoniously on top of the other, older letters that sat like orphaned children, waiting, longing, to be rescued. I usually felt sorry for those letters, wished the people they'd been sent to would give them a good home, but they weren't my problem today. I barely gave them a second thought as I took the stairs two at a time back up to my flat.

In my bedroom I had already laid out my birthday breakfast feast: fresh croissants with smoked salmon, three chocolate truffles and a glass of Möet.

Everything had to be perfect today. Everything. I'd planned it that way. After I'd devoured my special brekky, I'd stay in bed until midday, opening birthday cards while receiving calls from well-wishing friends and relatives. Then I had an appointment at the hairdresser to get my hair washed, deep conditioned and cut. I was going for a radical change – ditching my usual chin-length bob for a style with long layers and a sweeping fringe. After that, I'd come back home and get dressed up. I really was going to wear a dress of gold sequins that set off my dark skin in a spectacular fashion. I was going to squeeze my feet into gold high heels and I was going to brush gold dust over my cleavage. And then a few of the girls from work were coming round for drinks and nibbles before we went into town to dance the night away.

I slipped carefully under the sheets, not wanting to spill any of the special spread, then took a swig of champagne before I tore through my cards like a child. Around me the pile of brightly coloured envelopes grew as I tugged out the cards and smiled at the words written inside.

It wasn't dim of me, then, not to notice it. It was like all the others. Slipped in among the bundle, innocuous and innocent looking. And, like all the others, I didn't really look at it, didn't try to decipher the handwriting on envelope, ignored the picture on the front. I simply opened it, eager to receive the message of love that had been scrawled inside. My heart stopped. I recognised the handwriting before I read the words. The words I read with a racing heart.

Dear Kamryn, Please don't ignore this.
I need to see you. I'm dying. I'm in St Jude's Hospital
in central London.
Yours, Adele x PS, I miss you.

Slamming it shut I registered for the first time that the card had 'I love you' on it instead of one of the usual birthday greetings. The piece of glossy cardboard sailed across the room when

I slung it as though it had burnt my fingers. It landed on the wicker laundry basket and sat there staring at me. With its white front and simple design, and three treacherous words, it sneered at me. Daring me to ignore it. Daring me to pretend the words inside weren't carved into my brain like they were scored onto the card.

I took a slug of my champagne but it tasted like vinegar in my mouth. The croissant, carefully sliced and filled with smoked salmon, was like sawdust as I chewed. The truffles were paste on my tongue.

Still the card stared at me. Goading me. *Ignore me if you can*, it mocked. *Go on, try it.*

I threw back the covers, got out of bed and went over to the card. Dispassionately, I tore it in half. Then tore those pieces in half again. I stomped into the kitchen, stamped on the pedal bin to open it and dropped the remains on top of the rotting vegetables, the greasy leftovers and discarded wrappers.

'There. That's what I think of that! And you!' I hissed at the card and its sender.

I returned to my bed. That was better. Much better. I sipped my champagne and ate my food. And everything was all right again. Perfect, even. Just like it should be on my birthday.

Nothing could ruin it. No matter how much anyone tried. And they were bloody trying, weren't they? You don't try much harder than with that message, dressed up as a birthday card. Very clever. Very bloody clever. Well it wasn't going to work. I wasn't falling for that nonsense. I was going to carry on with my plan. I was going to make my thirty-second more special than my eighteenth, twenty-first and thirtieth birthdays combined.

Because when I am thirty-two I shall wear gold sequins and six-inch stilettos and brush gold dust over my cleavage, just as I promised myself ages ago.

★

The door was ajar and didn't protest as I gently pushed on it. I didn't knock. I never knocked on an already open door because to me it always said, 'Come, no knocking required.'

From her place amongst her white pillows she smiled as I stepped into view. 'I knew you'd come,' she whispered.

chapter two

Dolce & Gabbana. Even now, at what was probably one of the darkest hours of her life, Adele wore designer clothes – a white D&G T-shirt peeked out under the covers. She always did have more style than sense.

At one time, that thought, twisted as it was, would've been out of my mouth – callously uttered to her because she would've appreciated it. I couldn't today. Things had drastically changed between us. Firstly, I hadn't seen her in two years. Secondly, the last time I saw her, she had her fingers buried in her hair as though on the verge of ripping out her blonde locks from their roots, mascara was running down her face and snot was dribbling out of her nose. She was talking, stumbling over her words, saying things I didn't want to hear. I was grabbing my clothes and my bag and blinking back tears and trying not to collapse in a heap. Things don't go back to being normal after you part on those terms. Thirdly, she was ill.

We didn't speak as a nurse fussed around Adele, noting the readings on the machines, checking the lines on the drips, plumping up the pillows so they propped the patient upright. The nurse had a round, friendly face with big brown smiling eyes. She reminded me a lot of my mother, particularly because of the way she'd pulled her plaited hair back into a ponytail. She grinned at me as though she knew me, told Adele not to talk for too long and left us to it.

Still we didn't speak. 'Hi' seemed a pretty insufficient way to greet someone I'd sworn never to communicate with ever again. Someone I'd done my best never to communicate with again.

'That nurse reminds me of your mum,' Adele said when the silence had started to drown out even the hum of the machines.

I nodded in agreement but couldn't bring myself to talk. I just couldn't. This wasn't the Adele – Del as I called her – I'd come to see, this wasn't the Adele I'd braced myself to talk to after all this time.

I don't know what I expected, hadn't really thought about it when I got on that train to travel two hundred miles from Leeds to London, but I didn't expect her to look like this. I could close my eyes and see the Del I expected to see. That mass of curly honey-blonde hair, which was always trimmed to shoulder length, would be there. As would that smooth, healthy glow of her creamy-white skin. What would be the clearest thing about the image? Her eyes, which were the blue-grey colour of highly polished steel, or her smile, which would always light up everything around her? Whichever it was, behind my eyelids, the real Del would be there. So perfect and three-dimensional I could reach out and hug her.

With my eyes open, Del Brannon was different. Altered.

The Del who was propped up in bed had skin that was a blotched patchwork of grey, white and yellow. Her face was hollowed out from her weight loss, and under her sunken eyes, conspicuously missing their eyebrows, deep dark circles were scored. Around her head was tied a royal blue scarf, probably to hide her lack of hair. My body went cold. Her beautiful, beautiful hair was all gone. Stripped away by the drugs that were meant to make her well.

I didn't know she'd look like this. Frail. Like an anaemic

autumn leaf – so dried, brittle and fragile that one touch would crumble her into a million pieces.

'It's good to see you,' she said, her voice a low rasp that was probably as painful to create as it was to hear. 'I'm glad you came.'

'What's with the voice?' I asked.

'It's the treatment. Makes my mouth dry and my tongue feels like it's grown shag pile.'

'God, remember when we felt like that because we'd actually enjoyed ourselves by getting drunk the night before?' I commented, then mentally slapped myself. I didn't mean it the way it sounded – I was trying to express sympathy but it'd come out wrong.

Del's dry, cracked lips pulled up into a smile. 'Trust you,' she said. 'No one else has dared say something like that to me. Too scared of making me cry, I suppose. Too scared that I might break down and die on them. Trust you to break the taboo.'

'It wasn't intentional,' I replied, suitably shamefaced. 'Just being myself.'

'I wouldn't want you any other way,' she said.

'What's wrong with you?' I asked. That sounded wrong, too. Harsh. Unfeeling. Admittedly, part of me was still that woman who was picking up her belongings and swearing to herself she'd never be that hurt again, but most of me was broken-hearted. I was used to solving problems with action and here I was, staring at someone who was in pain, knowing I couldn't do a damn thing about it. That's why I sounded so harsh. I was helpless and I didn't 'do' helpless very well. 'I mean, you said you were . . . What are you ill with?'

'Leukaemia,' she replied.

'I thought only children got that,' I said before I could stop myself.

'That's what I said!' she exclaimed. 'You know, when the doctor told me, I said those exact words. It went down like a cup of cold sick, I can tell you.'

'Glad to know it's not only me who says inappropriate things,' I muttered loudly.

'Yep, even when I'm at death's door.' She said that so blithely, calmly. I had an urge to reach out, take hold of her bony shoulders and shake her. Violently. So violently that she was reminded what was going on. How could she be so laid-back about it? So comfortable with the notion?

I was still struggling to understand how someone who was my age, who went to the gym, who ate relatively healthily, who had never smoked, who drank as much as I had woke up one day to find there was a clock ticking over her head; discovered she was one step closer to knowing when she'd meet her maker than I was. I'd been wrestling with this thought since I read the card she sent me.

'It's all right, you know, I've accepted what's happening to me,' Del reassured me, as though reading my thoughts. 'It took a while but I'm here. I know it's going to take you a while to catch up.'

'Only a little while,' I said sarcastically.

'I had to get here quickly,' she continued, ignoring not what I'd said but how I'd said it. 'I had to make plans. It's not just about me. So, no matter how much I wanted to pretend it wasn't happening, I had to remember the most important person that needs taking care of.'

Tegan. She was talking about her daughter Tegan. How was she taking this? If I was having problems dealing with it, how was a clever little five-year-old coping?

'I suppose you've worked out why I wanted to see you,' she said after another long silence had passed.

'To make me feel guilty for ignoring you for two years?' I replied.

13

'Apart from that,' Del said, a sly smile playing around her grey lips.

'Well then, no.'

'After I'm gone . . .' Del paused, took a deep breath, 'I want you to adopt Tegan.'

'What?'

'I want . . . No, I *need* you to adopt Tegan after I die.'

I could feel the frown creasing my forehead, and my face twisting itself into an 'Are you mad?' look.

She stared back at me as if she expected an answer to what she'd just said.

'You're joking, right?'

'Do I look like I'm joking?' she replied, exasperated. 'If I was joking there'd be a punchline and it'd be funny. No, *Kamryn*, I'm not joking. I want you to adopt my daughter when I die.'

'All right, *Adele*, if you're serious, I'll give you a serious answer. No. Absolutely no.'

'You haven't even thought about it.'

'There's nothing to think about. You've always known that I don't want children. I told you enough times, I'm not having kids.'

'I'm not asking you to have kids, just my one.' Del inhaled deeply, a move that seemed to take all her strength and added to her grey colour. 'I've done all the hard stuff, morning sickness, losing my figure, twenty-four hours in labour . . . You just have to look after her. Be her mother. Love her.'

'Just' look after her. 'Just' be her mother. Like that was easy. And anyway . . . 'Del, we haven't even *spoken* in two years and now you're asking me to adopt a child? Can you see what's wrong with this picture? Why I'm having problems with this?'

'Tegan isn't "a child",' she snarled, instantly enraged. Of all the outrageous things I'd said since I arrived, this was the one

14

that got her goat; that made her so angry her steel-blue eyes seemed to pulsate with the defiance that now sat in them. 'She's your godchild. You loved her once, I refuse to believe that's changed.'

I couldn't argue with that. I had loved Tegan. I still loved Tegan.

I glanced at the photo on her nightstand. It was in a plain glass frame, a big close-up picture of Tegan and Del. Tegan had her arms linked around her mum's neck, holding her mum's face as close as possible to hers. They were both grinning at the camera. Tegan was a miniature version of her mother in every respect except her nose. The shape of her nose she inherited from her father.

'Kam, I still think of you as my best friend,' Del was saying. 'And you're the only person, the *only* person on *earth* I'd trust with my daughter.

'She was like your child once. And, I'm sorry to lay this on you, but I don't know how long I've got left, I can't afford to mess about. If you don't take her . . . What will happen to her? There's no one else. There's no one—' The whites of her eyes darkened with red and her chest started to heave. 'I can't even cry,' she whispered between heaves, 'because I'm not producing enough tears.' Instead of crying, she started to choke, each cough convulsing her thinned body.

I lay a hand on her forearm. 'Please don't,' I said, desperate to stop her. 'I'll think about it. But I'm not promising anything, all right?'

Del kept inhaling deeply until she'd calmed down. 'You'll really think about it?' she said when she was calm enough to speak.

'Yes. I'll think about it.'

'That's all I ask, that you think about it.'

'And I will. But only think.'

'Thank you,' she whispered. 'Thank you.'

We lapsed into silence. I should be going. She'd done the deed, had asked the unthinkable of me, so what was there to do but for me to leave, retreat and think about it as I promised?

'Kam,' she began. The way she said my name made me look at her and I knew instantly what she was going to say next. I didn't want her to say it. I wanted her to leave it. 'About what happened—'

'Don't,' I cut in, a warning note in my voice.

'You never let me explain,' she pleaded.

'Don't,' I warned again.

'Kam, listen to me. I didn't . . .'

'I SAID DON'T!' I shouted so suddenly and brutally that I even frightened myself. 'I don't want to think about it, I don't want to hear about it, and I *certainly* don't want to talk about it. It's over with. *Leave it.*'

It was a wound that hadn't healed. She'd been picking at a superficial scab, one that skimmed the surface of an injury that was so deep even the slightest jolt would have it gushing blood again. But still, I shouldn't have unleashed my anger like that. She *was* ill. She didn't have the strength to fight back.

'Just leave it,' I repeated in a calmer tone. 'Please.'

Del did as she was told and refocused her line of sight on the picture on her nightstand. She half smiled, but I could see the sadness tugging around her eyes. Tegan was everything to Adele. Everything. I could never fully understand that, I suppose. Tegan was important to me, but she seemed to be Adele's reason for living. Everything she did, thought and said was about Tegan. Nothing and no one came before Adele's child. The idea of leaving her must be more than she could bear. And how do you explain to a child that you're leaving them? How do you tell your child you're dying?

'Where is she?' I asked in an attempt to diffuse the tension in the room and the guilt in my soul.

She closed her eyes briefly, as though pained, before

16

delivering her next bombshell in a quiet voice. 'With my father and his wife.'

My heart skipped a beat. Were things so bad she'd really left Tegan with them? 'And how's that been?' I asked diplomatically, instead of screaming, 'Are you mad?' at her.

'Awful,' Adele replied. The whites of her eyes reddened again, she'd be crying if she could. 'They don't let me see her. Since I've been in here they've brought her to see me once. Once in four weeks. It's too far, they say, so they only bring her when it's convenient. I speak to her on the phone but it's not the same.

'I miss her so much. And I can tell every time I speak to her that she's becoming more depressed. More withdrawn. She can't understand why she can't be with me now that I need her most. My father and his wife don't want her there and she knows it. Kam, I want to be with my daughter. I've only got a little while and I want to spend it with her.' She looked at me, her steel-blue eyes beseeching me, asking me to solve this problem for her. 'I just want to see her. Before, you know.'

No, I don't know. I'm still playing catch up, remember? I'm not on that page yet, Del, I silently replied. 'Isn't there anyone else she can stay with?' I asked out loud. I knew she had no other family but surely she had some other friends? Anyone but her father and stepmother.

'No. When I first realised I was seriously sick, I wrote to you to ask if you could take care of Tegan for a while but you never replied.'

'I never opened the letter,' I replied honestly. I still had it, I'm sure. Shoved at the bottom of my knicker drawer like all the other correspondence from her – I was too indignant to open them but too cowardly to bin them. They sat in the drawer, growing older and dustier, unopened and mostly ignored.

'I guessed you didn't. I tried a couple of other people, but they couldn't take on such a big responsibility, so it had to be my father.' Del always called him that, 'my father'. To his face she called him 'Father'. Never did she call him 'Dad' or 'Daddy'. There was always a level of formality between them – even now, it seemed. 'When we moved in he was so hard on Tegan, but I didn't have the strength to fight him and his wife. If there was one thing I could do differently it'd be to take back what—'

'Do they still live in the same place, down in Guildford?' I cut in. I wasn't going to let her sneak up on that conversation again.

She shook her head slightly. 'Tegan got that stubbornness from you,' Del said. 'She's exactly like that, won't do or talk about anything she doesn't want to. I used to think she got it from me, but no, it's clearly from you. But yes, they still live down in Guildford.'

'OK.' I took a deep breath. *Can't believe I'm about to do this.* 'What if I go down and see her?'

Del's face brightened. 'You'll do that?'

'I'm not saying I'll adopt her or anything, I'll just go see if she's all right. OK? Just a visit.'

'Thank you,' Del smiled. 'Thank you, thank you, thank you.'

'Will she even remember who I am?' I asked.

'Course. She still draws you in pictures. Talks about you. And those anonymous cards and pressies you send on her birthday and at Christmas, I always tell her they're from you. She always asks when you're going to come back from holiday.'

'Holiday?'

'You left so suddenly I told her you had to go on holiday for a long time. Because then she'd think you were coming back. Neither of us could've stood it if there wasn't at least the hope that you'd come back,' she said. Her eyelids suddenly shut and stayed closed.

Anxiety twisted my stomach as time ticked by but she didn't open her eyes. The machines were still rhythmically bleeping so I knew she wasn't . . . But what if this was the start of it? What if this was the decline into . . .

Del's eyelids crept apart until they were thin slits, her sallow skin was greyer than it had been when I arrived. I was tiring her out. I should go. But I didn't want to. I wanted to stay with her. Be with her. Just in case . . . I wanted to sit here all day. All night. For ever.

'I'd better go,' I said, forcing myself not to be so silly. I couldn't do anything here. I'd do more good by bringing news of her baby. 'If I'm going to see Tegan today I'd better be making tracks.' I stood up, hoisted my bag on to my shoulder.

'Give her my love.' Del's voice was as weak as tissue paper. 'Tell her Mummy loves her.'

'I will,' I said. 'Course I will.'

I paused at the doorway, waiting for Del's reply. I got nothing. I turned to her and saw from the slow rise and fall of her chest that she was asleep. I watched her sleep for a few moments, fancying myself as some kind of guardian angel, watching over her, keeping her safe. Again I told myself off for being silly, then I walked out of the room. Walked out of the room, out of the hospital and into the nearest pub.

chapter three

Adele and I had known each other for nearly half of our lives – fourteen of our thirty-two years. We'd met in the first year at Leeds University, when we were assigned to work on an English assignment together.

I'd internally groaned when I heard that I was going to be studying with Adele Hamilton-Mackenzie. At eighteen I was a staunch working-class citizen and now I was being forced to team up with someone who was clearly from a well-to-do family, what with her having a double-barrelled surname and everything. Plus, she was bound to be a public school wanker with the kind of accent that would make me want to slap her. She turned her blonde head and sought out Kamryn Matika across the class. She smiled and dipped her head at me, I did the same before she turned back to the front. *God*, I thought bitterly, *she's bound to think the world revolves around her. And she'll try to order me about. No doubt about it, I'm cursed. And that curse involves me working with some silly slapper with an accent.*

At the end of the class, I gathered up my books and pens, planning to make the quickest getaway known to womankind, but as I straightened up from stuffing my belongings into my cloth rucksack, ready to hightail it out of the lecture hall, I was confronted by a slender eighteen-year-old who was dressed like a fifty-year-old in a blue polo neck and blue polyester slacks. I was taken aback by how quickly she'd appeared in front of me, it was almost as if she'd popped out of thin air.

She grinned at me with straight white teeth, and tossed her mass of silky blonde hair.

'Hi, I'm Adele,' she said, her voice as bright and lively as it was thorough-bred. *She's perky as well as posh, can my life get any worse?* I thought. 'How about we nab a coffee and talk about the assignment.' It wasn't a question, more a vague order.

'I think we should go away and think about it and meet up in a few days,' I replied through a teeth-clenchingly fake smile. No one ordered me about – vaguely or otherwise. Besides, which eighteen-year-old in her right mind actually worked on a project on the day they'd been given it? Not me, certainly.

In response, Adele's poise disintegrated until her shoulders were hunched forwards and her gaze was fixed desolately on the parquet floor. She wasn't as self-assured as she acted, and I wasn't as brazen and hard-faced as I pretended. I might start off giving that impression, might act cold and unapproachable, but I always let myself down when my conscience kicked in – I had no bitch follow-through.

'Not a fan of coffee to be honest,' I said, trying to sound friendly, 'how about we go get a drink in the college bar instead?'

'If you're sure?' she replied cautiously.

'Yup,' I muttered, feeling suitably manipulated, 'I'm sure.'

'What kind of a name is Kamryn, anyway?' Adele asked me without shame.

'A made-up one,' was my terse reply. I'd spotted her student union card when she'd been hunting for change in her purse earlier and knew for a fact that I was sharing valuable drinking and conversational time with Lucinda-Jayne Adele Hamilton-Mackenzie. So, her asking about my moniker when she was Girly Two-Hyphen Name was an audacious step too far.

21

'It's not a spelling mistake? Your name is Kamryn. K A M R Y N,' she spelt it out. 'Not C A M E R O N, Cameron like the boy's name?'

'Actually, it is. I thought it'd be fun to pretend it was spelt differently. I love people asking me about it. You're so wise, you caught me out. You're clearly Miss Marple's clever younger sister.'

Adele raised her left eyebrow slightly and twisted her lip-glossed mouth into a wry smile. 'You're not very friendly, are you?' she commented.

'I guess not,' I agreed. It'd taken her four drinks to discover I wasn't the sharing kind. Far too many people opened their hearts and lives at the drop of a hat, as far as I was concerned. Why give someone that power over you? Why endow them with the ability to hurt you that much? Let someone in and you were asking for an emotional kicking some day.

'At least you know it,' she said, and knocked back half her Malibu and coke in one dainty, lady-like gulp. 'But despite that, I like you.'

'I'm honoured.'

'No, I am.' She placed a slender hand above her left breast. 'I truly am.'

She stared at me with such a friendly, open expression that I couldn't help but bite the proffered bait. 'Why's that then?' I asked.

'You're lovely.' She even sounded truthful. 'I haven't met many lovely people in my life. So, when I do, I feel honoured. When I first saw you across that classroom I got an instant feeling of how lovely you are. You pretend you're all prickly but underneath, not even that far underneath, you're simply gorgeous.'

'Are you a lesbian or something?' I asked brusquely.

'No, I'm not,' she laughed. 'But if I was, I'd definitely fancy you.'

'I wouldn't blame you,' I lied. Not even short, fat, ugly men fancied me. And I couldn't blame them: I wore baggy clothes to hide my weight; I had never applied make-up to my dry, spotty skin; I only tamed the mass of frizz masquerading as my hair by plaiting it into shoulder-length black extensions. I had no illusions at all that I was beautiful, pretty or even able to attract the right sort of attention from men. Especially when on top of the paucity in the looks area, I was lacking the *je ne sais quoi* that attracted men to ugly girls: I wasn't funny, wasn't friendly and wasn't going to use sex to get attention. In short, the Wicked Witch of the West probably saw more duvet action than me.

'You're so full of shit,' Adele laughed. (Shit sounded odd, *wrong*, coming out of her mouth. From me, with my London accent, swearing sounded like any other word unless you emphasised it. From Adele's posh mouth it sounded like a mini rebellion. She spoke like she should be saying 'phooey!' or 'sugar!' instead of 'shit'. 'You're so full of phooey,' would've sounded more meaningful, not as if she was trying too hard to shock those around her.) 'You don't believe that for a second,' she continued. 'That's why you're so prickly. You think people don't like or fancy you, so you exude the impression that you don't care what others think. I've seen your type before. I'd say you were bullied at school by boys. And you were probably bullied because you're different from other people. And unlikely to change to fit in.'

I recoiled from her. *How did she know that? How? Is everything that had happened written on my face?* Were the taunts, notes, phone calls, scrawls on walls all there, plain for any passing posh princess to see? What would I do if it was? College, two hundred miles from where anyone knew me, had been my escape. My getaway. My chance to leave all those hideous years behind and reinvent myself. Was it all a waste of time? Did I have 'misfit' imprinted on my forehead?

23

I forced a smile so Adele wouldn't know how close to the bone her words had sliced. *What should I say? How do I retaliate?*

To my smile she said, 'One of my friends from school was like you. Bullied to the point where she had no confidence in herself at all and shut out all her friends because she didn't think she could trust them. Actually, she wasn't really a friend. I don't have that many friends if I'm honest.'

'Well you're bound not to if you keep saying things like that,' I sniped.

'I was simply saying,' she protested.

'Yeah, well, maybe you shouldn't be "simply saying", especially when you know nothing about me. And what makes you such an expert when you've clearly come from a perfect life with rich parents who could send you to all the best private schools?' I was being a bitch and I didn't care. I wanted her to back the hell off. 'Huh? What makes you such an expert on crap lives?'

She picked up her drink, slowly swirled it around, making the melting ice cubes bump together. She glanced at me for a long while, then stared down into her drink. 'My mother died not long after I was born because of complications from childbirth. My father never wanted children, as he told me almost every day of my life, and he blamed me for my mother's death. My father wanted nothing to do with me so I spent a lot of time with a childminder until my father married again. His wife is not my biggest fan and she's never made a secret of it.' Adele looked up at me, smiled. 'I don't have many friends because I'm too much. I try too hard, that's what my last best friend told me. I try too hard, which makes me hard work. But I can't help it. I don't know how not to be who I am. I've spent so much time with people who don't like me, I try to avoid upsetting them.

'I do know a bit about crap lives. It's not as bad as some but it's certainly not perfect.'

I suddenly felt like an accidental mass murderer. 'Sorry,' I mumbled. 'I didn't realise.' The worst part was that she hadn't been trying to make me feel guilty for how I'd judged her, she was simply being honest. Adele was lacking in manipulative guile. I had no bitch follow-through and Adele had no side to her. She was upfront and open in everything she did.

'It's all right,' she said, sitting up, tossing back her hair and flashing me a big, bright smile. 'You weren't to know.'

'Listen, Adele, if we're going to hang around together you've got to cut that out,' I said.

'Cut what out?'

'Being so damn nice all the time. It's not natural.'

Adele's steel-blue eyes lit up. 'You want to hang around with me, to be my friend?'

I shrugged nonchalantly.

She grinned at me in return. This posh creature called Adele, the one who spoke as though she had five plums rammed in each cheek, grinned at me. That smile not only lit up her face, it put an effervescent gleam in her eyes and a rosy glow in her cheeks. The radiance of that smile flowed from her to me and I fell for her. Deeply. I couldn't help but like her. She was going to be an important part of my world. She was going to help shape the person I was to become. I didn't know how I knew, I simply did. For some unfathomable reason I knew she was going to be in my life for a very long time.

We became almost inseparable because we grew up together. Once Adele settled into college life she settled into her personality. She found herself and who she was. She stopped dressing like a fifty-year-old – slacks never darkened her body again, she often had a strop that involved shouting, swearing and throwing things. But she finally killed the timid Adele I'd had that drink with when she had her belly button pierced.

I, meanwhile, lost weight, smiled more and murdered the

Kamryn that Adele had that first drink with when I refused sex with a gorgeous man because he was wearing paisley-patterned Y-fronts. But all that was to come. At that moment, she'd been enormously happy that I'd shrugged my consent at the possibility of us hanging around together and I was secretly overjoyed that someone thought I was lovely.

'Anyway, I thought we already were friends,' Adele said. 'Every stranger is a friend you haven't met yet, and all that.'

'Oh, shut up and get the drinks in.'

I stood up from the pub table, stone-cold sober. I'd intended to drink myself into oblivion, to make all of this reality – returning to London, seeing how ill Del was – go away, but at the bar, instead of ordering a double vodka and orange, my drink of choice when oblivion was required, I'd asked for a double vodka and orange without the vodka.

The barman had been unimpressed, thought I was trying to be funny and glared at me before he reached for a glass. *I'm not being funny*, I wanted to say. *It's just, I've got this mate and she's never going to drink alcohol again. I can't do it either, out of loyalty to her.* But he wouldn't understand. And why would he care?

As it was the orange juice sans vodka went virtually undrunk as I sat remembering my first meeting with Del.

I slipped on my red rain mac. I had to get to Guildford, should have made the move down there over an hour ago. I'd been delaying the inevitable, though. The second I got on that train to Surrey I'd be embroiling myself further in this. I hadn't intended to do that. I'd meant to come down here, see how ill she was then get back on the train to Leeds the second I left the hospital. If I missed the last train, then I'd find a cheap B&B for the night and get on the first train back. No hanging around, no visiting friends and family who I hadn't seen since leaving London two years ago. Now I was getting embroiled right up to my neck.

I hoisted my holdall onto my shoulder. *Come on, bird,* I cajoled myself, *it's Guildford or bust.*

Adele became a member of my family. Christmas, Easter and summer holidays if I went home, she came with me. Her father and his wife weren't bothered that she never went home, they, in fact, didn't even pretend to care what happened to her. If she called, which I was always amazed she did, she'd come off the phone in bits. Always crying and on the verge of vomiting, always wondering what she could do, how she could change to make him love her even a little bit. I got used to putting her back together, to reassuring her that she was wonderful and loveable because I cared for her, because lots of other people adored her. And that maybe, one day, he'd see sense. I never believed that for a second, but it was what she wanted to hear so I said it, and sounded convincing to boot.

Mr Hamilton-Mackenzie was never going to change, I knew that. Not when I heard about the depth of his resentment towards her. When we first met Adele would often get falling-down drunk and confess how awful her life had been before Leeds. She'd tell me about her father's quick-to-discipline attitude. About time spent in hospital with broken arms, fractured legs, a cracked jaw as a result of being 'punished'. Once he'd knocked her through a ground-floor window and a piece of glass had lodged itself in her back, narrowly missing her kidney – the glass had to be removed by surgery. Another time he'd hit her with the buckle end of his belt and gouged out a huge chunk of her left thigh, meaning she rarely wore skirts.

Amazingly, annoyingly, depressingly, no one suspected what was going on. Or, if they did, they looked away, not wanting to get involved. No one noticed, it seemed, what was going on behind the closed doors of the Hamilton-Mackenzie household. They accepted it when Mr Hamilton-Mackenzie, a respectable, clean-cut example of white, middle-class decency, despaired time and again at his daughter's clumsiness, her tomboyishness that got her into scrapes, her silliness that made her hook up with rough boys.

Like me, Del's escape was college. She desperately wanted to be loved by her father, and the only way I could help her was to pretend that he was capable of it and say that one day he would. When I told her that, whether she believed me or not, it kept the hope alive in her, and even I knew we all need hope to survive.

My family weren't perfect but they were bothered – very vocally so – if I didn't go home every few months; they did call me regularly for a chat and, because she was my friend, they accepted Adele into the fold. Adele found a new place called home with the Matikas. It wasn't her real home, it wasn't the love of her father, but every time my mum told us off for waking up the house when we came in at 3 a.m.; every time my dad reached into his wallet and gave her a tenner to buy herself something; every time my sister asked for advice about her love life, it was almost as good as her real home. She felt she belonged.

Obviously, only one thing could possibly come between us: a man.

chapter four

This was surreal.

Being in London, a city I had fled over two years ago. But not just London, this particular area of it. Waterloo.

I wandered across Waterloo's huge station concourse, memories slamming into me with every step I took. No one seemed to notice how freaked out I was. How I walked slowly, expecting to run into a younger version of Adele, or even myself. Commuters just hurried around me; announcements for trains continued being thrown out over the loudspeakers; life rushed on oblivious. Oblivious to the fact that this is the place where I used to come to meet Adele after work for drinks when we were both single. When she wasn't ill and thin, the shadow of a person lying in that hospital bed. She used to work just around the corner and I used to get the tube here from Oxford Street, where I worked, so we could travel home together after a few drinks.

Waterloo was also remarkable for another reason. This was the place where I met him. At a house party just up the road from here. Him, the man who came between me and Adele.

He wasn't just any man, though. He was Nate Turner, my fiancé.

Nate walked into my life one cold April night and said he

didn't want to walk out of it again. I told him to try that line on a woman who might believe it. 'I'm going to win you over,' he'd stated seriously.

'Better men than you have failed,' I'd replied equally seriously.

Eighteen months later we decided to get married. And three years after that we set a date for the following year. We didn't have the perfect relationship, more a perfect understanding. He put up with a lot from me, had to deal with my issues.

My 'issues' weren't immediately obvious. By the time I met Nate my outward appearance was that nothing bothered me, that year after year of being called fat and ugly hadn't done a thing except to spur me on to success. No one, except maybe Adele, knew that beneath my adult veneer, beneath my confidence and great job and ability to sleep with good-looking men, beat the heart of a terrified girl.

The outside world, and even to an extent Adele, was taken in by my outward appearance; the impenetrable, polished image that I diligently maintained. People truly believed I was cool and haughty, confident and capable. Nate had seen through me. He discovered almost straight away the thing that terrified me more than anything else. My ultimate phobia? People.

It'd started before the bullying at school. I suspected it was what triggered the bullying – those who terrorised me saw that there was something not right about me, that I didn't fit in, that every conversation was underlined with the fear that they'd discover I wasn't like other people, and they exploited that terror.

I didn't seem to have that thing that binds us, makes us human. I struggled to make those connections, struggled to form relationships, even platonic ones. I grew up in a big family, was close to my siblings, but for some reason I never quite knew how to react in certain situations. I was so worried about messing up, about saying the wrong thing, of inciting wrath, that communication became an exercise in terror. And it made me seem stand-offish, judgmental and, in later years, a hard-faced bitch. It wasn't that I didn't want to relate to others, it was just that I didn't know how.

Then I met Adele and found I could do the communicating thing. I started to believe that I wasn't defective. Broken. I could form relationships.

I'd been seeing Nate for a few weeks when he told me he knew my secret. We'd gone to one of his work parties and from the moment I walked in I knew I didn't fit in. I wasn't dressed as classily as the other women, I didn't radiate their insouciant style and I didn't work in broadcast media. I tried to make polite conversation but I knew with every word I was confirming how different I was, how out of place I was. When, three torturous hours later, Nate said, 'Shall we go?' I was out the door and hailing a taxi before he'd finished forming 'shall'. Later, Nate wrapped himself around me like a cat curls around its owner's legs and said, 'People terrify you, don't they? That's why you're so cold. I saw you tonight, you were trying to talk, to connect with people, but you had such fear in your eyes.'

I sometimes think people can see that I'm defective, that there's nothing there. Behind the job and clothes and make-up there's nothing to know. I sometimes think I'm this shell and I can't work out why people like me. And when I'm with strangers it reminds me of that. That I'm insubstantial. I didn't say that to him, of course I didn't. Even if I could get the words out, why would a casual fling want to hear that?

To my silence he added, 'You don't have to be scared. I'll always look after you. I think you're amazing. You're everything to me, babe.' That upset me so much I got dressed and went home.

31

Nate didn't seem to care that I wasn't 100 per cent strong, independent and capable all the time, that he was with someone who had the potential to become needy and dependent. He took me as I was, loved me whether I was nice or nasty. He dealt with everything I threw at him, and then some.

It wasn't one-sided though. I put up with a lot from him, too. He came across as laid-back and infinitely secure, but he was a mass of neuroses that I took on once I decided to give it a go with him. We had balance, Nate and I. A perfect symmetry of love, honesty and trust. With him, as I confessed to Adele after about six months, 'commitment' and 'for ever' weren't only concepts, they were a reality.

Saturday night.

It was a Saturday night two years ago. Del and I had put Tegan to bed with the intention of doing some wedding planning, seeing as my 'big day' was only two months away, but we'd been waylaid; distracted by four bottles of wine and a packet of cocktail sausages. Del was reclining on the brown leatherette sofa, having unbuttoned the flies of her dark green combats and tucked her vest top under and up through the bottom of her bra. Her stomach was disconcertingly flat, especially considering she'd given birth three years earlier. You could see the silvery stretchmarks across her creamy-white skin, but otherwise everything seemed to have returned to where it should be – she'd even started wearing the white gold body bar through her pierced navel again.

I was on the other sofa. I'd also undone the top buttons of my jeans, and taken off my bra, but my less than flat stomach and stretchmark-rippled breasts were hidden under a white T-shirt I'd borrowed from Del. I'd had to borrow the T-shirt because Tegan's bath earlier had resulted in me, my top and bra being soaked through.

Rather than sorting out the seating plan, we were talking about Del's dating. I knew Nate would go mad when I went home without a seating plan (when he'd offered to do it I'd gotten hoity-toity and had indignantly replied, 'Don't mind me, I was obviously mistaken when I thought this was my wedding too') but Del's dating was important. She'd recently met a man and was at the start of the dating ritual. That ritual that began with wanting to recount every detail and nuance of their first conversation, which was followed by the excitement of the second date. Then came the anticipatory days leading up to the 'sex' date. And then there was the continued excitement that were the fourth to tenth dates. Swiftly followed by the decline into one of them not calling the other, with its accompanying soundtrack of self-recrimination and wondering what was wrong with you. Del was at date six with this new man and interest wasn't as yet waning.

'He does this thing with his hips and it's . . . Wow,' she revealed. 'It blows my mind every time.'

This man, although he knew how to blow her mind every time, didn't know she had a child. If he got to date fifteen she'd tell him but this man wasn't likely to make it that far. She liked him, but he wasn't The One. Nor even The One Who Was Going To Be Around For Very Long, so she wasn't going to upset Tegan by introducing her to a man who would eventually be gone from her life. Del was fiercely protective of Tegan. Her daughter's life had to have as few disruptions as possible and anyone who got in the way of that was literally taking their life in their hands. She'd rather be single a lifetime than introduce Tegan to someone who wouldn't be around for long. And, she reasoned, as soon as she told someone about her daughter they were obliged to meet her.

'Nate does this thing with his mouth,' I revealed. 'He starts off licking my inner thighs really slowly, then he does this thing with his mouth . . . It's . . .' I grinned and sighed. 'Amazing.' I rarely shared the intimate details of our sex life with anyone, not even Del, but then I hadn't drunk two bottles of wine in a long while – I'd pretty much tell her anything at that moment. 'It's . . . I'm getting shivers down my spine just thinking about it.'

'Hmmm, I know,' Del agreed. Then froze. Everything about her froze the second those three words came out of her mouth.

My heart had stopped mid-beat and the breath was caught in my chest. Time seemed to stand still.

Del's eyes edged over to my area of the room, two discs of blue steel, now branded with terror. I exhaled but my muscles didn't unclench. I inhaled deeply. *No, I'm wrong,* I told myself. *Surely I was wrong. But I'd heard her. I'd heard the inflection of her 'I know'. She said it like she did. She did know. She'd been there. She'd done it. With Nate. She'd done it with Nate. His tongue had licked her inner thighs. His lips had . . .*

I sat up, put my feet on the floor to steady myself, then exhaled again. Long and drawn-out. Inhaled. Deep and slow. 'When?' I asked forcing the word out of my mouth.

Del didn't answer and, for a second, I thought she was going to deny it, was going to try to bluff her way out of it. Instead she closed her eyes for a moment, swallowed hard, then faced me. 'Long time ago,' she whispered, her eyes never leaving mine. 'Long, long time ago. Way long time ago.'

The breath caught in my chest again and I inhaled to try to get it moving, but my body was immobile. Frozen. Nothing would go in, nothing would come out, it hurt too much. 'How long for?'

'Once. Only the once.'

Tears pricked behind my eyes and my jaw muscles clenched themselves into a tight ball. I didn't feel like crying but the

34

moistness in my eyes, the pain in my jaw said I was about to bawl my eyes out.

Del sat up, ran her slender fingers through her hair, used the palms of her hands to rub at her wet eyes.

'Only the once,' she repeated.

Once. Only the once. The words didn't have any meaning. Did once make it any better than twice? Or fifty times? It was done between them. Was it less wrong because it was once? I blinked but my vision was still blurred by tears.

Why? I asked her silently.

Del sat hunched forwards on the sofa, her combats splayed open, elbows rested on her knees, hands in her hair, staring at the laminate flooring.

Why? I asked again in my head.

She continued to stare at the fake floorboards, obviously not hearing my telepathic questions. Lost in her own thoughts and her own world. A world where she'd confessed. She continued to stare at the floor. Then, she lifted her eyes, glanced at the picture of Tegan that sat on top of the television before returning her gaze to the floor.

It was an instinctive thing, a little thing that gave everything away. 'No,' I gasped, more to myself than to her. I was trying to convince myself I was being ridiculous; that my heart had skipped several beats for nothing.

Del's head snapped round to me as she heard my gasp. My eyes darted from Del to the photo to Del. Our eyes locked and her face drained of colour.

I shook my head, trying to dislodge the thought, trying to remove the very idea from my mind. My eyes flew back to the picture. From that smiling snapshot, Tegan's nose was a dead giveaway. She was Nate's child.

Everything fell into place, like the final pieces in a jigsaw puzzle. The pieces had been there all along, of course, I simply hadn't seen them. Hadn't seen the bigger picture until that moment when everything came into focus. Now I knew why Tegan looked so familiar. It wasn't because she was her mother's double, which she was in most ways, it was because she had the same ski-slope nose as her father, the shape of his large eyes, his sardonic twist of the lip. I'd seen those features all along, of course, but my mind hadn't made the connection.

I'd asked Del who the father was when she first found out she was pregnant. She'd tearfully told me that it'd been an accident, that he wasn't around, that he was a married man she'd met through work.

'Bastard,' I'd hissed.

'No,' she'd replied. 'He didn't mean for it to happen. Neither did I, it was an accident. No one's to blame.'

Every conversation we'd had about the father of her baby whizzed through my head: every time she said he wasn't capable of loving her, let alone a child; how she'd repeated that it was a mistake – the best thing that had happened to her – but still a mistake; all those hours she'd declared she didn't need the father messing her life up. And there was me, the surrogate father. The one who went to antenatal classes, who'd been in the delivery room almost gagging at what I saw, who helped out as much as I could – all the while encouraging her to tell the daddy because it was morally right, that even if she didn't want him to know, he had a right. He had to earn his bastard stripes by rejecting her and the child. And, I often said, Tegan might want to know. 'What are you going to tell her then? That you didn't want him to know he's a father so she wasn't allowed to have a dad?'

She'd replied, 'I'll worry about that when I have to.'

Now she had to.

I was a prize idiot. A big fat festering idiot who'd been lecturing her, pushing her to tell the love of my life that he'd knocked her up.

I launched myself off the sofa but once on my feet I found I was almost doubled up from the red-hot searing pain in my stomach. I was still winded by the shock. My face creased up as it all hit me full force.

Nate had a child. Nate had fathered my best friend's child.

I started to gather up my things: the damp bra I'd taken off; my belt that I'd discarded because it was cutting into my stomach; the notebooks I'd taken out to show seating-plan willing; the map of the tables; the coloured pens. I fumbled around for them, shoving them into my bag, running a hand through my black hair to neaten it. I spotted my socks slung on the floor beside the other sofa but I wasn't going near her so I shoved my bare feet into my trainers.

With shaking hands I pulled the wet top I'd taken off earlier over the white T-shirt. Then remembered the T-shirt was hers. My lying, cheating friend's. I ripped the top off, pulled off the T-shirt and threw it on the ground, then tugged on my damp top over my braless body.

'Kam, let's talk about this,' she pleaded. 'Please, Kam, let's talk.'

It was a half-hearted plea. I wasn't a talker when I was upset. I was the ignore-it-in-the-hope-it'll-go-away type. Besides, what was there to talk about? How good my fiancé was in bed? What marks out of ten we'd both give him? Ask if he knew Tegan was his daughter and was he still going to marry me? He'd done this awful thing but was planning to say 'I do' in two months' time. In eight weeks – EIGHT WEEKS – he was going to stand up in front of everyone we knew and declare that he loved me; that he was going to forsake all others. Except he wasn't, was he? He certainly hadn't in the past so why would he in the future?

'He doesn't know about Tegan,' Del said. Her voice was strong, clear, determined. She wasn't playing about. When it came to Tegan, she wasn't going to mess about. Especially not

37

with this. 'I don't want him to know,' she continued. 'I don't want to upset Tegan's life. Whatever else you do, don't ruin Tegan's life. It's not her fault.'

I wish I had it in me to call her names. To slap her face and pull out her hair. The best I could do was to walk out.

And never go back.

chapter five

'I'm here to see Tiga,' I said to the woman who answered the door to the five-bedroom detached house a fifteen-minute taxi ride from the centre of Guildford.

She looked at me blankly and then I remembered I was the only person on earth who called Tegan 'Tiga'. 'I mean, I'm here to see Tegan.'

A spark of recognition ignited in Muriel's eyes. She was Del's stepmother. A slight, fragile woman who looked as if one knock too many would snap her in two. Her greying hair had been set on big rollers and hairsprayed to within an inch of snapping. When I'd first met her she'd had a uniform style of dressing: some kind of tweed skirt, twinset and pearls combo. She didn't disappoint this time, even in this heat, at the height of summer, she wore a green jumper with a cardigan, her tweed skirt was brown and the creamy pearls sat at her wrinkled throat. She seemed so respectable, normal, even docile. However, pure evil pulsed through this woman's veins.

Del had shown me what this woman was capable of. I'd seen the silvery welts on Del's thighs from where her stepmother had put out cigarettes on her. The little finger on her left hand that hadn't grown straight after this woman had wrenched it out of its socket. The scar under her hairline on her forehead where Muriel had thrown a glass at her.

'I'm Kamryn. Tegan's godmother?' I said, flattening out my voice to hide my hatred. 'Lucinda-Jayne's friend?' Del had dropped 'Lucinda-Jayne' the second she got to college in favour of her middle name, Adele. When we graduated from college she changed her surname to Brannon, her mother's maiden name. To the people who met her after Leeds she was Adele Brannon. We'd had a big celebration when she finally changed her name by deed poll. Her father still called her Lucinda-Jayne and she wouldn't dream of correcting him.

More recognition blossomed in Muriel's eyes, although it should have been an inferno of recognition by now – I was the only one of Del's friends she'd met over the years. Del wasn't exactly rushing back to the bosom of her family at every opportunity so she only took one person back home with her – me.

'Yes, I remember who you are.' A slur streaked Muriel's voice. Was it sherry, wine or gin and tonic she'd been spending time with today? They'd been her best friends, her constant companions, when we'd met years ago. Obviously nothing had changed.

'So, can I see Tegan?' I asked, when it became clear she wasn't about to say anything else.

'She's not available right now,' she replied.

'She's out?'

'No. She's not receiving visitors.'

'A five-year-old isn't receiving visitors?' I replied, irritated and incredulous in equal measures. 'Somehow, I can't imagine her saying, "If anyone calls, tell them one shall be out."'

Muriel sneered down her nose at me as if I was something smelly and disgusting she'd trodden in. 'The little madam is being punished,' she said contemptuously, 'if it's any business of yours.'

'It is my business.' Every one of my words was carefully modulated to prevent me screaming. 'I'm her godmother. I've been asked to look after her if anything happens to her mother.'

'You will have to call another time because, as I explained, she is being punished.'

The woman moved to shut the door, and all the rage, the hatred and anger simmering inside erupted through the surface of my placidity. I lunged forwards, every muscle in my body tensed as the flat of my hand slapped against the blue door and held it open. 'Punished for what?' I said.

Having jumped slightly at my advance, Muriel glanced away.

'Punished for what?' I asked, a snarling edge to my voice.

Muriel said nothing.

'I'd like to see her.'

'She isn't allowed to see anyone.'

'I'm not leaving until I see her.'

She lowered her voice. 'I can't let you in. You don't know what Ronald will do to me if I let you see her.'

'You obviously don't know what I'll do to you if you don't,' I said in a tone that was menacing and scary, even to me. I was certain I'd heard that line in a movie but it'd been out of my mouth before I could stop myself.

Muriel's bloodshot eyes pinched together venomously but still radiated fear. I knew what she was capable of but only when dealing with a defenceless child, whilst she had no clue what I was capable of. To be honest, neither did I. In my thirty-two years I'd never hit anyone in anger but that didn't mean I wouldn't if I had to.

Muriel increased the poison in her glare and I hardened the expression on my face. She really had no idea how incensed I was. Travelling two hundred miles in a day, seeing my friend who was on the verge of death, now coming back to this place where Del had suffered so much . . . All of this had shaped my mood.

Muriel's body relaxed in resignation as she let go of the door, turned and headed up the large staircase, muttering just loud enough, 'It's not even as if we want her here.'

I let out a deep, silent breath of relief – *what if she'd made me front up to her for real? Best not to think about it.*

The house hadn't changed much since I'd last come here eight years ago. Del and I had made a flying visit to get the rest of the clothes and books she had left here, which had been an excuse. She'd lived without those things for years, why decide she desperately needed them now? I guessed that Del had returned to make peace with her father, to reach out to him one last time. He'd been ultra-polite because she'd had a guest with her but also excessively dismissive. It was one of the most chilling things I'd ever seen (and the second I was alone later, I called my parents for a quick chat). When we climbed into the back of the taxi Del didn't have to tell me she intended never to return there, I knew it. She'd done her best to reconnect with her family and now she had to leave it.

Nothing about the house had changed since that day: the same cream carpet lined the floors, the same magnolia paint covered the walls, the same depressing pictures of country scenes hung on those magnolia walls. The atmosphere was the only thing that was different – it had stagnated. Had become decrepit, barren, lifeless.

Muriel stopped outside a white panelled door. There was a key in the lock, which she reached for. Her liver-spotted hand paused at the key before she turned it. *They'd locked Tegan in? THEY'D LOCKED HER IN? Where did they think a child who wasn't tall enough to reach the front door handle would go if she left her room?*

Tegan's room was twice the size of my living room. The

walls were magnolia too but in here the carpet was royal blue. Two of the walls were lined with white bookcases and on each shelf sat dolls, play bricks, cuddly toys, teddies and books. None of them looked as if they'd been touched or played with; they were ornaments, perfect, untouchable relics to that thing called childhood. The neatly made single bed sat beside the large window that overlooked the wide expanse of garden.

Despite the brightly coloured children's belongings, the room was cold and uninviting. At the centre of the room was a small red plastic table and a yellow plastic chair, and at the table sat Tegan.

Even from a distance I could see everything was wrong. She sat stock-still on her chair, her small body rigid with fear. Her pale blonde hair hung around her face in dirty, unwashed clumps, her pink top was grubby and creased. And her eyes were fixed on the plate of food in front of her.

Shock punched me a fraction below my solar plexus. The last time I saw Tegan she'd been staring at me with big, enraptured eyes as I read her a story. She had been a child that took nothing sitting down, lying down or standing still. Everything was full-on where she was concerned. She was always wanting to run or play or read or laugh or to get someone in a hug.

'Tiga,' I whispered. I moved slowly across the room towards her. 'Tiga, it's Auntie Kamryn, do you remember me?' I bobbed down beside her and looked at her as I waited for her to reply.

A few seconds passed before she nodded. Nodded but kept her eyes forwards, fixed on her plate. The plate was loaded with age-greyed boiled potatoes, dried and shrivelled peas and a desiccated pork chop that was covered in a skin of white mould. The smell of the rotting meal assaulted my nostrils and I drew back, half-retching.

43

'So you do remember Auntie Kamryn?' I said, fighting the gagging in my throat.

Tegan nodded again.

'That's brilliant. And did Mummy tell you that you might come and stay with Auntie Kamryn for a little while?'

Tegan nodded.

'How do you feel about that?'

She raised her shoulders and lowered them. Then a tiny, hoarse voice said, 'Don't know.'

I slowly reached out to tuck a lock of her unwashed hair behind her right ear so I could see her face but before I made contact she flinched away from me into a cringe, her hands flying up as though to protect herself from an attack.

I recoiled back too, my heart racing with fear and horror. She thought I might hurt her. This small, frail creature thought I might hurt her. I stared at her and felt my heartbeat increase. Then I noticed her right hand – three red lines were streaked across its swollen palm. Around her right wrist were blue-black-purple bruises that looked like large handprints, as though someone had held her hand open as they whacked her with a cane.

It was those red lines marking her young skin that did it. Inside, I snapped. I wasn't even remotely close to screaming, lashing out or overturning furniture though. I was angry. Completely, totally angry. It spilled through me until I was calm. It dampened every other emotion until I felt nothing else. Every other emotion my anger was usually mingled with – outrage, hurt, indignation, pain, shock – were blotted out by this type of anger. It flowed through me and stilled everything.

I suddenly knew what I had to do.

I clamoured to my feet and Tegan relaxed from her cringe. I took big strides as I marched across the room to the white wardrobe and the white chest of drawers beside it. I yanked

44

open the top drawer, checked inside. It was filled with neatly folded tops. I grabbed a handful of tops and then slammed the drawer shut, opened another drawer, gathered another bundle of clothes. I yanked open the third drawer and took the vests and pants in there.

'What are you doing?' Muriel shrieked.

I ignored her. My arms were filled with brightly coloured clothes. I went to my holdall, wrenched back the zip and shoved everything inside.

'You can't do this!' Muriel screamed at me as I opened the wardrobe doors.

'Clearly I can do this,' I said, as I reached for a couple of coats and some shoes, 'because I *am* doing it.'

'I'll call the police,' she threatened.

My head whipped round to glare at her. 'Be my guest. I'd love to hear you explain why Tegan hasn't been washed in days, why she's sat in front of rotting food and how she got the marks on her hand. Actually, hang on, I'll call the police myself.' I chucked Tegan's clothes in the general direction of my holdall, reached into my coat pocket and pulled out my mobile. 'What's the number again? Oh yes, nine, nine, nine.' I punched keys on the phone. 'Do you want to press "call" or shall I?'

'Take her, we'll be glad to see the back of her,' Muriel spat before turning on her heels and storming out of the room, slamming the door behind her.

When the door shut behind her I waited a second to see if she was going to lock it, meaning I *would* have to call the police to get us out of there, but no, she just shut the door. I turned back to Tegan. Her face, with its tear-stained cheeks, ski-slope nose and pouty lips, was turned up to me. Her royal blue eyes that were ringed with red stared at me as though she thought I was insane.

I went to her, bobbed down beside her. I didn't get too

45

close for fear of scaring her again. 'Do you have a favourite toy?' I asked her.

She nodded suspiciously.

'OK, go get it and anything else that you love and bring it to me.'

Her eyes widened in alarm.

'We're going away,' I explained. 'You're going to come and stay with Auntie Kamryn.'

Tegan, although clearly tempted by the idea of getting out of there, was nobody's fool and continued to regard me suspiciously. We didn't have time for this. For all I knew Muriel was calling her husband. He could be on the way back. This was his house, his home ground so he'd have the advantage. And I couldn't be sure that he wouldn't become violent.

'Come on, Tiga, get your stuff and we can go see your mummy tomorrow.'

'Mummy?' Her pale face brightened. 'Mummy?'

'Yes, Mummy.'

Her chair didn't make a sound on the deep-pile carpet as she pushed it back and stood up. She went to her bed, got down on the floor and from under it she pulled a multi-coloured rucksack. She held the rucksack out to me. I grinned at her and she smiled back at me. This kid and I were singing from the same song book at last.

Time passed. I don't know how much but by the end of its passing, I was standing on the corner of a street in a town I didn't know very well, a child in my arms and half a dozen bags – including my holdall, her rucksack and four carrier bags – at my feet. I didn't have a clue where I – no, we – were going. I didn't have any cab numbers, didn't know where the nearest bus stop was.

'Do you know what today is?' I asked Tegan.

She looked into my eyes, as though nothing I said would surprise her, then she shook her head.

'It's my birthday.' It was too. Although this morning seemed a million years ago, it was still my birthday.

She nodded and managed a small, confused smile. 'Happy birthday,' she whispered, then rested her tired head on my shoulder.

'Thanks,' I replied.

It's also the day I'm going to be arrested for kidnapping.

chapter six

Light, the colour of twice-used bathwater, strained through the gaps in the beige curtains, trying to brighten my hotel room.

The coffee I held in my hands had cooled to a freezing black sludge, my body was stiff from sitting in the same position for a couple of hours and my eyes ached as I stared at the world that was coming alive outside. I could hear the birds tuning up for their dawn chorus, buses chugging along noisily, cars speeding by, plus the occasional police siren. I'd stopped thinking those police sirens were coming for me a couple of hours ago but my mind was still racing at 100 mph – it had been for most of the night . . .

Eight hours earlier, I'd been let into the room by a porter who brought up our bags and left them inside the doorway, slid the key card into the slot to work the electricity, switched on only side lights so as not to wake the sleeping child in my arms, then quietly shut the door behind him. I'd checked us into a hotel that was within walking distance of St Jude's Hospital. The room was sparse and small, but it had a double bed, a small cot bed for Tegan and a television – everything we needed.

As the door closed behind us I walked over to the cot,

Tegan was like an anvil in my arms, my biceps, elbows and forearms were frozen in pain because I'd been holding her for so long. The second we'd got in the back of the taxi that would bring us into central London, Tegan had climbed into my lap, wrapped her arms as far around my torso as they would go, rested her face against my chest and fallen asleep. The whole sixty-minute drive into town I'd had to restrain myself from breathing too deeply or shifting about in case I jostled her awake, although it had to be said she was doing a pretty good impression of being deeply ensconced in dreamland. She hadn't stirred when I'd shuffled and contorted my way out of the taxi, nor when I talked the receptionist through the registration form, nor when we came up in the lift to our room. She was likely to be out for the count all night.

I laid her gently on the cot bed, then nearly jumped out of my skin as her eyes flew open. My heartbeat, which was racing as though she'd leapt out at me from behind a door, took a few seconds to slow down.

With her dirty blonde hair fanned out around her as she lay on the tiny bed, Tegan's eyes didn't leave me as her pale oval face slid into a mire of fear. She was terrified. Wide awake and terrified.

Join the queue, honey, I thought. I was terrified too. The implications of what I had done were only just starting to hit me. I'd done something big and stupid and I was petrified because of it.

'What's the matter?' I asked cautiously. My fear that she might burst into tears outweighed all my other fears. I had no clue how to handle a crying child, except maybe to scream 'Shut up!'. In all the preceding years, with all my nieces and nephews, with Tegan herself, when a tiny person got crysome, I handed them back to the person responsible for them, secure in the knowledge that nothing I could do would appease them so I didn't have to try. In other words, I passed the buck back

49

to the person who'd chosen to become a parent, who'd chosen to deal with tears, snot and tantrums.

Tegan's visage of terror didn't slip, not even for a microsecond as she stared up at me.

'Do you want to sleep in the big bed?' I asked, taking a wild guess at what might be troubling her – apart from being abducted from the place she'd called home for the past few months and being held hostage by a woman she hadn't seen in two years.

Tegan nodded.

'OK, but let's have a bath first, all right?'

She nodded.

'And maybe something to eat?'

She nodded again. 'OK, good.' That was a plan. A good plan. I could work with this. Bathe her, feed her, get her to go to sleep. Sorted. I got to my feet, as Tegan sat up on the small cot bed. She pulled her knees up to her chest, wrapped her arms around them and watched me go across the room to the table with the phone and menu.

I picked up the laminated menu card and scanned it for something that she might like. It was clear that she wasn't going to speak to me so there was no point in asking her. Burger and chips seemed the easiest choice.

She didn't move as I did homeyfying things like turning on the telly, flicking through the channels to find something unlikely to corrupt her young mind and putting on a couple more lights. I searched through the bags, found her blue checked pyjamas, a clean pair of white knickers and a white vest. I lay them on the big bed and went to the bathroom.

It was a functional bathroom with possibly the tiniest showerhead in the world hanging over the bath, but it was clean and mildew-free, a miracle considering it had no window, just an air extractor in the corner. I pinned back the white shower curtain, then sat on the side of the bath to push the plug in and turn on the taps. Once the bath was half full, I drizzled in some bubble bath and agitated the water to try to make some bubbles. It wasn't as impressive as I would have liked, but it wasn't as depressing as a white hotel tub with just water in it.

I went back to Tegan and knelt down in front of her. 'Can we take off your clothes then?' I asked gently.

She hesitated, possibly unsure if this was the right thing to do. Then, resigning herself to it, she uncurled her body, slid off the bed and stood in front of me, patient and passive. I took off her jacket, then gently tugged her grubby pink top over her head. I had to stop myself from recoiling in horror. She was reed thin, she hadn't been fed properly in weeks. Her arms were like frail little sticks that hung from her scrawny shoulders; her ribs were prominent under her skin and her stomach was concave.

It wasn't just her thinned body. Her skin . . . Tears punched at my eyes and my lower jaw started to tremble. Her skin, her beautiful, beautiful skin was blotched and dappled with dirt and bruises and welts. Each of the bruises looked like the result of a slap, a punch or a grab. Each mark was long and straight, as though she'd been whipped with a belt.

My mind caved in on itself as my heart thumped and thumped in my ears. How could they do this? How could anyone do this? I never knew this sort of thing went on. I mean, I knew it existed, and I knew it was awful. But it wasn't real because I'd never seen it. It was like someone telling you the sun was hot. You knew it was hot, of course it was hot because it's a burning ball of gases, nevertheless, I'd never know, *believe* how hot it was until I'd stuck my hand into it. The same with this. I'd heard it all from Del, I'd seen her scars, but I couldn't know, I couldn't *believe* until this moment. Fat tears swelled in my eyes.

Stop it, I ordered myself. *Don't let her think you're disgusted by her, that it's her fault.*

51

I blinked back my tears and inhaled deeply through my nose. I couldn't fall apart in front of her – it wasn't fair.

I finished undressing her, fighting every fresh batch of tears that arose with every item of her clothing I removed. It was all over her: the dirt, the bruising, the marking. Once her last item of clothing was off, I wrapped her in a big white towel and went to lead her into the bathroom. I stopped, got down on my knees and enveloped her in my arms. 'You'll be all right, sweetie,' I told her. 'I'm going to take care of you, OK? I'm going to take care of you.' I had to let her know she was all right. This wouldn't happen again, she was safe now. She didn't react as I tried to hug away her pain. How still and silent she stood in my arms made me pull her tiny body closer to me.

While I bathed her I was constantly reminded of the last bath I'd given her. The one where she'd soaked me through and I'd had to borrow a T-shirt from Del. I was reminded because it was so different: there was no boisterous splashing, no giggling at the shapes the bubbles made, no trying to wet my clothes. She sat still and let me clean her bruised skin. I wished she'd give me even the slightest indication that she was there in the room with me but her eyes stayed fixed on a point on the tiled wall, her body not resisting any swipe of the flannel.

Her blonde hair fell in straight golden waves to her shoulders when I'd dried it and she was pretty damn cute in her blue checked pyjamas. Cute, but silent. A knock at the door made both of us jump, we looked at each other, then at the door. After a few fraught seconds I realised it was probably room service with our food.

Any hunger that had been lurking around my stomach had been knocked out of me when I saw Tegan's body but when the waiter slid the tray onto the big table, Tegan's eyes lit up as though she hadn't seen real food in an age.

I took the burger, chips and Ribena to her, then sat opposite her on the big bed as she accepted the plate and carton. She didn't move towards the food for a few seconds, then tentatively reached out and picked up the burger and moved it to her lips. Before she bit into it she looked up at me, silently checking it was OK.

I conjured up my brightest smile then nodded at her. *It's all right to eat,* I silently replied. She took a nibble of the burger and kept her eyes on me as she chewed. She took another look at me before taking another bite. I welded the encouraging grin to my face and kept it there the whole time while she ate. 'You don't have to eat it all,' I said several times, 'if you don't want to finish it, you don't have to.'

She did want to. She cleared her plate and drained the carton, then sat back, staring at me with big scared eyes. Tegan took all her cues from me, unsure what to do next – a case of the completely lost leading the completely lost. I didn't know what to do next, either. However, being the adult meant I had to pretend I knew what I was doing or we'd sit here all night, waiting for the other to navigate us into surer territory.

'Are you tired?' I hazarded.

She nodded. Good, she was sticking to the plan: bath, food, bed.

'OK, come lie down.'

The corners of her mouth turned down, then her jaw started trembling as her eyes filled with tears. *No, no, not crying! I can handle anything except crying.* Weariness was plain on her face, exhaustion was tugging at her features, her movements were slow and of one who was sleep-deprived, so why wasn't she eager to lie down and sleep?

'What's the matter, Tiga?' I asked.

'I be scared on my own,' she whispered, then cringed as though she expected me to explode at her.

'Do you want me to lie with you?' I asked gently.

53

She came out of her cringe but was cautious as she slowly nodded. Her surprise that I didn't start shouting was palpable.

'OK, you lie down and I'll take my shoes off.'

Tegan nestled down under the blankets, made sure I was lying facing her, closed her eyes, then fell asleep. Just like that. Out like a light. I waited until I was sure she was deeply asleep before I slid noiselessly out of bed and sat in the chair staring out of the window.

I shifted in the chair, arched my back to try to unknot it, blinked unseeingly at the window.

How had I got myself here? Here. Where this thing called adoption was a serious issue.

I'd left Adele's bedside determined to only *think* about it. And hadn't. It wasn't as if I had to think about it right away, so I had stored it away somewhere in my head to be brought out and considered another time. Except 'another time' had come around a lot quicker than I thought it would.

Less than twenty-four hours ago my biggest decision was which bra would maximise my cleavage in my gold sequin dress. My gold sequin dress. Now that was a memory from a distant age. Was that really me? Was it really me who was planning on dusting my cleavage with gold dust? Because if it was, then how could I be the same person sat in a hotel arm-chair thinking about adopting a child?

Me and child.

Kamryn and child.

Never meant to happen.

Children had never been in my sphere of destiny, not on my list of things to do. There were lots of children in my life – eight of them courtesy of my two brothers and sister – and whilst I loved each one of those little people with all my heart, they weren't enough to make me want to partake. The time limit factor was what heightened my enjoyment of being with

54

children – anything more than twenty-four hours with them was asking too much of me.

You had to be prepared to give up everything for children. *Everything*. Time, space, affection. I wasn't that altruistic and wouldn't pretend I was that way inclined just to look 'normal'.

When I was younger, most people thought my lack of interest in children was because I hadn't met the right man. The right man, they theorised, would conjure up in me the need to procreate. When Nate and I started talking about marriage, everyone – Del included – thought I'd change my mind. That this much-vaunted thing called 'maternal instinct' would kick in and I'd start cooing at kids in buggies, swooning over tiny clothes in shops and start planning which room in our flat would become the nursery. Because Nate, my husband to be, was meant to have been the inspiration I needed to crave the fertilisation of my eggs.

People constantly asked me when Nate and I would be having children and I replied, 'Erm, never.' There was, without exception, surprise then sympathy at my response, then I'd get a variation on, 'Are you sure you want to marry Nate when he doesn't want children?' I began to wonder if anyone had ever seen me as a person in my own right not simply as a baby-making machine. I usually informed these people: 'Nate and I aren't having kids. It's one of the fundamental things we agree on. You know, no voting Conservative, no buying Oasis CDs and no children.'

No children.

I put down the coffee cup on the floor by the armchair, hoisted myself upright. Careful not to bounce the mattress, I slid back into the bed. I lay facing Tegan, examining the contours of her face, seeing Nate. A smile spread across my face as I remembered the amount of times I'd done that to Nate over the years we were together: lay in the middle of the night, watching him sleep, resisting the urge to run a finger over his nose, or kiss his eyelids, or whisper 'I love you' in his ear. With Nate, I found it nearly impossible to hide my affection, especially when he was asleep and unlikely to witness my weakness for him.

My parents, out of everyone, were hurt the most by me cancelling the wedding.

They couldn't believe that, two months before their big day, it was all off. I had no illusions about that, it was *their* big day. It was what they'd been waiting for most of their lives. I'd thought they were going to throw themselves at Nate's feet and worship him when we told them we were getting married. Finally someone was willing to take their troublesome eldest daughter off their hands. All I had to do was not ruin it before I said 'I do' and then they'd be home free. I'd be someone else's responsibility.

So that phone call, the one I made from a hotel room in Leeds two days after I found out what had happened between Nate and Del, the one that went 'Nate and I have split up, the wedding's off and I'm moving to Leeds' was well received. Well received in that they didn't have a way to reach down the phone line and throttle me.

Cancelling the wedding was a typical Kamryn move as far as they were concerned. I could never get it right; couldn't do this one normal thing for them. I'd always dressed shabbily, I was never pretty, I'd never had boyfriends, I'd never fitted in, and now, the one thing, the *one* thing that would prove I was normal, was off. My siblings – both the older one and the two younger ones – had managed it, had gotten married, had settled down, had reproduced, so why couldn't I? What was wrong with me?

They'd told all their friends. Relatives from abroad were meant to be flying in. They'd done their share of helping me to prepare. My mum had been searching for the perfect outfit and there I was, saying it was all for nothing. All that hard work was for nothing. Although they never actually said it, I knew they were thinking, *What did you do wrong, Kamryn?*

My siblings and my friends were more understanding. Most of them said that if it wasn't right, it wasn't right, but I knew they all wanted to know the real reason for our split. Was he cheating? Was I cheating? Had he hit me? Had I panicked? Had he discovered something hideous about me at the last minute? Everyone was supportive but I knew I could never be honest with them. I could never say to another human being: 'My fiancé and my best friend made a child.'

That was what Adele and Nate had done. I wasn't simply hurt by them having sex, I was humiliated, disgraced and, ultimately, isolated. When you can't be honest with people, you can't ever relax with them in case you let something slip. I couldn't have stayed in London, among the friends and elements of that life, even if I wanted to. It would have been too hard on a daily basis hiding what had happened.

Tegan stirred and I held my breath in case she awoke. A dozen little expressions flitted across her face as her dream played itself out, then she settled back into sleep.

Del knew what a ginormous thing she was asking of me when she made the request to adopt Tegan. She knew I couldn't look at Tegan the same ever again. I sent her Christmas and birthday presents, I sent her postcards if I went abroad, I bought her little pressies that I posted off to London. All done from a distance. At no point did I have to look at her whilst I made those little contacts. To look at her would be to remember what my two favourite people had done. And to remember how I hurt the day it had all come out. How I'd hurt every day after that.

I gently brushed a stray strand of hair away from Tegan's face.

Could I do this? Could I adopt the child of the man I had been two months away from marrying? In sleep she looked so much like him. In waking life she had shades of him too. She might grow into her looks, might become more like her dad every day. Could I bear that? Every day, day after day, for the rest of my life staring at mini Nate, being reminded of my best friend and my fiancé making love.

This was all moot, though, wasn't it? There was no going back now. I'd taken Tegan from her grandparents in Guildford. I'd had to – she couldn't have stayed there a second longer – but I'd still taken her. That meant I hadn't simply said yes to adopting her, I'd screamed it from the top of my lungs.

chapter seven

Kamryn and I had a lot of sex without love or even real emotion in our younger days.

Of course, it wasn't the done thing, us being women and all, but we had our reasons.

My reason: weariness. I, Adele Brannon, was weary. Tired of meeting another new man, of hoping he was The One, of waiting for love to blossom between us, then finding he wasn't The One and love wasn't planning on paying us even a fleeting visit. So I decided to take the far more appealing route of chasing lust, on the way to love. If I waited to find love to have sex, well, I would never have gotten laid. I believed in love so whilst I waited for its arrival in my life, I concentrated on having the best sex with the best-looking men in London, just to pass the time, you know.

Kamryn, on the other hand, didn't believe in love. She'd experienced every type of being screwed over by men there was and had decided to give a little back – in kind. Years and years of being told you're ugly and fat will do that. She was very careful not to talk about the years before we met. She'd often say, 'It's over, there's nothing to talk about' but sometimes I'd catch her off guard and she'd reveal how deeply she'd been scarred by the things people used to say to her. Every day at school and then in sixth form, bombarded with abuse. And then at home, she'd get silent calls and notes. When I met her she was a good-looking woman, but as she got older, she got better-looking;

grew into her features and went from good-looking to striking. She had huge dark eyes, long eyelashes and this amazing smile. The tragedy being she never saw it, never believed it.

I remember more than once she confessed that no matter how much weight she lost, how many times she was called beautiful, she would look in the mirror and see a fat, ugly person. 'It's like for a few seconds I see what's there, then the haze disappears and I see this grotesque monster.' I'd been so shocked at that I burst into tears and she'd tried to reassure me that she was exaggerating, but I knew she wasn't. Years of hearing the same thing had done that to her and that's what had made me cry. She hadn't done anything to deserve that, but still, her mind was scored over and over with that belief. I wasn't surprised she was wary of people, didn't know who to trust. And that no matter how many times you told her, she wouldn't believe she was beautiful.

The worst part was the better-looking she got, the more she attracted men who seemed to be after one thing – to make themselves feel like real men by putting down a gorgeous woman.

It was the nice ones, the ones who'd sucker me in too, that hurt the most. They'd start off being lovely, treating her well, then they would erode her confidence, put down her looks, try to douse her spark. After she'd dated another creep for six months only for him to suggest she diet to trim down her size fourteen frame so she could fit into the size ten dress he wanted her to wear to his work do, Kamryn changed. He was the last of the men who would make her feel like nothing, the last of those men who would be allowed to behave as if she should be grateful they even glanced in her direction. After him, Kam refused to show her soft side to another man. She didn't have to say it for me to know that this went back to her school days. All the things people had called her during school and sixth form – Man-Ryn, Fugly (Fucking Ugly) and Mike Tyson – had left the type of scars that would never completely heal. All the men she dated during and after college seemed to prove her school 'mates' right; they made her believe that there was something fundamentally wrong with her and that love was going to pass her by. The only thing for it was to use men for sex and never let any of them get so close they could hurt her.

About eight years ago, everything changed. We were out clubbing and as usual we stood out — she with her curves, dark skin and feather-cut black hair, me with my slender frame, pale skin and masses of blonde hair. I was wearing shiny black trousers, a denim bustier top and my denim stilettos whilst Kam wore her black velvet jacket, dark blue jeans and white vest top. I'd forced her to complete the look with a pair of my black suede stilettos.

This club was a new one but seemed to be full of the same old disgusting men. I had to drink to compensate for the lack of talent, while Kam dispatched every man who approached her with her acid tongue and acrid expressions. One man, probably the sexiest-looking one in the club, did get close enough to her to move in for a kiss, but at the last second she turned her back on him and walked away. We left after that.

I was the drunkest of the two of us so in the taxi back to our flat in north London I was allowed to lay my head on her thigh and fall asleep while she stayed awake to get us home.

'I'm going to do it with Nate,' Kam said.

'I thought you'd already shagged him,' I replied, not opening my eyes.

'I have,' she said. 'No, I mean, I'm going to go out with him. Date him. Properly.'

'Is that why you didn't snog that man?' I asked, my interest was piqued, but not enough to make me open my eyes.

'Yes,' she mumbled. 'I . . . I think I might like him.'

My eyes flew open and I sat bolt upright but she turned away to stare out the window before I could see into her eyes. She'd met Nate at a party a few months earlier and for some reason had given him her real phone number. Since day one she'd been giving him the run-around. He'd call and she'd screen calls, only phoning back days later. If she did answer the phone she'd be very nonchalant and vague about when they'd next meet up. Most shockingly, even for her, she shagged him after their first official date – which was afternoon coffee in north London – because she'd been convinced it would get rid of him. Not Nate. He hung in there. He'd dismantled her defences, I didn't realise how successfully until that moment.

'What?' I said.

'I think I might like him,' she repeated, studiously staring out of the window.

Bloody hell! Those six words were her equivalent to 'I'm falling in love with him.' When she'd hardened her heart, Kamryn had chucked out all ambiguity about her feelings towards men. She knew which men she wanted to sleep with, which ones were just friends, which ones she would date but would never bed. For her to admit she wasn't sure about a man meant he was special.

'Really?' I said to her.

She nodded but wouldn't look at me.

'Wake me up when we get home,' she said. She was embarrassed and vulnerable, she'd exposed a part of herself that hadn't been seen in years: she was unsure about a man. Kam closed her eyes, rested her head against the window and pretty soon she was asleep.

I watched her sleep as the cab made its way through the dark London streets. I was still reeling. Kam was in love. Wow! I suddenly felt sick. What if he's a bastard? What if he loses interest once he's got her undivided attention? It's happened before, what if it happens again? Kam will never recover. I had to do something. I was extremely drunk, hideously tired and a little shaken up – obviously the perfect time to make a decision to protect Kam's heart. And that something was to tell the taxi driver in hushed tones to head for another address . . .

After three knocks and three rings of the bell, the door of the house in Tuffnell Park with eight stone steps leading up to it was answered. I'd dropped Kam off here a few times so I knew it was the right house. I'd asked the taxi driver to wait a minute while I went to get something.

'Adele?' Nate said as he opened the door. He was wearing jeans *and a T-shirt, and even though it was 3 a.m. he didn't look as if he'd been asleep. Nate was good-looking. Not as sexy as the man Kam had been dancing with in the club, but he had something about him. Strong features, sexily messy brown-black hair and big navy blue eyes. 'Is Kamryn all right? What's happened?'*

'She's in the taxi. I had to come here. I tell you —' I poked him in his chest — 'if you hurt my friend, I kill you. You treat her right or I kill you. No messing.' I added another chest poke for good measure. 'Proper, proper kill you.'

He didn't say anything but even in my drunken state I could tell he didn't believe me.

'I'm serious,' I reassured him, just as the heel of my left shoe slid off the step . . . For the longest microsecond of my life I was falling then Nate's strong hands were on my forearms and he was hauling me inside. My legs had turned to rubber so he had to practically carry me to the lounge doorway. He grabbed his wallet from the side. 'Wait here,' he ordered and disappeared outside. He returned a few minutes later followed by an extremely pissed off Kamryn. I'd graduated from standing in the lounge doorway to lying in the middle of the floor. My legs had stopped supporting me around the same time Nate had gone outside.

Kamryn stalked across the room, threw herself into one of the arm-chairs and sat glaring at me.

'I'm so pleased to see you both,' Nate said pleasantly. He even sounded as though he meant it. He was obviously a man of even temperament — I certainly wouldn't be pleasant if someone came round to my house in the small hours and started threatening me.

'You owe Nathaniel for the taxi,' Kamryn said, her arms tightly folded across her chest.

'I had to tell Nate to treat you proper,' I explained to Kam. 'Or I would kill him.'

'You got that message across,' Nate reassured. 'Thank you, it's always good to know someone will murder you if you offend them or their kin.'

'You should have seen how many men tried it on with sexy Kamryn tonight,' I said to Nate. 'All the men in the club were after her. You're not her only option, you know. This really good-looking one, he put his hand on her bum.'

Nate's eyes hardened and he fixed that granite-like gaze on Kamryn as jealousy crept over his features – he wasn't that even tempered.

'No, no, but she didn't do anything,' I said quickly. 'He tried to kiss her and everything, but she said, "Nooooo, I've got a boyfriend."'

'Del . . .' Kam threatened.

Nate turned to me. 'She said that?'

'Oh yes. She said, "I've got a new boyfriend, he's called Nate and he's so sexy, I really love him."' I pointed at him. 'She loves you, she loves you.'

'Del! Shut up!' Kam said, outraged.

'She loves you, she loves you.'

Kam leapt up out of her chair, stepped forwards but wobbled on the unfamiliar heels and fell flat on her face.

'Look, Nate, she's fallen for you!' I shrieked.

Nate laughed quietly. Kam crawled determinedly forwards on her hands and knees towards me.

'She thinks you're so lovely,' I shouted before she got to me. 'She said you're so funny and sexy. And you've got the biggest . . .' Kam's hand covered my mouth but I carried on speaking, 'Kenis. Hoove kot se geegest kenis ever!'

'SHUT UP!' Kam screeched, then she was on top of me, started tickling me with hard angry digs in the ribs to quiet me. I yelled out for mercy as I fought her off. After a few seconds, Nate came over to us and hauled Kam off me.

'Enough!' he decreed, holding back my angry best friend. 'Kam, I know Adele's making it all up – I've accepted that it's illegal for you to say anything nice about me. And, Adele, thanks for trying but I've got a pretty good idea of how Kam feels about me, so don't try to make

*me feel better. Besides, you don't want to piss off someone you share
a flat with, not on my account.'*

I pushed my lips together, made a zipping motion across them, then
clamped my hands over my mouth. Kam had stopped fighting in
Nate's arms and was staring at him. I think what he said had jolted
her, the fact he knew she wouldn't ever say anything nice about him
even though she liked him had thrown her. He smiled at her with deep
affection but in response she glanced away.

'Come on, I think it's bed time,' he said.

'No!' I squealed. 'We can't have a threesome!'

'No, darling, I mean, you can sleep in one of my housemates' beds.
They're all away. Come on.'

They took an arm each and hoisted me up, then helped me up the
stairs because I still had legs of rubber. I was deposited on the double
bed of a room that smelt of boys but was very tidy. I turned over,
kicked my shoes off, then snuggled down into the soft duvet.

'Are you all right there, Del?' Nate asked.

'Yup, am right. Just sleep here. On nice bed. No be sick or nothing.'

'OK. If you need anything, Kam and I will be in my room, right
next door,' Nate said.

'Actually, I think I'll stay here,' Kam stated, every word coated
with ice. Anyone would have thought he'd suggested she shave her
head, not go sleep with a man she was falling in love with.

Nate, who'd obviously heard it all before, said, 'Fair enough. Like
I said, I'm next door if you need anything. See you in the morning.'

Kam sat down beside me after he shut the door behind him, then
lay down with her back to me.

'Stop being such a hard-faced bitch,' I mumbled.

'Shut up and go to sleep.'

'Only if you're nice to Nate. He's lovely. He loves you.'

'You know nothing about it.'

'He loves you. I love you. You don't need to be a bitch no more.'

I fell asleep before she replied and the next thing I knew, the covers were pulled off me and I was being shaken. 'Come on, you silly tart, it's morning, we're off,' Kamryn said, shaking and shaking me.

'No, wanna sleep,' I replied, trying to shrug her off.

'Too fucking bad. We're leaving.' She pulled me out of bed. I sat up slowly, every movement making pain shoot through my head. I wanted water and more sleep, but if Kam wanted to leave, then we had to leave. I only realised how grim things were when I saw my shoes. They'd been transformed overnight from sexy fashion pieces I'd spent a month's wages on to denim instruments of torture.

'Yeah,' Kam said, indicating to the shoes she had on her feet, 'it's a bitch walking in them in the morning.'

We tottered along the brightening streets, huddled inside our light-weight jackets, looking every inch a pair of hookers who'd been working all night. Every step was agony and I often wore heels, so Kamryn, who lived in trainers, must've been going through hell. I took a side-long glance at her, expecting her to be highly pissed off as well as pained. She was dishevelled, tired and her eyes were bloodshot from lack of sleep but she wasn't cross. In fact, a slight, self-satisfied smile was playing on her lips. It could only mean one thing.

'Did you give him the good stuff?' I asked her.

'Oh yes,' she said with a smug sniff. 'He won't be walking straight for a week.'

Since I've been in hospital I've had a lot of time to replay bits of my life. That night is often dusted off and played. Especially the bit where she says, 'I think I might like him.' She'd told me first that she loved him – she didn't even say it to Nate until months later. I was so honoured she'd told me first that she was in love, it showed how much she thought of me.

I still hate myself for ruining what they had.

chapter eight

Duped.

Hoodwinked. Conned. Duped. Whatever you called it, it had been done to me. I hadn't realised it, it didn't even occur to me that it was possible until this morning when Tegan and I had shown up at the hospital.

I'd opened the door to Del's hospital room and as Tegan ran in and scrambled up onto the bed, Del smiled at me in a way that said she knew my answer was yes. That I was going to take on her child.

But, apparently, Del had always known the answer was going to be in the affirmative because the cheeky minx had already had the legal documents drawn up, naming me as Tegan's legal guardian. She'd also sent off for the relevant forms so I could get the ball rolling to adopt Tegan. These papers were stashed in the wooden locker by her bed, waiting for me to put my moniker to them. While Tegan was gabbling on at her mother and kissing her face, Del pointed me in the direction of the papers. When I'd opened the locker I found she'd rather thoughtfully put a pen in there.

'You might as well sign them now,' she said with a grin.

'Yeah, I might as well,' I replied. I hadn't said a word about what I'd found in Guildford. Nor a word about what I planned to do next. Come to think of it, I hadn't even said hello.

I'd read through the sheets in a cursory fashion, knowing there was no other way in which Adele could screw me over more than she already had, then resisted the urge to sign 'World Class Mug' instead of Kamryn Matika by the Xs on the various pages.

Even now, sitting in the corridor, holding onto a plastic cup of vending machine tea, I seethed a little. But only a little. All right, it was more than a little. I was scared. Confused. Majorly pissed off. This decision had been thrust upon me and I was feeling . . . What was I feeling? I'd spent most of the night galloping, jogging, walking, limping and crawling through a range of emotions and I'd finally ended up at a place called 'acceptance'. Which felt a lot like 'resignation'. I'd been chased down until I was trapped, held hostage in this situation: I couldn't take Tegan back to Guildford; I couldn't leave her to grow up in care. I had no other choices; no way out.

So, no matter what conflicting emotions were battling inside me, I had to do this. This was my little Tiga, after all. I'd held her minutes after she was born. I'd helped name her. I'd been there when she took her first steps. I'd almost cried when she pointed at me and said, 'Win take me,' when Adele had asked her if she wanted to go see Father Christmas one year. I had to do this. How could I not? This was Tiga. How could I not want to take her on?

Very easily, actually, the thought popped into my head before I could stop it. *You are a bad person,* I chastised myself. *A bad, bad person.*

A transformation had come over Tegan when we'd arrived. She didn't seem to notice the tubes and machines around her mother and had practically leapt onto the bed, throwing her arms around her mother's neck and covering her cheek in kisses. Having hardly said anything to me since Guildford, she was like a clockwork toy that had been finally wound up after weeks of idleness and was wearing herself down by chatting at super-speed, pausing constantly to kiss her mother's cheek.

I'd slipped out to give them time alone together. I'd forgotten about the bond between them. They were best mates, couldn't bear to be parted. Weren't whole without each other. How the hell was Tegan going to cope when . . .

I cracked another big split in the side of the plastic cup.

What if Del got better?

What if she made a recovery? Went into remission? I seized that thought, clung to it like a life buoy in the sea of despair and self-pity I was currently drowning in. Del would live.

Where was it written that she had to die of this? Had she tried everything? I mean, *everything*? Every treatment available? And I'm sure it wasn't my imagination that she was looking better. Brighter. Less grey and mottled and tired. That was probably Tegan's influence. Having her around obviously made Del feel a million times better, so we could build on that. She and Tegan would spend lots of time together. Her strength would improve and she would live.

About half an hour later Nancy the nurse took Tegan for a walk to the canteen so Del and I could talk.

'You could get well again,' I blurted at her the second the door shut behind Nancy and Tegan. I still hadn't mastered the tact-in-front-of-an-ill-person thing. 'I mean, you could get better.'

Del shook her head slightly. 'No.'

'You don't know that,' I said.

'Yes, I do.'

'Come on, Del, you can't give up. You can still beat this thing, I know you can. You're one of, no, you're *the* strongest person I know. Look how much shite you've had to overcome in the past, course you can—'

'Kam, it's too late,' Del cut in.

I wasn't going to be deterred and talked right over her.

'You've got to fight this. You *can* beat this,' I said. 'There are lots of new treatments, alternative therapies. Have you tried acupuncture, or—'

'Kam,' her voice was stern enough to halt my wild chatter. 'I've come to accept this, you will too.'

'But you've got to fight,' I whispered.

'I have been fighting. That's why I'm still here.'

'I can't believe you've given up so easily.'

'Kam, you don't understand . . .' her voice trailed off and she inhaled deeply. 'I want to live. *God* I want to live. I want to see my daughter grow up. I want to have all those teenage fights with Tegan that I was preparing myself for. I want to find cigarettes in her bedroom and have big stand-up rows with her about it. I want to wave her off to university. I want to be the one who gives her away at her wedding. I want to get married myself one day because, you know, I still believe in love.

'I want to have the time to sort out our problems. I thought we had all the time in the world. I thought I had all the time in the world. And now I know that I don't, I've got to accept it. I've got to . . .' Del paused, inhaled again. 'I want to live. But I'm not going to. I have to accept that or I'll be frozen. And I have to be active. I have to make as many plans as I can for Tegan. Do everything I can to make sure her life is sorted. And being with you is the start of that.'

I sniffed back my tears but still they broke free, tumbled down my face. I wiped at my eyes with the palms of my hands then dried them on my jeans.

'I've written her a load of letters,' Del was saying. 'Gotten twenty birthday cards. Twenty Christmas cards. I've written them all. It's amazing how much there is to say, even when you're writing them for the future. But the letters, they're for things like her eighteenth birthday. And her twenty-first. And when she's deciding whether to go to uni; some are just for those times when we'd have a chat. You know, well, you'll find out how much she likes to chat. Do you remember how she was like that? You'll find out.'

I bit down on my lower lip and dipped my head as she talked. She wasn't going to be here in a few years. In twenty years. In five years. Even in a year. That was a horrifying thought, knowing someone you loved wouldn't see the future. Wouldn't see if we managed to get another woman prime minister – this time a non-evil one. Wouldn't know how grey her hair would turn, how many wrinkles her face would be invaded by, how saggy her body would become. Wouldn't be around to see what type of person her daughter became. That was a humbling thought. My chest contracted; fresh tears escaped my eyes and drizzled down my face.

I might not be here in twenty years, in five years, in a year, but I didn't know it. I didn't have that clock ticking away so loudly in the foreground it drowned out everything. Del was going to die.

'I didn't want to make a video. I don't want her to for ever think of me like this. I want her to remember me as the healthy woman in the pictures, not someone who looks so grey and old and tired. So, the letters will help. I hope. I hope.' Del's eyes reddened, like they did yesterday when she wanted to cry. For someone who professed to having reached 'acceptance' she seemed to want to cry a lot.

'You've got to love her. Promise me. Even when she's really bad, or says something horrible, you've got to love her. Promise me. Please promise me.'

I brushed brusquely at my tears. Who did she think I was? *What* did she think I was? Of course I'd love Tegan, if I didn't I wouldn't even be considering this. 'Del, just because I stopped talking to you doesn't mean I didn't still care about you both.'

'I'm scared she won't have unconditional love. And that's all a mother wants for her daughter. For her to know there'll

71

always be someone there who loves her no matter what. Promise me that's what you'll give her – unconditional love.'

I nodded. 'I've always loved her. Why do you think I sent her pressies? And look—' I scrambled about in my bag for my wallet, pulled out the red leather purse – opened it and showed it to her.

As she relieved me of my purse, I noticed her hands were covered in skin that was paper thin, the veins underneath were blue and green, like wires in a cable leading up to the plug of her fingers. They were scarred with marks from where the drips had been. I glanced away, her hands distressed me.

Del opened my wallet and saw a picture of Tegan. I'd taken it on her third birthday, just weeks before I left London. I'd plaited her hair into two cornrows with a centre parting and she was wearing a pink pinafore with a white top underneath. She was grinning at the camera, holding her chin forwards having squeezed shut her eyes.

'You've always carried this?' Del whispered. 'Even after . . .'

'Yep,' I cut in. I'd put that picture in there when I moved to Leeds and realised I wouldn't be seeing Tegan again. It was the only one of the photos I had of her that didn't instantly give away who her father was.

I wanted, no, needed a reminder of her because in all of it, in all my hurt and anger and shock, there was one truth that was clear to me. One truth that was never blurred in my mind: it wasn't her fault. Tegan wasn't responsible for my fiancé and my best friend screwing things up. Besides, 'I've always adored Tiga. You know that, you said it yourself the other day. I couldn't stop loving her just like that.'

Del's body relaxed, almost as though one of her concerns, one of the things on her list of things to worry about had been dealt with. 'One more thing you must promise me,' Del said, still staring down at the picture under plastic in my wallet.

'What's that then?'

I felt her eyes staring hard at me until I raised my eyes to her. 'When you adopt her you'll change her name to yours, won't you?'

'Probably. To be honest I haven't thought about it in that much detail. I've only had twenty-four hours to make the decision, so I'll need a bit more time to refine the details.'

'But once you've done all that, you'll change her surname to yours, won't you?' Del asked again.

'I suppose,' I said with a shrug. 'Probably.'

'All right. Then you've got to let her call you Mummy, if she wants to.'

'You what?' I shrank back in my seat, stricken. 'Come on Del, that's . . . No. No. I can't.'

'Why not?'

'Because I'm not.'

'You're not her aunt but you let her call you Auntie.'

'That's completely different! You know that's completely different.'

'I want her to feel as though she's got another mother, that she's got someone who'll do all the mummy things with her.'

'She will have. But it's not right, her calling me Mum. It's not . . . It's not natural!'

'That's the best argument you've got?' Del raised what would have been her left eyebrow as she mocked me.

Rather shamefully, it was. What I was trying to say was, you couldn't replace a human being that easily and it wasn't right to try. Tegan had known her mother, she'd remember her. What was it going to do to her mind asking her to think of me as a new version of the woman she called Mummy? Tegan might love me, but she could never love me like she did her mother. Asking her to try would be wrong. It'd tear her apart, it'd confuse her in ways that we couldn't even begin to understand. I wasn't going to be responsible for screwing her up.

73

'You know that's not all I'm trying to say,' I replied.

'Come on, Kam, what do you think adoption means? It means you're becoming her mother, you're adopting a role. You're taking over from where I left off. I want her to think of you as her mother. And I want you to think of her as your daughter.'

'I will.'

'Not if you won't let her call you Mum.' Del stopped talking suddenly, rested her frail body and her scarf-covered head against the white pillows. I watched her inhale a few times, her skin paling with each inhalation. Her eyes slipped shut. She inhaled a few more times. 'If someone calls you beautiful often enough you believe it.' Her voice was as thin and fragile as tissue paper, the slightest interruption would tear it apart. She slowly opened her eyes. 'If someone . . . If they tell you something often enough you believe it. Self-fulfilling prophecy. I want that to happen to you and Tegan. If she calls you Mummy often enough you'll believe it. She'll be a part of you that you'll never . . . you'll never want to let go. She'll become your daughter.'

'She will be. You know that saying, "A rose by any other name would smell as sweet"? She can still call me Auntie and I'll be like her mother. I can't ever be her mother because she's got one, you. But I'll be the next best thing. I'll be the rose and still smell as sweet.'

'Please. Just think about it.'

'OK. I'll think about it. Only think though. I'm not promising anything.'

Silence came to us. Silence that she broke with, 'Kam, about Nate—'

'Del, please, don't,' I interrupted. 'I can't deal with talking about that on top of everything. I'm just about coping with all this. I can't handle talking about that as well. OK? Please. We'll sort it out another time.'

'Another time,' she echoed. 'Time's funny like that. Infinite. For ever. We aren't.'

'You say that, but no one has actually proved that time is infinite.'

Adele smiled. 'You're so obnoxious.'

'I try,' I smiled back at her. Then I verbalised what I'd been thinking through whilst I'd been waiting in the corridor. 'Look, you said you had a few months . . . I'm going to get time off work. If the doctors agree, I'll find a place to rent for the three of us and you can come home. I'll learn how to take care of you and you can come home. You know, till . . . Till . . .' I couldn't say it. I'd thought the word, considered what it meant, but I hadn't said it. Wouldn't say it. 'I want to be there with you at . . .' I swallowed. 'I want to be with you.'

'You'll do that?'

I nodded, my face buckling with emotion. I knew what I was offering. I couldn't say the word, but I was offering to watch her do it. I'd have to watch my best friend leave this planet. I'd baulked at the thought of taking care of a child, could I really sit with someone I loved and watch the life ebb out of her? I'd have to. Of course I'd have to. She had no one else. And she'd do the same for me if the roles were reversed. 'Of course I'll do that, Del,' I said. 'Of course I will.'

She held her hand out to me and I took it. It was cool to the touch, the skin papery and dry. I thought I might crumble it if I held her too tight. Our eyes met and for a second I felt like I was back in that college bar, back where I fell for her. Everything good about her, all her inner beauty radiated outwards at me.

'Count yourself lucky, mind,' I said with a cheeky smile. 'You know I wouldn't do that for anyone else, don't you?'

'I'm honoured,' she replied with a slight laugh, her fingers curling around mine, 'truly, I'm honoured.'

'No, I am.'

chapter nine

A week I'd been in London, although it felt like a lifetime. A lifetime of traffic-clogged streets, anonymous living and accents like mine. It was almost as if I'd never left. In that time, in the past eight days, the three of us – Adele, Tegan and I – had slipped into a routine. A loose one, but still a routine. Structure, no matter how small, was important for all of us.

We'd wake at fifteen seconds past the crack of dawn because Tegan liked to scramble out from under the covers, lie on the end of the bed, turn on the TV, find cartoons and stay in front of them for as long as I allowed her to. As soon as the TV went on, I would pull a pillow over my head, trying to blot out the high-pitched squeaks and clangs emanating from the screen.

After about an hour of cartoons, I'd drag myself from the double bed, stiff and kinked up because I'd have been on the edge all night scared to death I'd roll over and crush her. After my shower, I'd persuade Tegan into the bath. By the time we were both dressed, Tegan would be incapable with excitement because she knew she'd be seeing her mum soon.

We'd drop by the hospital for an hour or so until we'd exhausted Del, then we'd go house hunting. None of the houses or flats Tegan and I saw were right for us but today, the eighth day since I'd been here, I knew we were going to find somewhere. A nice three-bedroom ground-floor flat that would give Del her own space and Tegan and I our own rooms. Maybe even a garden for Tegan to play in now that summer had kicked in and the air was warm, the days bright with sun and positive energy. Today was the day, I could feel it in my soul.

Everything else I needed to change to fit my life around this situation had slotted into place. I'd asked for a six-month sabbatical from work, but they'd suggested I have the preceding week and the next two weeks as my annual leave, then work from home – home being the place I rented with Del and Tegan – three days a week. We'd get email, I could easily work from the London office of the department store I was National Marketing Manager for, and if I needed to go to Leeds then they'd schedule midday meetings so I had time to get there and back in a day. I'd find an estate agent to sort out renting my flat in Leeds. It was all going to work out. We just needed somewhere to live.

Despite my conviction about finding the right house, today hadn't exactly started well. My five-year-old charge hadn't roused from bed yet because she'd been up late, fizzing with excitement about the future. About the three of us being together. She'd begun to relax with me in the past eight days. Now she felt she could do things like turn on the telly without staring at me until I asked her what was wrong. Also, I guessed her mother had been talking to her about the longer term future because she'd ask things like, 'What's Leeds like?' and 'Can I have my own room?'

Tegan's latest idea was getting a cat. There was no way on earth that we were getting any kind of furry animal, not now, not ever. They were fine in the wild, but not in my flat, nor my realm of responsibility. I don't know where she got the idea from but it'd been one of the first things she brought up when we went to visit her mother yesterday.

She'd opened the door to Del's room, ran in, leapt up onto the bed and began her ritual of kisses. They started high up on Del's left cheek, got lower and lower, crossed her chin, avoiding the tube hooked through her nostrils, then went up to her right cheek. Tegan never seemed to notice her mum wasn't looking well or that she was connected to machines. And, yesterday, I wasn't surprised. Del looked amazing during our evening visit. She'd seemed stronger in the past few days, was even eating solid food and keeping it down. She seemed to last longer and longer when we visited before growing tired; her conversation wasn't punctuated with as many pauses to catch her breath or rest her eyes.

Yesterday, colour was back in her face, that mottled grey and yellow had faded, instead her skin glowed a healthy pink. The red had all but gone from the whites of her eyes and the sparkle was back in the steel-blue windows to her soul. She was almost normal. Apart from the navy blue scarf around her head, the thinned face and the lack of eyebrows, she could have been the Del I knew all those years ago. I'd grinned because she'd done it. She'd accepted that she did have a choice in this after all – she could get better, live.

'How you doing?' she asked. Her voice sounded far more substantial than it had been only three days ago, and my grin widened.

'I'm fine. I'm always fine,' I said. 'You look so well.'

'I feel well. Not well. Better. A lot better. You, on the other hand, look exhausted.'

'I'm fine, really.' I *was* tired, couldn't remember the last proper night's sleep I'd had, but hey, let's get everything in proportion. Terminally ill, a bit knackered – who should be complaining here?

'Please take care of yourself, Kam.'

'I am,' I replied.

'That'd be a first,' Adele said.

'I *am*.'

'Can we get a cat?' Tegan interjected.

'You'll have to ask Kamryn about that,' Del said, passing the buck rather neatly to me, even though she knew how I felt about all things furry.

'Can we?' Tegan asked me.

'Not right now, sweetie. We'll talk about it another time.' *As in never.*

Del pushed her lips together to hide her smirk.

'We saw a house with no upstairs today,' Tegan informed her mother. 'It was a bung-low.'

'That's nice,' Del said.

Tegan stretched out on the bed and rested her head on her mother's right breast, avoiding almost by some sixth sense the tube coming out of her torso and the drip in her hand. Del gazed tenderly down at her daughter's head, then back up at me. 'She's tired as well.'

'I know, but a day house hunting will do that.'

'She needs to be settled.'

'She will be. When we find somewhere that feels like home she can have her own room and she can see you any time she wants. Which is what you both need.'

'If we get a cat, can we call it Pussy Puss?' Tegan asked in a sleepy voice.

'Pussy's a good name for a cat,' Del said, trying to hold back her laughter.

'Yeah,' I said, 'it certainly is.'

'Can you imagine walking around the neighbourhood calling "Pussy, Pussy"?' Del giggled.

'Why are you laughing?' Tegan asked as her mother and I snickered like two schoolboys who'd discovered see-thru bras in the underwear section of their mothers' catalogues.

'Your Auntie Kamryn is just being silly that's all. Don't mind her.'

'No, sweetie, don't mind me.'

I knew why Tegan was so awake when we returned to the hotel last night – she'd had a snooze during the evening while Del and I thought up the weirdest, rudest names for pets that we could wander around the streets shouting out. Our favourite had been Your Hairy Butt, ('Your Hairy Butt, Your Hairy Butt, dinner time!') which made Del laugh so much I thought she was going to pass out.

When we got back to the hotel, Tegan had been fizzing, keyed up about getting a cat, about her mum coming home, about having fish fingers for dinner . . . Nothing was too trivial for her to chatter about. I'd watched her babble as she bounced on the bed. Then watched as she lay down as if about to sleep, then would suddenly leap up with something else to talk about. I marvelled at the transformation. Less than a week ago she wouldn't talk to me, now she couldn't stop. When she'd finally fallen asleep it'd been pushing 3 a.m. and I was whacked out myself.

I checked her sleeping form, a small crescent shape under the blue blankets, blonde hair splayed out around her face on the white pillow. *Maybe I'll leave her a bit longer.* Del was seeing the consultant this morning, anyway, so we had house hunting as first task of the day. I wanted to get on with it but Tegan obviously needed her sleep and a grumpy child was something I could do without.

A knock at the door made me jump. My eyes went to the LCD display on the clock radio by the bed: 07:55. Far too early for callers. Maybe it was the laundry woman. I bit my lower lip anxiously, I hadn't gotten our dirty clothes together for washing. I looked around at the room, ashamed. Our room was a bomb site. Stuff was all over the joint: new clothes that I had to buy because I hadn't brought enough down with me mingled in with old ones, outfits that Tegan didn't want to wear that I'd taken out but hadn't folded away, toys Tegan had been playing with. I wasn't the tidiest of people and living out of one room you really needed to be. I'd have to ask the laundry woman to come back later when I'd got our washing together.

I traversed several piles of clothes to get to the door.

Nancy, Adele's nurse, was stood on the other side of the door. She was wearing a buttoned-up beige mac, black tights, and sensible pink and white trainers. Her black plaits were loose and her face was free of make-up – it was also missing her usual bright smile.

I knew. The moment my eyes settled on her face I knew. But I also didn't know, I wasn't ready.

'Hello, Kamryn,' she said with a smile. Not her usually bright, sunny one, this one was warm but subdued.

'Hi,' I said back.

'Where's Tegan?' she asked.

'She's asleep,' I replied.

'OK, good. May I speak to you in the corridor?'

I nodded, looked around to check Tegan was still sleeping before I put my shoe in the doorway so the door wouldn't slam shut.

We walked to the end of the corridor, to where there were two tan leather armchairs and a glass side table upon which stood a vase of silk flowers. Neither of us sat in the armchairs and I kept an eye on the door to our room.

'I'm sorry, Kamryn,' Nancy began, and the bundle of butterflies that had been fluttering around my stomach plummeted through my body. 'Adele passed away in the night.'

'But she looked all right yesterday,' I said through the thick lump of emotion that had filled my throat.

'She was very, very ill.'

'But she looked better yesterday,' I insisted. 'She said she felt better.' In the face of such testimony, testimony from the one person who should know, how could this woman be telling me this?

'Adele looked better but she had been deteriorating for a long, long time. We were all surprised that she survived this long.'

This didn't make sense. No sense at all. We'd been laughing yesterday. Joking about pets called Your Hairy Butt. 'She wasn't on her own, was she?' My eyes frantically searched Nancy's tired face. It was the most important thing in the world right then, that she didn't leave, go on this new journey, all alone. Without someone there to help her pass into the next place she was going to go to. 'Adele didn't die alone?'

Nancy shook her head. 'No, I was with her. She said to tell Tegan she loved her and to tell you goodbye.'

'It should have been me, I should have been with her. I said I'd be with her.'

'She didn't want that,' Nancy said gently and laid a hand on my arm. 'She'd asked enough of you already. And, she was happy.

'Adele had been holding on because she didn't know what was going to happen to her baby. But when you came she was happy because her child would be taken care of and she could let go. That's why she was looking better, she wasn't as worried. She knew yesterday that she was near the end – after you had gone she said that if she passed away in the night, not to tell you until this morning. She didn't want to spoil the last memory you had of her laughing and joking by you watching her go. She just wanted you to remember the laughing.'

82

abandoned her. When she needed me most I'd turned my back on her. And she'd dwindled to that. To nothingness. I'd wanted to cry then but hadn't.

Then came the tears for what had happened to Tegan. I could've saved her from all that pain, all that violence, if I'd opened just one of Del's letters. Had talked to her even once and found out what was going on. Every bruise and mark and welt on Tegan's thin little body was scarred on my soul. I'd fought those tears when I first bathed her because I had to be strong, I had to hold it all together. Now, though, every ounce of strength was gone and all that was left was a big pool of sobbing.

I didn't feel better. Each sob didn't release pain, it brought more of it. More of the things I'd hidden from, had pushed away, pushed down, pushed behind me were cascading out in an embarrassing mess. Mess. I was making a mess. And I couldn't stop.

Tegan was still asleep.

She'd hardly stirred in an hour and I'd had to stare hard at her chest several times to check she was still breathing. She was so peaceful in sleep, probably the calmest she'd been since we'd got here.

I'd been lying next to her for what felt like an eternity. I didn't want to wake her. If I woke her, I had to tell her. I had to let her know, and that was going to be . . . I didn't know how I was going to do it.

I'd calmed down. I wasn't calm, just *calmer,* no longer hysterical. I hadn't realised until I started crying how unbalanced I'd felt, how I'd spent two years on the edge of hysteria, always wanting to let it out but unsure if I started if I'd be able to stop. Now I'd stemmed the flow of tears, had washed my face, had bathed my eyes in enough cold water to take away the redness and puffiness.

Tegan opened her eyes suddenly, making me jump. She always did that. She could be fast asleep then her blue eyes would be open and staring intently at you.

'Why are your eyes red?' she asked. So much for taking away the redness with cold water.

I brushed her hair off her forehead, exposing the soft white skin on her forehead.

'I've been crying,' I replied.

'Why?' she asked, tilting her head deeper into the pillow in a questioning gesture.

'I'm sad.'

'Why?'

I inhaled deeply, felt the tightness of emotion compressing my lungs. 'I'm sad because of your mummy.'

'Mummy?' Tegan sat up. 'Are we going to see Mummy today?'

I shook my head. 'No, sweetie,' I said.

'I want to see Mummy.'

My lower jaw trembled as I watched the little girl with dishevelled hair and creased pyjamas who sat asking me with big confused eyes why I was keeping her mother from her.

'Tiga, when your mummy said you were going to live with me, where did she say she'd be?'

'In heaven with Jesus and the angels,' Tegan replied. Just like that. As though heaven was only around the corner, and Jesus and the angels could be found hanging out in the local park.

'Did she say why?'

'Because she was ill and Jesus and the angels would look after her.'

'I'm sorry, sweetie, your mummy's gone to be with Jesus and the angels.'

Tegan shook her head. 'No she hasn't. She's in the hospital.'

'She was yesterday. But today she's gone to heaven.'

'When is she coming back?'

'I'm sorry, Tiga, she's not coming back.'

'I DON'T BELIEVE YOU!' Tegan shouted and I recoiled at the volume of her voice. She scrambled out from under the covers and leapt off the bed. 'I don't believe you. I want to see my mummy. I want to see my mummy.'

'I'm sorry, you can't,' I said quietly.

'I want my mummy,' she screamed. 'I want to see my mummy!'

I sat on the bed, frozen as Tegan stood in the middle of the floor, her pyjamas hanging off her thin body, flinging her arms up and down and stamping her feet, screaming.

Her cries got louder and more anguished.

I didn't know what to do. Try to hold her? Leave her to scream it out? Run away and hide? That was the strongest urge: to bury my face in the pillow, to cover my ears and wait for all of this to go away. I didn't know what else to do. Nancy had offered to stay whilst I told Tegan but I'd said no, she'd done enough already, I couldn't impose upon her any more. Now I wished she had stayed. She would have known what to do.

I kept repeating that I was sorry but Tegan didn't hear me. She just screamed and screamed, stamping her feet and flailing her arms about. On and on. 'I WANT MY MUMMY, I WANT MY MUMMY, I WANT MY MUMMY, I WANT MY MUMMY.'

Trampling clothes and papers and other items littering the floor, I crossed the room to her.

'I WANT MY MUMMY, I WANT MY MUMMY, I WANT MY MUMMY, I WANT MY MUMMY.'

I slipped my arms around her even though she fought me, hit out with her tiny fists, each of them connecting with my body but not hurting.

'I WANT MY MUMMY, I WANT MY MUMMY, I WANT MY MUMMY, I WANT MY MUMMY.'

She bucked and twisted, as wild and vicious as a cornered animal, still screaming, but I held on to her until her rage subsided and she went limp in my arms – her head flopped onto my left bicep, finally exhausted from crying and yelling and begging for her mother.

'You've still got me,' I said, holding her close and gently stroking her back.

'Don't want you,' she whispered in a tiny, hoarse voice, 'want my mummy.'

chapter ten

The handle to door of my former bedroom turned and the door slowly opened. I watched as more of the corridor of my parents' house came into view and Tegan stepped in. She was dressed in a calf-length, black satin dress with a full skirt, embroidered bodice and long sleeves that my mum had bought her. She had shiny black patent shoes on her feet and white socks that ended mid-calf. Mum had also tied black ribbons into the twin bunches in Tegan's hair. The black was tragically striking against her whey-coloured skin and pale gold hair, it brought out the dark strands of colour in her royal blue eyes, gave her a regal air. Her beauty brought a lump to my throat instead of a smile to my lips because she wasn't going to wow people at a party but was attending her mother's funeral.

Since we didn't need to be in town any more, the day after Adele . . . The day after it happened, Tegan and I packed up and moved to my parents' house in Ealing, the outskirts of west London. The plan was to return to Leeds a few days after the funeral. After today.

Tegan had reverted to the fearful silence that had shrouded her when I'd taken her from Guildford. This silence, however, was splintered with sadness and the worry of what would happen to her now; what she would do without her mum.

She refused to speak to me unless absolutely necessary, and

when it came to meals we'd play the guessing game, with a nod at the right place, but no shaking of her head if she didn't want it. Despite not speaking to me, I always had to be in her sight and if I left her company for too long, she'd seek me out, apprehension smudged onto her face, until she could touch me. A brush of her short fingers on the back of my hand, a slight stroke of my hair, a nudge against my abdomen, just to make sure I was real. Solid. There. I'd find her sitting outside the bathroom if I went for a shower. The day I nipped down the road for a bottle of water and to make some calls, I'd returned to find her sitting beside the front door, clutching her knees to her chest, her eyes like two chips of dark sapphire on a snow plain as they stared into the mid-distance. She'd curled her arms around my thigh and rested her head against it when I walked in, and I accepted that I couldn't leave her alone again.

We slept in the same bed, if we were watching TV she'd climb into my lap, put her arms around me and rest her head against my chest, she'd often fall asleep like that. We were virtually inseparable. The silent duo, because I didn't feel much like speaking either. My usual way for dealing with things was sleeping, and right now all I felt like doing was escaping into another realm, especially when I was arranging a funeral. A funeral for my best friend. For the woman I couldn't remember saying a proper goodbye to. Every time I thought of that, my stomach would implode, clenching in on itself until it was a tight, solid ball of pain. I didn't get to say goodbye. I couldn't remember the last expression on her face – did she smile? Did I smile at her? I couldn't picture her face. Couldn't hold onto the image of her, not when it was the ill face. When I looked at Adele in the hospital I didn't see the ill person, she was transformed into a cream-skinned, curly blonde stunner with steel-blue eyes and a killer smile. Had I seen that smile before I left? I couldn't remember. I couldn't hold onto the image of her because I'd not been seeing Adele as she was, simply a memory of the woman she used to be.

In the here and now, Tegan stood in the corner of the room, leaning her right shoulder against the wall, staring at me, waiting for me to finish getting ready. My dress wasn't anywhere near as beautiful as hers – it was a simple straight up and down, ankle-skimming linen creation with a V-neck and short sleeves that I'd grabbed in a dash to Ealing Shopping Centre. I hadn't brought enough clothes with me for a long spell in London and I certainly hadn't been prepared for a funeral.

'I like your dress,' I said to her.

Tegan said nothing, although her impassive blue eyes remained on me.

'And I like your hair bunches. My mum used to put my hair in bunches too. But I had three – two at the front, one at the back.'

Her eyes never left my face.

'I used to have different coloured ribbons tied to each bunch. So did my sister, you know, Sheridan. My mum would plait them and then tie a ribbon around them. Remember how I used to plait your hair?'

Nothing. Her blue eyes watched me but her mouth didn't move to reply.

I looked down at my shiny black shoes, trying to control the expression on my face. It was hard enough coping with every-thing else, and the funeral would be a nightmare, but it'd be a million times worse if Tegan continued her campaign of silence against me.

It wasn't her fault, though. She didn't know how else to be. What do you do when you're five years old and your mother dies? And in her place is a strange woman who you haven't seen in two years, claiming she'll take care of you?

91

I stood, painting a smile on my face as I reached my full height. 'What do you think of my dress?' I asked.

Her eyes roamed from my face to my feet, then back up to my face but didn't betray her thoughts, and since this question required more than a nod for an answer, she didn't tell me what she thought.

'Do you like it?' I rephrased.

She nodded and turned the corners of her mouth up nearly managing a smile. I almost wrapped her up in my arms as a thank you for acknowledging me, for taking this small but significant step on our road back to verbal communication.

'It's not as pretty as yours,' I stated.

The corners of Tegan's mouth returned to a flatline but I remembered the twitch of her lips when she smiled at me. That would keep me going for a couple of hours. 'OK, I'm ready, finally. Let's go.'

chapter eleven

Adele Brannon
(formerly Lucinda-Jayne Hamilton-Mackenzie)
died recently after a valiant battle with leukaemia.
She is survived by her daughter, Tegan Brannon.
The funeral will be held on 31 July at 4 p.m.
St Agnes's church, Ealing.

In the grey-brick, Catholic church Tegan sat motionless and impassive beside me, watching the people who stood in the pulpit, talking about her mother. I wasn't sure she knew what was going on – I'd explained that a funeral was where you said goodbye to someone who'd died – but like everything I'd said to her since her cry in the hotel room, she'd given no sign of understanding what I was talking about. Nevertheless, now she was silent and still, as though she sensed the gravity of the occasion.

I, on the other hand, couldn't, wouldn't sit still. My body, hot and coated with a film of sweat under the black linen dress and matching jacket, wouldn't stop fidgeting. The wooden pew beneath me, smoothed shiny by hundreds if not thousands of bums over the years, was uncomfortable, unsuited to long periods of sitting. Even if it had been a comfy armchair, I wouldn't have sat still. To sit still would be to agree with what had happened. I would be telling the world that I approved of Adele being taken away from us. That this dying business and accompanying funeral were acceptable to me.

The church vibrated with the presence of hundreds of people. *Hundreds*. Hundreds of them had come to pay their last respects – Adele had thought she'd be lucky if she got enough people to make a football team turning up.

'I tell you, leukaemia sure helps you find out who your friends are,' she'd said with her characteristic laugh. Her humour had stayed at the edge of the gallows in those last few days. Always saying things that only the terminally ill were allowed to get away with. I usually laughed, but some of the things Adele came out with horrified even me. 'I don't blame people for not coming to visit, though. Who wants to sit in a hospital room and be reminded of death?' she'd continued. 'Besides, how do you react when you find out someone you vaguely know is knocking on heaven's door? You can't mourn them when you don't know them, can you? And what do you say when you visit? "Sorry we didn't get to know you, now it's too late"?'

'Suppose,' I'd mumbled, eager to the change the subject; desperate to stop her using the 'D' word.

'One of my biggest regrets is that I don't know that many people. I wish I'd made the effort to touch more lives.'

She had touched lives, I wish she'd known that. The church was filled to capacity, with two rows of people standing at the back. People did care and did remember because they had dusted off their black suits, black dresses, black skirts and tops and, like a steady stream of mournful ravens, had flocked to St Agnes's. I'd only contacted a couple of the places where she worked, put notices in her local paper, another in a couple of the media trade magazines, and one on our university's website. Word of mouth must have done the rest.

My whole family was here, even my older brother who lived and worked in Japan and hadn't known Del that well had

94

flown in for it. And my sister's family had driven down from Manchester to be here. Nancy, Adele's nurse, had come and brought her husband.

Adele's father wasn't there. Wasn't there, didn't want to be there, hadn't even sent flowers. He didn't care. That was the stark reality of it. Of all the things from the past few weeks, his reaction had caused me a disproportionate amount of hurt.

I'd rung Mr Hamilton-Mackenzie to tell him what happened on the day Adele died, and after a long silence he'd said, 'Thank you for letting me know.' He hadn't asked about Tegan, hadn't shouted about my raid on their home and I guessed it was the shock. His only child had died and it had shaken him in the same way it had me; had reminded him that he hadn't seen her in the weeks before her death and now he'd never get the chance.

'I'll let you know about the funeral arrangements,' I'd said and he thanked me again before hanging up.

A week later, three days ago, I called him again.

'Kamryn,' he'd said warmly when he answered the phone, 'how are you?'

I'd been thrown; thought for a moment I'd dialled the wrong number. 'As fine as can be expected in these circumstances,' I said cautiously.

I heard something catch in his voice as he said, 'I know. I'm still coming to terms with this myself.'

'I'm calling about the funeral,' I said, the evil thoughts I'd had about him melting away like ice left out in the noon-day sun. I was right, death had made him accept that he loved his daughter; he was going to redeem himself.

'The funeral, ah, yes.'

'It's on Friday. I've done almost everything that Del could-n't do herself . . .'

'Del?' he interjected, his voice stern.

'I mean Lucinda-Jayne. She made most of the arrangements with the undertaker – she wanted to be cremated – and I've sorted out the details. But if you want to add any readings or hymns let me know and we can work it out.'

Silence. I fancied I could hear him pulling himself together, trying to suppress the tears in his voice, trying not to fall apart before he could tell me what he wanted. 'I won't be attending. Neither my wife nor I will be attending.'

'Why?' rose up in my throat as a protest, but I stopped myself in time. I'd nearly fallen for it. Fallen for his game. This was why Del was always broken up after every phone call. Why every time she spoke to him she believed he might have changed, because he knew how to lure you in, to con you into thinking you were conversing with a decent person – then he'd turn on you, like a snake hypnotising its prey before administering the lethal bite, and you were powerless to resist even if you'd experienced it all before.

I took a deep breath. 'OK,' I exhaled. I had no strength to argue with him, nor even to talk to him. What was there to say to this man? How was I meant to get through to him? By begging? Was I meant to beg him to come to his own daughter's funeral?

He had no idea how difficult the preceding week had been. That one of my many tasks was identifying Adele's body. I hadn't flinched in the morgue when I was asked to confirm that the person lying motionless in front of me was the woman who used to throw her head back and laugh; the friend who had once rugby tackled me for the last packet of crisps in our flat; the girl who'd often be found adjusting her bra straps, fiddling with the top button of her jeans, rebuckling her belt, twisting her hair round her fingers while she grinned.

The person in front of me was lifeless. No expression on her pale grey face. Her lips were pressed together, her eyes closed, her hair nothing but thin blonde wisps on her head. I'd stared at her, lying on a hospital trolley, serene and delicate. *Will she be cold if I touch her?* I wondered. Would she be as cold and fragile as she seemed? Because that's what she looked like, frozen and frail, not at all like my friend.

No, I'd almost said to the hospital official, *that isn't Lucinda-Jayne Adele Hamilton-Mackenzie. And she isn't Adele Brannon. And she certainly isn't Del. That person isn't anyone I know.*

I'd done that. The first dead body I'd ever seen was of my best friend. Did Mr Hamilton-Mackenzie think after that I could find it in me to beg him to come to his daughter's funeral when I'd done something so devastating?

'It's not right that I should have to bury another member of my family,' he was saying in a voice designed to break the heart of anyone who didn't know how many times he'd put Adele in hospital. 'I buried her mother. Isn't that enough? Haven't I done enough?' He paused to swallow a couple of audible and expertly pitched sobs. 'Lucinda-Jayne was the last of my family and I can't say goodbye. You understand, don't you, Kamryn? Don't you?'

'What about Tegan?' I replied, my voice as even as a sheet of glass. 'Isn't your granddaughter a member of your family?'

He paused. The pause elongated itself into silence, which became a yawning chasm of arrogant righteousness: he was right and nothing would make him think otherwise, not even something as glaringly obvious as the truth.

'Goodbye,' I eventually stated, and hung up. That was it. The end. He'd never challenge me if I tried to adopt Tegan. He'd never try to get in touch and, while I was relieved and grateful, that was when the sadness had started to stab at me. *Why didn't he love his child?* I found myself asking. *How could anyone not love their child? You might not like them all the time, but when they died . . .*

I slipped an arm around Tegan's shoulders and pulled her towards me as a sudden need to remind her that I was there for her seized me. I held her to my body hoping I could transmit how much I cared about her through the closeness of our touch. She didn't react, not even to resist, she sat still and silent.

I refocused on the priest, listening to his speech about life and death, and Adele. He hadn't known my friend, he was repeating what I'd written for him. But he went beyond what I'd noted, he talked about the warmth he felt when he spoke to those who knew Adele. How wonderful a friend she must have been because so many people had travelled from all over the country to pay their last respects. He moved on to explain about her being a mother, saying how a parent would always want to live to see her child grow up, but he was sure that Adele's daughter, Tegan, would be in good hands.

I wouldn't count on it, mate, I thought before I could stop myself. That would have made Adele laugh. 'Trust you,' she'd have guffawed, 'only you would think like that at my funeral.'

The final prayers were said, the final hymn sung. I got up with the rest of the congregation and turned to follow the four men – two of them my brothers – who picked up the oak coffin with its brass plaque declaring ADELE BRANNON, hoisted it on to their shoulders and began carrying it out of the church.

I tore my eyes away, couldn't look, it didn't seem real. Adele in a box. Adele not walking and talking. Gone. Instead, I cast my line of sight to the back of the church, away from the faces of people sat around me. I couldn't make eye contact with any of these people and hold it together. If I saw even one teared-up face, I'd lose it. All the hurt I'd pushed down and away since I'd cried in the hotel corridor would come spewing out and I wouldn't be able to contain it.

The doors at the back of the church were opened and suddenly it was summer again, hot and bright; the bleak winter of the funeral melting away as light was shed on the dark atmosphere inside. As I gathered my mind together, searching between the black suits for something to focus on, I saw him. His tall frame dressed in a black suit with a black shirt and tie, his grief-bleached skin, his agonised features, his softly spiked-up brown hair. I gasped, my body momentarily rigid with shock.

I craned forwards, squinted to get a better look before he disappeared out of the doors. It was him. It was definitely him.

Nate.

There was a small service at Ealing West crematorium that only my family came to. Words were spoken that I didn't hear. Slowly the box was pulled away from us, pulled away behind the heavy black curtain, disappearing, inch by inch until all that was left were the black curtains swishing together.

It was over. I looked up at the funeral director who'd made it happen. *Do it again. Please, do it again.* I pleaded with my eyes. *I wasn't ready. Please rewind so I can pay attention this time.* I'd stepped out of my body for a moment, and now she was gone. I bit my lower lip and didn't move out of my seat as everyone filed out. Once I was alone – Tegan had gone with my mum and dad – I stepped out of the pew and stood in front of the curtain, where she'd disappeared.

A million thoughts were speeding through my mind, each leaving a burning groove where it ran. Adele. Tegan. Work. Heaven. Death. Life. Leukaemia. Hotels. Nate.

I was ashamed to admit I'd been thinking about Nate.

What was he doing there? He was at a friend's funeral. *How did he know she was gone?* He probably saw the notices in the trade press – he was a radio producer. Every question had an obvious answer. It hadn't occurred to me that he'd turn up. What did it mean? Did it mean anything? Was he in love with her? But they both said it was just the once. And I'd assumed they hadn't seen each other in the two years since I'd left them.

I'll never know for sure, of course. Never find out what really went on . . . What was wrong with me? Why was I thinking about this stuff? I should be thinking about Del. But Nate kept wrestling his way into my mind.

I could remember the last time I saw Nate more clearly than the last time I saw Del. I remember the silence with Nate. How he'd stared at me with haunted eyes as I walked out of the door. I'd been expecting everything to end with a row but it was depressingly quiet. And slow. I always thought if you found out you'd been cheated on, had been cuckolded, that you'd want to lash out, but I hadn't. It wasn't in me. I'd walked out of our flat the day I collected my belongings, knowing it was the last time I'd see him, so I'd looked back to take in his unshaven chin, unwashed hair and sleep-deprived eyes. I listened to him say, 'Don't go' then I walked out.

I had no grand finale with Adele, no curtain call or fade to black. It was another day, another goodbye. Another entry on the list of 'see ya laters' we'd uttered to each other over the years. I'd wracked my brain and still I couldn't remember what I'd said to her. Did I say goodbye? Did I hug her? Did I say the very disposable 'see ya then'? I couldn't remember and it was breaking my heart. I knew I didn't have much time left with her, so why didn't I take in every detail? Why didn't I hang onto every second?

The ball of pain in my stomach contracted suddenly, as though an iron fist had been driven deep into the area below my solar plexus. I doubled over, clutching my stomach, trying to hold myself together. *How would I have said goodbye if I knew that was the last time I would see her?* I don't know. I would have looked at her, I know that. Had I anyway? Did I turn around and look at her? *I can't remember.* I could summon up the look of her from years ago – from college, from after college, from our working years, but not from just a week ago.

Nate. I was thinking about Nate, too, because I didn't want to think about what came next.

Next.

I wish I was a better person, could face this head on, seize the day, seize the rest of my life. Embrace the idea of taking on a child. Del did it. When she'd found out she was pregnant she'd been shocked, of course, and had wailed about not being able to do it, but a few days later she'd accepted the reality, had obviously thought it through and decided she could do it. And she did it. Brilliantly. I'd thought it through, looked into the future, and all I could see were bleak times. Hardship. Sacrifice. Years and years of being responsible for someone else.

I was the woman who sometimes ate a packet of Maltesers for dinner. The woman who was dreading going home because my flat was a tip. I'd left in a rush all those weeks ago, expecting to go back the next day. Meaning there were clothes everywhere, receipts and papers and magazines and cards and partially unwrapped birthday presents littering my bedroom and lounge floors. New types of mould growing in my fridge, if not on the worktops. Light bulbs had probably blown. On top of that, a hundred and one things would have to change about my life so that I could slot Tegan in to it. So that I could make her a new home.

Let's not forget Tegan wasn't talking to me. There'd be the two of us in a house of silence. Mum had suggested that I leave Tegan in London for a few days whilst I arranged everything back in Leeds. But no. Even if she didn't fall apart at the idea of me not being around, I couldn't do without her. She was the last connection I had to Adele and I needed to hold onto that link whether it was communicating with me or not.

Footsteps on the blond wood floor made me straighten up and quickly wipe tears from my eyes. Clearing my throat, I inhaled, scrabbling to recreate the serenity I'd been projecting for the past few days. Everyone thought I was being strong, that I was brave and undaunted; the reality was Kamryn Matika was faking it. I'd painted on this attitude and everyone in the vicinity had fallen for it. I pulled back my shoulders and straightened my back, another deep inhalation stroked more calm into my muscles.

I jumped slightly as a hand slipped into mine. I looked down at the hand, small, perfectly-formed, surprisingly cold. They were chubby, pink fingers that I'd marvelled at when she was born. I'd stared at them, amazed that even though she was hours old her hands looked as though she'd lived fifty years – they had wrinkles at the knuckles and creases on her palms, just like adult hands.

My eyes moved from Tegan's hand to her face. She was looking up at me, her blonde bunches hanging backwards as she tipped her head right back. Her big blue eyes were fixed on me. I tried to smile at her as she studied me. She opened her mouth, licked her dry lips, then she spoke, her voice small and wavering as each word came out. 'Are you my new mummy?'

I nodded. 'Yes, sweetheart, I am.'

'double promise
for ever and ever,
amen?'

chapter twelve

'What do you think of your new home?' I asked Tegan.

She was sitting at the very centre of my cream sofa, wearing a denim dress with a white T-shirt under it. The bruises on her arms had faded away now so she could wear short-sleeved tops without being self-conscious, and without me wanting to cry at what she'd been through. Tegan's blonde hair was in bunches, and she was clutching a rag doll called Meg she'd had since she was a year old. Meg had black wool hair, an orange face and body, big brown eyes surrounded by spiky eyelashes, and a navy blue dress. Meg's hair was also in bunches secured by elastic bands.

'It smells,' Tegan replied honestly.

The girl on the sofa was right. My flat reeked of fish and the other rubbish from the bin, which, day after day, had been breaking down into their odorous parts as though resentful at having been neglected for the six weeks I had been in London. From the doorway I surveyed the room. The place seemed to have grown messier: papers and magazines littered the floor, an upturned shoe in the corner, post that I hadn't finished opening on my birthday perched precariously on the arm of the sofa.

'Apart from the smell,' I said to Tegan, pushing the chaos and its resulting shame to the back of my mind.

Tegan's face asked me if I was mad. How could she imagine something that was there not being there? That was like asking her to fly to the moon.

'Hang on,' I said. I left the living room, clambered over our bags that littered the long narrow corridor and entered the kitchen. I recoiled at the stench – it was so overpowering it could strip paint off walls, and the air above the bin area shimmered in the August heat.

Holding my breath I took the rubbish to the black wheelie bin outside, then returned to wash my hands in the bathroom. Another finger of shame needled me as I noticed the toothpaste spots on the sink taps and the dental floss stuck to the side of basin. This messiness had to stop I realised as I dried my hands on the white hand towel. Now there was someone else to consider, tidiness had to become a habit rather than a rare occurrence; I had to learn to be fastidiously neat, repeat the mantra 'A place for everything and everything in its place' until it became as much a part of my life as brushing my teeth. I returned to the kitchen and opened the big sash window, letting in the heavy, windless air. The smell would soon disperse, the normal smells of a house would be restored.

On the sofa, Tegan was doing that thing she did so well – sitting still and silent. Waiting. Waiting for me to take the lead, to tell her what came next. The tragic part being I really didn't know. I hadn't worked it all out. Life had become a list of events I had to get through: identifying body, funeral, collecting Adele's belongings, moving back to Leeds. One step at a time until the last thing on the list was crossed off. And here we were, in Leeds. That also meant the plan had stopped. I didn't know what came next. Life, yes. But how?

'This will be your room,' I told Tegan.

She glanced down at the sofa then back up at me. *What are you talking about?* her expression said.

'We'll take out the sofa, put it in the smelly kitchen. Except

I'm hoping it won't be smelly by then. We'll get you a bed, you can have a telly. Not this telly, because it's far too big, we'll put that in the kitchen too. No, we'll get you a small telly, and a video recorder so you can watch your videos and things. And we can paint the walls whatever colour you like. I'm sorry, you can't have wallpaper because it'll end in tears – when I was little, my mum and my dad almost got divorced over wall-papering . . .' Tegan watched me as I rambled. 'Anyway, you decide on the colour, but only on a colour you can live with for a long time, not a scary one that will give you nightmares. Not that I'm saying you're not allowed to have nightmares, I just don't want to do anything that will encourage them.

'Anyways, back to your room. Yeah, we can paint the walls, I'll get you a rug or something because this laminate flooring, although it looks very nice, is pretty cold in the mornings. I'll take out the desk, put that in my bedroom, it should fit in there. And we'll use the kitchen as a living room as well as a kitchen. It's big enough, thankfully. Does that sound all right to you?'

Tegan stared at me.

'Am I talking too fast?'

She squeezed up her nose and mouth and nodded, her bunches bouncing as she confirmed that I was a gabbling fool.

I exhaled deeply, plonked myself down beside her on the sofa. 'Sorry,' I said. 'I just want you to . . .' That sounded like I was putting pressure on her. Saying that if she didn't feel instantly at home, she'd be wrong. She'd upset me. 'Sorry,' I repeated although she didn't know why I was apologising.

We'd got the train to Leeds this morning. My parents had offered to drive us up here but I'd said no. I wanted a clean break from London, for us to start as we were going to go on – just the two of us. 'It'll be easier all round if we get the train,' I'd said. 'You can come and visit another time.' I'd hired a man with a van who had set off before us with Adele's boxes, our biggest bags and everything else we couldn't carry. He'd shown up as our taxi from the station had turned into my street. The boxes were currently piled up in the communal hallway downstairs, awaiting a place in the flat. My flat had seemed huge two years ago when I moved in, but I had accumulated a lot of possessions: books, CDs, videos, DVDs, magazines, electrical equipment, knick-knacks I wouldn't be parted from, so now space was going to be an issue. I would have to find a place for the few possessions Adele had left behind. When I'd arrived at the storage facility, I'd been horrified that her unit was the smallest they had, and even then her ten boxes hadn't made a dent in the space. Her whole life, her thirty-two years, had fitted into ten boxes. Most of the boxes contained things she wanted me to pass on to Tegan. Adele had never been a hoarder, never accumulated knick-knacks or keepsakes, and she made sure she didn't take up any more room than necessary now she was gone. Well, as gone as she could be. I had her ashes in one of my bags. I wasn't going to scatter them, I'd have them buried near us so Tegan and I had somewhere to go if we wanted to lay flowers or visit her.

'I like the windows,' Tegan commented quietly. I'd been blessed not only with large rooms in my flat but also with six-foot-high sash windows in my bedroom and the kitchen, and two large windows in what was going to be Tegan's room. They were gorgeous . . . But were they a potential danger?

Stop worrying, I warned myself. Tegan had managed not to fall out of any windows so far, why would she start now?

'Thank you,' I replied. 'I like the windows too. Listen, we need some food and some other bits like a new toothbrush, shampoo and stuff for you, so how about we go shopping? How does that sound?'

'I like that idea,' Tegan said in her small voice.

'You're not tired from all the travelling?' We'd only been in the flat a few minutes but I wanted to get moving. Constant motion stopped me thinking about how things could go wrong, what we'd lost, what this situation truly meant.

'No,' she smiled, 'I'm not tired.'

'Well that's just what I wanted to hear.'

Conspiracy. There was some kind of conspiracy.

A shampoo conspiracy. Who knew you could get so much shampoo?

I'd been up and down the aisles of the supermarket, looking for shampoo for Tegan's hair and discovered there was a lot of the stuff. Since I got my shampoo from the hair salon over in Roundhay where I had my hair straightened every six weeks, I never went down these aisles – I never needed to know what types of shampoo there were out there for white hair. And how it related to a small white girl's hair. Scanning the shelves, I'd noticed most of the bottles with their fancy names that I remembered from television adverts, were for adults. They had ceramides and fruit oils and other things I knew nothing of. Would they be good for a child's locks? In the hotel I'd just used the small bottles the cleaner left every morning, but I wasn't sure if that was a good practice long-term. And my shampoo probably wasn't good for Tegan's hair. When we lived together, Adele often swiped my shampoo if she ran out, but that wasn't that often. And Adele's hair was curly and strong, it needed lots of moisturising she told me. Tegan's hair was bone straight, each strand fine and fragile, like delicate silk threads. I didn't want to damage it, to replace the mane of silk threads with a bird's nest of straw-like locks.

Why didn't Adele tell me about things like this? I thought, anxiety clawing at me. Was this the thing that was going to crack my veneer of calm? Not the body identification, not the funeral, not receiving the urn of Adele's ashes, but the inability to find the right shampoo.

It wasn't simply shampoo, though, it represented much more. How little I knew of my young charge. She had likes and dislikes that I hadn't a clue about. Television shows she didn't want to miss, others she could go the rest of her life without seeing. Food she was allergic to, others that she wouldn't eat because she simply didn't like them. Events and phrases that would cause her temper to flare. Products that were good for her hair. Tegan was a universe of thoughts, emotions, needs and wants that I had no access to.

I leant against the trolley, visually ransacking the shelves for something that would do, each second that passed stoked the fires of insecurity burning inside me. 'Do you remember which shampoo you used to use?' I asked Tegan who was standing beside me, holding onto Meg. She looked up at me and shook her head.

How can this be so hard? I asked myself. *It's only shampoo.* It's literally shampoo. I should just pick one and be done with it. But I wouldn't just 'pick one' for me. It had taken me years to find the right one for me, I should afford Tegan the same respect. *Get a grip, Matika, it's only shampoo,* I intervened with myself.

From the corner of my eye I saw a supermarket helper approaching. She was younger than me, didn't look as though she had children, but her straight hair was a similar shade of pale gold blonde to Tegan's. She might be able to give me some pointers. 'Excuse me,' I said, stepping into her path.

Her small brown eyes remained unfriendly despite the smile she spread on her face as she asked, 'Yes, madam?'

'I was wondering if you could help me? I'm trying to find the best shampoo for a child's hair.' I indicated to Tegan who dutifully smiled at her. 'I was wondering if you could tell me which is the best one?'

'Oh, um . . .' the woman began, turning to the shelves.

Before she could finish her reply a voice cut in, 'Don't you know?'

We looked to the source of the voice and a mumsy-looking woman, about forty, with a round body, dressed in a blouse and a flowery skirt was staring at us.

'Sorry, were you talking to me?' I asked.

'Yes. Don't you know which shampoo you should be buying?'

What's it to you? I thought. 'Erm, I've never bought it before,' I replied, trying to restrain myself from being out and out rude. I turned back to the supermarket helper, shutting the interloper out of the conversation.

'Why didn't you ask your employer before you came out?' the woman continued, ignoring the fact I'd shut her out of our conversation.

I ignored her for a moment, then what she said filtered into my mind. I spun back to her. 'Why would I ask a marketing director about children's shampoo?' I asked with a frown.

'Her parents will obviously know what shampoo they use.'

Oh, it was suddenly clear: a black woman with a small white girl, could only mean that I was staff; an au pair. *Do I look like an au pair?* I glanced down at myself: I was wearing baggy navy blue jeans, a red top that had cut-away sleeves and a slashed neck and black trainers, on my back was a black leather rucksack. If you didn't know me, you wouldn't look at me and think I was a successful thirty-two-year-old National Marketing Manager, that was true. However, no one who looked at me would think I had the temperament to be a nanny. More than a few people had told me that I had a stand-offish air about me, that friendliness wasn't what they thought of when I came to mind. Who would *pay* me to look after their child? And, anyway, why couldn't I be her parent? Why did this woman look at me and instantly think employee? I could be Tegan's stepmother, for all she knew.

'Well, her parents don't,' I said through tight lips. The supermarket helper sidled away, perhaps to get security in case things got physical, but probably because she didn't want to be caught in the crossfire if we did start chucking bottles at each other.

'Where are her parents?' the woman asked, as though she fully expected me to spontaneously confess that I had snatched the child beside me simply because she'd challenged me.

'What's it to you?' I asked calmly, although a rivulet of indignant venom ran through the words.

'What are you doing with that child?'

'If you must know,' I snapped, 'she's my child. I'm her parent.'

'You?'

'Yes, me.'

'Do her parents know you're trying to pretend she's your daughter?' The woman raised her voice, drawing attention to us. Other shoppers instantly tuned in, keeping up the pretence of looking at nappies, cotton wool, baby food and feeding bottles while keeping a close eye on us.

'I'm not pretending anything,' I hissed.

'Then what *are* you doing?' she said, just as loudly.

What am I doing? I'm struggling to deal with all this, is what I'm doing. I'm doing my best not to break down in tears because I can't find the right shampoo. I'm just about managing to stop myself from opening a bottle of vodka every night and drinking until my best friend is alive again, my fiancé isn't a cheat and I'm still living in London being Regional Marketing Manager of the company I've given seven years of my life to.

Tegan tugged on my jeans just above the knee until I looked down at her.

'I like this one,' she said, holding a bottle of shampoo in a bright orange container up to me. I hadn't even noticed she'd wandered away. I took the container and, aware that everyone

112

down the aisle was watching me, took my time in reading the label. I wasn't really taking in the words, wasn't reading the ingredients, I simply wasn't going to be intimidated. No one was going to make me run and hide, no matter how much I wanted to. I grinned down at Tegan who, surprisingly, smiled back up at me, before I dropped the shampoo into the trolley.

The woman's question, 'What are you doing?' still hung in the air. I looked back up at her and smiled sweetly.

'What am I doing? I'm buying shampoo.'

Tegan slipped her hand into mine and, pushing the trolley, we strode away from the aisle with our heads held high.

My heart was racing in my chest and thudding loudly in my ears. This was going to happen a lot in the coming weeks, months and, probably, years. Outsiders were going to question my status in Tegan's life, they weren't going to instantly believe I was Tegan's legal guardian, her 'parent'. Since I'd sent the adoption papers off, I'd found out that it wouldn't be straight-forward to adopt Tegan. It'd take months, possibly years. I had an array of official hoops to jump through, a mountain of forms to fill in, masses of personal information to disclose to any stranger who asked, but even then it might not be enough. Cross-racial adoptions were very, very rare, especially this way round, a black woman adopting a white child. I had to do it, though.

As Tegan's crying subsided that day in the hotel, as she stood limp and helpless in my arms after learning her mother had gone to heaven, a moment of clarity came over me. There was something I could do to make it up to Adele for not being there at the end, for not helping out when I could have done. There was one way I could prove to Tegan that she really did have me – I had to adopt her. Not merely take her on, be her legal guardian, but make her part of my family. Be her mother like Adele wanted. From what I'd found out so far, however, I might not be allowed to.

'Mummy Ryn,' Tegan said, making me jump out of the thoughts I'd been immersed in. I frowned down at her.

'What did you call me?'

'Mummy Ryn,' Tegan repeated as though I was mad, as though it was every day she called me 'Mummy' when she'd been calling me Auntie Ryn most of her life.

'Why did you call me Mummy?' I asked.

Her little face looked for a moment as though it was going to scrunch up in tears. 'You said you are my new mummy,' she whispered, her royal blue eyes filling with tears, her voice accusing me of lying to her.

I crouched down to her height, willing her not to cry. My last experience with her weeping had been harrowing and we'd both taken mental blows from that, it'd taken hours for us calm down. I didn't want her breaking her heart in the middle of a supermarket over something as trivial as what she called me. 'I am,' I reassured her pale face. I stroked her hair and tried a smile to calm her.

She shook her head, 'But you are not my real mummy. My real mummy has gone to heaven. And she's not coming back.'

A lump rose in my throat. 'That's right,' I agreed quietly.

'So you are not Auntie Ryn no more.'

'I suppose not.'

'You are Mummy Ryn,' she concluded. I was impressed with her reasoning skills, it proved how intelligent she was. I'd forgotten that about her, how even when she was three Tegan could put forward a good argument to change her bedtime.

'OK, I'm Mummy Ryn. What did you want to ask me?'

Tegan sniffed, wiped at one of her teared-up eyes with the back of her hand. 'Am . . .' she gulped. 'Am I allowed to have some chocolate?'

'Yes, but only if you eat all your vegetables as well.' Responsible adults were meant to say things like that, weren't they?

Her heart-shaped face suddenly brightened with a smile. She shook her head, 'We haven't got no vegetables,' she giggled, pointing to the food in our wire-framed trolley.

I decided we weren't going to buy vegetables today. It'd been so long since I heard soft little gurglings rise up from her throat in a giggle and so long since I saw her face spread wide in a smile, there was no way I could force vegetables on her now. 'You've got me there,' I agreed with a grin. 'No vegetables today. But tomorrow, we're going to start eating healthily. OK?'

She nodded. Then, before I could stand up, she slipped her arms around my neck, gave me a quick squeeze, then let me go. She went back to her position beside the trolley and stood there, cradling Meg in both arms, staring off into the distance as though she hadn't hugged me at all.

As I straightened up I remembered the one time I'd been on a boat and how I'd clung to the side, feeling as though my insides were being churned over in a solution of bile and brine. That violent nausea rose and fell in my stomach again. *What will we do if I'm not allowed to adopt her?*

chapter thirteen

I had this life before I got Del's card and went to London and inherited Tegan. It was a life of work. Nothing but work. It was what kept me sane when I moved to Leeds.

My job title was National Marketing Manager for Angeles, the department store. The chain had begun a hundred years ago as a haberdashery store in Leeds and the head office was still based there, not in London. We had branches in every major British city and our long-term goal was to overtake John Lewis as the country's biggest department store chain. I'd started in the London store as a regional marketing assistant and had worked my way up to my current position as second in command for the entire company's marketing department – main role: running the in-store magazine, *Living Angeles*. I did everything from picking the magazine's theme for the month to signing off the finished copies. I'd helped the National Marketing Director, Ted Payne, set it up and, two months before my non-wedding, the plan had been for me to spend a month in Leeds co-ordinating the magazine's launch. After I left Nate and Adele, I'd asked Ted if I could accept the job as National Marketing Manager that he'd been offering me since we'd met. When he agreed, I'd then pushed my luck by asking if I could work out my notice for the London job in Leeds.

In the past few years the magazine had grown from being published once a season to coming out every month. My workload had tripled, but I didn't mind – work was my life.

When I'd finally bought my flat in the Leeds suburb of Horsforth, three months after I left London, I had to force myself to go back there, night after night. All my life I'd lived with people: my family, then Adele, then Nate. The echo of a permanently empty flat was something I had to psych myself up to face every time I left the office. It seemed too big for me. I'd not really been paying attention when I bought it. The cavernous kitchen with high ceilings and coving was twenty-five feet long but seemed to stretch for miles. The living room and the bedroom were the same, no longer than fourteen foot each but a depressing expanse of space with only me in it. The night I finally received the bunch of keys to my new flat, I'd sat on the lounge floor and felt the terror descend. The flat was empty of furniture because I hadn't even thought about buying any, the walls were painted in off-white colour that I hated, but the silence was the most terrifying thing of all. It was that dark shape you were always afraid of in the blackness outside your bedroom window when you were little; the monster in the wardrobe; the thing without a name that lived under the stairs. I wasn't cut out for living in silence and solitude. I wasn't cut out for this. I'd hunched forwards as the terror solidified into tears. I was all alone in a huge flat. I had to start again.

I knew I had two choices at that moment: buckle under the strain of it all or spend as much time as possible at work. I didn't see the flat in daylight for months. I'd get into work for 7 a.m. and leave around 10 p.m., then would be too tired to do anything but crawl into bed. I'd even work weekends, just so I wouldn't be alone in the flat.

As time wore on, of course, I eased off the manic work schedule and made some real friends at work, one of them was

Betsy Dawali, who I shared a glass-walled office with. The other was my boss, Ted Payne. I was closer to Ted than anyone else at work.

Ted was fifty or so, one of those older men whose neat white hair, barely lined, strong-jawed face made him exceptionally attractive. It wasn't simply his looks though, Ted had an unwavering decency, and a calm, straightforward way of talking that made him incredibly sexy.

The night he came to visit me after my return to Leeds he wore an expensive, immaculately pressed navy blue suit with a white shirt and red tie. He sat on my sofa, staring into a glass of white wine. He'd destroyed his neat, work-day appearance by loosening his tie, and raking his hand through his white hair. But whilst he'd relaxed his facade, he'd been unsettled since he walked in the door. He never met my eye for any length of time and had cast his eyes down as soon as he accepted a glass of white wine with a thin smile. I'd settled myself down on my big red beanbag with a glass of wine and watched Ted avoid looking at me.

I didn't like to see him like this. He'd always been steady and strong, not hesitant and nervous. He always knew what to do in any situation. Ted had been the one who had arranged everything when I'd asked for a sabbatical for six months so I could take care of Adele – he'd come up with the idea of me working three days a week from home. When I called him after Adele died to tell him I'd fostered a child, he'd organised for me to have both compassionate and maternity leave.

Ted raised his head, studied me for a long moment. 'Kamryn,' he began and I held my breath, scared of what he was going to say. 'I have some news. I didn't want to worry you whilst you were away. I'm . . . I'm leaving.'

The glass slipped in my hand and I clutched it tighter to stop the wine spilling onto my carpet. He was leaving me, he was walking out of my life. Ted's dark eyes held my gaze for a lot longer than was strictly necessary – there was something else. Something final about this. 'Why do I get the feeling I'm never going to see you again?' I asked cautiously.

'Ava and I are moving to Italy, starting again over there.'

Not only leaving the company but leaving the country, too. 'That's . . . It's great for you. Sorry, that sounds fake, but it's not. I am really pleased for you, but I'm also feeling sorry for myself. I'll miss you.'

'You'll hardly know I'm gone,' he said with a laugh.

I didn't laugh. Ted knew how much he meant to me.

Since we'd met six years ago and worked on a project in London together, Ted had been offering me a job as his second in command. Although he knew I was settled in London, he'd offer me the job saying, 'One day, Matika, I'll wear you down.' Just over two years ago, three days after I found out about Nate and Adele, I'd pre-empted his usual offer and asked if the position was still open. He'd been shocked. It'd showed on his face, in his slight frown, but he'd asked me no questions, simply told me what I'd have to do to formally apply and gave me the job almost straight away. When I'd stepped into my new role, we were setting up *Living Angeles* so we worked many a late night together, would order in food and then he'd walk me back to my hotel.

One particular Friday night he walked me back to the hotel, wished me a good weekend and left me in reception. I went to the room that had been my home while I was meant to be finding a flat and sat on the edge of the bed in the dark. Scared and alone and unable to do anything except wring my hands. Minutes later there was a knock at the door. I took my time answering it because I could barely move. It was Ted.

'Kamryn,' he said, his face creasing in concern, 'are you OK? You've been a bit down these past few weeks but today you seem even more . . . What's the matter?'

119

'It's my wedding day tomorrow,' I confessed. The burden of that had been weighing on me for most of the week. I was meant to be marrying Nate the next day. 'I'm meant to be getting married tomorrow.'

He hid his surprise behind a look of deep concern, as he said quietly, 'Oh, Kamryn.'

I nodded. 'But it's over. I'm not getting married. I'm all alone.'

He folded his arms around me and I crumpled. He led me to the bed and lay with me all night, holding me, stroking my hair as I swung between silence and quiet sobbing. In the morning, I looked at him to say thank you and found him staring at me with the same look of intense concern he'd had when I'd opened the door. Silence and understanding swelled between us, then he bent his head and kissed me. He kissed me and I decided to go with it. I knew he was married and that while he and his wife, Ava, had split up recently they were talking about getting back together, but I still decided to go with it. I was tired of feeling loss and pain and loneliness as I had done the preceding weeks, I wanted to feel something else. Anything else. Even for a few minutes. Even if it would only compound my problems. I reached for the button on his shirt but he stopped me. 'I–I . . .' he stuttered, 'I'm sorry. I'm back with Ava. I'm sorry.'

I was relieved. Unburdened. I hadn't been sure I could go through with sex and now, thankfully, I didn't have to. Ted took me in his arms again and said he'd stay as long as I needed him. We spent most of Saturday lying on the bed and I even fell asleep. He left on Sunday and, although we never mentioned the night again, we were closer. He'd seen a fragile side of me and I saw the same side of him six months later when his wife left him again and I'd spent the night watching him drink himself into oblivion then making sure he got home safely. We had a friendship that was mutually supportive, I'd always notice if he wasn't around.

'It's going to work out with you and Ava, then?' I asked.

'Absolutely.'

The troubled expression belied the conviction of his reply. 'This is what you want, isn't it, Ted?' I asked, worried that he'd been pushed into this decision by his wife. She'd left him several times in the twenty years that they'd been married but he always took her back because, he said, 'I love her.'

'Yes, Kamryn, it is what I want.'

'So, what's up? What aren't you telling me?'

'There's no easy way to say this . . .'

'Just say it then.'

'They've already found my replacement. I've been working with him on a handover for the past couple of weeks.'

The glass of wine slipped in my hand again. 'You mean I've not even been given the chance to apply for the job? Don't they think I'm up to it?'

'It's not that, Kamryn, you know you can't do this job now that you've got a child, not with all the late nights and travelling to London and Edinburgh.'

The heat of indignation began in my feet and burned its way up through my body to the tips of my hair. 'That's why? Because I've got a child?'

'No one has said that officially. They want someone new, someone who's going to be able to put in the hours, look at the company's marketing strategy with a fresh eye and make some big changes. You can't do that if you've got to leave on time every night, you know that, Kamryn.'

'This wouldn't be happening if I was a bloke, would it? No one makes judgements about men's dedication to the job once they become fathers. A man can work all the hours God sends and still be seen as a good father because he's providing for his family. Or he can leave on time every night and his boss won't question his commitment, they'll simply think he's a good father who wants to spend time with his children. It's win-win if you're a man.'

'We all make choices, Kamryn,' Ted stated calmly, unruffled by my rant. 'I'm not saying what they've done is right, but would you really want to miss out on the time with Tegan? She's only going to be this age once, do you want to miss out on that? Especially when she's just lost her mother and will need you. How would you feel if you squandered the hours you could spend with her at work?'

Although the man in the blue suit was right, the resentment still thudded through my veins. 'That should have been my choice, it's my life, after all. I'm annoyed that I didn't even get the chance to apply, to prove I was up to it. Who are they to make decisions about my life? I've worked for Angeles for seven years and this is how I get treated? Who do they think they are? Who do they think I am? Do they think I'm going to take this lying down?'

'It's a testament to how much the company respect and like you that they were willing to let you work from London, then gave you all this time off for compassionate and then maternity leave,' Ted reasoned.

'That's also what alerted them to the fact that my priorities might have changed.' I took a mouthful of wine, held it there, letting the sharp tang of the pale liquid seep into my taste buds before swallowing. 'God I'm pissed off,' I stated, my whole body slumping in resignation. It wasn't simply the job. It was the sense of powerlessness that had engulfed my life. Everything was out of control. First I couldn't do anything to stop Adele . . . *going*. And then I didn't stop Tegan from being hurt by her grandparents. I had motherhood forced upon me and now my job, the one thing that always kept me sane, the thing I could rely on to remain constant had been snatched away from me. I wasn't mistress of my own destiny any more; circumstance had taken a sledgehammer to all my best-laid plans. I had no control over any part of my life. And I wasn't even allowed to complain about it. Wasn't allowed to tell anyone who would listen how wronged I had been, how unfair everything was, I had to put up and shut up – stiff upper lip and all that.

'What's the new Marketing Director like, then?'

'Luke Wiseman? He's ambitious,' Ted stated diplomatically. It got worse. 'He was headhunted for the position.' And worse. 'From a management consultancy firm.' And worse. 'He's a Harvard Business School graduate. He's got lots of ideas, which is what Angeles needs.'

'I suppose you're right.'

Ted sat back, relaxed now that he'd imparted the grave news about my working life. 'How's parenthood?' he asked, his eyes alight with interest. Ted and Ava didn't have children, and it was their infertility that had dismantled their marriage. Ava couldn't conceive children and she'd been against adoption, but she wanted Ted to have children, so she repeatedly left him so he could find someone else.

'It's fine,' I said. I couldn't tell Ted how much I was struggling – he'd give anything to be in my position, to be a parent, to have a child asleep in the other room, knowing he was going to take care of her.

'Does "fine" mean you're barely coping?'

'No, it's not that bad. I've just got a lot of other stuff to deal with.'

'Tegan's mother?'

'Yeah, that among other things.'

'Would you like to talk about it?' His brown eyes were laced with that concern he had shown the night we kissed.

'To be honest, no. Tell me all about your plans for moving to Italy and, most importantly, when I can come visit.'

Hours later, with a taxi waiting outside for him, I saw Ted out and we shared a brief, friendly hug.

'You'll make a good parent,' Ted said as we stepped apart.

I gave him a wan smile in return. 'Thanks.'

'You will, I know you will. I have every confidence in you.'

'Thanks, boss. I'll see you in a few weeks.'

'Yes, you will.' Ted began down the stairs, then stopped. 'Oh,' he said and spun back. 'I forgot to tell you, someone called for you while you were still in London. Very pleasant young man. He wanted to know if you were going to the funeral. What was his name?' Ted clicked his fingers, trying to recall the name. He needn't have bothered, I knew exactly what he was going to say.

'Oh, yes, Nathaniel Turner.'

chapter fourteen

My walls. My beautiful white-with-a-hint-of-cream walls.

That's what hurt the most about all this. The walls. Losing the sitting room wasn't so bad – it wasn't as if I had built the room from scratch. It was the loss of the walls I'd spent hours and hours painting that hurt. I had made the bricks and mortar mine when I painted the walls. And now it was going to go.

Tegan stood with a paintbrush in one hand, a pot of red paint at her trainered feet and a mix of happiness, excitement and apprehension on her little face. I'd tied a blue and white scarf around her head to protect her hair. She'd been worried about wearing her pink long-sleeved top and blue jeans for the job, but I'd reassured her that this was what adults wore to decorate. And just to prove my point, I'd dusted off my old decorating gear – dark blue combats, a pink T-shirt, and a yellow and white scarf to tie around my head.

'Am I really 'lowed to paint on the wall?' Tegan checked again. She'd asked me that five times in the past minute.

'Yep, any colour you want.'

I'd taken us to a DIY store yesterday and we'd bought a host of stencils – animals, stars, moons, suns, dolphins, fish – and paints in red, blue, brown, yellow and green. It was marginally cheaper than painting the whole room again. Not necessarily financially cheaper, simply less costly in terms of my time and sanity.

'Can I paint a fish there?'

She pointed to the space under the window. I'd had to lie on the floor to get right under the window sill to cover the old paint on the walls under there. Now it was going to be graced with a fish. 'What colour do you want to paint it?'

She looked down at the open pot of red paint that was releasing fumes into the hot room. The windows were wide open but the cream fabric blinds that hung at them didn't move because there wasn't even the slightest stir of wind in the air. 'Red.'

'Go on, then,' I said. I picked up the fish stencil, attached it to the wall with tape, then stepped aside for the artist to do her work.

Tegan took one more look at me to confirm that it was all right to do this, and made a stroke in the middle of the stencil. Each of her strokes were short and stubby, nervous and hesitant, carefully placed so she wouldn't go outside the edges, until the fish was filled in.

The fish looked bereft on the wall, one lone splash of colour in the wide ocean of cream-white.

'OK, who's next?' I asked.

'An elephant,' Tegan decided.

'What colour?'

'Blue?' she asked.

'If the lady wants blue, the lady can have blue.' I got down on my knees, picked up the screwdriver, inserted it under the lid of the blue pot of paint and prised it open. The rich, deep blue glinted up at me. I carefully placed the lid on the newspaper covering the floor.

I went to the stereo as Tegan coloured in the elephant stencil, flicked on the radio. I found an easy-listening station, one that would fit with the sun streaming in through the open windows and the warm, humid air. When I'd opened the window earlier I'd been struck by how fragrant the air was, and closed my eyes as I inhaled the outside. I'd forgotten how different the atmosphere was up here. London, much as I loved it, much as no one was allowed to slag it off to my face, much as it was my 'home', was saturated with the urgency of life down there. The frantic pace of being a capital city seemed to stain the air. Leeds was a city but without the frenzy.

The pling, pling, pling of Peter Gabriel's 'Solsbury Hill' started and I flicked the radio up a few notches so it filled the room and the flat. I'd moved all the furniture into the middle of the room when Tegan had been asleep in my room last night. I'd dismantled my desk and put my iMac on the floor in the corner of the bedroom. Old white and cream sheets covered the furniture. I glanced over at Tegan, whose little body was hunched forwards, tensed as she carefully painted her elephant. I could feel rather than see the concentration on her face. I could imagine her little tongue poking out from between her pink lips, her brow furrowed, her eyes crunched up in concentration as she made blue marks on the wall. I smiled and cranked up the stereo another notch or two.

It took most of the afternoon to encircle the room with animals. Tegan was very particular and wanted to make sure each animal was equally spaced and all the same height from the ground, meaning I had to get the ruler out and ensure each animal was the same distance from its neighbour. Personally, I would have lived with any imperfections but not Tegan. She was precise in almost everything: at night, she had to sleep on the same side of the bed; she ate her dinner from the centre of the plate outwards; when she took her shoes off when she came in, she placed them neatly at the same place by the kitchen door every time. I just kicked mine off and pushed them aside so I wouldn't trip over them.

We stood beside the covered furniture and looked at our handiwork. It was pretty. Tegan's ark of multicoloured animals. She was good at painting, it had to be said. Probably got it from her mother. But then her father had been good at art too. Nate was always scribbling things on pieces of paper. We'd sit in pubs and at the end of the evening, we'd find he'd sketched someone across the bar on a beer mat. At home, while we were watching TV, there'd be the scratch, scratch of his pen on paper as he doodled. It was his way of burning off nervous energy. Some people smoked, others bit their nails, Nate sketched.

Since I'd seen him at the funeral, Nate had been inhabiting my mind. Any space that wasn't occupied with thoughts of Tegan, Adele and how I would cope, was filled with Nate. I hadn't thought of him much since the day I collected my belongings from London, there was a part of my mind I'd consigned him to, a place I could ignore, but now he'd breached that, was reaching into every free recess. He'd called me. Had discovered that Adele was gone and had called me. Was he hoping for a reconciliation? Or to use this as a reason to start talking to me again? Or was it simply to find out if I was going to the funeral?

'Like A Virgin' came on the radio and shoved Nate aside, replaced the image of him in black with the image of Madonna in white, gyrating in a highly non-virginal way as she did in the video. I cranked up the stereo until Madge's voice was on the verge of distorting with the volume. I glanced down at Tegan who was staring up at me with a confused expression on her face. *Is this suitable listening for a five-year-old?* I wondered. *Ah well, too late, she's heard most of it.* I didn't understand the words when I'd first heard it all those years ago and I was a teenager.

I held my hand out to her and she slipped her blue, red, green and yellow splattered fingers into my palm. I started rocking my hips, swaying my head in time to the music. I moved her hand with mine and she followed suit. Our bodies moved in time to the music. Dancing and moving in the room of heat and paint fumes. I lifted her hand up in the air and let her twirl a couple of times, then I grabbed both her small hands and rocked her arms. Unexpectedly, she threw her head back and laughed, a giggle that was part-way between a belly rumble and a gurgle. It lifted my heart. I grabbed her, pulled her into my arms and started jiggling around the room with her. She was light in my arms, light but so much more substantial than she had been.

She started laughing even more, throwing her head right back and rocking her body in my arms as though she was dancing too.

'Like A Virgin' segued into Cyndi Lauper's 'Girls Just Wanna Have Fun', and I put Tegan down as we both simultaneously threw our arms in the air and started moving our bodies side to side. Tegan even knew some of the words and sang along to the chorus.

'This is my mummy's favourite song,' Tegan laughed. And then stopped as she realised what she'd done: she'd brought up her mother when neither of us had mentioned her in the past week.

I stopped dancing too, my heart drumming hard in my chest. Cyndi carried on singing her heart out but Tegan and I stood staring at each other, every word of the song like shards of glass scraping across our skins.

Moving stiffly, I went to the stereo and flicked it off. The silence was sudden and brutal. I didn't know how to handle moments of sudden remembering like this one. I'd done the best I could to read up on how to help a child deal with death but reading was no substitute for experience, of which I had none. And none of the articles had explained what to do in moments of sudden remembering. When you were having fun even though your mother, your best friend, was gone. None of them explained how to handle the twin emotions of guilt and resentment. Guilt at forgetting for a minute that this horrible thing had happened and finding a droplet of enjoyment; and resentment aimed at your loved one for leaving you. And then more guilt for feeling that resentment. And then more resentment for that guilt. It was a spiral that I stayed on the outside of, thinking around it like you would walk around a puddle in the road – you knew it was there but you were going nowhere near it. Thinking around these feelings meant, though, that I didn't have the vocabulary to speak to Tegan about it. I didn't know how to explain to her that it was normal to feel this; that she was allowed to be angry and upset and confused and hurt. And that despite the pain that had surrounded us, sadness wasn't mandatory twenty-four hours a day, laughing was permissible.

I pointed to the expanse of cream-white on the chimney breast. 'OK, so what are we going to do there?' I asked, having fortified my voice with false courage. Neither of us had started to cry so we had to press on, wait until we were ready to let some of our feelings out.

Tegan shrugged her bony shoulders, crossed one leg over the other and sat down on the floor beside the paint pots.

'Ah, come on, you can do better than that,' I coaxed, sitting down beside her. How was I supposed to explain to Tegan that it was all right to be happy sometimes when I was struggling with that concept myself?

Her big royal blue eyes glistened in her pale, heart-shaped face as she stared up at me. The corners of the mouth that had been pointed upwards in a grin seconds ago, were turned down.

'How about a sun?' I said. Her eyes stared back at me. 'A big yellow sun. And maybe a house?' She shook her head. 'OK, a big yellow sun. How about some hills? Some green hills.' She nodded. 'OK, a big yellow sun, some green hills. Anything else?'

'A tree,' she whispered.

'OK, trees. I think I can paint trees. What else?'

'Chocolate flowers.'

'OK. So we've got a big yellow sun, green hills, trees and chocolate. Do you mind if I make the flowers into those red and white swirly sweets instead? We won't have enough brown paint after the trees.'

She stared at the wall for a few seconds, then returned her gaze to me as she nodded in agreement.

'I think your mummy would have liked the sun and the hills and the trees and the flowers that are really sweets,' I said. We couldn't just pretend Del didn't exist. We had to find a way to talk about her, no matter how painful. 'She'd be able to paint them a lot better than me,' I added.

Tegan's damp, inquisitive eyes stared at me for a long, quiet minute. 'My mummy drawed lots of pictures,' she eventually said.

'Yup, she certainly did. And she was very good. Come on then,' I said, getting to my feet. 'Once we've done this, we'll go buy you a bed.'

'Is this really my room?' Tegan asked, from the doorway. I stood behind her, watching as she slowly turned her head, careful not to miss anything as she visually ingested her new space. It'd taken us another week to get ourselves sorted out, for Tegan's single bed to be delivered, for Betsy, the woman I shared an office with at work, to send her brother, Brad – a sulky fifteen-year-old who for some reason did whatever Betsy ordered him to do – to come around and help me shift furniture. The cream sofa was moved into the dining end of the kitchen, and sat with its back beside the doorway. My beanbag was placed in the corner at the bottom of the alcove, where I'd built in bookshelves. Brad helped me move the twenty-eight-inch telly into the kitchen, too. It sat opposite the sofa. Betsy was the grateful recipient of the large table that had sat at the dining end of the kitchen. It'd cost a fortune, even with the staff discount I got from Angeles. It had maple wood legs, frosted glass top and came with six matching chairs that had fancy frosted glass backs. There was no way I could keep it, instead I got a small, wood table that marked the living area from the kitchen.

The computer, printer and other paraphernalia had been relegated to my bedroom. The real problem had been my books. I had over five hundred of them on three sets of white shelves in the living room. It'd taken me nearly eighteen months to get around to buying those shelves and putting my books on display, I was loath to give it all up so quickly. In the end, what didn't fit onto the bookshelves in the alcove, was piled up on the floor beside the telly, a leaning tower of books. On the other side of the telly, my pile of videos and DVDs. The only other storage I had were five cupboards that were flush to the wall in my corridor, but half of them were now filled with Adele's boxes. The small telly that had been in the kitchen was now in Tegan's room.

The room she stood staring at. Her bed was made up with a single duvet that had a light blue sky and cloud scene on one side and came with matching pillows. Beside the window stood a light wood wardrobe. Under the window sat a matching drawer unit for her undies, socks and foldable clothes. I'd used carpet tape to fix two large red and white rugs – one under the TV stand and another under the bed – to the laminate floor.

On the other side of the fireplace sat a large toy box. She also had a shelf for the books I knew she loved to read and have read to her. To finish off I'd spelt out 'Tegan' on the door in brightly coloured letters.

'Yup, it's all yours. You can do anything you like in here,' I replied, deciding that the 'within reason' was implicit.

'Really and truly?' She still hadn't moved from the doorway.

'Absolutely. Are you going to go in?'

She took tentative steps into the room, then sat on the bed.

'Now I thought you might like to try sleeping in your own bed tonight, but if you want to still sleep in with me, that's fine too.'

'I like this bed,' she proclaimed. 'It's big enough for Tegan.'

'Cool. Now, I'm going to make a cup of something to drink. Why don't you try out your television and video?'

Tegan nodded eagerly and jumped off the bed then scuttled across the room to the small television that sat with a new video player I'd shelled out for.

Shelling out was something I'd been doing a lot of recently and it was scaring me how expensive everything was. I hadn't been the most sensible person when it came to money. I paid my mortgage on time, I mostly paid my bills on time, and I spent far too much on going out. But, despite my job title, I wasn't raking it in. I'd always lived with an overdraft and a credit card. (Nate had been the sensible one when it came to money, but few of his frugal ways had rubbed off on me.) Now that I had two mouths to feed, clothe and take care of, I was struggling.

Del, much as I loved her, had been appalling with money. It took her dying for me to realise how careless she was. And, I admit it, how irresponsible. *Irresponsible*. There, I'd thought it. Del was irresponsible. She loved her daughter, there was no doubt about it, but she hadn't provided for her in any way. They'd lived in the flat Del and I had rented when we first moved to London. And they'd given up that flat, when Del's condition became chronic, to move in with her father and his wife.

She had no savings – just a great clothes collection. She'd

been freelance most of her working life because she needed to be flexible when it came to childcare, so she had no life insurance or any other kind of financial back-up plan for this eventuality. The one sensible thing she did was to take out insurance on her credit cards so they were paid off when I sent the companies her death certificate.

I suppose, like me, she thought she had all the time in the world to start being a financial adult. If it hadn't been for three solid months of browbeating from Nate I wouldn't have started a pension. Without realising it, I thought I was going to live for ever, and that at some point, when I was older, I'd accept I wasn't going to live for an eternity and sign up for pensions, savings, start reading the financial pages of the papers and not blank out when ISAs were mentioned.

That still hadn't happened. And it hadn't happened for Del, either.

Things were going to be tight for us.

I took my time making the drinks, giving Tegan the chance to familiarise herself with her new space, and by the time I returned she'd tucked Meg up in the bed, and had arranged all the books on her shelf into height order.

'I like this room,' she informed me as she took the cup of Horlicks I'd made her from my hand and sat on the floor in the middle of the room. I sat opposite her and looked around, this room wasn't as grand as the room she'd had in Guildford, but it was hers, no bad memories attached. Speaking of memories . . .

'I'm glad you like the room, Tiga,' I said. 'I've got something for you.'

'A present?' Her eyes lit up.

'Sort of,' I said. I jumped up and went to the kitchen to retrieve the memento I'd dug out when Tegan was asleep last night.

'I know this might make you sad at first, but I think you

should have it up anyway.' I held out the picture of Adele and Tegan that Del had kept on her bedside stand in the hospital. The pair of them had their heads pressed close together, Tegan's arms wrapped around her mum's neck, the two of them beaming out from behind the plain glass frame.

Tegan hesitated, her eyes wide and scared as they stared at the photo in my hand. Eventually, she set down the cup of Horlicks and took it from me. She held it in both hands, her loose hair almost hiding her face as she gazed down at it, but I could still see her lips were turned down.

'Your mum was very pretty, wasn't she?' I ventured.

She nodded without looking up.

'You don't have to put it up, sweetheart,' I said to her, frightened that I'd pushed her too far too soon. 'I'll put it to one side if you want.'

What had I been thinking? I didn't want to look at pictures of Adele all day, why would she?

Tegan stood, went to the television and placed her picture on top of it. 'I think it should be there. Is that OK, Mummy Ryn?'

I nodded and smiled. 'That's perfect, sweetheart.'

chapter fifteen

Rustle, flick went the papers as the headmistress leafed through them. I sat in silence as I watched her while Tegan, of course, was still and silent in the comfy chair beside me.

The headmistress, oblivious to our nervous gazes, stopped at one page, squinted down at it even though her glasses were on her face, then raised her head and graced me with a full-on look. I felt my face stiffen with worry and she fired me a professional, practiced smile that widened her oblong face, then she dipped her head and resumed study of the file in front of her. My heartbeat increased a fraction as I followed her gaze as she read from the pages encased in a beige folder. *How had they got so many papers, so much information, when I hadn't provided it? Nor filled in any forms.* In fact, when I'd called the school to find out how I went about registering a child for the next term, they had said I had to give them my child's name, former address and the name of her former school – but I didn't need to fill any forms in.

'None at all?' I said.

'No,' came the reply.

'But doesn't that mean anyone can show up at any time and say, "I've got a child and I want them to go to this school?"'

'They need to live in the catchment area and, of course, there needs to be room,' the school secretary replied.

'So anyone who lives in the catchment area can show up at any time and say, "I've got a child and I want them to go to this school?"'

'Essentially, yes.'

'That doesn't seem right,' I said.

'Why?'

'Because it's harder to join a supermarket loyalty card scheme, what if an impostor shows up?'

'An impostor child?'

When she said it like that, it sounded like I was being mad, but fundamentally, it seemed wrong. I had been raised finding it difficult to join any kind of group – Girl Guides, student union, bank, jobs – there were always forms to fill in, information to dole out, pieces of yourself to distribute to the world at large. This should be harder. As a result, I'd asked to meet the headteacher because I needed to make life difficult for myself. And also because I wanted to get to know the place, I didn't want to launch Tegan into a new environment, one that would become a huge part of her world, without seeing it for myself first. I wanted to visualise where she was talking about when she told me about her day, I wanted to check that all the things I'd read about the school being decent and safe were true, that there weren't in fact open manholes, and water running down the walls. My request had been made a week ago, when I had still believed that I needed to check if the school met my standards. As the days passed that feeling dissipated and I'd started to worry about the possibility of rejection. Of me doing something, appearing to be something that would make them decide they didn't want Tegan after all. That fear had grown until it solidified in my mind as not just a possibility, but a certainty. This morning I'd made us change our clothes two, maybe ten, times, finally settling on a black skirt suit with a white vest top for me and a red denim dress with a white T-shirt

137

underneath for Tegan. I'd used straighteners to defrizz my hair, and combed it with a side parting into my usual bob. Tegan's hair I'd combed back into a ponytail tied with a red ribbon.

I'd had to keep letting go of Tegan's hand to dry sweat off my hands as we walked from our flat to the primary school. I couldn't remember approaching any kind of meeting with this amount of trepidation, but a mule-like kick in my stomach as we were shown into the headmistress's office had confirmed that I was capable of feeling even more fear.

Mrs Hollaby, the headmistress, was hovering around the fifty age mark, judging from the creases in her oblong-shaped face and the grey-white hair looped up into a low bun. Her clothes, however – a white T-shirt with a bright, paint-splatter print of the school's name, and stone-washed, elastic-waisted jeans – clashed with her looks. They also made me feel inadequate and overdressed.

I straightened up in my seat, forcing myself to exude the confidence that had convinced the board of managing directors at Angeles to green light my magazine idea. My eyes probably gave me away, though, they revealed that I was fretting over where she got that file and what was disclosed in those pages. Did it tell about Adele's death? Did it confess who Tegan's father was? Did it explain the woman who was once down as next of kin had abandoned them?

'Mrs Matika . . .' Mrs Hollaby began as she raised her head to me.

'It's Ms Matika,' I cut in.

'Ms?' she replied, the slight inflection in her voice questioning my marital status. Was I divorced or one of those *liberal* women.

'Ms, Miss, they're so interchangeable,' I replied. 'I was never married but I never wanted people to know that. It's none of their business. I mean, men don't have to advertise their marital status, do they?' I added a nervous laugh that rang hollow and flat around the room and confirmed that I was unbalanced.

'I see,' she stated.

'Call me Kamryn.'

Her face creased into another of her professional, practiced smiles – rather than reassure me, it shivered a chill up my spine. 'Kamryn.' She made my name sound like a statement. 'It's a shame your partner wasn't able to come along.'

'I don't have a partner,' I replied quietly.

Mrs Hollaby frowned. 'You are, then, Tegan's parent?'

'Yes, I am.'

'Her only parent?'

'Yes,' I said.

Rustle, rustle, flick, flick, went the papers as 'Miss' searched through them again, trying to find an answer, trying to explain why Tegan with her white skin and blonde hair had brown-skinned, raven-haired Kamryn for a parent.

I watched her hunting for that kernel of information and wondered for a moment if I should leave her blundering around in the darkness of this situation like a barely woken woman searching for a light switch. I couldn't, of course. I had to enlighten her, those in charge had to know what had happened for Tegan's sake.

'I'm Tegan's legal guardian,' I stated clearly and precisely, making it known that I didn't want to discuss this in front of Tegan. To reinforce my point, I glanced at Tegan. She sat in the centre of the chair, her arms folded around Meg in a hug, while her eyes intently watched 'Miss'. She seemed fascinated by this woman, as though she was a new species she had discovered.

'Miss' understood my reticence and reached out her long hand for the phone receiver. I watched her fingers tap in a number, then asked for someone to come into her office. A few minutes later a young woman with waist-length brown hair, who wore the same bright school T-shirt and blue jeans entered the room. After a short conversation with Mrs Hollaby, she bobbed down in front of Tegan and introduced herself as Maya. She asked Tegan if she wanted to come and meet some other children at the playgroup.

Tegan's head snapped around to look at me, her eyes were widened in what appeared to be alarm.

'You don't have to go if you don't want to,' I reassured.

Her eyes widened a fraction more, but in the royal blue of her irises her black pupils were still large, which meant she wasn't scared, she wanted to go but wasn't confident enough to say so in front of two strangers.

'You're allowed to if you want. Do you want to?' I smiled encouragingly.

She nodded.

'Go on then,' I said. 'I'll come find you later, OK?'

Her lips moved up into a smile, 'OK,' she replied before she slid off the chair. Holding Maya's hand she left the room.

I watched them go, another kick of fear almost winding me: what if I never saw her again? I didn't know anything about this Maya person, what if she wandered out of the school with Tegan?

'She'll be fine,' Mrs Hollaby said to the back of my head.

I resettled myself in the chair, faced her. 'I know. I just worry.'

'I can see that.' She arranged her face into a concerned expression.

From a place deep inside me I sighed, breathed out all the air in my lungs as I resigned myself to this. To letting a complete stranger into my life. Since Nate and Adele, I hadn't opened up to people. Ted had known a bit about me, but I was careful not to reveal too much. Share too much and someone could hurt you. 'I'm Tegan's legal guardian,' I began. I inhaled.

140

Little steps. I had to take little steps. 'Her mother, my best friend, died recently. I've inherited Tegan. I'm responsible for her.'

'Miss' got up, came around the desk and sat in Tegan's chair. The seat, which had seemed huge with Tegan in it, was smaller around an adult form. She clasped her large hands together, scrutinising me like she had studied the papers in Tegan's file, searching my face as though the words of my story would slowly present themselves on my features. She looked poised to hug me and I drew back a fraction. 'I'm going to adopt her because that's what I promised her mother I'd do.' No one else knew that. Everyone thought that I was taking care of her, no one knew that I was going to make her a Matika. 'Her mother only d— Left us a few weeks ago, but I've got to get moving with adopting her.'

'This must be very difficult for you,' she said.

'Am I that obvious?' All bravado in my voice was ruined with a quiver of emotion, this was more difficult than I thought it would be.

Her eyebrows knitted together in concern and a sympathetic smile sat on her lips. I looked away, to protect myself from her sympathy. Sympathy was the one thing I could live without – I would have no strength when faced with the kindness of strangers. I fixed my gaze on a point beyond her shoulder, to the large window and the world beyond. Everything was so bright today. Bright and sunny. It was summer, everything was alive, lively, kissed happy by the sunshine.

'Do you have a social worker?' Miss asked.

'I, erm, haven't had time to do that yet,' I said, still not looking at her. 'I've been trying to sort out the flat so that Tegan could have her own room. And then there was the shampoo saga, which I won't even go into. And with the painting and moving and furniture and shampoo, I've only

141

had time to do this. To register at a school. I thought that if I got her into a school you might be able to recommend a playgroup or something that she can go to during the summer holidays for when I go back to work. But I will get a social worker. I promise.'

She touched my hand and I jumped in surprise, then tensed in case she tried to hug me. 'I'm not berating you, Kamryn. I was asking because they can help. That's what they're there for. Not only with the adoption, but also with any problems you're having. They'll also help you find someone for Tegan to talk to.'

What does Tegan need to talk about? I wondered as alarm bells sounded in my ears. 'Grief is hard on everyone,' she stated. 'If Tegan is finding it hard to express that she might need someone else to talk to. You will need a social worker for the adoption, however.'

'OK. Yes. I think I knew that.'

'What about a health visitor?'

'Tegan's not sick,' I replied, alarm bubbling up again.

'A health visitor will talk to you about a whole manner of things. They're for you as well as your child. If you have any worries about being a parent, they can help you.'

'OK.'

'There is help available, you simply have to ask for it.'

I couldn't ask for help, it was all I could do to explain my situation, revealing I was struggling as well would be impossible.

'One of the other parents here is going through the adoption process as well,' Miss said. 'I could talk to her, see if she'd be willing to share her story with you.'

I withdrew from her again, not sure which was scarier, a hug or the thought of being set up with another person, like a parental version of *Blind Date*.

'You're not the sharing kind, I take it?' she astutely observed.

I smiled. 'No, I'm not.'

'Very well.'

'So, do we, I mean, does Tegan get in? Does she have a place here?'

She nodded. 'Yes, she lives in the area and it's been a pleasure meeting her, she seems a lovely child.'

'She is. And about the playgroups?'

'Yes, of course. We have a playgroup here. It runs from eight to six-thirty. We give the children breakfast, lunch and a light snack in the afternoon before they are picked up. We have activities during the day and reading, drawing and nap time.'

'It costs, right?'

'Yes.'

No matter the cost it wouldn't be as expensive as a child-minder. I'd crunched and crunched the numbers, stripping back our budget so we only bought clothes every other year and ate nothing but pasta and home-made tomato sauce, and still there would be a financial shortfall. A playgroup was the only thing I could afford, I would simply have to work through lunch to ensure I left on time every night, and then take work home to do after Tegan was asleep. 'Do you have places?'

Mrs Hollaby's wrinkles deepened as she smiled. 'We'll make a place for Tegan.'

I threw my arms around her neck, squeezed her in gratitude, as I cried, 'Thank you! Thank you so much!' Something had gone right. Something small, but significant. Mrs Hollaby's body stiffened in my hold and I caught myself. Realised what I was doing and let her go. 'I mean, thanks, that's great,' I said calmly. 'Shall we go find Tegan now then?' I said. The head-mistress's office, the world it encompassed, felt wrong and that was because Tegan wasn't in it. I was so used to her being beside me, or across the room from me, in sight – in her

143

waking hours, we were never apart longer than it took for me to have a shower – that I felt unsettled without her.

We walked along corridors with blue, rubbery floors and cream walls. Noticeboards with bright, child-created artwork lined the spaces between the huge windows. I gave the pictures a polite once-over as I passed, pleased I could pick out a cow or a horse or a dragon or a person from the better efforts.

The sun almost blinded me as I crossed the threshold into the playground, its brightness causing me to squint. I scanned the corners of the playground for Tegan. I knew she'd be alone, clutching onto Meg and praying for me to come get her. I couldn't spot her. My eyes ran over the playground again: she wasn't by the drinking fountain. Nor by the base of the climbing frame. She wasn't at the edge of the playing area. Nor stood forlornly against the red brick wall. My heart jumped in fear. What had Maya done to Tegan? Had she stolen her. I was on the verge of grabbing the headmistress and demanding she produce my child when I spotted Tegan standing with four girls. The five of them were engrossed in an intense conversation, their voices lowered, their faces as serious as jurors on a murder trial. Tegan's group were all her height, two with pitch-black hair, one with blonde hair, another with red-gold hair. Tegan was the prettiest, I decided, even though I could only see the back of two of her companions. She didn't need time to grow into her looks, she was already striking. As if guessing I was mentally crowning her the beauty of the school yard in my head, Tegan looked up. Our eyes met and she beamed at me. She lifted Meg in her right hand, waved the rag doll at me, then without waiting for a response, submerged herself in the conversation again.

'Looks like she's fitted right in,' Mrs Hollaby commented.

★

144

'I met lots of people,' Tegan said. She held onto my hand and swung it as she skipped along the pavement. Meg swung along in time in Tegan's other hand.

'That's nice,' I said. I glanced down and found her staring up at me.

'I met Crystal. She's got a brother called Cosmo. He isn't as big as she is. And I met Ingrid and she's got a big brother called Lachlan. I haven't got a brother, have I?'

'No,' I replied.

'And I met Matilda. She's got lots of brothers and sisters. She's got a sister called Marlene. And a sister called Maree.'

'They're the same name.'

'No they isn't. One is called Marlene and one is called Maree. That's not the same name.'

'Oh, OK.'

'And she's got a brother called Declan. And a brother called Dorian. And a brother called Daryl.'

'That's a lot of brothers and sisters.'

She nodded, her ponytail bobbing. 'I know. Matilda said was I coming back tomorrow. Am I going back tomorrow, Mummy Ryn? Is I 'lowed to go back tomorrow?'

'Not tomorrow, next week. Did you like it there, then?' I asked.

'Yes.'

'You don't mind going back?'

'No. I want to go back.' She was excited. 'I've got lots of friends. Crystal and Ingrid and Matilda.'

I never made friends that quickly as a child, I didn't make friends that quickly as an adult. Tiga? No problems.

'OK, you can go back.'

Her face was taken over with a huge grin that fired a shard of jealousy into the heart of my chest. I'd been tearing myself apart because she was out of sight for ten minutes, and she couldn't wait to be away from me.

'Are you going to come and play for the whole of the time next week?' Tegan asked.

'No, I'm going to work.'

In the middle of the pavement Tegan stopped swinging my hand and halted her skip. 'Why not?' she asked, panicked; horrified that I wasn't going to be around. I'd wanted her to feel something, to at least miss me, but not this terror.

'I have to go to work.'

'Why can't you come with me?'

'Because I'm an adult and adults have to go to work. But you can play with your friends all day then tell me about it later.'

'Are you going to come later?'

'Yes, in the evening. And then you can tell me who else you met and about their brothers and sisters.'

'Do you promise you'll come afterwards?' she asked.

'Yes, I promise.'

'Double promise for ever and ever amen?'

'Yes,' I replied. She stared at me until I said, 'Yes, I double promise for ever and ever amen.'

Tegan grinned at me and started skipping again. One foot in front of the other: skip, hop, hop, skip, along the pavement. Her bare legs, crowned with red open-toe sandals, dancing up and down.

'Shall we get some food and sit in the park for the rest of the day?' I asked her.

'Yes,' Tegan said. 'But we have to go home first, don't we?'

'Why?' I asked her.

'Because you have to change your pretty clothes.'

'Yes, I suppose we do.'

Tegan's lips pulled back over her little white teeth and her cheeks became full and round as her grin widened. Her eyes crinkled up and sparkled. The rosé glow on her cheeks and luminescence in her eyes reminded me of Adele. Reminded me of that first proper smile she'd fired at me. How struck I was by that smile. And then I realised Tegan had said, 'We have to go home first.' 'Home.' She'd said it without any prompting from me, which meant she was feeling settled at the flat. Settled with me.

'Guess what?' Tegan asked.

'What?'

'Crystal's got a cat.'

'he doesn't look like a monster'

chapter sixteen

I hesitated outside the ninth-floor office, my hand raised to knock.

On the other side of the door was Luke Wiseman, the new Marketing Director of Angeles. He'd summoned me via email to his office to have a 'chat' (his word, not mine) the third day of my return to Angeles.

The thought of coming back to work had turned my emotions into a pendulum that swung constantly between fear and excitement. Fear gripped me every time I remembered that I'd been away for so many weeks I might not remember what to do. Then the pendulum would swing to excitement because I'd been away for so many weeks I might not remember what to do, meaning work would be a different type of challenge. Then I would be afraid again because I was going to be miles away from Tegan. I'd spent two days without her while she was at playgroup, but once I was back working in the city centre, being with her would be dependent upon traffic and public transport, I couldn't just walk around the corner to get her. Then I'd be excited again because I wouldn't have to watch hours of children's television so I'd be able to stop speaking and thinking in the overemphasised way the presenters did.

Between the anxiety and anticipation, lay the knowledge

that I'd be meeting Luke Wiseman. He was my boss, the person I would work most closely with, and he was also my first ever work nemesis – the only colleague I'd known to get a job I should have been given. His presence at Angeles would be rubbing my face in my failure to make it to the top.

On my first day back at work, Tegan, who hadn't been blighted by nerves on her first day at playgroup (she'd been excited on the way there and then incredibly chatty that evening), had given me an extra big hug at the school gates. 'Have fun at your work,' she'd told me, like I was the child and she was the adult.

The train ride into Leeds city centre after that had been nerve-racking, all I could think about was not being intimidated by Luke Wiseman – by the time I'd reached my tenth-floor office I was flitting between wanting to throw up and deciding to slap him the second I met him to show who the real boss was around here. I'd found out ten minutes later that he was in London until Friday.

Friday. Today.

Once I knew I wouldn't be forced to deal with my arch enemy, I relaxed at work, enjoyed people dropping by to tell me their news, to find out what I had been up to. Betsy, who'd been alone in our office for nearly two months, acted as though I had returned from a year living abroad when she saw me. She'd spent the day offering to make the tea and running around the desk to engulf me in bear hugs. 'You could have me up for sexual harassment,' she said at one point, 'I'm so tempted to snog you.'

'The feeling's mutual, mate,' I'd replied, a little surprised but immeasurably happy that I'd been missed. We were friends Betsy and I, but I'd always thought it was a work thing. It was nice to know she actually cared. 'But without the snogging.'

Ted had left yesterday in his usual dignified, understated manner. At lunch he'd asked me to accompany him to the sandwich shop. Once there, he'd confessed he wasn't returning to the office, couldn't stand the extravagant goodbyes Angeles staff usually held, so 'Goodbye, Kamryn. I'll keep in touch.' And that was it, no more Ted.

Now I had to conquer Luke. I took a deep breath, steeled myself, then knocked on the door. Seconds later, a baritone voice bid me enter.

I took another deep breath before entering the spacious white-walled office. The blinds were pulled down over the window behind the desk to shield the computer from sunlight. I looked around, investigating what Luke had changed about the office. The large yucca plant still sat in the corner, the position of the desk had stayed the same, the blinds were still cream, the meeting table in the corner still had four blue chairs around it. He hadn't made an imprint upon the place, almost as though he had no need to show it was his domain. If it was mine, I would have put up the covers of *Living Angeles*, I would have added a couple more plants, I would ha— *Stop*, I chastised myself. *Luke has the job, the office, you have to accept that.*

The man behind the desk didn't stand as I entered. In fact, he sat back in his chair, stretched his tall body and made no attempt to hide the fact he was sizing me up. I was more discreet as I scrutinised him. His features, strong and well-defined, looked as though an artist had spent hours chiselling them smooth into his clear, tanned skin. His nose was straight and strong, his eyes equally spaced apart, his jaw a smooth line that curved down to his chin. The black hair on his head had been razored to a grade one, which made his face all the more striking. Around his succulent lips was a thin, line moustache that ran down the sides of his face into a beard. What stood out about him, though, were his eyes – a bright, clear, burnt orange-hazel colour, that reminded me of brown, highly polished amber. He was dressed in a white shirt with the top button open and the sleeves rolled up to above his elbows, and smart beige trousers. From the stretch of his body I knew he had a gym-made physique. I recognised his type, I'd worked with many of them over the years, he was Mr Career. He was dynamic, thrusting, über-ambitious and anyone who worked with him had to give 150 per cent or he would take it as a personal insult and finish their careers.

While I appraised him, Mr Wiseman's hazel eyes flicked over me, took in my raven-black, chin-length bob; my dark brown eyes; my unmade-up mouth; my slender neck, my body hidden beneath a plain red shirt and straight-leg black trousers; my unpainted toes peeking out of wedge-heel sandals. After he'd looked me up and down, his eyes hardened with distaste. Clearly he wasn't impressed with what he saw.

'Sit down,' he ordered.

'Why, is this going to take long?' I replied, matching his hostile tone.

He smiled suddenly, catching me off guard with an unexpected display of charm. 'Please, Kamryn,' he said warmly, as he indicated to the seat opposite his desk, 'take a seat.' *It's too late for the charm now,* I thought. *I saw the revulsion in your eyes, I know what you think of me.*

'I'd rather stand,' I said, returning his charming smile with one that reached the tips of my hair yet was 100 per cent fake. 'I've got a lot of work to do.'

My reply wiped a layer of shine off his glossy smile. He studied me for a moment, obviously trying to work out how to deal with me. 'What are you doing tonight?' he asked.

'Sorry?' I replied, wrong-footed. *Is he asking me out?* Had I read him completely wrong? Had that expression really been his way of covering up his attraction to me?

'I've been having dinner with all the heads of departments to pick their brains about what they think of the marketing of

Angeles, see if they have any ideas on how we can improve things. You're the last on my list . . . Of the marketing department. So I thought, if you're not busy tonight, we could get it out of the way.'

I was impressed at the number of insults he'd managed to cram into that minuscule monologue.

1. 'Last on my list.' *Just in case I doubted that I would be last on every one of his lists.*
2. 'If you're not busy tonight.' *Of course, I was bound to be dateless and friendless on a Friday night.*
3. 'Get it out of the way.' *I was like a smear test to him: unpleasant but necessary.*

'Dinner tonight should be fine,' I said, through my fake smile.

'I'll meet you in the foyer at six-thirty,' he said, trying to outsmile me.

'Should be fun.'

'Shouldn't it just,' he muttered as I shut the door behind me.

I arrived in the foyer at six thirty-two, according to the huge clock that sat above the receptionist's area. Luke was there, all six foot two inches of him, wearing a beige mac over his trendy clothes. When I emerged from the lift he raised his arm and looked at his watch before shooting me another of his fake smiles – anyone would think I was a couple of hours late.

'I'm not late, am I,' I stated as I halted in front of him.

'Just a couple of minutes,' he replied curtly.

'Right. Well, the lift took a bit longer than I thought it would.'

'I didn't think it'd be your fault,' he said.

'I'm glad you know me so well.'

155

'I've booked us a table at a restaurant around the corner for –' he paused to look at his Rolex – 'seven minutes' time. We'd better hurry if we don't want to be even more late.'

'Right.'

We turned right out of our corner building, went down onto The Headrow and crossed the street onto Vicar Lane, then took a left into King Edwards Street. The air was thick, heavy and humid, everyone we passed in the street seemed subdued and drowsy, ready to curl up and fall asleep in some quiet corner. I carried my red mac in my arms, fighting the urge to close my eyes and give in to the sleepiness tugging at my senses.

We arrived at a small French restaurant I'd walked past a few times but had never entered. The air was fragrant with garlic and tomatoes, and soft music played as we stepped into the dimly lit interior. Everything about the place oozed intimacy. That surprised me. I'd half expected him to take me to a scuzzy burger bar where he'd order me the cheapest burger on the menu and say that if I wanted a fizzy drink I'd have to buy it myself.

After handing our coats to the maître d' Luke and I were seated at a table for two in the centre of the crowded restaurant. The second we were given our menus we both ducked behind them, hiding from each other. I scanned the ivory-coloured card, deciding that if I had to spend time with this man, then he was going to pay top dollar for it. I found the most expensive dish on the menu – lobster – and opted for that. And crab for starters.

When the waiter arrived, to Luke's credit, he requested a pricey bottle of red wine. To his detriment, he didn't ask me if I wanted wine, let alone the colour I might prefer. I hated red wine, so asked for water instead. We ordered – one of Luke's eyebrows arching up at my choices – gave our menus to the waiter and then sat back.

'So, Kamryn, tell me about yourself,' Luke said. I mentally sifted though his voice, trying to untangle the threads of geography in his accent. It was a network of American – an East Coast/New York inflection, and southern England – London – and, if I wasn't mistaken, English Midlands, possibly Birmingham.

'What do you want to know?' I asked, keeping my line of sight focused on the stem of my wine glass to avoid meeting his eye. Every time I glanced at him I saw the naked disgust on his face. Something about me repulsed him. My looks? My body? My continued existence in this world? I wasn't sure which one riled him so or why he'd taken against me in such a short amount of time, particularly when he had the job and I didn't, but he made no effort to hide his dislike of me. In fact, he wore it like a badge, something he wanted to be defined by: 'My Name Is Luke, and Kamryn Turns My Stomach'.

'Anything you want to tell me.'

'All right, I'm thirty-two. I've worked for Angeles for seven years now. Five years in London, two years up here. I set up *Living Angeles* with Ted, it actually came from my idea, but I don't like to brag. Erm, that's about it. Except to say, I love my work and I'm sad that Ted has gone.'

Mr Wiseman's left eyebrow slowly arched up as he regarded me with the same distaste he would a drooling green alien. 'I meant, tell me about you,' he said patronisingly. 'Your life. Not your work. Are you married? In a long-term relationship? Do you have kids?'

I'm supposed to know that's what you meant, am I? I thought. 'No, I'm not married,' I replied sarcastically, 'I don't have a boyfriend and I don't have—. JESUS CHRIST!' I leapt up, knocking the chair over. Other diners had stopped eating, drinking, talking and stared at me in surprise. I ignored them, fumbled under the table until I found my bag, grabbed it, then ran out of the restaurant, not bothering to say another word to Luke.

Tegan. I'd forgotten her. I'd actually forgotten her.

I ran out onto the pavement while one hand ferreted about in my black leather bag for my mobile. My fingers closed around it and I snatched it up to dial the school's number. I pressed the 'on' button and nothing happened. The battery was flat, obviously why they hadn't called me.

Panic clutching at my chest, I ran down Vicar Lane in the direction of the train station, mentally calculating how long it'd take me to get there.

What will they do with her? Will they leave her on the pavement until someone arrives? I didn't know any of the other parents to call and ask if they'd take her. She'd be sat there, waiting, thinking I'd forgotten her. Which I had.

I spotted a yellow taxi light on top of a car and almost threw myself under the wheels as I bellowed, 'TAXI!' He screeched to a halt in front of me and I leapt into the back seat telling him where to go. I added, 'And I'll pay you double if you get me there in under fifteen minutes.'

'Emergency is it, love?' the portly driver asked.

'The stupid cow who was meant to pick up my child from school forgot and so she's there. All alone. I need to get to her.'

'Bloody hell!' he replied, and sped off.

As we hurtled through the streets, the driver pushing the speed limit whenever he could, I fingered my useless mobile while gnawing on my bottom lip.

'It'll be all right,' he reassured.

I couldn't reply, I was choking on my guilt. I'd actually forgotten Tegan. *How? How could I forget? How?*

The imposing red-brick building of the school was deserted when we arrived. No cars parked outside, no children or parents milling around. The metal gates were shut, and fear spiked my stomach. I handed the driver twenty-five pounds, all the money I had on me, and leapt out onto the pavement. Guilt was compressing my chest, making it impossible to breathe, while fear squeezed my heart. I ran to the school gates and tentatively pushed one, found it was unlocked. I sprinted the short distance to the big blue doors and with a gentle push that opened too.

'Tegan?' I called. My voice echoed down the emptiness and I had another clutch of fear. *What if she isn't there? What if someone saw her stood alone outside and took her?* 'Tegan?' I called again.

Her blonde head poked out of a classroom at the end of the corridor. Her face lit up and she grinned with sudden delight as she saw me, then the smile evaporated and her face slunk downwards into sullen disappointment. I ran to her, threw myself to my knees and then scooped her up.

'I'm sorry,' I said into her hair, grateful that I had the chance to hold her again, that her small form was safe in my arms. 'I'm so, so sorry.' Tegan stayed silent and motionless in my embrace.

Maya, the teaching assistant who had been there the day that we'd first visited the school, emerged from the classroom. 'She thought something had happened to you,' Maya explained. 'Especially when we couldn't get you on your mobile.'

'The battery's flat. I'm so sorry. I got caught up at work. I'm sorry. It won't happen again. I didn't realise the time until it was really late. I'm sorry.' I pulled Tegan away, looked her full in the face. 'I'm so sorry, Tiga.'

Maya bobbed down to our height, stroked Tegan's hair. 'We were all right weren't we, Tegan? We drew some pictures.'

'I'm sorry I've taken up your time as well,' I said to Maya.

'These things happen,' Maya replied, adding with her tone: *But it'd better not happen again.*

'OK, Tiga, come on, let's go home. We'll have a pizza and watch a DVD. Does that sound like a good idea?'

She nodded automatically, as though she didn't care either

way. Maya handed me Tegan's pink and lilac school bag, then stood as I did.

'Thank you for taking care of her,' I said.

'She was no trouble.'

Tegan gave me her hand and smiled at Maya, who said goodbye, and we started down the corridor. Before I opened the door, I stopped and took her in my arms again. 'Tegan, I'm so sorry. I did a terrible thing tonight and I promise, promise, *promise* it won't happen again. OK?'

She nodded but didn't speak.

I gazed into her five-year-old face, her blue eyes strained with sadness and fear. I'd done that. I'd terrified her. Made her think she'd been abandoned. 'I promise you, I won't do this to you ever again.'

Silence. Silence like that day I took her from Guildford, when she didn't know if she could trust me. She was scared of me again. Wondered if I would let her down, if I would walk away and leave her, especially after she'd made me double promise for ever and ever that I would come back every evening. Tegan wasn't sure if I'd be there when she needed me. Nor if this part of her life was going to unravel like the life she had with her mum before they moved to Guildford, and then mutate into a nightmare like the Guildford life had. Tegan was suddenly adrift in this new existence, unsure if she'd ever see solid ground again, and all because I wasn't used to letting anyone know what my plans were. It'd been so long since I'd had to check in with anyone about what I was doing, I hadn't even thought . . . That had to change because this certainly couldn't happen again.

I pressed a kiss on Tegan's forehead, stood up and we began the journey home.

chapter seventeen

'I am sorry, all right?' I said to Tegan, as I shook cornflakes into a white bowl and placed it in front of her. 'It won't happen again.' She said nothing, simply stared at her breakfast and waited for me to splash on milk. Once I did, she picked up her spoon, shovelled cereal into her mouth and chewed as though I didn't exist.

She was five and already an expert at the cold shoulder. I'd been subjected to her stubborn jawline and haughty silence for more than fourteen hours now. Indignation, hurt, anger were all conveyed by her muteness. I was sorry. I hadn't slept last night because of my guilt, but I couldn't get that across to Tegan. Nothing I said seemed to convey how sorry I was, and that it wouldn't happen again. I couldn't stand another hour of this silence, let alone the rest of the weekend. *What if she never forgives me?* I wondered as I watched her eat. *We'd live in this atmosphere for the next fifteen years or so. Years.*

'Look,' I pulled up a chair beside her, 'I'm sorry. I'm truly, truly sorry. It won't happen again – I promise. I . . . I'm sorry. You see, there's this nasty man at my work called Luke who doesn't like me. That's all right because I don't like him either, but I've got to work with him. He's my new boss. So I'm f— filled with dread.'

Tegan nonchalantly spooned milk and orange-yellow flakes

into her mouth. 'I had to go for dinner with him and he's awful. So arrogant. He's horrible.'

'Like a monster?' she asked, finally acknowledging me. I was obviously speaking her language.

An image of Luke with hairy eyebrows, talons for hands and huge drooling fangs flashed across my mind. 'Yeah, exactly like a monster.'

'Oh,' she said and nodded with some sympathy for my predicament.

A knock at the front door made us both jump, we looked at each other, wondering who that could be. We'd had no visitors since Tegan moved in, especially not someone who didn't buzz beforehand. The person knocked again and I hurried to answer it.

Luke, tall and imposing, stood outside my flat. He'd poured himself into a pair of loose-fitting blue jeans and a white T-shirt that skimmed over his muscular chest. His D&G sunglasses were hooked into the neck of his T-shirt.

'Luke! Oh f-f-damn!' I'd all but forgotten that I left him sitting in a restaurant having ordered an expensive meal.

'Yep, that's the effect I like to have on a woman – especially one who enjoyed my company so much she ran out of a restaurant.' In his arms he carried a red mac, from the missing button on the sleeve, it looked very much like my red mac.

Before I could start to explain, Tegan appeared beside me, linked her arms around my right thigh and stared up at Luke.

'Who's this?' Luke asked, crouching down to Tegan's height.

'This is Tegan,' I replied. 'Tegan, this is Luke from my work.'

Luke smiled, a genuine smile that moved his eyes into friendliness, one that was yet to be aimed at me. Tegan had that effect on adults. They would look at her and grin because her eyes were an unusual blue, her skin was a perfect butter-white, her lips were a candyfloss pink. People looked at Tegan and smiled because they couldn't help themselves. 'Pleased to meet you, Tegan.'

162

Tegan blinked back at him, studied his face, his close-cut hair, strong features and hazel eyes. Then she turned her head up to me, a slight frown knitting her forehead. 'He doesn't look like a monster, Mummy Ryn,' she informed me. Luke turned his face up to me too and raised a questioning eyebrow; I glanced away, my whole body burning with shame.

'You left so suddenly last night, I just wanted to check you were OK,' Luke said, standing up and towering over me again. 'I tried your mobile but it was off, so I asked your friend Betsy for your address. I hope you don't mind. Oh, and I thought I'd return this.'

I relieved him of the red rain mac I'd forgotten in my haste to leave the restaurant last night. 'Thanks, and yes, we're fine.'

'We're going to the zoo,' Tegan piped up, her eyes fixed on Luke.

'Are you?' Luke asked her.

'Yeah, are we?' I said.

'You said we could go to the zoo,' Tegan accused.

'Yes, sometime. Not today.'

'I'll leave you to it, then,' Luke said.

'Mummy Ryn,' Tegan said, 'Luke can drive us to the zoo in his car.'

'No he can't,' I replied quickly.

'Why can't I?' Luke asked indignantly.

'You might not even have a car.'

'How do you think I got here?'

'I'm sure you've got better things to do on a Saturday than drive us to the zoo.'

'Nothing that can't wait.'

I had to do this, didn't I? I had to let her have her way on this because I'd terrified her last night. A day looking at animals was the least I could do. 'Thanks, Luke, a lift to the zoo would be great,' I managed through gritted teeth.

'What's your favourite animal, Luke?' Tegan asked happily.

163

'Elephants,' he said, his eyes lingering on me for a moment longer than was strictly polite.

'Will there be elephants at the zoo, Mummy Ryn?'

'I suppose so.'

'You can see the elephants, Luke,' she said with a giggle, although she was still clinging to my leg, using me as a human shield.

'I'm sure Luke's got better things to do than come around the zoo with us,' I repeated, not holding out much hope.

'Like I said, nothing that can't wait.'

This munchkin had well and truly screwed me. I reminded myself never to upset her again. 'You'd better come in while we get ready,' I conceded.

As expected of a sunny Saturday during the summer holidays the zoo, which was about fifteen minutes outside of York, had hoards of people flocking towards it – and it wasn't even midday when Luke pulled up into the overflow car park.

There were people in summer clothes – cut-off jeans, shorts, vests, T-shirts in bright pastels and muted fluorescents – everywhere. Visitors weaved around each other, making odd patterns as they followed the paths around the animal enclosures. Tegan, who I'd dressed in loose pink trousers with lilac butterflies, a matching pink T-shirt and pink sandals skipped happily along between me and Luke, holding my hand. Every inch of exposed skin on her body had been slathered in sunblock. Her hair was in a high ponytail around the base of which I'd twisted a red silk flower. She'd been beside herself with happiness at it and kept running to the mirror in my bedroom to check it out – she had no idea that it was a way for me to instantly spot her if we got separated in a crowd.

Tegan had done most of the talking during the ninety-minute drive, asking Luke questions about the zoo. I was silent in the front seat, trying not to slump into a sulk at having to spend the day with this idiot. Luke and I spoke when we absolutely had to which was only when I asked him to stop so I could buy some drinks and to thank him when we got out of the car.

Fluffy pink candyfloss was installed in Tegan's hand and she flitted away into a world of her own, starring at the creatures behind glass and high fences.

'I take it she's the reason you left so suddenly last night,' Luke murmured as we rested our bodies against the glass wall separating us from the chasm that surrounded the lions' den.

'Yup,' I replied.

He checked Tegan wasn't listening, leaned towards me, pressing his body against mine so he could whisper by my ear, 'You forgot her?'

I nodded and he jerked his body away in disgust. 'I take it you haven't been doing this very long.'

I moved my head to look him squarely in the face, I'd already been shamed by a five-year-old, he couldn't make me feel any worse. 'You take right,' I said.

He returned my gaze, steady and straight. With the laughter of children, the conversations of adults, the cries of babies, the sounds of animals as a backdrop, our mutual dislike grew. The seeds had been planted yesterday afternoon, had been watered in the evening, and were now sprouting roots while strong green shoots pushed up through the earth. A few more hours and this feeling between us would blossom into an orchard of full-on hatred.

'Mummy Ryn,' Tegan said, tugging on my hand, forcing me to break the confrontational eyelock with Luke.

'Yes, gorgeous?' I said. She'd finished the candyfloss and the only evidence that it'd ever existed were the small fluffs of pink at the top of the stick in her hand. Not a speck of it was on her mouth or face, no bits stuck to her top.

'Can we go see the monkeys?'

'Absolutely,' I replied.

We set off for the monkey enclosure on the far side of the zoo, around the winding stone path and to the left.

'About work,' Luke said as we walked.

'Hmm–huh?' I replied.

'Do you mind if we talk now seeing as our conversation was cut short last night?'

'Course not,' I mumbled. Actually, I did mind. I minded very much. This was Tegan time, but I couldn't say that. I had to prove to my new boss that a child hadn't slowed me down, that I was efficient and capable.

'You and Ted had a very close working relationship . . .' Luke stopped, allowing the statement to hang in the air, a big black stain of accusation I was expected to be desperate to scrub away.

'Yes, we did,' I replied without shame.

'I see.' He was unimpressed because my reply had, apparently, confirmed his suspicions.

'Of course, most people thought we were at it at every given opportunity,' I whispered so Tegan wouldn't hear. Luke's eyes fixed for long seconds on my face. 'Some people even suggested that I'd slept my way to a position I had before I even moved up here.'

'I never accused you of anything,' Luke defended.

'I never said you did.'

'I'm simply concerned that the marketing department won't work as well now that Ted has gone.'

'You mean you'd heard the snide remarks about how Ted carried me in this position then presumed I'd done the deed to get my job.'

We stopped at the chimpanzee enclosure and Tegan's eyes almost doubled in size, her face taken over by wonderment. 'Monkeys,' she breathed.

166

'With you being head of all the marketing departments in our company, I'd have expected that you'd go out of your way to get on with your second in command, not judge them before you've even met them,' I said in hushed tones.

'If you'd been around to meet maybe I wouldn't have had to rely on third-hand stories and gossip about your morals to make my assessment,' he hissed back.

'Yeah, you're right,' I admitted.

Surprised, he narrowed his eyes, trying to decipher the slight in what I'd said. There wasn't one. He was right, but I wasn't going to use Adele as a sick note.

'You want to know the worst part about the rumours? Ted is, and always had been, devoted to his wife,' I said. I gave Luke a long up and down look. 'He's a decent man.'

Luke tried to force me into another eyelock and was greeted with an 'Oh purl-ease!' expression. Ignoring him, I crouched down beside Tegan.

The chimpanzee enclosure was filled with trees, their thick, sturdy branches reaching out to the sky. To one side sat a cave-like hut. Five chimpanzees sat in the branches of the trees; two pairs, and one on its own. The pairs were engrossed with grooming each other, searching through their partners' thick black fur for nits. The fifth sat still, staring into space.

'A baby monkey.' Tegan pointed. I followed her finger to the hut area where a female chimp cradled a baby chimp in her arms. The mother gazed down at the baby and I fancied that I saw a smile on her simian face.

'That's her mummy, isn't it?' Tegan said.

'Yes, sweetheart,' I replied. Everything started closing in on me. I was aware of everything: the pungent aroma of animals; the stickiness of the day; the clamminess of my skin . . . All of it crowding in on me. I was drowning, being submerged in a reminder of my best friend and what had happened to her. That I'd seen her grey, emaciated body lying on a hospital trolley, the spark of the woman I knew extinguished. That she was gone.

'Her mummy hasn't gone to heaven to be with Jesus and the angels, has she?' Tegan murmured, her voice low and matter-of-fact.

'No, sweetie, she hasn't.'

The diminutive blonde inhaled, her little shoulders rising as air expanded her chest, then her shoulders fell as she expelled air in a deep exhalation. Her eyes glazed over as though she was calculating something. I wished she would talk to me; tell me what she was feeling. The intense agony of being suffocated by the reminder of Adele's death I'd just felt was probably nothing compared with what she felt. I wanted her to tell me, to let me know how she felt. If she was hurt or angry or sad or in pain. She might not be able to articulate all her feelings, but if she tried . . . Like it was easy for me. When was the last time I spontaneously shared an emotion?

'Can we see the snakes?' Tegan asked, coming out of her revere.

'Do we have to?' I whined.

'Yes,' she replied, 'I like snakes.'

How and when she'd seen enough of snakes to make an informed decision, I didn't know. 'OK,' I said, standing up, 'we can see the snakes.' I looked down at the leaflet in my hand, mentally plotted a course to the reptile kingdom from our current position.

'I'll get the ice creams,' a man said right beside me. I started a little before I realised he was with us, that it was Luke who had spoken.

'Mummy Ryn wants chocolate ice cream,' Tegan told him. 'She likes chocolate.'

Luke gave me a derogatory once-over. 'Yeah, I can see that.'

'Right, so, Kingdom of the Snakes,' I said, 'go on then, Luke, take us to your leader.'

chapter eighteen

We spent most of the day like that, Tegan dictating the order in which we saw the animals, Luke and I discussing work in hushed tones and taking every opportunity to snipe at each other. Tegan was oblivious to the atmosphere between her two accompanying adults, happy to be surrounded by non-human creatures.

In the car back to Leeds Tegan came up with the idea of a picnic in the park. It was late afternoon and she was too buoyed up to simply go home – she wanted to cram as much excitement into the day as possible.

'How about we save the picnic for another time, sweetie?' I replied. 'We'll have a mini one when we get home.' At home, I could rid myself of the man next to me.

'O-OK,' she replied, disappointment in her voice. 'Can Luke come?'

'If he wants to,' I replied, knowing he would. Knowing it'd be too much to hope for him to slink away.

'Do you want to come to our picnic at home?' Tegan asked the back of Luke's head.

His eyes flicked to the rear-view mirror, and his face once again lit up with a genuine smile at the girl in pink and lilac with her red flower in her hair. 'That would be lovely, thank you, Tegan,' he said.

I let us in to our flat and Tegan led Luke into the kitchen area. I busied myself making the picnic while Tegan and Luke sat at the dining table playing. They made a hundred-piece jigsaw, and then Tegan got Luke to inspect her collection of ten classic cars. Next, Tegan got out her box of papers, and her red plastic bucket of pens and pencils and they drew pictures of the animals we'd seen at the zoo. In the depth of their playing, the picnic was forgotten. I left the sandwiches, salad and pop beside them on the table and flopped onto the sofa to watch television. Every so often I'd glance up, see the pair of them: he, a grown man, bent forwards, coloured pen in hand, concentrating on his drawing; she a smaller figure concentrating just as hard on her work of art. He was taking this seriously. Had thrown himself into playing with Tegan with the same intensity he would devising a new marketing strategy for Angeles. Had it been anyone else, his interest would have been endearing, but because it was him, I decided it was nice that Tegan had someone her own mental age to play with.

The second the clock hit eight o'clock I flicked off the television, stood up and announced, 'OK, Tiga, bedtime.'

'Do I have to?' Tegan whined before letting out a huge yawn. Her tiny face was pale with tiredness and her eyes were virtually shut.

'You can hardly keep your eyes open. Come on, bed.' I turned to Luke. 'You'll have to go, Tegan really does have to go to bed.'

'OK,' Luke said, putting down his red pen and standing up.

'Will you come back tomorrow?' Tegan asked Luke, her tired eyes fixed on him.

'If I'm allowed to,' Luke replied.

Two sets of eyes shifted to me. 'Time's ticking on,' I said, tapping my watch while neatly sidestepping the issue. I wasn't going to be made the bad guy because I didn't want to spend my free time with someone from work. Someone I didn't even like from work.

'You have to ask Mummy Ryn if you can come back tomorrow,' Tegan informed Luke. Her mouth opened, gaping into a yawn, her tiny hands clenched into fists as she stretched into it. 'She won't get cross. Mummy Ryn never gets cross, not even when I painted on the wall.'

'Is it OK if I come back tomorrow?' Luke asked.

'If you've really got nothing better to do,' I replied, without looking at him.

'Nothing that can't wait,' he confirmed.

Don't do us any favours, eh, mate? I thought. 'Right, that's settled. Bye then, Luke.' I moved to Tiga and picked her up from the chair. She clamped her legs around my waist, laced her arms around my neck and snuggled her face against my neck.

Reluctantly, Luke moved towards the door. 'Bye, Tegan,' he said.

'Bye bye,' she whispered. 'See you tomorrow.'

As the door shut behind Luke, I placed Tegan on her bed. She was like a floppy rag doll as I tugged off her clothes and replaced them with her red and white gingham pyjamas. I pulled back the white top sheet on her bed and helped her slip inside. Her face nestled down into the white pillow, her hair lying in a wavy formation around her face.

'Na-night,' I said.

'Na-night,' she whispered.

I reached for the bedside lamp, ready to shut out the orangey-yellow glow that lit the room.

'You don't like Luke,' Tegan said.

My hand held the cord to switch off the light. Maybe she hadn't been as oblivious to our animosity as I'd thought. 'He's all right,' I said.

'I like him,' she stated.

'I know you do, Tiga.'

'Can he be my friend?'

If he must, I wanted to say. Instead, I held my tongue.

171

Waited and waited . . . Soon her chest was moving slowly up and down in sleep. I waited a few more minutes, just to make sure she was asleep, then I slipped out of her dark room, pulling the door almost shut.

We'd had fun today. And she seemed to have forgotten how much I let her down yesterday. I flopped down onto the sofa, laid my head on the armrest and closed my eyes. Despite Luke, we'd had the first bit of fun since Adele left us. I thought again of Luke. Tall, handsome and incredibly charming – to Tegan. I had to admit, she'd had fun *because* of Luke. Tegan had taken to him, almost instantly. She'd laid eyes on him and decided she wanted him around, a kind of love at first sight. Maybe there was good in him, somewhere beneath his arrogance and his dislike of me there could be a decent person. One I could warm to. If Tegan liked him, then maybe I could too.

I awoke and the house was shrouded in middle-of-the-night silence. People had crawled back from pubs and clubs and the other places they'd visited and were now settled for the night. The outside world was quiet and calm; still and silent. I blinked, groggy and exhausted, confused about where I was. My face was damp, I realised. I raised my hand to my cheek, stroked away the clamminess of tears. I'd been crying in my sleep. Again. Seconds passed before I could fight my way through the fug of slumber to work out why: Adele.

I sat bolt upright. Tegan. Was the house, the world, so quiet because something had happened to her? I got to my feet, left the living room and went to Tegan's bedroom door. Carefully, I pushed it open and poked my head in. Tegan was in the same position I left her – face in profile on her cloud-covered pillow, hair splayed around her, hands up beside her head. She was sleeping peacefully. At least it looked like she was asleep. It could be . . . I squinted hard at her, willing her to move, to

172

make a sound, to let me know she was still with me. Finally she inhaled, then slowly exhaled. I exhaled too. She was all right. Still here.

I removed my head from her room, pulled the door back into place, then stumbled back to the living room to turn off the lights.

Being a parent was exhausting. How anyone with a child closed their eyes at night and went to sleep when the world was beset with danger, I didn't know. How could you relax for a second when the fear that something might happen to your child was hanging over you?

I staggered to the bathroom at the end of the hall, looked into the mirror over the sink. My eyes were puffy from the crying, the skin on my right cheek was tight from lying on a damp, salty patch on the sofa armrest for so long. I rinsed my face in cold water, then reached for the cleanser on the glass bathroom shelf. I squeezed a dollop into the palm of my hand, rubbed my palms together to create a white foam and washed away the signs of misery. As I straightened up, I caught my reflection. My face was clean but I could still feel the slick of tears on my cheeks, a residue of the pain that had leaked out when I was asleep.

The sleep crying had to stop. It was no good for my eyes, no good for my skin. No good for my mind because I woke up more exhausted than when I went to sleep.

Rivulets of water trickled down my cheeks, forehead, nose, over my lips and down my chin, where they pooled together into drops that spotted my white T-shirt. Sleep crying came, of course, from not being able to control myself. Once I entered dreamland, I couldn't focus on something else. Couldn't ignore the guilt that shadowed my every thought. I'd let Adele die with unresolved issues between us. I'd let her go without allowing her talk. Anguish wrenched through me whenever I thought that Adele's last moments on earth might have been filled with her wishing I'd let her explain. It ached physically to think that when she asked Nancy to tell Tegan she loved her and to tell me goodbye that for a flicker of a moment she wondered if I still hated her. If I still blamed her.

The thought that her last moments might have been consumed with those doubts because of my pride and stubbornness was so unbearable I couldn't examine it too long. I had to shove it aside and away, bury it in thoughts of work and making our money go further and watching television and cleaning the flat. Anything to avoid the gut-wrenching, big-dipper feeling that I had wronged my best friend; that I had managed to mortally hurt someone I cared about.

Even if I couldn't forgive her, I could at least have listened. Let her explain. Because I'd never believed she was in love with Nate when she slept with him. Nor that she even fancied him. Nate would've been too nice in Adele's eyes; she wanted a bastard she could tame – and Nate, as she knew him, wasn't in need of taming.

I shut off the taps, reached for a couple of cottonwool pads from the roll lying on the bathroom shelf and in long strokes I dried water from my face.

I did a bad thing in not giving Adele a chance to explain. I stopped looking at myself in the mirror, couldn't gaze at the face of someone so awful any longer. *I am a bad person. No matter what I do, I am a bad, bad person.*

chapter nineteen

'So, this is where all the cool kids hang out,' Luke commented as he reclined on my picnic blanket. He broke a brown bread chicken salad sandwich in two and slipped a section between his lips.

Luke meant it literally, of course. The last Saturday of the summer holidays, a few select members of Tegan's playgroup had a picnic in Horsforth park. They played rounders, ate food, drank pop and generally enjoyed themselves before the new school term started. I'd basked in the reflected glory of Tegan's popularity. I'd never been part of the cool or popular anything, but Tiga was. The other children – Crystal, Matilda and Ingrid – were the core gang, and with their brothers and sisters, we ended up with nearly twenty children. My basking had lasted right up until she demanded Luke's number to invite him.

'Do we have to?' I'd whined.

'Yes, he'll really like it,' she'd replied. He had, of course, accepted and said he would bring the food. He had more money than sense because it looked like he'd picked up his local Tesco and emptied several varieties of sandwiches, dips, crisps, sausage rolls, mini sausages, chocolate bites and biscuits into a picnic hamper. It was sufficient for everyone at the picnic with enough left over for dinner for the rest of the week.

Despite that, it hadn't made me like him. There was very little my boss could do to endear himself to me. I was comforted by the fact the feeling was mutual. Relations between us had declined in direct proportion to the amount of time we spent together. 'I've never seen two people who dislike each other as much as you two,' Betsy commented after a meeting with Luke.

'It's not my imagination then, it is a two-way thing?' I asked.

'Too right! It's not even that smouldering hatred that's a cover for wanting to shag each other stupid, it's actual, genuine hatred.'

'Yeah, I know.'

'Did you wrong him in another life or something?' Betsy mused.

'Not that I can remember.'

'He's perfectly pleasant to the rest of us . . . Why does he hate you so much?'

'He thinks I look like a dog,' I replied. My stomach flipped as I voiced this thought. I'd always known it, the look in his eyes the first time we met had told me so, but I hadn't named it. Now I had, I couldn't deny it. His sole reason for not liking me was he thought I was ugly.

The worst part was, I couldn't leave him at work, couldn't find a way to consign all thoughts of him to the walls of Angeles, because Tegan kept asking him to come back. Three Saturdays and two Sundays in a row he'd dropped by to play drawing or jigsaw with Tegan. And the one weekend he couldn't visit, he came by in the evening the following week. I suspected he'd started visiting because he wanted to check I was treating Tegan properly, but now he just liked coming over to see her. Tegan hadn't been this taken with anyone for as long as I could remember so I found it impossible to turn him away. I was stuck with him. I had grown to respect his friendship with my five-year-old. There was nothing about him that suggested he had an ulterior motive for hanging around, and whilst I didn't leave them alone together, it was mainly because there weren't too many places to go in my flat, not because I feared what he would do. Despite how much he disliked me, I could glean that Luke was one of the good guys. We restricted our sniping to work hours – outside of the nine-to-five we spoke very little. Or at all. Like now.

I lay back on the red, green and blue tartan blanket, propped up by my elbows, my legs outstretched and my head up so I could see the kids running around. Most of the other parents got involved with the game, were on a team with their child, hit and chased the ball, tried hard to get rounders. When it came to that sort of thing, I was a back-seat parent. 'So, this is where the cool kids hang out,' Luke repeated.

'Yup, my kid is really cool,' I replied.

Luke said nothing, and we lapsed into the silence that was usual when we saw each other outside of work. After a few minutes, he tried again, 'So . . .'

If you add, 'this is where the cool kids hang out' again, I will punch you, I thought. But he didn't. He left the sentence at that one word. That one, simple word: 'So.'

'So . . .?' I questioned, turning to him. His lithe body, clothed in knee-length chino shorts and a white T-shirt, was also stretched out on his back, propped up by his elbows. His D&G sunglasses hid half his face.

Embarrassment swept briefly across his features. We had nothing good or even inane to say to each other. I returned my attention to the game. Tiga was wearing blue tracksuit bottoms with a white stripe down the side and a red T-shirt, her blue baseball cap was pushed firmly down on her head. She stood near first base, her body poised to catch the ball when the pitcher threw it to the batter. I was so proud of her at that moment. Not only was she good at games, she was a natural at fitting in, and she threw herself completely into the activity – there were no half measures with Tegan, she gave 100 per cent to everything she did.

'Why does Tegan call you Mummy Ryn?' Luke asked.

I refocused on him. 'Because I am. I didn't give birth to her but she thinks of me as her mother.'

'I meant the Ryn part. Why Ryn and not Kamryn or even Kam?'

'When Tegan was tiny, people often called me Kam, which I hate,' the second the words left my mouth I knew he would call me Kam until the day I died. 'And, I was always correcting them, saying, "Ryn. My name is Kam*ryn*." Tegan thought my name was Ryn because she heard me say it so many times. So when she started to speak she'd call me "Win" then it became Ryn. And stuck.'

'That's a good story,' Luke said, he even managed a small, genuine smile. 'What do her friends call you?'

'I don't know, "That Weird Lady Who Lives With Tegan"?'

Luke's face creased up as he laughed out loud, which made me laugh. We both laughed while looking at each other. Maybe he wasn't so bad. 'You know, you should smile more often,' he mused. 'Your smile suits you. And if you lost a bit of weight . . .'

My expression hardened as my grin evaporated. I jerked myself upright, raised my knees, hunching forwards, trying to hide my frame. I stared down at the blanket, my face hot with embarrassment, my eyes burning with a desperation to start crying. He thought I was fat as well as ugly. But I didn't understand why it hurt when this man said those things. I'd heard them all my life: overtly and subtly men had told me those things and I'd white noised them. Made them insignificant in the grand scheme of things. But this man could hurt me. Was it because no one had been so blatant about disliking me in years? Was it because I was concentrating so hard on staying strong I had no real defences against an attack of this nature.

'I didn't mean that the way it sounded,' he justified, not recanting it: he might not have meant it the way it sounded, but he still meant it.

I hid my face and my hurt from him. I wasn't going down this road again. It'd taken years for me to build up some confidence, to believe I was worth something, I didn't need to let this man do this to me.

Trying to blank him from my mind, I glanced up, just as a yellow tennis ball whizzed through the air at me. I ducked my head away but Luke wasn't so quick and the ball glanced off the side of his face, knocking his glasses skew-whiff before it landed on the blanket. Unfortunately, it wouldn't have caused him anything more than the slightest sting.

Everyone from the game waited expectantly, their bodies frozen to see how Luke would react. He peeled off his sunglasses while raising a hand to his face, then he grinned at the players. Everyone in the rounders game laughed, and Luke jumped up to his feet, picked up the ball. Throwing, 'I'll just return the ball,' in my direction, he sped off across the grass to join the game. Once he was gone my body unfurled as I relaxed. He had that effect on me, every time I was with him I was on edge, waiting for the next insult, for the next look. I lay down on my side, propped up on one elbow, watching Tiga. Every few minutes she would take her eyes off the game and seek me out. As we made eye contact a toothy smile would spread across her face, she'd lift her right hand, wave it briskly at me, wait for me to wave back and then return to the game.

There might be better ways to spend a Saturday, but at that moment, I couldn't think of a single one.

We've got a long walk home, I thought once the game had broken up. Tegan looked as if she was going to fall asleep where she was kneeling, helping me to pack up the leftover food. I was starting to wonder how we would get all this back without Luke's help. He'd said, 'I'll be right back,' and had headed off in the direction of the park's loos when the game had finished, and I was eager to leave before he returned.

Maybe I should just leave the hamper. I glanced at Tiga, her messed up hair peeked out in unruly, random strands from under her blue baseball cap as she concentrated on resealing food in packets. There was no way she would let me leave behind something of Luke's.

'Excuse me, Mrs Brannon?' a female voice said from some-where above us. Tiga and I both glanced upwards.

Beside us stood one of the mothers from the picnic, one of the people I often saw when I arrived at the school to collect Tiga. We'd only ever exchanged smiles on those days we made eye contact. She had a slender face with accentuated cheek-bones, warm brown eyes and shoulder-length raven black hair. She was a full-size version of one of Tegan's friends.

'Mrs Brannon?' she repeated.

I got to my feet, brushing bits of grass and dried dirt off my hands. 'I'm not Mrs Brannon. I'm Ms Matika – Kamryn Matika. Tegan's guardian.'

'I see,' she replied, although lines of confusion criss-crossed her eyes.

'It's complicated,' I said. 'And you are?'

'Mrs Kaye, Della Kaye.' She paused. 'I was wondering . . . You see, Matilda – I'm her mother by the way – she keeps asking if Tegan can come to her house, I mean, our house.'

'Of course,' I said, then realised I'd been hasty. Who was this woman? Where was their house? 'I mean, Tegan's never men-tioned . . .' Tegan's eyes were filled with apprehension as she stared up at Mrs Kaye, anyone who hadn't heard the conversa-tion would think she was being told off by her headmistress. 'Tegan?' Her fearful gaze switched to me.

'I know you're really busy at your work,' Tegan deflected.

'I wouldn't mind you going to your friend's house,' I said. 'You can go any time you want.' I turned to Mrs Kaye. 'Any time she wants. When would be convenient for you?'

'I was thinking,' Mrs Kaye began, 'Matilda and Tegan are best friends, what if I take Tegan when I pick up the girls and she stays with us for a couple of hours every afternoon until you come home from work? It'll be easier for you when school starts again next week and the kids have to be picked up by 4 o'clock.'

'Erm,' I replied, hijacked by the kindness of the offer.

'Really, it's no problem. We'd love to have Tegan over.'

'And you wouldn't mind?'

'I look after six children already, one more won't make a difference.'

Tegan was still looking fearful, maybe she didn't want to go to Matilda's house, which was the real reason she didn't mention it. 'How about I talk it over with Tegan and then get back to you?'

Mrs Kaye seemed pleased with this, then after giving me their phone number and saying her goodbyes, she walked away.

As I watched her leave, a heavy, lead feeling filled my mouth and weighted down on my chest. Why hadn't Tegan asked me this? What else was she keeping from me?

I unfolded the blanket, sat down then patted the area of wool beside me. 'Let's sit and talk a minute,' I said, trying not to let my hurt come through in my voice. Tegan bit her inner lower lip as she crossed her left leg over her right and sat down.

'Tiga, you know you can tell me anything, don't you?' I said. I thought about what I'd just said, I'd told her she wasn't scared of me. 'I mean, Tiga, I don't mind if you want to go to your friends' houses for a few hours after school. I mean, somewhere along the line you, you,' I licked my lips, 'you can even stay over at their houses. You just have to tell me and we'll arrange it.'

'But I know you're busy,' she said in a small voice.

'That doesn't matter. We'll find a way around it. I mean it, if you want to go to your friends' houses or . . .' My voice trailed off as I realised that she'd probably missed out on more than a few birthday parties because she hadn't told me about them. 'Or anything. Just tell me and we'll find a way to get you there. OK?'

Tiga thought about it for a second, two, three . . . Then nodded. 'OK,' she said, her voice even quieter.

'I'm not cross,' I clarified. 'Not even a little.'

Her shoulders fell suddenly as she relaxed.

'Do you want to go to Matilda's house after school, then?' I asked. It would save us a lot of money on the after-school club if she did. Plus I could relax a little about getting back after work – I wouldn't take advantage of the Kayes' generosity, but I would-n't want to disembowel the whole of the UK's rail system every time a train was even slightly delayed. I'd have breathing room.

'Would I be 'lowed?' she asked.

'Yes, sweetheart, as long as you want to. And if you don't want to, all you have to do is tell me and you can go to the after-school club as planned.'

'OK, I want to go.'

I grinned at her. More than anything I wanted her to have a friend apart from me. And not just Luke. Tegan needed people outside of our little unit, even I could see that. Content as I was with my limited circle of friends and previously work-centred life, it'd be criminal to recreate it in a child as gregarious as Tegan. I had to get her to trust people, after her recent experiences, that wasn't going to be easy.

'Good, I'm glad,' I said to her decision to go to Matilda's after school.

'You're not sad?' Tiga asked.

'Not if you're going to be happy. And I'll make sure Mrs Kaye knows that you have to ring me every day at four-thirty.' This was our agreement since the incident where I forgot her. Every day she rang me to find out what time I was going to pick her up, what we'd have for dinner and to tell me what she'd done so far that day. In other words, to make sure I never forgot again.

'Right, come on,' I said, moving to the picnic basket. 'Let's get packed away before Luke reappears.'

'Can Luke come to my house for his dinner?' she asked.

'If he wants,' I replied.

'I'm sure he will,' Tegan said firmly. She exhibited an unusual boldness where Luke was concerned, she wouldn't ask me if it was all right to go to a friend's house, but with Luke coming to dinner, no hesitation.

'Like I say, we'll see if he wants to.'

'Does he like coming to our house?' Tegan asked.

'I suppose so, he does it often enough.'

'Then he'll want to come for his dinner.' That was such logical reasoning I had to remind myself this child was only five.

'We'll see if he wants to.'

'You'll see if who wants to what?' Luke asked, causing my heart to lurch. I'd had my head buried in the hamper so I could pull faces without Tegan seeing and hadn't heard his approach.

I removed myself from the hamper, looked at him. Even after rounders he looked immaculately turned out: his shirt was still brilliant white, his shorts without so much as a hint of a grass stain, his legs, covered in wiry, light brown hairs, had tanned a little in the dying embers of the summer sun.

'Erm, well, we were wondering if you wanted to come over for dinner?'

Luke's face lit up in uncensored delight and I got a glimpse of what he must have looked like as a child when given the

183

Christmas present he'd begged for. How his cheeks must have rounded up when his plump lips pulled back into a grin, how his hazel eyes must have brimmed with happiness as he stared at his parents, unable to speak with joy. What happened, I wondered, to turn that delight-filled boy into this abundantly arrogant man?

'Would I really be allowed?' Luke asked.

'Yeah, sure, why not,' I replied.

'That'd be great,' he proclaimed. He turned his grin on Tegan who beamed back at him.

'It's only leftover picnic food you know, nothing fancy,' I warned, his joy suggested he expected a specially created meal.

'I know,' he replied with a happy shrug of his shoulders. 'Here, let me help.' He dropped to his knees and finished off the packing. When we'd done – had packed up the hamper, folded up the basket and collected all our rubbish – we got to our feet and he hoisted the wicker basket onto his shoulder. 'I moved the car nearer to the park edge so it'd be easier to get our stuff to it.'

I nodded, held out my hand for Tegan. She slipped her hand into mine, clutching onto her rounders bat with the other. Before we started to follow Luke across the grass, Tegan tugged my hand so I would come down to her level and she could whisper in my ear.

'See,' she said, 'I told you he'd come for his dinner.'

chapter twenty

Since my return to work, I'd noticed that the office I shared with Betsy had become a drop-in centre for the other women who worked in the non-retail departments. I think it'd started whilst I was away, people coming by to keep Betsy company, and it hadn't stopped. Especially when they realised that my work machine days were behind me and I wasn't going to look disapprovingly at them if they spent too long in our office, discussing non-work things. I wasn't as close to the boss, like I had been with Ted, so I wasn't an extension of him away from the directors' floor. And, I had changed. I wasn't engaged in work. Cruising was the wrong term for it because I knew I did a good job – I'd soon be out on my ear if I didn't, Luke would see to that – I simply didn't become involved in work. Not like I used to. The marketing director's job going to Luke was only part of it. The main part, the other 90 per cent, was a feeling of futility; pointlessness. I knew it was connected to Adele, but hadn't allowed myself to examine it closely – or at all. I carried on, getting by, not taking any of the satisfaction I used to get from work. It had been my life for so long, now it was something to do to pay the bills and feed Tegan. Which meant any distraction, no matter how small, was appreciated.

'The thing is,' Betsy was saying on the Monday after Tegan's school picnic, 'I think I could fall in love with him.' She was talking about a man she had met a week earlier. She'd just shown Ruby from the accounts department, one of our most frequent visitors, a text from this man. I'd seen it three times already, and it was still filthy no matter how many times I saw it. 'There's such a connection between us,' Betsy continued. 'I've never felt like this about anyone.'

She'd said that about the last man she'd met, two weeks before. And the one before that. For someone who had a hard-nosed edge and brain for business, Betsy was also impressively flighty. Betsy's dark brown eyes were staring off into the distance and she twirled a lock of her shiny, shoulder-length black hair around her forefinger. 'I think he might be The One.'

A memory stung my chest as I watched Betsy. Adele had said that more than once, with that same expression on her face. We'd had these conversations so many times in the past. 'He's so gorgeous. I've never met anyone as gorgeous as him.' Adele would have said something like that, too.

'Oh please, you always say that,' Ruby dismissed.

'I do not!' Betsy protested, swinging her feet up onto her desk.

'You do. Oh my God, I've never met a girl who falls in love as much as you do. You look at a man and you start plotting marriage.'

'Kamryn, tell her I don't always do that,' Betsy protested.

'I don't always do that,' I stated seriously to Ruby.

'You two! You'd think neither of you had ever been in love.'

'Just cos we're not complete love sluts like you,' Ruby replied, 'don't try to put us down.'

My office partner folded her arms across her chest and stuck out her lower lip in a partial huff.

'Oh bless you,' I said with a smile. 'I do know what you're talking about. It's like the icing on the cake when a bloke's gorgeous as well. But looks aren't everything,' I paused for effect, 'agility and imagination in the sack are.'

'Glad to see you're using company time to discuss important marketing issues, Kamryn,' Luke's deep voice stated. None of us had heard him approach our office, nor enter, because he hadn't bothered to knock. He'd simply appeared from nowhere, almost like a malevolent black cloud that waited until you left the house without a coat or brolly then emptied a monsoon upon you.

My heart flipped over and my stomach spiked with ice as I looked at the vision in charcoal grey that stood in our office doorway. The first time in years I say something like that at work, the first time I step out of my work persona within the walls of Angeles and he, of course, was around to witness it. This would become another piece of evidence that I was the unprofessional, unsuitable underling that he had to get rid of.

Betsy took her feet off her desk and sat up straight in her seat, Ruby leapt up and grabbed a piece of paper, pretending it was what she had come for. Both of them shot me looks of sympathy – they both knew what was coming next from Luke: at best a sarky comment; at worst a verbal warning about maintaining standards of professionalism with the staff I managed.

Ruby scuttled out of the office without uttering another word, Betsy sat frozen, staring at me. 'Betsy, would you mind giving Kamryn and me a moment alone, please?' Luke said, firing her a smile of pure charm.

Reluctantly, and looking on the verge of tears, Betsy got up and exited our office, leaving the door open behind her. Luke entered the spacious glass-walled office and stood beside my desk, effectively towering over me. To stand up, I realised, would be to directly challenge his position as the alpha bastard in this office and would result in this bollocking being more vicious than necessary. To remain sitting would be to allow him to dominate me. I chose the third option, to get up and go to the door to shut it.

When I turned back to him, he seemed to occupy the entire space beside my desk with his open-legged, folded-arm stance. As usual, his eyes flicked over me in an unimpressed manner, and I immediately felt dishevelled: my black hair wiry and wild; my black trousers and black silk wraparound top shapeless and unflattering; my body lumpen and unappealing. Luke had the effect of making me feel unkempt and unattractive; being with him reminded me of being at school, hearing all those things they used to say about me all over again. Feeling as though the words ugly and fat were watermarked into my skin – hard to see but there.

'Yes?' I asked, folding my arms across my chest and straightening up to exude confidence. This was my office, it had been my castle for over two years before his arrival, no one was allowed to make me feel like this in it.

'Look, Kamryn,' he began, 'we got off to a bad start.'

I paused, peered at him in surprise and mentally replayed what he said. When my mind refused to believe what it'd just heard, I said, 'Pardon?'

'I said, we got off to a bad start.'

'Yes, I suppose we did,' I replied, wondering when the bollocking would begin. 'But whose fault was that?'

He inhaled, paused. 'Mine.'

'I suppose I wasn't completely blameless,' I conceded.

'We've got to work together and see each other outside of work because Tegan likes me being around.'

I contemplated him in cautious silence.

'After Saturday . . . With the dinner invite . . . I was so incredibly touched. And I got to thinking about all this and how stupid it is. And I hoped we could work out our problems; see if we can find a way to get on.' I must have looked sceptical because he said, 'All right, maybe not get on but not wind each other up.'

'OK,' I replied.

'Right then.' He paused, inhaled and exhaled deeply. 'I'm sorry for acting as though you couldn't do your job. I'd just heard so much about you that I thought you'd be this dynamic, pretty young thing who was eager to please. Instead . . .' his voice trailed away and he grimaced slightly, as though he couldn't believe he'd begun to expose his uncensored thoughts again.

'Oh, please, don't stop now, I want to hear it all. "Instead . . ."?'

'Instead, you turned up and you seemed kind of scatty. Not what I expected at all. So, sorry, I shouldn't have judged you like that.'

I said nothing.

'And I'm sorry, also, for listening to those ridiculous rumours about you and Ted. That's not the way I usually work.'

'Thank you for saying all that, it's very gracious of you. And I want to apologise for calling you a small-minded, tiny-dicked, arrogant wanker who got his job by licking arse rather than by hard graft,' I replied, even though my heart wasn't in it. What Luke had said had hurt and I was disgusted with myself for letting it needle me.

'You never called me that,' he pointed out.

'Oh, I did. In my head. Lots of times. In fact . . . Sorry, I just did it again.'

Luke's expression softened a little, a sliver of amusement danced around his lips. 'It wasn't only me,' he commented. 'You weren't exactly friendly when we first met.'

'No, but I'm sure you'd have got past that a lot quicker if I was some blonde goddess or girlie brunette.'

His eyes fixed on my face in a manner I knew meant he was desperately trying to stop himself giving me another once-over. 'Your kid's so cool,' he said changing the subject.

'Is that a dig?' I asked. 'I'm not cool but Tegan is?'

'Are you always this paranoid?' he asked.

189

'Just cos you're paranoid, doesn't mean people aren't out to get you,' I replied.

'I was simply making a statement of fact. Your child is cool. You can't help but like her . . . And that's not a dig, it's a statement of fact.'

'Yes, she is a lovely girl,' I agreed.

'Right, well, I'd better let you get back to work – and put Betsy and Ruby out of their misery.' We both glanced out of the office at Betsy who was wringing her hands as she pretended to have a conversation with Ruby at her desk while they both watched the office. When they saw us look their way they both fell over themselves to look otherwise engaged.

'So, we wipe the slate clean and start again?' he said, turning at the door.

'Yup, I believe that is what we have agreed.'

Luke smiled, not a charming one but not a caustic one, either. 'I do mean it, you know.'

I returned his smile. 'Me too.'

When I returned from a meeting with the head of the children's department later that day, I found a Twix bar on my desk with the note,

Tegan said you like chocolate.
Luke

'you have to kiss
luke too'

chapter twenty-one

Light flooded my senses as I opened my eyes a fraction. I had to immediately snap them shut again. It was too painful. Even with my eyes closed there seemed to be gallons of light pouring into my head, squeezing my brain in a death grip.

I reached out for a pillow to cover my head but my fingers couldn't located one. Odd. I usually had lots of pillows in my bed. It slowly dawned on me I hadn't moved my arm at all. I'd lost the use of my limbs. My mouth and my head and my eyes all felt swollen and tender. And the pain made me feel like throwing up. I had the beginnings of a migraine – I could still think so I wasn't in the grip of a proper one, yet.

I didn't have time for a migraine. I had a child to prepare for school; I had to get ready for work. The fist around my temple tightened.

Maybe Mrs Kaye would come over to take Tegan to school? I wondered before dismissing the idea. She had six children to sort out, she couldn't take on another at such short notice. I'd have to brave it out, force myself to put the migraine behind me for a little while.

I gasped as the fist clamped tighter around my head.

Or maybe Luke? He'd come and take Tiga to school – he'd do anything for her. And for me too, it seemed.

He'd been true to his word about starting again and in the

two weeks since the picnic hadn't snapped at me or dismissed any of my ideas out of hand. He'd also suggested we have daily meetings in his office to discuss our revamped marketing strategy. I'd begun to look forward to these because it was almost as good as working with Ted. I felt like part of a team, involved again. And the apathy and feelings of futility eased for a while. I was the old Kamryn, focused on work and work alone for half an hour. Luke and I weren't friends or anything, just colleagues. He had started to trust my opinion, to accept that I really did know my job and that if I'd been given the chance to apply, I would have been a serious contender for his position. The times we saw each other outside of work we did actually speak about non-work things. Some way down the line our relationship could become a proper full on friendship. In the spirit of our newly negotiated peace and harmony I was sure if I picked up the phone he'd be straight over to take Tegan to school. All I had to do was reach out and pick up the phone.

Time passed. And I still couldn't move. Not in bed and certainly not to pick up the phone. The alarm went off and my body contracted in agony. I didn't even have the energy to shut it off so I had to wait for it to stop. I must have fallen asleep again because the next thing I knew, Tegan was stood by my bed.

'Mummy Ryn,' she said, taking hold of my arm and pulling at it.

'Hnghhh,' I replied.

'It's time for us to get up,' she sing-songed.

'I– I can't,' I replied.

'But I have to go to school.'

I managed to open my eyes, and focus on the girl in the red gingham PJs. She was looking at me with deep disapproval and slight irritation – the same way my mum used to at me when I dawdled about getting up for school in the mornings.

194

'I'm not feeling well,' I managed through my swollen mouth and its heavy-weight tongue.

'You're sick?' she asked.

'Yes, Tiga, I'm sick. I'm sorry.'

Her eyes doubled in size and she turned and fled. Ran out of my bedroom before I could form the word, 'Wait.' Even though I could barely lift my eyelids, I had to go after her and find out what was wrong.

Summoning all my strength I raised my arm, gripped the edge of my sheet and pulled it back. That small movement sent spikes of pain shooting behind my eyes. I had to rest for a few seconds before I moved my legs off the bed and sat up. They touched the floor and the soft pile felt like needles on the bottom of my feet. I swayed as I stood up, and had to hold onto the bedside table to steady myself.

I grabbed onto the wall and moved across my bedroom, keeping myself upright by holding onto the wall with the flats of my hands, propelling myself forwards. When I reached the window, I had to hold onto the radiator to keep myself moving and then I was back holding onto the cool white walls. *Come on, come on,* I urged myself. I finally reached the door and grabbed the door frame, launching myself out of the bedroom and into the corridor.

I headed along the corridor, which, after the turn from my bedroom, was mercifully straight. I held onto the cupboard fronts as Tegan's bedroom, my target, loomed into view – a shining beacon of hope in a dark night.

One more step, one more step. I launched myself away from the wall and made it – I was finally standing in Tegan's doorway.

She was sitting cross-legged on her bed, clinging onto Meg as though her life depended on it while rocking back and forth, her face contorted with the pain of unshed tears.

'Tegan, what's the matter?' I said, leaning against her door frame to keep myself upright.

'You're ill,' she said, still rocking and staring at a spot on the floor. 'You're ill and you're going to heaven to be with Jesus and the angels and my mummy.'

'What?' I asked.

'You're going to heaven like my mummy,' she accused.

'Tiga, I'm not, it's only a migraine, a headache, it will go away. It w—' My words were cut short by the buzzer sounding, which caused agony to explode in my head. I couldn't ignore it, if it sounded again, it would probably finish me off. 'Wait here,' I said to Tegan.

'Hello,' I said into the white intercom.

'It's Luke,' the voice on the other end said.

What's he doing here at the crack of dawn? I hadn't called him despite my thoughts earlier. I buzzed him in and opened our front door to him.

He appeared seconds later, wearing the same blue shirt, navy blue tie and black suit he'd been wearing at work yesterday. He was brandishing a smug grin and a twinkle in his eye.

'Hi, I was seeing someone in the area and thought you might like a lift to school and wor— Jeez, you look awful,' he said as I stepped back to let him in.

'I thought we'd gotten over you thinking I was a dog,' I joked. Tegan came out of her bedroom, having heard Luke's voice.

'Kamryn?' Luke said. His voice sounded as though he was whispering at me from the end of a long tunnel. 'Are you going—'

More pain exploded in my brain, and the world was suddenly an array of pulsing pink, blue, green and yellow flashing lights. Then everything was white.

Slowly, I prised open my eyes, and didn't instantly snap them shut. The light didn't puncture my head with stars of agony like it did earlier. Spikes of pain still tore at the area behind my right eye but the nausea was gone. Something cool and damp lay across my forehead, taking away the burning from the migraine. I reached up to touch it, it was a flannel.

'Ahhh, you're awake.' Beside my bed, Luke sat on one of the kitchen chairs, a book in his hands, one foot resting on the wooden base of my bed. He laid the book down on my bedside table and examined me with concerned hazel eyes.

'Where's Tegan?' I croaked.

He indicated to the space on the bed beside me. I turned my head, she was in her pyjamas curled up like a cat beside me, clinging to Meg even in the depths of sleep.

'She didn't want to leave you.'

'I passed out?'

Luke nodded. 'When you keeled over you gave me a scare, but she was hysterical. She started screaming about you going to heaven like her mum. She refused to go to school, said if she left you would go to heaven without her.'

I stared down at her, watching her troubled little face as it slept. Suddenly her eyes flew open, making me jump a little. She sat up, blinking at me.

'Are you better?' she asked, her face and body tensed as she awaited my reply.

'A little bit,' I replied, trying – and failing – to make my voice sound normal.

'Hey, T, why don't you go get Kamryn a drink from the kitchen? I've put one on the table,' Luke said. To me he added, 'T said you had a migraine so I rang the doctor and she said you should get lots of fluids.'

Tegan shunted down to the end of the bed, then got off by turning around, putting a foot on the wooden base, then putting the other foot on the floor. Her feet pounded the carpet as she ran out to the kitchen.

The second she disappeared, Luke threw himself forwards in

his seat. 'I take it Tegan's mother died recently?' he said in low-ered tones.

I nodded.

'How recently?'

'Very.'

'Kamryn, you can talk to me.'

We had ceased hostilities, we had pleasant conversations and, at some point, he and I could become real friends, but right now he was getting nothing out of me.

Tegan returned to the room, holding a straight glass in both her hands, her tongue poking out the corner of her mouth as she took small steps, walking slowly and carefully, so as not to spill any of the glass's contents. I struggled upright, the flannel falling from my forehead as I sat up.

Luke retrieved the flannel and left. A bathroom tap spurted to life seconds later. I took the glass from Tegan, lowered my head, drank. The water soothed and cooled as it flowed into my mouth and down my throat. I gulped down a couple more mouthfuls. 'Thank you,' I said.

'Are you going to be better?' she asked, rocking from one foot to another, twisting her petite hands together. It never occurred to me that she would make the connection between my illness and death. That she'd think I'd go the same way as her mother. But why wouldn't she? Most nights I'd wake up and have a moment of terror that had me rushing to her bed-room to double check she was all right. Irrational fear in the wake of a death wasn't so irrational, and it certainly wasn't the reserve of adults.

'Between the water and the flannel, I'll be better in no time,' I said. Tegan twisted her mouth to one side, and regarded me with suspicion – convinced she was not. Tegan needed someone she could rely on, I realised as I watched her reaction to my reply. Someone who'd be there when I wasn't. Luke returned, bearing the orange flannel. He moved to lay it on my forehead then thought better of it. 'Here,' he held it out to me.

'I'm going to be fine,' I reassured Tegan, reaching out my free hand to her. She slipped her small hand into mine and I was transported back to the day of the funeral. The day I held her hand in mine, suddenly frightened at this new responsibility. Responsibility for a life. I had to ensure she reached adulthood, that she was happy and healthy and intellectually stretched as she made that journey. Single parents were constantly being held up as pariahs in society, but they should be hailed as heroes – bringing up children on your own without falling apart was a miracle to me. I'd only been doing it for a couple of months and I was struggling. Much as it grated my self-sufficient mind to admit it, I needed someone.

Luke patted his legs. 'Jump up, T, and we can read to Kamryn before she goes back to sleep.' She did as she was told and Luke opened my book – J. G. Ballard's *Drowned World* – at where I'd shoved a bookmark in.

He started reading, encouraging Tegan to follow the words with her finger. I closed my eyes. His voice was smooth as he formed the words my favourite author had written. Luke took the glass from my hand as I slid down in bed and felt myself drift into sleep again. My eyes flittered open for a second and the image of Tegan sat on Luke's lap, staring at the book, while he read to us, was one that stayed with me into sleep.

When I awoke again Luke was still sitting by my bed, reading. I removed the damp flannel from my forehead, and the movement alerted him I was awake. His face creased into the affectionate smile he usually reserved for Tegan. 'Hi,' he said. I moved my arm but Tegan wasn't beside me.

'I convinced her to go watch telly,' he said when he spotted what I was doing. 'She only agreed to go if I stayed here and she comes back every few minutes to check you haven't gone anywhere.'

The spikes of pain were blunted now, only a dull throb signalled my earlier torture, but I still moved stiffly as I sat up. 'Thanks, Luke. Thanks for everything.'

He leant forwards, picked up the glass of water and handed it to me. He watched me drink and took the glass away when I'd finished.

'I called Tegan's school earlier, explained the situation, and I told work we wouldn't be in for a couple of days. You're sick, obviously, so I'll work from home.'

'Why?'

'It's clear that you need someone to take care of you both.'

'I don't *need* anyone,' I snapped.

Luke gripped his lips together rather than rise to my anger. 'Well, I thought I'd stick around if that's all right.'

'Everyone at work's going to think we're shagging now.' I pulled the covers up to my neck, I was braless in a white T-shirt in front of a man who had issues with my body.

'There are worst things for people to think.'

'Are there?' I replied.

Luke glanced down, embarrassed. Something occurred to me. He lived in a two-bedroom flat in Alwoodley, so for him to be in Horsforth meant he was travelling in the wrong direction for work. 'Why were you in the area again?'

'I, erm, was visiting someone.'

'You're wearing the same clothes as you were yesterday.'

'Yeah, I haven't been home.' We made eye contact and I knew exactly what he meant.

'Blonde or brunette?'

'Blonde. Pretty. Amazing body. Not afraid to use it.'

'Good for you.'

'I think we should talk.'

'What are we doing now?'

'Kamryn, I'm well aware I've been a pig to you, but you haven't been the easiest person to get along with. And now I'm beginning to understand why – you're grieving.'

I stopped looking at him, stared at my off television.

'I don't pretend to understand any of what you're going through, but I do know that bottling it up isn't good for you or for Tegan.' That touched a nerve – was I hurting Tegan by not being honest about my emotions? By hiding from my pain.

'I always thought that Tegan was someone you'd fostered after you hadn't really thought things through. And no one at work seems to know that much about you, which is strange when you've worked there for years. Ted wasn't talking. Your friend Betsy won't tell me a thing, but I get the impression she doesn't know that much anyway.'

'What makes you think I'd talk to you, then?'

'You owe me.'

'For what?!'

'Hey, I caught you when you fainted. I carried you to bed. I calmed Tegan down. I called the doctor to find out what to do. I . . . I even told work that you were ill. Now if that isn't stuff worthy of a reward, I don't know what is.'

'I'll buy you a drink sometime.'

'Seriously, Kamryn, you can talk to me. It'll go no further.' He paused, waited for me to unburden myself. I said nothing.

'OK,' he said with a sigh. 'I was engaged to be married. I met her at Harvard. I've travelled a lot so we've been together on and off for ten years – whenever I returned to New York we got back together. This last time we were together for three years.' Luke reached into his inside pocket, pulled out his wallet, flipped it open and showed me her picture. She was pretty, of course. Long blonde hair, immaculate skin, shaped eyebrows, soft pink lips. She was more than pretty, she was stunningly beautiful. And the way her brown eyes sparkled at the camera, she was obviously in love with the person who'd taken the picture. Obviously in love with my boss. He flipped the wallet shut and returned it to his pocket. 'Her name is Nicole and we'd actually set a date for the wedding. Then I was offered a job in London. I assumed she'd want to come with me but she said no. When I decided to turn the job down she told me not to because London wasn't the issue, her feelings for me were. She loved me but, at that time, she couldn't commit to moving across the world with me. She wasn't sure it would work out between us. So, I came alone. We speak every week and I still carry her picture, as you just saw, and . . .' He stopped talking and stared at the carpet for a few seconds. Then he raised his burnt-orange hazel eyes. 'And I cling to the hope she'll change her mind about us. There. No one else in England knows that. I'm trusting you to keep it to yourself because even eighteen months down the line it still hurts. I still want her back.'

While he'd been talking, I had to hide my horror at Luke, my boss, humanising himself right before my eyes. He had shared with me. Me. Of all people. That must have taken him a lot to do. He'd done it though, to get me to do the same.

But opening up . . . It terrified me. Especially to him. But he had done it to me. Also, this wasn't about me, it was about Tegan. She loved this Luke man. And today proved I needed a back-up person; someone I could rely on to take care of her if I wasn't around. He was it. I stared at him for a moment, my heart racing in my chest. *This is for Tegan.* 'OK,' I began. I told him the tale. Starting with the night I found out about Adele and Nate to the moment he walked into our lives. Luke didn't say anything, didn't ask questions nor request clarification, he simply listened with a face of stone, occasionally stroking the patch of his line beard that sat in the groove below his lips. When I'd finished, he nodded his head.

'You've been struggling to cope with all this on your own?' he asked. He whistled long and low. 'I'm surprised you haven't had a complete breakdown, no wonder you've been such a prickly bitch.'

'What's your excuse for being an arrogant bastard?' I replied.

'It's my nature,' he shot back.

I smirked at that.

He smiled back and said, 'I'll make us dinner soon.'

'You don't have to. You can go, I'm feeling better.'

'I don't have to, but I want to. If you let me, I'd like to help out.' His sincerity surprised me. Yes, his story had made him human, vulnerable even, but this was making him a nice human.

'Why?'

'Because I like Tegan.'

'There's got to be more to it than that.'

'Maybe there is, maybe there isn't. I'll tell you about it one day.'

Luke was saved from further questioning by Tegan, who came bounding in and leapt up onto the bed.

'Are you better?' she asked as she arranged herself beside me.

'Much, much better. I can even get out of bed and come into the living room.'

Tegan beamed. 'Really and truly? Luke said you would get better.'

'I won't say this very often, but Luke was right.'

She slid down onto the floor. 'I can put one of my DVDs on.'

Throwing back the covers, I stood up. I had to make it look good – didn't want to scare her again. Luke stood, and moved forward as though to help me but the scowl I shot him forced him back.

Tegan took my hand and slowly led me to the living room

where we collapsed on the sofa together. 'Whilst you're up, put the kettle on, Luke,' I said.

'Yeah, put the kettle on, Luke,' Tegan giggled. She snuggled into me and I wrapped my arm around her.

'What did your last slave die of?' he mumbled as he did as he was told.

'Answering back,' I replied.

He glanced at me over his shoulder and I managed a smile. Holding my eyes with his, he grinned back. *I could grow to like this man*, I realised. *I could grow to like him a lot.*

chapter twenty-two

'If you could just wait in the other room while Tegan and I have a chat.' The social worker was good. She made what she said sound as damn close to a request as you could get, but we both knew it was an order.

I moved out of the living area, which, like everything else in the flat, had been polished and wiped to within an inch of its life. I'd taken the whole day off work, even though the home visit was in the afternoon, so I could finish the cleaning in the morning. After the cleaning I'd put on a pale pink, silk dress, the most expensive item in my wardrobe, a dress I knew suited me, pulled out to impress that social worker. Tegan had bunches in her hair and was wearing her favourite outfit of the moment: an A-line blue denim dress over a white, long-sleeved top. She also had fluffy bunny slippers on her feet.

In my bedroom, I sat on the bed, pulled my knees up to my chest, accepting the fact the social worker had to find out if I was ill-treating Tegan. She needed to know if Tegan liked being here with me, if I was good enough. And she couldn't do that if I was sitting there. But then, would Tiga say anything even if I wasn't in the same room? She was funny, friendly and gregarious, but also incredibly closed. We were similar in that respect. While her mother had always labelled herself 'too much', 'too open', Tegan was guarded. Very cautious about revealing what was going on inside. She'd never mentioned what happened in Guildford, how much she suffered at the hands of her grandparents, would she admit if she was unhappy with me?

My stomach flipped a little as I wondered what the woman would ask. Would she ask leading questions, try to get things out of Tiga that could be perceived as reasonable parts of everyday parenting cock-ups? Like forgetting she existed that one time? It'd only been once but I hadn't forgotten, I doubt Tiga had either. And what about collapsing a few weeks ago and scaring the living daylights out of her? I hadn't done that on purpose either, but that didn't mean it hadn't scarred her for life.

I chewed on my lower lip. What if Tegan hated being with me? I'd never considered that, not properly. I was always worried about her missing her mum, but what if all along she simply didn't want to be with me? What if, no matter what I did or said she'd rather be anywhere but here? The only thing in her life she'd chosen was Luke. He'd become a part of her life – *our* life – at her insistence, no one had forced him upon her like they did me. And she loved him. Every second of every day when he was around she was enraptured with him. He was like summer holidays – he represented fun and freedom; I was like school – I represented timetables and discipline. Would she tell the social worker that?

Thirty torturous minutes later, I was allowed back in. Tiga was grinning as I sat down on the sofa. She climbed into my lap and made Meg kiss me on the cheek. 'Meg loves you today,' she said, climbed off my lap and wandered out the room. I turned my attention to the social worker, who hadn't written down that exchange on her notepad. In fact, she'd packed away her pad and pen and was just staring at me. She was thirtyish, with straight brown bobbed hair, thin lips and flat eyes.

I couldn't read her: not her body language – her hands were clasped together in her lap; nor her face – she had a half-smile on her lips and her brown eyes were steadily fixed on me, but that could mean anything.

'So, do I pass muster?' I asked.

'That wasn't the reason for my visit,' she replied. Her look progressed from vaguely impassive to one that suggested she could see every evil thought I'd ever had.

'What was the reason for your visit, then?' Had she been instructed to steer clear of the fact that Tegan was white? There was nothing they could do about me taking care of her because it was a request in Adele's will, but they could turn down my adoption application. They could prevent Tegan becoming a Matika and never say that our different colours was the real reason why.

'How are you finding all this?' she replied, expertly avoiding my question.

'Fine,' I replied.

'It's not a strain?'

'No, not really.'

'It'd be understandable if it was, Kamryn, this must be hard for you.'

What has Tegan said? 'No harder than it would be for anyone else,' I replied.

'And how are you finding working full-time and taking care of Tegan?'

'Fine.'

'It must be tiring?'

'Must it?' I replied, facetiously, remembered who she was and added, 'It's fine.'

'Picking up Tegan from school isn't a problem with the hours you work?'

'No, she goes to a friend's house after school and I pick her up from there.'

'Children often fall out, what if that happens with her friend? What would happen there?'

'There's an after-school club at the school. I'd have to leave work earlier to pick her up by six but then I'd just work through lunch.'

'And you wouldn't mind that?'

'Are you trying to say I should give up work or something? Because I can't afford to – and if I work part-time things would be even tighter than they are now.'

'Are you struggling financially?'

'Who isn't in this day and age?' I was becoming riled. Why was this woman determined to twist everything I said? To make me feel as though nothing I did would be good enough?

'Who's Luke?' she asked, changing tact.

'He's my boss,' I replied cautiously. 'Tegan met him once and they got on really well.'

I saw a slight twitch in her eyebrows.

'He's a good guy,' I added hastily. 'I wouldn't let him near Tegan if I thought there was anything dodgy about him.'

'Tegan said he was her best friend,' the social worker stated.

'Hmm, they do get on . . .' *So, he's her best friend, huh? I thought jealously. Who am I? Jo-Jo the Dog-faced Boy?*

'She also said that you never get cross with her.'

'Did she?' I replied. 'Is that bad?'

'No, simply unusual. Do you seriously never get cross with her or are you holding back?'

'Tiga's the best behaved child in the world, she hasn't done anything to make me cross with her. Not ever.' I paused to consider this. 'That's true, actually, she's really well behaved.'

'You think she's holding back?'

'Maybe . . .' Fear spiked in me. 'I've never thought about it. She just always does what she's told. No questions, no back-chat. I never considered she wouldn't disagree because she's frightened of me. That's what you think, isn't it? That she's sacred of me. I wouldn't hurt her, though. Not ever.'

'I didn't think for a second you would,' the social worker said. 'I just wonder if she needs counselling to help her come to terms with her mother's death.'

'That's not a thought, is it? It's an order,' I said.

Her smile would have been friendly if her eyes hadn't remained like gimlets in her pale face. 'I wouldn't say that.'

'What would you say? That if I don't get her counselling, you're not going to recommend that I be allowed to adopt her?'

'Why don't you think about it?' she said, not answering my question. *Deliberately* not answering my question. *Again.* She stood. 'I'll schedule another meeting with you in a couple of months, see how the pair of you are getting on together. It was lovely to meet you both.'

Bitch! I kept thinking. I wanted to stand in the middle of my living room and scream it at the top of my voice until all my inner venom was out. *BITCH! BITCH! BITCH!* She'd said, without saying it, that I wasn't good enough; that I wasn't taking care of Tegan properly. That we needed to bring more people – *counsellors* – into our lives. And that she would screw me over if I didn't comply. In my more rational moments, of course, I knew that she was only thinking of Tegan and how counselling would help her, but most of the time since that woman had left had been crammed with the urge to scream 'BITCH'. I knew I wasn't doing brilliantly before she showed up but now I knew I was doing it all wrong. I wasn't helping Tegan to deal with her mother's death, I wasn't bringing her up to be a healthy, happy adult, I was holding her back, potentially damaging her.

'Mummy Ryn,' Tegan asked.

'Yes?' I snapped, then heard my voice and stopped. Took a

deep breath, stopped staring unseeingly into the cupboard of tinned food and turned to her. She'd been sat at the table painting pictures since the social worker left and now looked at me with a paintbrush in one hand, Meg hooked in the other arm. She didn't look damaged; her body wasn't tensed, her eyes weren't filled with fear, her skin wasn't grey with unhappiness. But who knew what pulsed beneath the surface, how much damage I'd caused. 'Yes, Tiga?' I repeated.

'What time is Luke coming back?'

'About ten o'clock.'

She put down the paintbrush, soundlessly counted, 'Eight, nine, ten,' on her fingers then protested, 'But that's after my bed time.'

'I know, but he's driving up from London, there's no way for him to get here earlier.'

'That's not fair.'

'He might come over tomorrow.'

'But I'm painting him a picture.'

'I'll give it to him if he comes here. I'm sure he'll love it.'

'But I want to give it to him.'

'Then give it to him tomorrow.' I returned to searching the depths of the cupboards, staring at cans and packets, bottles and jars, waiting for inspiration to strike. I heard scuffly sounds behind me as Tegan climbed down from her place at the table.

I thought she might be coming to join me, to sit on the counter and stare into the cupboard as we often did before I started dinner. Instead she asked, 'What if he doesn't come tomorrow?'

'He probably will,' I threw over my shoulder. 'He usually comes over on Saturday.'

'But what if he doesn't?'

I don't know! I almost shouted. I took a deep breath, this wasn't her fault, I reminded myself. My mood wasn't her fault. I spun towards her and found she wasn't halfway across the kitchen but right behind me, clutching onto her bowl of dirty paintbrush water. And as I turned, my legs connected with her hands, knocking the bowl free of her fingers. The contents splashed out, splaying its wet, grey tendrils over my lap. Tegan gasped a tiny shocked gasp before she fell into a terrified silence.

I stared down at my dress. I'd spent so much money on this dress. It'd been my first purchase when I'd moved to Leeds after I left Nate and Adele, it represented me starting again, doing normal, simple things like shopping again. I loved this dress. Now it was ruined. Just like the rest of my life. Ruined. Destroyed. Nothing I could do would fix it.

'I'VE HAD ENOUGH OF YOU!' I screamed. 'YOU'RE DOING MY HEAD IN!'

I felt Tegan's body jump at the sound of my voice, then she froze – literally petrified by my anger.

I wanted her to go away. I *needed* her to go away, to get away from me before I said something that couldn't be taken back.

'Go to your room,' I whispered, controlling my voice.

Without a protest, I heard Tiga's footsteps retreating as she left the room. But I didn't move, I was frozen with fear. Fear for what I almost said . . . I almost said that if it wasn't for her, I wouldn't have social workers looking down their noses at me. If it wasn't for her, I would be Marketing Director of Angeles, it'd be me travelling up from London right now, not Luke. If she wasn't here, I'd be free to do what I wanted instead of always having to think first about childcare arrangements. I wouldn't have my day structured around her and I wouldn't always be wondering if I was going to fall down at the next hurdle.

Tears swelled in my eyes, collected on my eyelashes then dripped down onto the floor. I didn't really feel my knees hitting the lino but there I was on the floor, the silk dress thirstily soaking up the puddle of dirty paint water. I covered my face with my hands, trying to rock myself better as I thought about how many more ways I could screw this up.

'Tiga,' I whispered sometime later as I pushed open her door. 'Tiga, I'm sorry.'

She sat on her bed, her knees pulled up to her chest, clutching Meg.

'I didn't mean it. I'm really—' I stopped speaking as I noticed her usually neat room was in a state of orderly disarray: her drawers and wardrobe had been emptied of clothes. Piles of neatly folded clothes sat in front of the wardrobe and drawers. Her multicoloured holdall had been retrieved from under her bed and sat open on the floor, a few clothes already in it. My heartbeat quickened and my stomach tumbled. Had the social worker told her that if she didn't like living with me, she could go live elsewhere? Was she leaving me?

'What's going on?' I asked, panicked. 'Why have you started to pack?' I stepped over the holdall, knelt down in front of Tegan. 'I'm sorry,' I said, searching her small heart-shaped face and blue eyes for some semblance of understanding. For some hint, however slight, that I could talk her into staying. 'I didn't mean to shout at you. I was angry with myself not you. I'm sorry.' She didn't move, simply held onto Meg, almost as though I hadn't spoken. 'Tiga, please believe me, I am sorry. I am truly, truly sorry.'

'Please,' she whispered, then stopped, obviously terrified of what came next.

'Please . . .?' I echoed.

'Please don't make me live at Nana Muriel's house,' she said, then cringed down, lowering her head to be close to Meg.

'Why would I make you live with Nana Muriel?' I asked. Of all the things I thought she was going to say, that wasn't it.

'Because I was naughty,' she replied. 'I don't want to go to Nana Muriel's house. I want to stay with you.'

'Is that why you got your clothes out?' I asked.

She nodded. It had never occurred to me that Tegan thought returning to that hell in Surrey was an option. I thought she knew she was stuck with me, for better or worse. Was that why she was always so good? Never questioning, never arguing, never throwing a tantrum? Because she thought I might send her back to being beaten and starved?

'Tiga, me and you . . .' I paused as her face creased up in absolute terror, waiting for me to pass sentence on her. I started again, my voice as soft as a wish, 'Tiga, you're going to stay with me until you're all grown up.'

The lines and creases of her face relaxed a fraction.

'You never have to see Nana Muriel again. Even if you're really naughty you're staying with me.'

Her eyes eased up to look at me at last.

'I'm going to look after you for ever and ever,' I stated. That thought once again sent panic stampeding in my chest. 'Tiga, this is your home. Even when you're all grown up, wherever I am will be your home. I . . . I'll always want to take care of you. Do you understand?'

'Even if I'm naughty?' she asked.

'Even then,' I said. 'Not that I'm encouraging it,' I hastily modified. 'If you are naughty we'll find a way to work around it. But you'll still stay with me.'

'I'm sorry I was naughty,' she said.

'You weren't naughty, it was an accident.'

'I'm sorry.'

'It was an accident, you didn't do it on purpose. And I'm sorry for shouting at you.'

'Luke won't see your pretty dress now,' she stated.

I was puzzled for a moment, searched her face to see if she knew. If she'd picked up on how my feelings for her best friend, my boss, had changed. She stared back at me, oblivious. She didn't know that since my migraine four weeks ago, something had fundamentally changed between Luke and me. He'd not only become human, he'd become a man in my eyes. Our meetings at work had become chats, at the weekend he'd often stick around after Tegan went to bed and we'd stay up drinking tea and talking until three or four o'clock in the morning. Tegan didn't know that I'd started to have unsettling thoughts about him. Thoughts about me and him and, yes, all right, sex. No, he wouldn't see me in my pretty dress and that was good. The thoughts I had weren't to be encouraged, let alone indulged. 'That's probably for the best,' I admitted to her.

'So, are you going to stay with me?' I asked, banishing Mr Wiseman from my mind.

Tegan scrunched up her nose as she nodded.

'Good. I'm really, really glad.'

Tiga reached out with Meg and made the rag doll kiss my cheek. 'Meg loves you a lot today,' she explained.

'I'm starting to get that. Shall we put away your clothes, sweetpea?' Another nod. Tegan slid off her bed. 'And, as a special treat, you can stay up and see Luke.'

Her eyes widened with the delight. 'Really and truly?'

'Yup,' I replied, knowing she'd be asleep before eight-thirty. Nine, tops.

chapter twenty-three

The allure of seeing Luke was, in fact, the strongest stimulant known to Tegankind – she was wide awake at ten-fifteen when he buzzed. I'd texted him to say Tegan was waiting up for him so could he come by on his way home, and he'd replied no problem.

I peeled myself off the sofa to answer the door, tiredness weighing down on me like an anvil but Tegan, bedecked in her red gingham PJs, clambered to her feet on the sofa and started bouncing up and down.

Luke entered bearing gifts. Like a dad who felt guilty about having to travel for work, who thought toys and other trinkets would be a compensator for his absence, Luke always bought Tegan something when he went away – even if it was for one night. This was his biggest hoard yet, though – he was weighted down with five plastic bags in each of his big hands.

'Jeez, how much have you spent?' I asked as he bustled past me.

'Erm, not much. One of my friends works for a toy company.'

I raised an eyebrow at him. 'Oh yeah? She sounds like a great friend,' I said.

Luke glanced away the second I said 'she' then studiously avoided making eye contact with my area of the room again. Guilty as almost charged, obviously.

'Come on, T,' he said, 'let's see what's in the bags.'

Tiga stopped bouncing and, holding onto Luke's arm, she climbed down onto the floor in front of the bags. Happiness flashed up in her eyes like twin beacons in a storm. All the jealousy I'd felt at how he'd come by his bounty was replaced by gratitude. She needed this, needed someone to make a fuss of her, to buy her presents and make her feel special.

Item by item, Luke emptied the bags in front of her and, I could have kissed him for this, most of the toys were educational. If not educational, then books – novels that were quite advanced for her age but she would love because she became completely involved in stories, the more complicated the better; drawing pads and colouring pens; felt-tips and crayons and colouring pencils; a couple of teddies and a game of Junior Scrabble.

'Are they all for me? Really and truly?' Tiga asked.

'Who else would they be for?' he replied.

'Am I 'lowed to keep them?' Tegan asked me, her royal blue eyes streaked with apprehension that I might say no.

'Of course, sweetpea,' I replied.

'Thank you!' she screeched and launched herself at Luke, who was knocked backwards, caught unawares as we both were. She started bouncing up and down on his abdomen, not seeming to notice the 'Ouf!' sound he made every time she connected with his stomach.

'Look, Mummy Ryn! I'm jumping on Luke!' she giggled. I smiled. This was the old Tiga. Affectionate, lively, bouncy. Luke brought that out in her; he was like a time machine for her personality. No wonder she wanted to be with him all the time – he made her joyful again. 'Mummy Ryn, am I 'lowed to kiss Luke for a thank you?' she said, increasing her bounce rate.

'If Luke doesn't mind.'

Tiga looked at Luke. 'Course I don't mind,' he said, winded, 'just don't jump on my tummy any more, OK?'

'OK,' Tegan said, disappointed. She leant forwards and planted a smacker in the middle of his forehead, just like he did to her whenever he kissed her goodnight or goodbye. She sat back, looked expectantly at me.

'What?' I asked, wondering what I'd missed.

Tegan sighed theatrically, as though I was being deliberately obtuse. 'You have to kiss Luke too,' she said in a slightly exasperated voice.

I took a horrified step back while accidentally making eye contact with Luke.

'I don't mind,' Luke said, his eyes shining with humour.

'He doesn't mind,' Tegan encouraged.

'Yeah, well, I'm sure he doesn't want to spoil your special kiss with mine.'

'Coward,' Luke mouthed at me.

'I think you should give him a few more bounces for me, though, Tiga.' Her face lit up and his contorted in horror. 'Yeah, a few really big bounces, right on his tummy.'

'OK!' She took up her task with admirable gusto.

'Have you been crying?' Luke asked over an hour later. He'd read Tiga four stories and listened to her rabbit on for a good ten minutes until her wind-up mechanism had finally unwound itself and she'd fallen asleep. He now removed the book I hadn't tidied away from the sofa, slid it onto the floor before he sat down. I was on the other end of the sofa, I'd been half watching telly, half wondering if I should start washing-up, completely listening to Luke and Tiga talking in her room.

I turned to Luke. He was exhausted: his eyes were pinkshot, his blue shirt was rumpled and the creases on his thirty-five-year-old face seemed more pronounced than usual. I didn't reply to his question because I was stunned he'd asked it.

'Have you?' he repeated.

I'd checked my face in the mirror before he'd arrived and

my eyes weren't red or puffy. How could he know? 'Why do you ask?'

'You've got that look in your eyes. You used to have it a lot when we first met. I used to think it was disdain but now I know it was because you were crying a lot in those days – now I know it's because Adele had just passed away. And that look is back.'

I couldn't tell him why I'd been crying, no one could know about it. Especially not him, he who could make Tegan so happy. I didn't want him to know I didn't have his skill with her.

'So, who was this woman you were shagging in London?' I asked.

Luke paused as a host of emotions – shame, delight, embarrassment, guilt – flitted across his features. 'I take it the social worker's visit didn't go well,' he ploughed on, determined to get me to open up.

Not as determined as I was to keep schtum, however. 'I'm guessing she was a new conquest judging by how much she heaped on you?'

Luke's eyes remained fixed on me for a moment as he calculated something. 'I didn't mean for it to happen,' he said, admitting defeat, it seemed. 'I, well, I kind of . . . you know some things get mixed up in your head? I liked her but she's not my usual type of, well, you know, and I've been thinking a lot lately about what my type is and if I've been a bit rigid in only going for one sort of woman. And I guess I got my emotions jumbled up with my logic and one thing led to another, really. Nothing to write home about but—'

'I shouted at Tegan,' I blurted out. I couldn't bear to hear any more.

'Is that why you were crying?'

I nodded.

'It's OK, you know, we all lose our tempers every now and again.'

'You don't understand, I lost it. I said I'd had enough of her, I told her she was doing my head in. I . . . I almost told her that she'd ruined my life.'

'But you didn't, that's what's important.'

'So it's not important that I think that?'

That stumped him. 'Ryn –' I liked that since we'd become friends, he'd taken to calling me Ryn too – 'it's not going to be easy, this. It's hard enough when you plan for a child but when you haven't, well it's going to be a hundred times harder. And, it's a horrible fact, but she has ruined your life. The life you had before has been dismantled, so it's been demolished, ruined. But that doesn't mean it's bad ruined. There are good ruins – look at the Acropolis. They're good ruins. People pay good money to see them cos they're good ruins.'

Bless him for trying.

'What did the social worker say?'

I gave him a brief rundown.

'Bitch,' he spat at the end of it. *Ah, I might have given him the Kamryn-spun version.*

'Maybe she didn't say it quite like that. She didn't actually say that Tegan only likes me because she's got no other option and that she's just grieving for her mother so counselling might help her to see that,' I conceded.

Luke smiled. 'I didn't think she had but she obviously added to you being upset earlier, that's why I called her a bitch.'

Over the past few weeks, I'd learnt more about Luke's story. He'd grown up in Birmingham but had gone to college in London. After university he moved to Boston to study at Harvard Business School, then he settled in New York to begin working in banking. He'd returned to London, then moved to Scotland for a couple of years. He'd worked in Japan for a year, then he'd decided to go to New York again and began working in management consultancy; and then returned to London working for the same American company, having split up with Nicole. Then he was headhunted by Angeles. From the sound of it, his thirty-five years had been unsettled, he was always moving, trying new things. Part of me admired that pioneering spirit, part of me wanted to ask what he was running away from. I couldn't though, we'd only recently ceased hostilities, asking such personal questions wasn't allowed. Support was allowed, though. And he was offering it to me.

'She was so scared,' I said, shaking my head trying to dislodge the image of her face. 'I did that. I nearly gave her a nervous breakdown.'

Luke edged across the sofa, placed his hand on my face, stilled my head.

'It's going to be OK,' he reassured, his warm hand on my face punctuation for his words. 'You're a good person.' His voice dropped a fraction. 'You're a great person.'

My eyes traced the contours of his face, taking in the smooth arcs that looped into his big eyes, the sloping lines that created his mouth, the solid shape that formed his nose. *I like him*. The thought hit me like a mallet on the head. I did. I liked him. I'd had sexual thoughts about him but I'd assumed that was because he was the only man in my life. This was more than sexual attraction. I liked him. His hand on my cheek, quickened my heartbeat. I liked this physical contact, it was comfortable and comforting.

Luke traced the outline of my face with his eyes, too. I wonder if he saw something different from when we first met. My black hair was longer now but cut into a long-layered style with a fringe that swept from right to left across my face. My eyes hadn't changed from their chestnut brown, although there were a few more shadows under them, my nose was still the same small, flat, broad shape; my lips still plump. I hadn't changed much at all, but he didn't look at me the way he used to. The disgust had gone. Replaced by what would seem to the untrained eye, the eye that wasn't privy to the history between us, affection.

The silence fizzed with expectation. We were meant to kiss. His head was meant to move closer and his lips were meant to meet mine and my day would be complete . . . A complete and utter disaster. I was pretty certain he wasn't attracted to me. He liked me as a friend, he might even bed me, but he wasn't attracted to me like I was to him. And he still loved Nicole. No matter what was happening now, he still loved his ex.

'I'd better get on with the washing-up,' I said, jerking my head away and standing up. He didn't move as I went to the kitchen area. 'Have you eaten?' I asked over my shoulder, without looking back to see his reaction to my fleeing the scene.

'Erm, no,' he replied. I heard him get up.

'There's pasta left, if you want some?' I retrieved a dinner plate from a cupboard, heaped on the penne pasta in a home-made tomato sauce. Luke took his dinner from me then went to the table. He moved to pick up his fork, realised he didn't have one and turned just as I held one out to him. We exchanged intimate smiles, the type that couples gave each other, and I felt that kick again: more than lust, less than love; a reckless cocktail of emotions that would end in fantastic sex – and trouble.

Two minutes later, I rolled on rubber gloves and moved plates out of the sink. I pushed in the stainless steel plug and turned on the hot water. As I refilled the sink with plates, Luke appeared beside me holding his plate, nothing but streaks of pasta sauce on it.

'Did you inhale it or something?' I asked, taking the plate from him and submerging it in the bubbly water.

'I didn't realise how hungry I was until I started eating – and although your pasta deserves to be savoured, I couldn't help

221

myself. I never can, every time I have it I can't get enough, quickly enough and have to wolf it down.'

What? I gave him a suspicious sideways look. 'Is that your way of saying I'm a good cook?'

Luke turned fully to me, his face innocent and sweet, especially now it was beard-free. 'Not a good cook, a great cook.'

He's flirting with me, I thought with a mental smirk. That in itself was comical. The fact he was so bad at it made it hysterical.

'Wash or dry?' he asked when I didn't respond to his ridiculous statement. His large but nimble fingers undid the pearly buttons on the sleeves of his blue shirt and he rolled up his sleeves.

'Neither, you must be knackered, why don't you head off?' It was best he left now and spared us both the embarrassment of my feelings and his flirting.

'Won't hear of it. I ate so I help to wash up.'

'OK, dry.' I handed him a tea towel and returned to cleaning off the first dish with a green and white sponge, rinsed it, then handed it to Luke who dried it. We worked in a companionable silence for all of thirty seconds before he broke it with, 'You're such a good mother, I don't know how anyone could ever doubt you.'

I gave him another sideways glance and found he was vigorously drying off a plate. He was nervous. Mr Arrogance himself was nervous about flirting with me.

'Tegan is such a lovely child and that's mostly thanks to you. You're a great influence, you care so much for her and you encourage her. It's—'

'All right,' I said, dropping the plate I was cleaning into the sink, 'stop now. You make me sound like Mary Poppins, Maria from *The Sound of Music* and Supermum all rolled into one. I'm not. I'm Kamryn. Who keeps screwing up.'

'You're so hard on yourself,' he commented with a shake of

his head. 'I noticed that quite early on, you're very critical of yourself when you've no need to be. You're a fantastic person and mother.'

'Luke . . .' I threatened.

'It's true,' he protested. His face stared straight at me, not a hint of a smile.

'If you say so,' I conceded, picking up the plate and soaping it again. I rinsed it off and handed it to him. Seconds later, he launched into, 'You don't give yourself enough credit for how good a parent you are. And how much of a difference you've made in Tegan's life. And the difference you've made in my life. I've changed so much and that's because of—'

'Are you flirting with me, Mr Wiseman?' I injected with a deadpan face, nonchalantly soaping the dish in my hands. 'Because if you cram any more compliments into that soliloquy, I might think you are.'

He slid a plate onto the worktop. 'Are you winding me up, Ms Matika?'

'You're an easy target when you keep chucking such over-the-top compliments at me,' I said. Before I could wonder what he or I would do next, I felt Luke's strong hands on my waist, spinning me towards him and suddenly his lips were on mine in a swift, breathtaking kiss. Taken aback, it took me a couple of seconds to respond, to kiss him back, to raise my arms and link them around his neck. While his lips parted mine and his tongue pushed into my mouth, Luke's muscular body pressed mine against the sink, and his hand moved up my top, slowly caressing my lower back, as his knee slipped between my legs. The rubber gloves stuck to his skin and soapy water dribbled down my forearms but neither of us cared as we kissed.

We broke apart, our chests heaving in unison, our eyes staring straight into each other's. He had beautiful eyes, even

223

when I didn't like him I'd thought that. The burnt-orange brown gave them an unusual intensity, which seemed to be on fire as he stared at me. I reached up, brushed my lips against his mouth gently, briefly, and pulled away. He smiled, his grin drowsy with desire, then bent his head and brushed his lips against mine. 'Bed?' he whispered after he pulled away.

I nodded.

Luke unwound my arms from his neck, pulled off the gloves and dropped them on the draining board. One last kiss and he took my hand, leading me out of the lounge door. We both instinctively turned towards Tegan's room so I could peek in through the gap in the door, double check that she was OK. She lay on her front, her face in profile on her cloud-covered pillow, her tiny arms resting up on each side of her head, her hands clenched into tight fists. I waited until her chest rose and fell so I knew she was asleep. I pulled the door a little closer to, then we headed down the corridor to the other end of the flat to my bedroom.

The moment I shut my bedroom door Luke grabbed me again, kissing me ferociously while my hands explored the smooth, firm contours of his body. Each touch exploded more desire in my veins. This was how my fantasies often started – me caressing his body as he kissed me, then us undressing each other and then . . .

There was no doubt about what was coming next as Luke took off his shirt, revealing the defined muscles of his chest and arms. I gasped inside not only at the perfection of his body but also at the thought that I was going to have sex. With Luke. The Boss. All those rumours circulating at work about him and me would become true in about five minutes.

He climbed on top of me, lifted my white T-shirt and pressed a kiss on my belly button. My body jerked with the intense pleasure at having a man's lips on my skin and this time

I couldn't contain my gasp. Luke raised his head, grinned at my response to him before tugging my T-shirt over my head. He threw it aside before returning his lips to my stomach, his kisses moving higher and higher until his mouth covered my left breast. I closed my eyes, arched back my body and sighed as I gave in to bliss, courtesy of Luke Wiseman . . .

chapter twenty-four

'Why have you got your clothes on?' Tegan's voice asked in my ear.

'Hmmmm?' I replied.

'Mummy Ryn,' she persisted. 'Why have you got your clothes on?'

I'm never, ever going to have a lie-in again. I thought with a desperate sadness. *It's going to be like this for the next ten years. And then, when she's a teenager, I'm never going to sleep because I'll be worrying about her going out and coming home late or, worse, not coming home at all.*

Tegan's small fingers gripped my forearm, shook me. 'Mummy Ryn, why have you got your clothes on? Did you sleep in them?'

I don't know, did I?

I slipped an arm down and felt my legs. They were indeed covered in my jeans. I definitely had my bra on because I could feel it digging into my ribs. And I had my T-shirt on. *Hang on, didn't Luke take that T-shirt off?* I wondered through my drowsiness. *LUKE!* I sat bolt upright, causing Tegan to jump back in shock. I glanced down to my right, expecting to see his sleeping form, but instead, that side of the bed was empty and remarkably crease-free. It didn't look as though I'd even rolled over it in the night.

'Do you always sleep in your clothes?' Tegan asked, and began her process of climbing up onto the bed: right foot on the wooden base, haul herself onto the mattress by clinging to the covers. I absently helped her up as I ransacked my memory. The last thing I remember, Luke was covering my body in hungry kisses. We were going to have sex. That obviously hadn't happened, not from the state of both the bed and me.

'No, sweetheart, I don't always sleep in my clothes. You've seen my pyjamas,' I said. Tegan struggled her way under my covers.

'Why aren't you wearing them?'

'Because I was too tired to get changed.' And there it was, the unpleasant truth. I cringed at the thought of it: I'd been lying under an incredibly good-looking, semi-naked man and I'd fallen asleep. That was bad enough; the fact that full years had passed since I'd slept with someone made it even more humiliating. The last person I'd kissed was Ted in the hotel room; the last person I'd had sex with was Nate the day before I found out about Adele. Both occurrences were more than two years ago.

In that time, sex had never been on the agenda. I'd been so intent on working out who I was since I'd become Kamryn Matika: single and best friendless, that sex became something I'd do when I'd pieced myself back together. And love, which was always lagging behind sex for me, wasn't even a consideration. The first hurdle would have been sex, allowing myself to be intimate with someone new when only one man had seen me naked for more than half a decade. Allowing someone to kiss and touch and enter me. Allowing myself to be physically vulnerable again. I'd thought that would be easy, but obviously not. Because when sex came a-knocking, I sparked out.

'Who is your letter from?' Tegan asked, pointing to the bedside table. A piece of folded paper was propped up against the base of my bedside lamp with my name scrawled on it. I picked it up and found it was in fact two pieces of paper – the one underneath had *Tegan* on it. I handed the note to her, which Tegan read out loud.

> 'Dear T,
> Thank you for the picture of me at the zoo. I will put it in my house. I hope to see you soon. Look after Ryn, she is very tired. Love, Luke.'

I looked down at my own note and read it silently.

> Hi Ryn,
> I decided it was best I leave in case Tegan came in – there'd be a lot of explaining to do if she found us asleep together. Thanks for dinner. Let's wash-up together again some time, yeah? See ya, Luke.

'Is that from Luke as well?' Tegan asked.

I bit down on my lower lip and, with a half smile, nodded. Each time I thought about our first kiss lust deliquesced my insides. I could have done it with Luke. Despite the worries I'd had last night, I could have started my sex life again with him. That was a liberating thought. It meant I had moved a step along the road to getting over Nate.

Tegan twisted her mouth to one side and frowned at me. 'Do you like Luke?' she eventually asked.

'Yes, I like Luke,' I replied, curling my arm around her and pulling her into the nook of my body and underarm.

'Do you like him lots and lots?' she asked.

'Um, yeah,' I replied, gazing down at her.

'More than you like me?' she asked.

'Of course not!' I screeched, horrified that the thought had even occurred to her. I pulled her even closer. 'Tiga, I love you.' That was the first time I'd said it to her. 'I like Luke, but I LOVE you. I'll not love anyone like I love you. Not ever.'

'Really and truly?'

'Yes. I promise. You're my first child. My only child.'

She grinned. 'I like you too,' she confirmed. 'But I like Luke more.'

chapter twenty-five

'We won't do anything,' Tegan said.

I raised an eyebrow at the little girl sitting on Luke's lap, he in turn was sitting on my big red beanbag. They were both staring at me as I stood in the living room/kitchen doorway.

'You expect me to believe that?' I replied, in case she didn't realise what the raised eyebrow meant.

'We honestly won't do anything,' Luke said, in the same tone she had used. It'd been a fortnight since Luke and I first kissed and then didn't have sex because I'd fallen asleep.

The morning after, he'd shown up and acted as though nothing untoward had gone on between us. He'd taken us out for a drive and chatted away like normal. I bought us ice creams and we fed some already plump ducks in Roundhay Park. Even when Tegan fell asleep while we were driving home he avoided all chat about the night before. By the time I let us into the flat I started to wonder if he *had* flirted with me, if we had kissed over my dirty dishes, if he had started to undress me. My only proof something had happened was the note stashed under my pillow but even that seemed ambiguous after a day of his nonchalance. My paranoia grew until I decided, as Tegan got ready for her bath, that I'd imagined it all. My fantasises had taken over to the extent that I didn't know where they ended and reality began.

After Tegan had been bathed, read to and convinced to go to sleep, Luke had flopped down on the sofa beside me. 'She's knackering, especially when she's knackered,' he said.

'I know,' I replied. 'Right, I'd better get on with doing the washing-up.'

Before I could get up, he grabbed my wrist, pulled me back saying, 'Oh no you don't.' He pushed me against the armrest and kissed me, his mouth firm and insistent against mine. 'I knew I had to keep it together today,' he explained in the gaps between kisses. 'If I mentioned it or even looked at you too long I knew I wouldn't be able to control myself.'

I sighed in relief. 'Oh, thank God. I started to wonder if I imagined it all.'

'No, you didn't.' He kissed me again, deep and slow. 'I'd like us to go to bed, but only if I won't send you to sleep.'

'Are you going to hold that against me for ever?'

'Not for ever, but for a while, I think I'm entitled.'

And that was it. We went to bed and I didn't fall asleep until after Luke had gone – I wouldn't let him stay because I didn't want Tegan to find us in bed together.

Adele had been so cautious about men and Tegan. Very few men met her daughter – he had to have long-term potential before that happened. Adele wanted Tegan's life to be as uninterrupted as possible, didn't want her daughter to become attached to a man who would be gone if the relationship ended. Once again I'd screwed up; had gone about this the wrong way. 'My' man was in our lives before I'd bedded him. If it didn't work out, we'd still have to see each other because Tegan would think the world was coming to an end otherwise. So, even after two weeks, we were keeping things under wraps, trying to work out if we had anything beyond sex going for us. I didn't like lying to her, even if it was lying by omission, but it was better than her thinking we were going to be playing happy families only to

231

find that after a few weeks Luke and I didn't feel much for each other.

Although, all the signs were good. He spent at least three nights a week at our place. I enjoyed his company. And his body. And his kisses. He was affectionate and tactile when we were talking in bed. He focused all his attention on me when we were alone together and he often sent me texts to say he was thinking of me. I enjoyed it; I responded, but it was sex. Nothing more. That wasn't completely true. It was more than physical sex, it was emotional sex too. It was a blend of lust and like that meant I did think about him when he wasn't with me but every kiss, every touch, every nice word skimmed the surface of my heart, none of it penetrated. He had yet to break through to who I was. Still, it was great to have him around. Especially at times like this, when I was going to wash my hair. Usually Tegan sat on the loo seat reading or talking to me so I knew she wasn't setting fire to herself or breaking something whilst I washed my hair. Today, Luke had offered to sit with her.

'Are you sure you'll be all right?' I asked again.

'Yes,' they chorused. It was their innocent eyes and calm faces that made me nervous. I wasn't trusting at the best of times but when the two of them seemed so eager to get rid of me . . .

'We're not going to break anything,' Luke reassured.

Now why did he have to say that?

'We promise,' added Tegan. 'Really and truly.'

I sighed silently and slunk away to the bathroom. I had to trust them, didn't I? If Luke was sticking around, was going to be a bigger part of my life, I had to trust them.

The chrome showerhead spurted out water, and I watched the fine spray arc into the bath, filling the bathroom with the sound of swishing water. I knelt down, put my head over the bath and drenched my hair. I dropped the showerhead into the

232

bath, then raked shampoo through my waterlogged black locks. *Gosh*. The thought swept through me as I lathered up. *Gosh*. I was relaxed. Still inside. It was such an alien sensation.

I was always so frantic, rushing: trying to fit lots of things in whilst thinking of Tegan, and what she might want for dinner, if she needed new clothes, if she was all right, if she was bored, if she was hurting, whether I should let her start Saturday morning karate classes like she wanted. Relaxing wasn't something I did very often. And relaxing at the office wasn't an option, either, especially now the new marketing director (Luke) had brought in a host of initiatives and ideas that had doubled my workload. We were going to be expanding *Living Angeles* to have separate magazines for the homes, clothes and children's departments. Plus an online shopping guide. And, as marketing person in charge of publications, I was overseeing these things. Since all this extra work had started, I rarely took a lunch break, after Tegan was in bed I'd spend more hours on the computer until Luke lured me to bed. Sometimes I'd even get up after he'd gone and work some more. My life was frantic. Calmness, like this moment, was a state I rarely experienced.

I vigorously washed out the shampoo. A quick towel dry and I slathered on the conditioning treatment. I had to wait ten minutes for it to fulfil its promise to smooth down cuticles and lock in shine thereby giving me beautiful hair. I checked the clock on my bathroom radio. Ten minutes. I could use the time to curl up on my bed or I could go check up on those two . . .

Walking in bare feet on a soft-pile carpet meant they couldn't hear me approach the living room, nor notice that I stopped to watch them through the gap between the doorframe and the hinge. They were still sitting in the position they had been ten minutes ago – Luke on the beanbag, Tegan snuggled back on top of him. On her lap sat my blue and green globe. Luke's right index finger was pressed on the globe as he pointed something out.

'It was very hot,' Luke was saying. 'So hot, in fact, I got sunstroke.'

'What's sunstroke?' Tegan asked.

'It's when you don't drink enough water but spend too much time in the sun without being covered up properly and you get ill. I had to spend a few days in bed getting better.'

'Did you nearly die?' she asked.

'No, but I was poorly.'

'My mummy died,' Tegan said.

My heart stopped. She hardly ever mentioned her mum to me. I did wonder, after the social worker's visit, if she avoided talking about her mum because she feared I'd get fed up and send her back to Guildford. I wasn't sure if I should bring Adele up, either. Everything I'd read about bereavement and children said to let the child come to you with their questions, but sometimes I wanted to check how Tegan was doing. To ask if she wanted to talk about Adele. If there were any feelings or memories she wanted to share. Cowardice, fear of upsetting her – fear of upsetting myself – stopped me. I wouldn't even know what to say. Would Luke?

'She's gone to heaven to be with Jesus and the angels,' Tegan added.

'I know,' Luke replied, 'Ryn told me. Do you miss her?'

Tegan bit her inner lip, then nodded. 'Sometimes,' she said in a small voice, 'I want to tell her things and I can't. I wanted to show her my homework with the special star because I did it so good. But I can't. My mummy can't see it.'

'Have you told Ryn this?'

'No,' she said in such a whisper I had to lean my head closer to the door to hear her. 'She cries about my mummy going to heaven. I don't want her to be sad.'

How does she know I cry about Adele dying? I never did it in front of her. I never cried in public, full stop. It was always in the dead of night, when I was alone. I'd bury my face in a pillow to muffle any sounds and cry. Never loudly. Maybe I wasn't as discreet as I thought. Maybe, like Luke, she picked up on the emptiness in my eyes after I'd cried.

'I know Ryn is sad, but she'd be sadder to know that you're not telling her something that upsets you. If you want to talk about your mummy, then tell her. She won't mind. She loves you. Promise me you'll talk to her?'

Tegan said nothing for a moment, then nodded. A short, decisive nod.

'Really and truly?' he asked.

'Yes, Luke,' she said.

'Good girl.'

Tegan spun the globe, stopped it with her finger. 'Have you been there?' She pointed to another green bit on the globe.

'Australia,' Luke read. 'No, but I was planning on going there one day. Maybe the three of us could go together.'

'You and me and Mummy Ryn?' Tegan gasped. 'On a plane and everything?'

'Yes, if Ryn's up for it.'

Tegan visibly sagged at the thought. 'No, she won't want to go.'

'Why not?'

'Because she can't do her hair.'

Luke, the git, laughed.

Luke's six-foot-two body wrapped around my five-foot-six frame was something I'd started to get used to. It felt natural to have his clammy skin pressed up against mine, his long, sculpted limbs curled around me. One of his hands would lazily stroke along my forearms as he nuzzled into my neck. That night, he was even more clingy, his face cosseted against my neck. Sex had been different as well. He'd stared down at me the whole way through, his eyes large and sorrowful, as though on the verge of tears. Afterwards, he'd cradled me close in his arms, as though I might evaporate if he didn't hold on tight enough. 'Ryn,' he began.

'Hmm?' I replied. I steeled myself because his voice, low and hesitant, told me he was about to say something awful. He took my hand in his, kissed each of my knuckles. It was going to be extraordinarily bad news.

'I'm sorry for how I treated you,' he blurted out.

'Eh?' I replied. That was the last thing I expected to hear. I'd been preparing myself for terminal illness or being transferred abroad or even that I was going to be sacked, not 'I'm sorry'.

'The things I said to you, how I used to look at you, the things I thought . . .' He paused, wincing as though replying them in his head. 'I'm sorry. I'm so sorry. I was so wrong. You're beautiful. Inside and out. I don't know why I couldn't see it before. You're beautiful. I look at what you've done for Tegan and how you treat me despite what I was like . . . I'm sorry, I'm truly sorry.'

'Ah, it's over with. And you were probably right. I mean, I am a bit of a—'

'Don't,' he cut in sternly, putting his fingers over my lips to stop me talking. 'Don't make a joke of it. I couldn't bear it. I hate myself for how I was.'

'It's all right,' I hushed. 'You weren't the first, I doubt you'll be the last.'

'How do you bear it?'

'It's been the same all my life, I don't let it bother me.' Luke's arms tightened around me. 'Seriously, it's not a problem. I've developed a thick skin where I don't believe anything that anyone says. That way, I know that no one can get to me because if it's not true, it can't hurt me.'

'Does that apply to good things, too?'

I thought about it. About how it took me ages to accept

anything that Nate said – and he always said the loveliest things. From day one he called me beautiful. Said he could feel the warmth from my smile. More than once he'd told me I was his dream woman. But it was years before I believed him, before it sunk in that he meant it, and when I accepted he genuinely loved me, I started to rely on hearing his compliments, which made it all the more painful when they were gone. 'I suppose.'

'That means you don't let yourself feel anything.'

'No, I feel plenty. I just don't let other people's beliefs and attitudes upset me.'

'So you don't believe that other people like you?' he asked.

'I didn't say that, I said I don't let it affect me. If people like me, that's fab but it doesn't stop me from existing. If they don't, that's fab too cos I don't care and still I'm existing.'

'That's such a sad way to live.'

'Luke, if you grew up being told *every day* that you're ugly, fat, stupid, a man, a dog, you can either grow a second skin and not rely on anyone else for your happiness and self-definition, or you can let it bury you. Guess which I did? I had to. It was a survival instinct.'

'But you don't need that survival instinct any more.'

'Yeah, you say that, but I met this bloke not too long ago who took against me because I'm not very pretty and I'm not thin. Now if I'd discarded my survival instinct I'd have been a mess at a time when I needed to be strong.'

'I'm sorry. And you are pretty. You're *gorgeous*. And your body is divine. You're divine.'

'You don't have to say that. It's all right. It doesn't bother me.' *Much. It doesn't bother me much.* I never said that out loud because I never wanted that modifier to be real. And if I said it out loud it became real. It would bother me more a whole lot more.

'I grew up in a children's home,' Luke said.

237

That was one of the many reasons why Luke and Tegan got on so well – they had a talent for the random. On the nights when I put her to bed, her chat before and after the story would flit from what she did at school to what ingredients I should put in fairy cream pie should I decide to make it one day to how I should brush my teeth twice a day. Now Luke was doing it.

'Really?'

'That's why I know that living with a survival instinct is a sad way to live.' *That's why you were so keen to help out.*

'Oh.'

'Both my parents are alive, you know? They just put me in a home. You see, my mum's English and comes from a very rich family. She met my dad, who's Spanish, when she was sixteen. Thirty-six years ago that wasn't the done thing, so when she got pregnant her family threw her out. My dad was only eighteen but they tried to make a go of it. It was too hard though and when I was about two my mum left, went back to her parents. My dad was less capable than she was. He tried, but he was only young himself. He kept going for years and we did have some good times. He was a laugh to be with, and we'd do some fun things. I remember he'd take me to the zoo. And we'd go see some of his relatives who lived near us, have these brilliant Spanish meals. It was amazing, you know, all the language, the laughter, the smell of the food. I felt like I belonged somewhere. He'd always pretend to his family that he was doing OK, but a lot of the time we were just about getting by. I'd go to school sometimes, other times I'd stay at home and wait for dad to get out of bed. He wouldn't get out of bed for days, wouldn't get washed or dressed. Of course, now I know he was depressed but at that age, I didn't. I tried to keep going.

'When I was seven, social services took me away because I hadn't been to school for weeks. I'll never forget that day, I was crying and calling for my dad but he didn't do anything. He sat there and watched them take me away.'

A sudden need to protect Luke, the little boy taken from his family, rose in me, I rolled over and slipped my arms around him, held him close, stroked his cheek as he continued his story.

'When they took me to the home, I was terrified. I'd stopped crying but I couldn't speak. They found me foster homes, lots of them. Some were good; some were awful – how they let kids stay in those places, I don't know. But it didn't matter either way because I always behaved badly so I could get sent back to the home. It's stupid, but I thought that if I was at the home, my dad would come get me. He'd know where I was. He hadn't been to visit me once in the time I was there, but I still believed he might.

'When I got to ten, no one would foster me. No one wanted a troublemaker mixed-race boy of ten. And because of that, I stayed at the home. That's when I realised my dad wasn't coming for me. So I calmed down. Became a good boy. Not because I wanted someone to adopt me but because I knew it was the only way to get myself through it. I decided not to rely on anyone, just to focus on doing well. And when I left the home at sixteen, I was in a good way: I'd done ten O levels. I left there, got a bedsit, got a part-time job, managed to do four A levels and got into university.

'I'd also learnt a few other lessons in that time. Like, that my mum didn't want me.' He paused, inhaled a couple of times to control himself. 'I found out who she was and found out that she'd moved to Perth in Australia years earlier. I wrote to her, telling her about myself, and she wrote back saying she'd moved on. She'd put all that stuff – she actually called me "stuff" – behind her, and told me not to contact her again.'

I gasped at her cruelty.

'I took that pretty hard. I couldn't work out what was

wrong with me. Why she didn't want me. It took me another two years to get up the courage to call my dad. He agreed to see me, which I took as a good sign. But he wasn't interested, either. He'd remarried, had two young kids and he didn't need or want me in his life. That was worse, you know, Ryn. I'd spent so much time with him, I could remember the good times we had. And he barely raised an eyebrow when I said I was going to university.'

'Have you seen him since?'

'Yeah, I go see him whenever I can. It's got worse over the years, not better. I think he feels guilty that he didn't get to know his son when he had the chance and now he's too proud to try.'

'You've got to keep trying though.'

'Ah Ryn, you don't understand – he doesn't like having me around. He won't even tell his children that I'm their half-brother. He told them that I'm the son of a man he knew years ago.'

I gasped again.

'I'm scared that if I say something to them, he'll cut me off completely and I couldn't bear that. At least now he sees me. Something is better than nothing . . .' Luke's voice cracked.

'Oh, babe . . .' I said, holding him close. This explained so much about Luke. His arrogance, his constant strive for perfection, why he'd moved so much – Luke never felt wanted. I understood, now, why he was so angry with me when he thought I'd half-heartedly fostered Tegan – he knew what it was like to have someone do a botch job on bringing up a child.

'Sorry,' he said.

'Don't be sorry, I understand.'

'No, you don't. I'm so in awe of what you're doing. Despite everything you've told me about how Tegan came about, you're still looking after her.'

'Thanks.'

Luke's fingers took hold of my face and his translucent orange-hazel eyes stared straight into mine. 'I mean it. I want you to believe me. You're awesome. You've stopped Tegan becoming me.'

'You're not so bad,' I replied. Luke was a damaged man, I realised. He'd never had a home, never thought he was wanted by anyone. He'd never felt he belonged anywhere, so work and being successful had become his reason for living.

I pressed a comforting kiss on Luke's mouth and he kissed me back, hard. His desperation and sadness came through in his kiss and then in the way he gently rolled me onto my back, climbed on top of me and started to make love.

Afterwards, I was tempted to ask him to stay. He shouldn't be alone when he'd revealed so much of himself, had shown me a part of him very few people had seen. But, Tegan . . . I couldn't risk her finding us together. Luke took the decision out of my hands by getting up, getting dressed. 'I'll see you,' he mumbled over his shoulder as he walked out the door. That was the type of disposable goodbye you'd say to a stranger you never expected to see again; the type of goodbye I feared I'd thrown at Adele the last time I'd seen her. If Luke left like this, we might lose him. He would feel so vulnerable that in this time alone he might decide to put us at a distance to protect himself.

From my bedroom window, I watched Luke leave my building. He opened the door to his black car and got in. Instead of reaching for the ignition, he leant over the steering wheel, cradled his head his hands and started to cry.

As I watched his broad shoulders shaking, I was slowly tugged back a few months. Back to the hotel room, holding Tegan as she screamed her heart out because her mother had left her and she was suddenly faced with the stark reality that she had no one else in the world. I'd been overwhelmed then by a need to protect her, to prove that someone did love her by adopting her. That feeling was back. I wanted to protect Luke, to put my arms around him and hush away his tears. I wanted him to know someone did want him. Someones – Tegan and I – would be lost without him. I picked up my mobile and dialled his number. He picked up after the fourth ring. Snuffling back tears he mumbled, 'Hello?'

'Come back,' I said.

'But Tegan . . .' he protested.

'You can leave before she gets up. Just come back.'

He came back and fell asleep in my arms. I stayed awake, stroking his face and making sure we didn't oversleep.

chapter twenty-six

'Is Luke your boyfriend?'

I was putting Tegan to bed. I'd bathed her, got her into her PJs then, in a rather controversial moment, she'd gone into the living room/kitchen, said 'Na-night, Luke' and put her head forward to receive a kiss. Controversial in that Luke always had to see her off into the land of nod if he was there. After saying goodnight and receiving her kiss, she took my hand and led me to her room. Now, as she lay tucked up under her covers, I understood why – she wanted to ask me grown-up questions.

'Why do you ask that?' I replied, laying aside the novel we were reading. She was tucked up under her rainbow duvet, her clean hair hidden under a pink, silk headscarf. Like most black women, I wore a scarf at night to protect my hair from the ravages of sleep, when Tegan saw mine she had wanted one too. She wouldn't believe me when I told her she didn't need one, and when I'd realised to deter her I'd need to go into a long discussion about the structure of different types of hair, I decided a scarf was the easiest option. The top of her blue and white sheep pyjamas peeked out from the covers. Her face, like the rest of her, had filled out a bit of late so she had five-year-old cheeks that plumped up when she smiled.

'Because Regina Matheson said that if a man and a woman see each other all the time they're boyfriend and girlfriend.'

'Does she now,' I replied. There was no way of getting out of it now, I had to tell Tegan the truth. But how? The other reason I'd been delaying, had let six weeks pass without telling her, was that I didn't know how to explain it to her. 'Would you mind if Luke was my boyfriend?' I asked.

'No!' she screeched, hiding her face behind her hands.

'OK . . . but if you did, you would tell me, wouldn't you?'

She took her hands away from her face and giggled in an almost musical way. 'Do you kiss him?' she asked. 'Like on TV?'

'Sometimes,' I replied cautiously, unsure if I should be having this kind of conversation with a child.

'Do you like kissing him?'

I *really* shouldn't be having this discussion with a five-year-old. 'I wouldn't do it if I didn't like it.' I moved to switch off the light. 'Goodnight now, Tiga.'

'Is he still my friend?' she asked. I stopped mid-move and sat back.

'Of course Luke's still your friend,' I stated. 'He'll always be your friend.'

'Are you still my new mummy?'

'Yes, sweetie.'

'But you're not my real mummy are you?'

'Why do you ask me that?' I replied, terrified of what she might say next. Would she accuse me of trying to replace her mother? Would she tell me that I was failing in my new role? Or would she ask why her mum wasn't coming back?

'Because Regina Matheson said you can't be my real mummy because we aren't the same colour.'

'Did she.'

'Yes. You're black, aren't you?'

'Yes.'

'And I'm white, aren't I?'

'Yes.'

'Regina Matheson said you couldn't be my real mummy.'

244

Deep inside, in the space below my ribcage and above my stomach, a rage started to burn. I wanted to meet this Regina Matheson. To crouch down, gaze into her face and order her not to fill Tegan's head with such terrors. That things were bad enough without her telling Tegan that she didn't belong with anyone.

'And she said I don't have a real family because I don't have a daddy.'

The rage exploded into flames. This girl was unbelievable. What other half-truths had she filled Tegan's head with?

'Well, you know what, I bet Regina Matheson doesn't know if her mummy wants her all the time,' I said. I'd heard this somewhere and was going to bastardise it for my own purposes.

Tegan's eyes widened in wonder.

'Her mummy is stuck with her. So's her daddy, for that matter. No matter what she does, they have to keep her, but I chose to have you with me. And I don't have to keep you but I want to. I want to keep you all the time and no matter what happens I'll always want to keep you with me. Do you understand?'

Tegan nodded.

'Don't get me wrong, I'm sure Regina's mother loves her very much, but she didn't choose her. She got what she was given, whilst I picked you.'

'Are you glad you picked me?' she asked in a quiet voice.

'I'm not only glad, I'M ECSTATIC!' I screeched and fell on Tegan, tickling her. Her little body bucked under my tickles and the lovely sound of her laughter filled the bedroom. 'Oh dear, I think Tiga needs more tickling!' I dived for her again. She kicked her legs, and shook her head, laughing with all her body.

I sat back and let her breathe. She giggled some more while I smoothed the covers back over her body.

'My mummy tickled me,' Tegan said.

'I know,' I said, trying to smile. My throat constricted

suddenly and my eyes began to sting, like they did whenever I thought of Adele. I swallowed the feelings, doing what I always did and thought of something else. Anything but Adele.

'What does heaven look like?' Tegan asked, her eyes heavier and her voice sleepier than they had been a minute ago.

I slowly shook my head. 'I don't know,' I replied.

'Does it look like that?' She pointed at the picture on the chimney breast opposite her bed. We'd painted it so many eons ago I'd literally stopped looking at it, but now I saw it with fresh eyes. The emerald fields, the green-topped brown trees, the big yellow sun, the white clouds on blue sky, and the red and white swirly sweets for flowers. It was a good picture, even if I did paint it. It'd be lovely if heaven was like that, but I'd never given heaven much thought. Not even after Adele's death. I knew how I felt about religion – that for the most part I believed there was a God, a higher power – but I always thought that heaven was maybe clouds. No, I didn't think that. I didn't know what I thought because I never thought about it. The picture was as good a scene of heaven as any, I suppose.

'Maybe, sweetheart. But I don't know.'

'My mummy would like it if it was.'

'Yes, she would, but I think she'd like a few clothes shops, too.'

Tegan's face scrunched up as she nodded and laughed.

'Right, madam, are you going to sleep? It's way, way past your bed time.'

'OK,' she said sleepily.

I leant forward, pressed my lips against her cool forehead. 'Goodnight, gorgeous.'

'Na-Night, Mummy Ryn.'

I wandered into the living room and started as I found Luke sprawled on the sofa watching television. I was so surprised I couldn't help, 'Oh,' escaping my lips.

'Oh?' he replied cautiously.

We had an honest friendship – *relationship* – but no one would take kindly to being told you'd forgotten they existed. And I had. In the talk of Adele, I'd forgotten he was in the flat.

'I mean, oh, you've washed-up,' I covered.

'Wasn't I meant to?'

'It's not that . . . I'm tired.'

He flicked off the television, moved his long legs off the sofa onto the floor, got up. 'In other words, you want me to go.' Luke stretched out his body, throwing his head back and arms out. His white T-shirt rode up, flashing his muscular stomach.

'I didn't say that,' I protested half-heartedly.

'You didn't have to, your face says it all.'

'Yeah, well, my face has been lying for years, so I don't know why you choose now to believe it.'

Luke put his head to one side and his hazel eyes narrowed slightly. 'How about you go cry in the bedroom, I wait here until you're calmer and then we start again?'

'Don't patronise me,' I spat.

'Or, you could tear a few more strips off me but let's do it in the bedroom so T doesn't hear.'

'Or you could f-off home.'

'Or I could f-off home.'

Nate used to do this. Used to ride out my moods with an incredible amount of stoicism, refusing to rise to any type of bait. Luke stuck his hands in his jeans pockets, his head still on one side as he waited for me to decide what would be the best move.

'I feel so guilty,' I stated. Talking. That was the best move. Sharing with my boyfriend.

'For?'

'For everything. For not being there when Adele needed me. For not taking care of Tegan sooner. For thinking twice about taking Tegan on. For not being with Adele when she died. For being so bad a mother I forgot Tegan that time.

For not being able to raise her how her mum would have done.

'And all the while there's some silly bint of a child at school telling her that I'm not her real mother and I never will be. So obviously she's going to feel abandoned because not even I'm her real family . . . Do you think I should complain to the school?'

'Not right this second, no,' Luke said.

'If you keep patronising me . . .'

'Sorry,' he said. 'OK, let's deal with these things one at a time. I know this isn't what you want to hear, but counselling could be the step forward you need.'

'Counselling for me?' I said, when I finally realised what he meant.

He nodded.

'Why would I need counselling?'

'Tegan's not the only one who has lost someone she cared about. And, unlike Tegan, you had a lot of unresolved issues. You need to talk them out, to someone who isn't me . . . And before you think I'm palming you off on someone else, all that stuff with your ex that you didn't sort out with Adele, I suspect you won't want to talk to me about them either. A professional might be able to help you put it all in context. Which might alleviate some of your guilt.

'OK, Tegan missing her mum is natural. There's nothing anyone can do about that, you're not especially blighted in that respect. And, finally, you worrying about her not thinking of you as her mother – she calls you Mummy.'

'Because her real mum told her to.'

'But she still does it. And not just to you, by the sound of it. When she calls the office she asks for Mummy Ryn, doesn't she?' I nodded. 'And, for this girl at school to have said this about you not being her mum, she must be calling you Mummy Ryn when you're not there. She truly thinks of you as her second mother.' I must have looked unconvinced because he added: 'There is one way you can fix that.'

'What, go back in time and give birth to her?'

Luke rolled his eyes. 'Ryn, I know the social worker freaked you out, but I think you should focus on adopting her again. Get T counselling, get the relevant forms, do whatever it takes to make her a Matika.'

I sighed internally. It was all right for him to say 'do whatever it takes' because he didn't know. Even Luke who grew up in the care system, didn't know what 'whatever it takes' would entail. He didn't realise that to adopt Tegan, I would have to contact Nate.

'tell me again, please
tell me again'

chapter twenty-seven

Whose idea was it to come up to town on a Saturday?

Even when I was childless and single I avoided central Leeds on the weekend unless I had no other choice. Working in a large department store meant I had access to everything from clothes to homeware, books to computer accessories. Anything else was left to Morrisons in Horsforth, and even then I was careful not to go there at the busiest times.

Today, however, we were pushing our way through the crowds of the St John's Centre, having been driven into town by his Royal Highness Luke Wiseman. He who had decreed that we should come up here for the day. 'It'll be fun,' he said, in hearing range of Miss Hedonist herself, Tegan Brannon, knowing that once she was on side I wouldn't refuse. Nor even protest. I was in the filthiest mood known to womankind but holding it in, trying not to show my irritation that a trog in a miniskirt – despite it being almost NOVEMBER – hadn't said 'Excuse me' to get past, she just shoved me out of the way. I even attempted a smile when a man wearing a blond toupee on top of his brown locks walked into me and didn't seem to notice.

'I want to look at furniture in John Lewis,' called Luke, who had Tegan sat on his shoulders, as I pushed open one of the glass doors at the bottom of the St John's Centre and exited.

Outside was saturated with cold. White plumes of expelled air rose up from the people huddled in coats, hands pushed deep into pockets, heads down against the wind that clawed frost across any exposed body part. In less than twenty steps I had crossed the ice-slimy brick pavement and pushed open the glass door to Angeles's biggest rival up north. I held the door for Tegan and Luke who were right behind me, then crossed the entrance to the next set of glass doors. Pushing that one open and stepping through, I held it for them then carried on. I was assailed again by people. The chill that had attached itself to my skin and clothes evaporated and I was instantly too hot.

I was striding towards the escalator when another woman who didn't seem to know it was winter what with her outfit of micro-mini and big woolly jumper, bashed into my shoulder with her shoulder while, at the same time, her plastic Tesco's bag, which had something heavy and glass in it, connected with the bony bit of my shin. The crack rang in my ears as the pain knocked stars behind my eyes. Instead of apologising, like most people would, she shot me a filthy look then stalked on. 'Do you wanna break the other fucking leg too?' I turned to shout at her until I caught sight of Tegan and Luke heading through the crowd, the pair of them smiling at the shoppers they passed. The insult dried up in my mind. I couldn't do that sort of thing any more – I was a responsible, example-setting parent.

I returned to my leg, and allowed myself a loud but soundless, 'Ow!' as I bent to rub at my damaged shin. *I may never walk again*, I decided when my fingers connected with the afflicted area and pain jolted up my leg. 'Bitch, I should've taken her down,' I hissed, then straightened up, managing to knock into another solid human form.

Does anyone else want to fucking knock me about, or what? I screamed inside, swivelling my glare to the latest person to make my hit list. My body was jolted again, this time not in pain but in shock. My heart stopped beating and the breath caught in my chest as my eyes focused on the man in front of me.

Nate.

Like twin beacons of astonishment, my name flashed up in his eyes: Kam. He said it too; breathed the single-syllable word between his plump, pink lips: 'Kam.'

Weeks had passed since Luke had convinced me to refocus on adopting Tegan and I still hadn't made steps towards contacting Nate. I couldn't. Every time I thought of him, of his face at the funeral, of forming words to speak to him, my mind would blank it out and I'd retreat into denial. I couldn't do it.

Nate was exactly as I remembered him: his brown-black hair softly sculpted into short peaks away from his face. His skin still smooth. His navy-blue eyes that could effortlessly unearth my deepest-kept secret. His nose, straight with its small upturn at the end. His mouth, my favourite part of his face, like firm marshmallows made from a mould of Cupid's bow. My eyes swept over his face again. He hadn't changed a bit.

'It is you, isn't it?' he asked when I didn't speak. 'I'm not hallucinating or anything, am I?'

I shook my head, unable to jumpstart my vocal cords.

'You haven't changed a bit,' he continued.

I moistened my lips, ready to attempt a reply, when Luke – Tegan sitting on his shoulders, her gloved hands holding onto the fingertips of his bare hands – appeared beside me. He looked at me, saw the imprint of shock on my face, and turned to the person I was focused on. Luke took in Nate's wide forehead, his big eyes, soft mouth and the full-size version of Tegan's nose, and his heartbeat almost visibly tripled. 'We'll wait for you over there,' my lover mumbled, then navigated the pair of them away from us before Tegan had a chance to speak.

Nate blinked at me a few times. 'What are the chances?' he asked as though we hadn't been interrupted.

'Nathaniel,' I finally uttered.

'Nate,' he corrected, searching my eyes for a flicker of a memory. 'You're the one who started calling me that, you can't go full name on me now.' He smiled at me and my stomach turned to jelly; quivering at the bottom of my abdomen.

'Nathaniel,' I repeated, using a firmer tone as I grappled for control of the situation. Before the funeral, the last time I'd seen him was the day I returned to London for my belongings and left him – the day my eyes were dry, red holes in my head and he looked like he hadn't slept in years – in this moment there was every danger the shock of this meeting would consume me. 'What are you doing here?' I asked.

'I live here,' he replied.

'What? In Leeds?' I recoiled, he couldn't, he just couldn't. Having two hundred miles between us had always been a comforting factor in our break up – there was no chance of running into him.

'Yes. No. I mean, no. I live in Tadcaster. Halfway between Leeds and York.' He pointed over his shoulder, as though Tadcaster could be found in the haberdashery department. 'I, erm, got a job as group scheduler at Yorkshire and Pennines FM. Erm, about a year or so now.'

'OK,' I said, outwardly nonchalant, internally appalled: I'd spent the past twelve months walking around playing Russian roulette with bumping into him. That thought was nauseating.

'Obviously you still live up here,' he said.

'Obviously.'

Nate's expression changed, the shock was whisked away, replaced by sadness. 'How are you coping since . . . ?' his voice trailed. Since . . . Nate like everyone else, me included, avoided that word, skirting around it like a pothole in the road. Pretending it wasn't there, as though death wasn't as bad, as devastating if you didn't utter the word.

I shrugged. 'I'm fine, I guess. How are you?'

'Much the same.' Our eyes slotted together like a key slipping into a lock, and I was free-falling, cut adrift in time. I didn't know when I was, if I was back four years ago, gazing into Nate's navy-blue eyes, wondering why he loved me; why he was so good to me. Then I was falling again – further back, meeting him for our first 'date' and seeing his eyes crinkle up as they saw me. I almost surrendered to the falling. Almost stepped forwards expecting his arms to loop around me while I immersed myself in the closeness of his warm body. It'd be so easy. All I had to do was let go of the ledge of reality I was clinging to and plummet into my history like Alice tumbling down the rabbit hole. Let it happen. Feel it all again. *Pull yourself together!* I snapped at myself, wrenching my sensibilities back into the present.

'I did think about getting in touch,' Nate said carefully. 'I didn't know how you'd react, though, if it'd just add to it all.'

Enough Adele talk, I decided, lowering my head to my scuffed, tan leather boots. I raised my left foot and rubbed the tip clean on the back of the right leg of my jeans, effectively distancing myself from him. Nate couldn't understand how lacerated I felt most of the time, no one except possibly Tegan could understand. That every day that I didn't simply stop, frozen with grief, was an excellent day. I was holding myself together with strands of denial, by ignoring the pain. If I visualised my feelings, the pain of them would be like long deep grooves scored onto the surface of my mind by guilt and regret. And if I thought about it for too long, if I allowed myself to glimpse the immense, unfathomable, acuteness of my feelings, I would become petrified. If I allowed myself to experience even a sliver of what I suspected I felt, I wouldn't be able to carry on living. It would consume me. So I constantly consigned my feelings to another place, another time, a debt I'd pay at a later date. The interest was mounting, but I had no resources to pay right now. Nate, simply by being there, was smearing salt-coated guilt into the wound, asking with menaces for me to pay some of what I owed. Talking about it would result in a breakdown.

Understanding almost straight away that I wasn't talking about it any more, Nate changed the subject. 'Boyfriend?' he asked.

I raised my head. 'Sorry?'

'That guy.' He inclined his head in Luke and Tegan's direction. I followed his line of sight. A little way away, standing in front of a glass case of expensive, delicate silver jewellery, Luke was unselfconsciously dancing, bobbing from one foot to the other, holding onto Tegan's hands and bouncing her on his shoulders as he moved in time to Elvis's 'Little Less Conversation' that played over the store's speakers. She giggled loudly as her hair, loose around her face and topped by her furry black hat, moved like golden waves in time with the rhythm. They were two of the happiest people in the store; even the grumpiest shoppers grinned a little when they walked past the jiggling pair. 'Is he your boyfriend?'

'Yeah,' I smiled, proud that he was my man because he so unreservedly loved Tegan.

'And that's his daughter?'

I tore my gaze from them to frown at Nate, searching his face for a sign that he recognised her. Nothing. A blank expression accompanied his question as he awaited my reply. I wasn't surprised he didn't recognise Adele's daughter. We had virtually lived with them, but Nate wasn't interested in children – he had a voracious appetite for adult company, loved socialising and being with people, but children, who he didn't know how to communicate with, nothing. He would watch

Tegan performing one of her dances if we made him, but he'd always have one eye on the television or on the paper or staring into space. When I told him she'd said her first word, he'd managed to say, 'Really?' in such a way that he almost convinced me he was interested.

'No,' I replied to his question about Luke and Tegan. 'He's looking after her.'

'Oh.' He smiled slightly at me. 'Cute kid.'

I moistened my lips, ready to utter, *Your kid*, then realised that it wasn't the right setting: John Lewis of a Saturday afternoon, with hundreds of people milling around, wasn't the ideal place to discover you were a father. Very few places would be ideal but this was less perfect than most.

Should I tell him anyway? I wondered, staring up at him. What if Nate wanted in on her life? Not likely, considering his apathy towards children, but it still worried me. My instincts told me not to tell him at all, to leave him in the happy state of ignorance within which he'd existed for six years. He was her father though, and Tegan had a right to know him, to have him in her life, especially after losing her mother.

In the years before I left, I had repeatedly lectured Adele on Tegan's need to know her father. Now I knew how simplistic – unenlightened – I had been. I'd had no idea, no comprehension of what living under the threat of Tegan having a father was like. Even if 'daddy' didn't want to lure her away, he could reject her, which would permanently damage her. Rejection by a parent – there was no bigger betrayal. Besides, Tegan, right now, had the complete family set. My parents were her grandparents – she called them Nana Faith and Grandpa Hector, my brothers and sister were her uncles and aunt, their children her cousins. When she went to visit my sister's children in Manchester she always came back regaling me with tales of the fun they'd had together. She wasn't lacking in relatives and people who cared for her. Nate was blood though.

Blood and genes, her connection to the great biological pool of life. The codes of her molecules had been written by Nate's body and by his parents' bodies before him. We couldn't give her that. Not me, not my family, not Luke. She and Nate had an indelible connection. Even if I didn't want him in my life any more, I owed it to Tegan to tell him.

'Look,' I said, managing to initiate sustained eye contact, 'we should talk, properly . . . About everything.'

Surprise leapt onto Nate's face. 'You really want to?' he asked cautiously, wondering if I was toying with him.

Want to? No. Have to? Yes. I nodded. 'Have you got a number I can reach you on?'

He delved into the inside pocket of his camel-coloured wool coat and took out his battered black wallet, removed a business card and handed it to me. The small white card had all his contact details – work number, mobile and email – on it. I pocketed it as we said brief, stiff goodbyes. We turned away in unison and I walked towards Tegan and Luke without looking back.

'Who's that man?' Tegan asked as I approached them, Luke stopped his dance and looked at me.

I stared up at Tegan. Her cheeks were pink from her laughter, her royal blue eyes danced with curiosity and excitement, and her lips were parted in a blissful half-smile. For Tegan, things didn't get much better than this. 'An old friend of mine,' I replied.

'He doesn't look that old,' she observed sagely. 'Not as old as Luke.'

'Cheers, madam,' he muttered, raising his amber-brown eyes to her in mock ill-humour.

'I mean, he's a friend I knew from a long time ago.'

'Did he know my mummy?' she asked unexpectedly.

'Yes, he did.'

'Does he know she's gone to heaven to be with Jesus and the angels?' Tegan always made Adele's death sound as though she'd gone to join a pop band; like we could expect an impromptu performance from them featuring a special chorus sung by Adele Brannon.

'Yes, sweetheart, he knows. And he was sad, but he's glad he knew her before she went to heaven.'

Tegan beamed at me, which threw me. I'd expected her to be upset, instead she seemed happy; completely unfazed. 'He's a nice man. Can we see him again?'

I felt Luke's eyes burning symmetrical holes into my face as his expression echoed, *'Well, can we?'*

'Maybe,' I replied, ignoring Luke's unwavering gaze. 'We'll have to see.'

Eight years ago, I entered a café in north London and found it was virtually empty, apart from the man running a grubby dishcloth over tabletops and a woman who sat at the back alternating sips of coffee with drags on a cigarette as she stared into space. The third person in there was Nate. My date. He sat at a table with his head lowered, engrossed in a broadsheet newspaper. I checked my watch to confirm I was on time because, judging from how far he'd got into his newspaper, and the empty white mug of coffee on the table beside the paper, it was obvious he'd been there a while.

My stomach tumbled over itself, unexpectedly gripped with nerves. I hadn't been bothered either way as I'd come down here for our first date, having met him a month earlier, but now there was a mass of fidgety, agitated butterflies crawling over each other inside me. 'Hi,' I said.

My date glanced up. A grin expanded his friendly face, crinkling up his eyes. I was taken aback by how happy he was to see me. He stood up and in doing so, towered above my five-foot-six body with his lithe, six-foot-two frame.

'Hi,' he said, still grinning.

'I'm not late, am I?' I asked.

261

'Nope.' He shrugged his black T-shirted shoulders. 'I was just so excited I got here early.'

'Oh,' I replied, unsure what to say to that.

'You're more beautiful than I remembered,' he said.

I stopped myself checking over my shoulder to see who he was talking to, then allowed myself to slide into the compliment. It didn't sound creepy or contrived, his sincerity made what he said sweet. 'What, this old face?' I joked. 'I've had it years.'

He laughed, a warm, indulgent belly rumble, and then walked around the square table to pull out the padded black chair for me. Impressive, but not overly so. I wasn't about to go into an Adele-style swoon – I'd met charmers before and under the glossy smile and polite manners, they were still your common or garden bastards.

We ordered coffee and a chocolate-chip muffin that Nate cut into eight segments, like you would an apple, so we could share it. And we talked. When I eventually got home I couldn't remember what about, it was the type of talking that was interrupted only by laughter and pauses to ingest the valuable information we'd just received.

When he nipped to the toilet some time later, I caught myself smiling as he walked away – and was horrified. I was falling for it. His charm and his wit had begun to win me over. But I knew what was going to happen. At some point, he was going to revert to type. He'd want to change me, control me, or leave me, and it'd be worse if I'd invested emotion in him beforehand.

By the time he returned and I had drained the chocolatey coffee dregs from my third cappuccino, I had formulated a plan. In the past few hours I'd learnt a thing or two about this Turner man and I knew how to eject him from my life. I placed the mug on the table and made direct eye contact with him. 'Coffee back at your place, then,' I stated.

Nate sat back. 'Um . . .' he mumbled with a slight grimace, not meeting my eye. After all his confidence and 'you're so beautifuls' was he rejecting me?

I sat forwards in my seat. 'Um?' I repeated.

His grimace creased into a complete face cringe. He *was* rejecting me. *Did I imagine the full-on flirting, the shy smiles and the lingering looks?*

'You don't want me to come back with you?' I asked.

'No! God, no! I mean yes! I do! More than anything, I do. It's just my house is a mess and I don't want you to judge me on that. And I don't have any milk or sugar or coffee . . . I haven't been to the shop for a few days. I suppose we could stop on the way—'

'Nate,' I cut in, 'do you have condoms?'

He nodded.

'Then I don't care what is or isn't in your kitchen. We're going back for sex. Or, shall I put it like this, if we go back to your place you're going to get lucky.'

'Oh, right,' he said. 'Right. Do you want to go back now?'

I moved my head up and down.

'Waiter, the bill!' Nate called, almost breaking his neck to go pay.

Later, much later, Nate pulled me towards him, wanting to cuddle before he drifted off into sleep. I, meanwhile, wanted to get as far away as possible from him. The plan had gone a bit wrong. My scheme: shag him, leave, wait for him to never call, hadn't worked. Instead of the detachment that accompanied a one-night stand, I was *feeling*. I had emotions flowing through me. Affection. Passion. Tenderness. Every time I glanced at Nate's face the word *inamorato*, 'lover', came to mind. The full, rounded meaning of that. The one you loved, with your body, your mind, your soul. The one you gave everything you were to. Which was insanity – I'd met Nate twice in my life.

I'd never had sex like that in my life, though. Our first kiss had been tentative – we'd sat on the end of his bed, knowing what was coming next. After our second kiss, he'd slowly caressed his thumb over my lips, erotically searing in the mouth touch while I stared into his eyes. After that it'd been a one-way trip into pleasure. He'd covered my body in kisses, he'd slowed me down with his expert foreplay technique, and by the time we got to mainplay I was biting my lower lip to stop myself calling out his name.

I didn't want this confusion. I didn't want to be feeling for him. I wanted everything clear cut, like it always had been. I slipped out of his hold and frantically picked up my clothes, started getting dressed. I shoved my legs into my black cotton knickers, pulled them up. Fastened on my black bra. Then my jeans were on and being buttoned up. I was belting up when Nate realised what I was doing and sat up. 'Are you going?'

Pulling my top over my head muffled my reply.

'Sorry, I didn't catch any of that.'

'I said, yes, I'm going. Places to do, people to be.'

'Oh, OK.' He rested on his elbows watching me search for one of my socks. 'I had a great time, Kamryn. The whole afternoon, it was amazing. I haven't talked like that for years.'

'Uh-huh,' I replied, locating my errant sock under his bed, snatching it up and rolling it on my left foot.

'There's a Sherlock Holmes retrospective down at the National Film Theatre,' he said, while I grabbed my jacket and shrugged it on, 'I know you like Sherlock, so we could go along? Have dinner and go for a walk along the river afterwards . . .?' As he talked, I was tying up my shoelaces.

'Kamryn,' he said gravely, as though it'd finally dawned on him what my departure meant. 'Will I ever see you again?'

That threw me. I'd expected that this would put an end to it. That he'd think I was a slut because I slept with him on the first date – I'd offered him sex before we'd even kissed for

God's sake! – and then would tactfully avoid mentioning us making contact again. Which was why I was so upset at enjoying sex with him. I wouldn't see him again. And that had hurt, more than I expected it to.

'Will I see you again?' he repeated. I revolved slowly to look at the man in the bed. He was delicious: his usually neatly spiked hair, now mussed up, his blue eyes heavily post-coital, his mouth slightly bruised from kissing. *Inamorato*. I could do this again. In a heartbeat I could. I bit my lower lip for a second, scared. *But what if he's playing me for a fool?* I wondered. *I couldn't bear it. Not with him.* I remembered his thumb running over my lips, and I thought, *He's worth the risk.*

I kissed the palm of my hand, then blew the kiss at him. 'We'll see,' I said, before picking up my bag and leaving.

'That was him, wasn't it?' Luke said as I flopped down onto the sofa beside him. We'd done our usual tag team of Tegan's bath (me) and story (Luke) but I'd had to go in after the story to reassure her I would think about buying her the pair of pink trainers we'd seen earlier. I didn't know how I'd afford them, but I'd find a way. Now Luke and I could talk, and judging not only from what he'd said, but his rigid posture, it wasn't going to be easy.

'That was *Tegan's father*.' He whispered the last two words in case madam, who had pin-sharp hearing, was still awake.

'Yes,' I stated.

'Did you tell him?'

'Call me strange, but I don't think John Lewis is the place to tell someone they've got a daughter, do you?'

'Are you going to tell him?'

'Probably.'

'So you're going to see him again?'

'Yes,' I replied.

He closed his eyes momentarily. 'Why?'

'If I'm going to adopt Tegan, I have to get Nate's permission.'

'His *permission*?' he repeated, affronted. 'Are you joking?'

'I never knew this until after I got all of Adele's things but his name is on Tegan's birth certificate. And because I know where he is – that he's still alive – I need to get his permission. He's Tegan's surviving parent so he has to sign away all rights to her. Social services try as much as they can to keep families together. There's so much emphasis nowadays on belonging, knowing where you come from. And the fact she's white isn't going to help my case. So I need as much as possible, in writing, to show that both Tegan's parents want me to adopt her. It'll be harder to turn me down that way.'

'Why didn't you mention this before?'

'Because the last thing I wanted to do was contact Nate. I always knew I could get hold of him through his parents if I wanted but I didn't want to.'

'You still feel a lot for him,' Luke stated. 'That's why you didn't want to get in touch with him, you were scared of your feelings.'

'That's ridiculous,' I replied. 'I admit if we were still together we would have been married two years by now so my feelings wouldn't have changed. But we're not married, we're not even together, so my feelings are completely different.'

Luke studied my face, uncertainty billowing in his eyes before he glanced away. I stared at his profile, watched the muscles in his jaw pulsate like a rapidly beating heart as he pumped his teeth together. I knew how he felt: jealous. Scared. Unworthy. I used to feel that way about him sometimes when he'd open his wallet to pay for something and I'd spot the picture of Nicole, his gorgeous fiancée, grinning at me; reminding me that he still had feelings for someone else. That whilst we had great sex and spent a lot of time together, Nicole was Plan A, and I was Plan B. A few weeks ago, I don't know when exactly, I noticed Nicole had left his wallet. And her spectre stopped hanging over our relationship. I'd been able to relax, to concentrate on building a relationship with my boyfriend, to work towards allowing him to penetrate my heart. And I his. Now he was in a similar position, although he was at a greater disadvantage. Whilst I'd been wrestling with a picture and memories, Luke would be grappling with a human presence.

'That doesn't change us, though,' I said, desperate to reassure him. 'I . . . I love you.'

I didn't. Of course I didn't. I cared for him but it was too soon to tell if it was love. I'd learnt about love from being with Nate, and I knew it wasn't this; it wasn't constant doubt. With Luke there was always disquiet. Should we be together? What would have happened if not for Tegan? Neither of us fooled ourselves, Tegan was our Cupid: without her we'd still be sniping at each other, making everyone around us miserable with our mutual hatred. And if he hadn't decided to change his type, he wouldn't have kissed me. I was never sure which came first – his changing of type or him liking me and deciding to change type. I was never brave enough to ask, either.

In the grand scheme of things, I felt a lot for Luke. I didn't look at him and think *inamorato*, didn't want to give everything I was to him, but I was fond of him. And, we were here. Together. No matter how we'd got here, we were here, he was a part of my life. A life I could grow to love. I could love him. I just didn't. I had to say it though – 'Needs must when the Devil vomits in your kettle,' as Adele often said.

'I do, you know?' I repeated to his silent face and sceptical eyes, 'I love you.'

'That's good to know,' he said, his whole body finally relaxing. He bent and pressed a kiss on my mouth, pressed another onto my forehead, then pulled me into his arms and settled back against the sofa.

There were lots of things you were supposed to say when someone tells you they love you but 'That's good to know' wasn't one of them. A chill breezed through me. Maybe I was wrong, maybe I was still Plan B.

chapter twenty-eight

'I like your orangey dress,' Tegan commented as she jumped on my bed. She bounced as though the springs were in her legs not the mattress – high, but controlled.

'Thank you,' I replied from my place sitting on the edge of the bed. Nerves tumbled around my stomach like a washing machine stuck on a spin cycle; and every so often my hands would break into a tremble.

'You look very pretty,' Tegan decided and flapped her arms up and down like a flightless bird trying to take off as she bounced.

'All right, T, enough,' Luke said, coming over to the bed, picking her up and swinging her under one arm. 'Leave Ryn to get ready in peace.'

'I don't mind,' I told him, our eyes met, then darted away from each other as though that simple action had burnt us. We'd found it difficult to make prolonged eye contact for the past few days – even in bed we didn't look at each other too long for fear of betraying our true feelings. Him, his fear; me, my uncertainty.

'Where are you going?' Tegan asked, swinging happily from her position under Luke's arm.

'I told you already,' I said.

'Tell me again.' She hung her head back until all I could see was the soft, butter-white flesh of her throat. 'Please! Tell me again.'

'I'm going to dinner with that man we saw in John Lewis,' I said, aware that every word slashed at Luke's already fragile ego. Tegan's head came forward, she was pink in the face. 'Are you going to talk about my mummy?' she asked.

'A little bit.'

'Will you tell me what he says?' She scrunched up her nose and mouth as she nodded, willing me to agree that I'd tell her everything.

I wouldn't be telling her anything – I couldn't discuss what caused my fiancé and my best friend to sleep together, nor explain that he was her father, nor relay how he reacted to the news that he was a parent.

'If Ryn can tell you, she will,' Luke said. 'Does that sound fair?'

'Suppose so,' she replied.

I glowered at Luke, resentful that he'd appointed himself my mouthpiece. He shrugged off my glare by asking, 'Do you want us to drive you into town?'

I shook my head.

'We won't come in, we'll just drop you off outside.'

'I'd rather get the train.' That matter was closed as far as I was concerned.

'Where's he taking you again?'

'I told you, I'm meeting him at the restaurant where you and I had our first disastrous dinner, remember?'

My boyfriend hadn't said it, but in the past two days he'd been acting as though my arrangement to meet Nate was us rekindling our relationship. He feared I'd leave the flat his girlfriend and return Nate's fiancée. That was why he wanted to drive me into town – it'd be half an hour of him remind-ing me of his existence; his relationship with Tegan; what I'd be giving up if I went back to Nate. His question was a test

270

to see if I was thinking of this as a date. I wasn't. The only make-up I'd applied was a little mascara, my 'pretty dress' was the scoop-neck, ankle-length, red and orange silk number that Luke had bought me to replace the dress destroyed by Tegan's dirty paint water. I'd worn it, not because it was flattering – it wasn't particularly – but because Luke had bought it. I was showing him he would be on my mind because his gift was on my body. I wore heels because the dress would look stupid with trainers. And that was as much of an effort as I'd made – there was nothing else I could do to reassure Luke short of not going. And I was going to do this. I had to see Nate.

'Right, I'd better be off.' I stood and took Tegan from Luke. She clamped her legs around my waist in a vice-like grip. She'd had her bath and was in her pyjamas so her skin smelt clean and bubble-bathy, and her hair had a shampoo fragrance. I carried her out of the bedroom and into the corridor.

'OK, baby, make sure you behave yourself for Luke . . . On second thoughts, don't!' We laughed conspiratorially as I put her down by the kitchen door. 'Seriously though, make sure you go to bed on time and that Luke brushes his teeth before bed.'

Tegan giggled her tinkly laugh again. I unhooked my long black coat, buttoned it on, then bent and hugged Tegan. She slipped her arms around my neck and kissed my face. 'You smell like sunshine,' she said before releasing me.

'And you smell like chocolate pudding and I need to tickle you!' I laughed as I gently tickled her ribs. This was our thing; our in-joke that meant we were close. A unit. She had lots of them with her mum and now we had one, which was a giant step forwards in our relationship – we were bonding, moving closer to being mother and daughter.

Tegan squirmed away, ran to Luke and wrapped her arms

271

around his legs. I straightened up and faced Tegan's unhappy protector. 'Thanks for Tegan-sitting, Luke, I really appreciate it.'

He gave a short nod. 'Have fun,' he blurted out as my fingers turned the Yale knob.

I'm not going out for fun, I wanted to shout at him. The silent worrying had reached my limit now, one more thing and I was going to sleep with Nate just to make a point.

'Have fun,' Tegan echoed.

'Thank you,' I replied and stepped out into the corridor. 'Bye.'

'T, go put on a DVD, I'll see Ryn off.'

Tegan did as she was told and Luke stepped out into the gloomy corridor with me. Neither of us moved to hit the communal light switch as I waited for him to say something. Seconds crawled by and he was silent, simply stared at me. 'See ya,' I finally said and turned away.

'Ryn,' he said, took my arm, pulled me back. In the pause that followed he touched a tender kiss on my mouth. 'I love you,' he said as he pulled away. He hadn't said that before. Not since I'd said it. In fact, I hadn't expected him to say it. I'd decided that his reply, 'That's good to know', had made his feelings clear: he didn't love me and I should get used to it. There'd been no other explanation as far as I could see. Now he'd upended my certainty about his feeling by saying this. By saying those three words. And he'd tainted it. Because no matter what happened next, I would always wonder *why* he'd said it. If he'd been motivated by genuine feelings or because he was scared I was going to sleep with someone else. Did he love me or did he simply want to control me?

Luke stood still and silent, waiting for my reply and I knew I had to say it back. I had to reconfirm I loved him. I opened my mouth and replied, 'That's good to know.' My answer was a reminder that whatever we both felt, whether we loved each other or not, he wasn't the only one who could be cruel and withholding of their affections. He wasn't the only one who had feelings.

He recoiled in surprise and hurt, his fingers slipped away from my arm. And I left without looking back.

chapter twenty-nine

Hazy. That's the best way to describe events following my departure from Adele's flat after her accidental confession.

I remember stumbling out of the ground-floor flat, dazed, unable to work out what to do or where to go. I recollect making it home and feeling safe because Nate was out drinking with his ex-housemates. I vaguely recall deciding to go to Leeds because I was meant to be going up there in a couple of days anyway for my four-week stint setting up *Living Angeles*.

I can't conjure up any memories of packing, but I must have done because I took clothes with me. My clearest memory was of the note I scrawled in blue ink on the telephone notepad and left on our kitchen table:

I know what you did.

Five words that would explain everything: why I had to go and why I wasn't coming back.

I know a taxi took me to Victoria coach station, but I don't remember the two hundred mile journey to Leeds, nor convincing the Holiday Inn to let me check in two days early. The next time I came to, I was lying fully clothed on my hotel bed, staring blank-eyed at the television. The phone had rung for a few minutes before I realised what the noise was, and reached out to answer it.

'There's a Mr Turner to see you, madam,' the receptionist informed me. I had arrived in the dark, but for some reason it was light. A glance at my watch told me it was early afternoon. I had no idea where the last fifteen hours had gone. The world had carried on without my knowledge.

I almost said, 'I don't want to see him,' then thought better of it. Nate's stubbornness would have him sitting in reception until I did see him. I couldn't hide in my bedroom for the rest of my life, and he would stay there until I saw him. 'I'll be right down,' I mumbled.

When I checked my face in the bathroom mirror, I was shocked at the woman who stared back at me. She was red-eyed and patchy-skinned from lack of sleep. Her hair was wild and her face was puffy. She looked weary. I dragged a comb through my black hair before I returned to the bedroom and flipped open my silver suitcase, which was lying unpacked on the floor by the bed. I selected a red jumper, pulled it on, and then added a black cardigan as an extra layer of armour.

Nate stood as I approached him in the hotel's reception. Dark circles ringed his eyes, his hair had been haphazardly spiked up and a five o'clock shadow was progressing across his chin. His clothes were crumpled, probably from the drive. He looked fragile, as though one harsh word would shatter him.

'I called every hotel in Leeds until I found you,' he explained.

'Let's go into the bar,' I replied, my voice calm and controlled.

We sat in two armchairs opposite each other at the back of the small bar. The lighting in the bar was subdued and the air was stale with the odour of a hundred thousand cigarettes.

'Come home,' Nate said the second we had taken our seats. 'Come home and we'll talk and sort this out.'

'There's nothing to sort out. I know what happened with you and . . . and . . .' my voice snagged in my mouth as what I was saying played out in my mind. It was too horrible to name.

'Kam, it's not what you think,' he said.

'What do I think?' I asked.

'We weren't having . . . It was once. Just once.'

'That's not what I was thinking, *Nathaniel*,' I hissed. 'What I was thinking is that you cheated on me and it's over.'

'Come home and we'll talk properly.'

'No, I can't. I can't talk to you. Not about this. You aren't who I thought you were. And that place isn't my home. Not any more.'

He reached across the table to take my hand and I jerked my body away from him. I used to love him holding my hand, the way his strong fingers would engulf my hand while his thumb caressed the centre of my palm. Nate could touch me in so many different ways and make me comfortable, calm. But not any more.

'We can't be over just like that,' he implored. 'We've been together six years, we're getting married in two months. It can't be over just like that. We have to talk about this.'

'OK, let's talk. Was she better than me? Sexier? More willing? Quicker to orgasm? Up for—'

'Stop it,' he cut in, 'it wasn't like that.'

'What else is there to talk about?'

'How much I love you? How much I want you back? How I'll do anything to make it right between us. Anything.'

'Anything?'

'Anything.'

'Then go away and leave me alone.' I got to my feet, tiredness made my head swim, my hearing echoey. 'I want nothing more to do with you.'

Nate closed his eyes as though he couldn't believe he'd walked into that one.

'I'll come back for my stuff soon. I don't know when yet, but soon. I'll leave the furniture and anything we bought together. I'll just take my books and CDs and DVDs, the rest of my clothes. My stuff that I moved in with. And I'll want half the flat money so I can get somewhere of my own. I'll keep paying the mortgage until we divide it all up so that there's no discrepancy with the payments. Our solicitors can sort that out, we can communicate through them so we don't have to talk again. If we sort it out quickly we can get on with our lives. And please, if you ever felt anything for me, please don't tell my parents why the wedding is off. I'm going to call them and tell them, but don't say it's because . . . Please. I'll die if anyone else knows. Just say anything but that. And, and, I think that's it. Bye, Nate.'

He stood, too. 'That can't be it. We've got a wedding planned. Why don't we put it on hold for a few more months until we sort it all out? This doesn't have to be the end.'

'Yes, it does. You know it does. That's why you never told me. You knew it'd be the end because we could never . . .' My face crumpled. I'd wanted to get away without crying. I shook my head and pulled myself together. As I wiped at my eyes I spotted the platinum and ruby engagement ring still on my finger. Nate had designed it. It had a solid band, with a hexagon cut stone at its heart. Despite everyone telling him an engagement ring should have a diamond, he'd chosen a ruby because red was my favourite colour. I'd not even thought of taking it off, it was such a part of me I'd forgotten it was there. I yanked it off, placed it on the glass table beside Nate's chair. 'Bye, Nate.'

He dropped heavily back onto his seat as I walked away. The last time I saw him was when I went to get my stuff three months later. He was there as I packed, but he didn't say anything. And when the removal men came later and took away my boxes he still said nothing. It was only as I was leaving that he spoke. He said those two words, 'Don't go,' and I stopped, turned to look at him because I knew it was the last time I'd see him, and then I walked out.

He'd done what I wanted and left me alone. It *was* what I wanted. I needed them both to leave me alone so I could rebuild a life without them. Adele had tried to get in touch, but I hadn't realised why until I saw her. Now I was going to dinner with Nate. And I was terrified.

chapter thirty

Like he did in that hotel lobby, Nate rose from his seat as I approached him at the restaurant table. My heart was thumping in my chest, staccato-beating in my ears, blocking up my throat.

His navy-blue eyes met mine as I reached him, his mouth turned up slightly in a nervous smile. 'Hi,' he said, moving around the table to me, placing his hand on my waist and kissing my cheek.

'Hi,' I replied as I received the kiss. We'd spent six years making all types of physical love, now the only form of touch we were allowed was the offering and receiving of perfunctory kisses. It seemed wrong somehow.

After we'd sat at our places, seconds of silence followed as we busied ourselves unfolding napkins, stealing unsubtle looks at each other. He looked good. His thirty-five-year-old face was strong and lacking in any excess fat. His brown-black hair now looked more black because he'd gelled it up into more pronounced spikes than the last time I saw him. His skin was that smooth, gold brown that always surprised me because he had navy-blue eyes and his parents – and Tegan – were a very pale white.

The waiter arrived with menus, poured water into our glasses. He told us about the specials and before he had a chance to leave, we ordered food. Nate and I were the fastest orderers on earth, we wouldn't waste valuable time messing about, we'd make a decision and stick to it. The waiter wrote down what we wanted, then walked away, leaving us alone. Leaving us to our evening together.

Nate sipped his water, I played with the base of my wine glass. Both of us were silent, waiting for the other to speak first.

'This is like being on a first date,' Nate said with a slight laugh, lifting his eyes to meet mine.

'Yeah, except we never really went on dates, did we?'

'We had coffee!' Nate protested.

'That ended back at your house.'

'I thought all my Christmases had come at once,' Nate said. 'Literally. When you invited yourself back to my place, it was better than I could have imagined.'

'I couldn't believe you actually thought I was inviting myself back for coffee.'

'I didn't, I was just so surprised that you'd come out with me at all, the idea that you'd let me touch you . . .'

'Yeah,' I agreed.

'Even then we both knew we were meant to be together, didn't we?' He was serious. When it came to us, Nate always said things like that and meant it because, according to him, Fate had thrown us together. The party we met at, he told me, he hadn't wanted to go to at all. His friends had persuaded him and when he arrived and saw me he realised that he'd met his soul mate. The woman he was going to marry.

'No, Nate, that's what you thought,' I clarified. 'I had altogether different motives – namely putting you off me.'

'What?' He drew back, alarmed and distressed in equal measures.

'I thought – hoped, I suppose – that you'd think I was easy cos I slept with you straight away and you'd disappear.'

'Oh.' Nate sat back, stared down at the white tablecloth, took another sip of water as he considered his reply. That was cruel and unnecessary, I realised. I'd purposely dismantled what was obviously a good memory for him. I opened my mouth to add that I'd only done it because how much I liked him had scared me, but his eyes darted up from the table, silencing me. 'Nothing you did could have put me off you,' he said. 'I'd already fallen for you in a big way.'

It was my turn to focus on the white cotton tablecloth. That was typical Nate, if he wasn't combating one of my moods with stoicism, he'd be earnest about how he felt. And that would make me feel awful. We'd had three full-blown rows in our six years together and all of them were started by him because if he snapped at me, I didn't let it go like he did – I'd snap back and things would get vicious. If I snapped at him first I'd be greeted with patience or honesty.

'Why so embarrassed, lady?' he teased. 'It's true. You know it's true.'

Our starters arrived and we silently watched the waiter place big white plates in front of us. I'd ordered strips of smoked salmon on a bed of rocket and Nate had gone for the roast vegetable soup topped with roasted almonds. Neither of us moved towards our food even when the waiter had gone. He was waiting for me to say something after his honest, calm reaction to my cruelty. He was waiting to find out if I would revert to the über-bitch he met or the sporadically nasty woman he almost married.

'That night was pretty confusing for me, too,' I confessed, concentrating on the way the rocket cradled the pink shreds of fish in its spiky hold. 'In fact, it totally shook me up.' I finally met his gaze. 'When I got home that night I knew I had to see you again, and soon, because no one had ever touched me in the way you did. I never slept with anyone else after that night.'

'I thought . . .'

'Yes, I gave you the impression that I had a couple of other men on the go but I didn't. I couldn't think about being with anyone else – after that coffee it was only you.'

Nate's face softened into a smile of surprise. He was still grinning as he picked up his spoon and started to eat. I picked up my fork, used its prongs to toy with the salmon strips but never once brought it to my mouth. Eating with my spin-cycle stomach was not an option. I watched the bowl of the spoon, filled with thick beige soup, disappear into Nate's mouth.

The memory of crying when we decided to get married came back to me. Crying because I'd finally realised what unconditional love felt like. Not only to receive it but to feel it. I'd known for a while I loved Nate but at the moment he accepted my proposal, I acknowledged what that meant. That I wasn't broken, I was like other people, I could feel, I could connect. And my heart was privileged enough to experience love. My heart had been hand-picked to find the one man I could love. And I had him to love for the rest of my life.

Nate glanced up from his soup, caught me watching him and beamed at me, his eyes crinkling up like they did on the day we first met for coffee. I grinned back and the tension lifted and we fell back into the ease and comfort we'd had on our first date.

chapter thirty-one

We talked and talked about nothing. I know it was nothing because when the waiter brought us the bill and our coats (we hadn't asked for them, he simply wanted to go home, what with it being well after closing time) we knew virtually nothing new each other: he didn't know about Tegan, that I'd seen him at the funeral nor that my boyfriend was called Luke. I didn't know how he'd found out about the funeral, if he was seeing someone, or why he had slept with Adele.

'May I walk you home?' Nate asked as the lights around the room were dimmed and the last few chairs were placed on tables.

'You can't walk me all the way to Horsforth, that's miles. And how will you get back to Tadcaster?'

'Details,' he dismissed with a wave of his hand. 'It's too late for a drink elsewhere apart from a club and you can't talk in those places. But if we walk, we can also talk.'

'All right, compromise, we walk until we get tired, then we can get a cab.'

We stepped out onto the street, into a navy black night that was spotted with neon street lights. I inhaled deeply, the chilled air shooting through my nose and setting my insides alight with cold. We walked along the empty street in silence, paused at the end of the block to check for traffic, then crossed. It was past midnight and I hadn't come even close to doing what I'd set out to do. As we continued down the road towards Hyde Park I stole a look up at Nate. His line of sight was fixed on the horizon, his hands deep in his pockets.

'I can feel you watching me,' he said, and halted, turned to me. I stopped too. 'I remember how often you used to do that, especially when you thought I was asleep.'

'You knew?'

A short nod of his head, a small smile playing on his lips.

'Why didn't you tell me?'

'Because I liked it. Why would I stop something that I liked?'

Nate took a step closer, still staring at me, his hands reached out. 'Look at you,' he murmured, his white breath curling up and away into the night as he spoke. I expected him to take my face in his hands, instead, he pulled my collar from inside my coat. He patted the wide triangles down in place, all the while staring into my eyes. I was transfixed, hypnotised by him. He gave a small laugh, his smile widened, turning him into the man I'd lived with. 'Look at you,' he breathed again. His hands slid down, across my collarbone and then down, between my breasts to the top button of my coat. 'You're done up wrong.' I glanced down. In my haste to leave the restaurant, I'd done up my coat buttons incorrectly. I looked up into his eyes.

'Oh,' I said with a small laugh that died halfway through its tiny existence.

His eyes fixed on mine, Nate's nimble fingers gently undid the first button. His fingers brushed down the wool and cashmere mix of my coat to the next button, he pulled that one open. His fingers continued down my body, until they reached the next button and then again, until the final button was open. Once my coat was open, Nate pulled it together again, then slowly buttoned it up.

'Thanks,' I murmured, my breathing laboured from, I told myself, the thinness of the cold air. Not from lust and longing. Not from wanting him to kiss me.

'Not a problem,' he said. He moved closer. Near enough for me to smell the aftershave on his skin; feel the rise and fall of his chest. He raised his hands and adjusted my collars, smoothed them into place but didn't take his hands away. He dipped his head, 'Kam,' he whispered as his lips touched mine.

'Ryn,' I said automatically, pulling away.

Nate pulled his head away too, his eyes searching mine, 'You're not going to make me call you by your full name, are you?' he asked.

'No, it's just no one calls me Kam any more, it's Ryn.'

'I'm not going to call you what he calls you.'

'It wasn't him who started it,' I replied.

Nate's lips grazed mine again and for a second, I wanted to fall into it. To let it happen. To kiss him.

I pulled back again. 'Nate,' I interrupted, 'I need to tell you something.'

'After,' he replied, moving in to continue the kiss.

'No.' I moved my head and his lips hit my chin. 'I need to tell you something,' I insisted.

Nate scrunched up his eyes as he lowered his head. He took his hands off me and rubbed his face. He always did that when he was nervous or agitated. Eventually, he reopened himself to me. 'I don't want to hear that you're going to marry him,' he said, clenching his fists. 'I CAN'T hear that you're going to marry him.'

'This has nothing to do with Luke,' I said, seeing him flinch at the mention of my lover's name.

'Go on then,' he said, steeling himself.

'I don't know how to say this . . . I think we need to sit down,' I said.

'OK,' he agreed. 'There's a park down the road.'

We walked the ten minutes to Hyde Park in silence, then sat on a bench not far from the entrance. The wind swirled around us, nipping at our already chilled skin. Nate sat facing forwards but close to me, trying to leech some of my body heat. I sat with my body slightly turned towards him.

'It's about Tegan,' I began.

Nate swivelled towards me, a frown on his face. 'Adele's daughter?'

I nodded, paused, hoped it'd sink in right then and there. He was a clever guy, why would I be bringing Tegan up if he wasn't her father?

His eyes suddenly lit up with knowledge, dispersing the frown. 'Oh, God,' he murmured. 'I'm such an idiot.' He slapped his forehead. 'That was her, wasn't it? That little girl the other day, that was Tegan. I didn't even recognise her. I was just so . . .' He waved his hand in the air near his head. 'I was all over the place because you were there. Shit. That was her. She's so grown up. How is she after . . .? You know, with everything?'

I was surprised at his concern. Nate had never shown much interest in Tegan before. He'd babysit with me sometimes, he'd occasionally read her a bedtime story, but he and she never had that much in common. 'She's OK. We have our off days and our better days, I'm meant to be getting her counselling.'

'*You're* meant to be getting her counselling?'

I nodded. 'Tegan lives with me. I'm bringing her up. I'm her legal guardian.'

'*You* are?' Nate was incredulous.

I bristled. 'Yes, me. What of it?'

He reached out, rested a calming hand on my forearm. 'I didn't mean anything, it's just, we were both determined not to have children and now you're her legal guardian. It's more than I could do.'

'There was no one else. And I'm her godmother, and I had to take on the responsibility no matter what I thought my life was going to be like. She was always precious to me and there was no one else.'

'You're a better person than I am. Is that what you wanted to tell me?'

I shook my head. 'It's about Tegan's father.'

His eyebrows lurched up in surprise. 'Her father? Is he around? Did you find out who he was?'

I nodded.

'And is he going to be involved in Tegan's life?'

'I don't know, I haven't told him yet. I can't find the right words. I don't know how he'll take it.'

'Not very well, I'd imagine,' Nate mused. 'Do you want me to come with you? Is that what you're trying to say? Because I will. It's the least I could do. For you and for . . . for Adele.'

'Oh my God, Nathaniel, when did you get so thick?' I snapped.

'I don't understand,' he said.

'Nate, it's you. You're Tegan's father.'

chapter thirty-two

Tegan's face moved in sleep. Her lips were slightly open, her hair hidden under the pink silk scarf. I liked watching her sleep. Sometimes, after I'd been to the loo in the middle of the night, I'd creep in here and watch her dark blonde lashes flutter against the soft white skin under her eyes, her pupils moving rapidly under her eyelids as she dreamed. That was one of the privileges I had now she was in my care. I could keep a curious vigil of her sleep. Bask in how beautiful she was. How peaceful she looked. How well she was growing up.

I turned away, a lump in my throat, she looked like Nate when she was asleep. Awake she was mini–Adele, slumbering she wore her father's face.

It was past 4 a.m., I'd let myself into the flat a couple of minutes ago and sneaked straight in to check Tegan was all right. She was, of course. I sniffed back a drizzle of snot – all that hanging about outside was giving me a cold. It wasn't only that, though. Conflicting, confusing emotions that coursed through me with the velocity of a recently undammed river were fighting to be released as a torrent of tears. I reached into my pocket for a tissue, and my fingers nudged up against my tights, which I'd hastily shoved in there before I got a cab home from Nate's place. A new wave of tears swelled in my eyes as I thought of the brave smile on his face as he kissed me goodbye. *How am I going to explain all this to Luke?*

Nate stared at me, his expression had frozen the second the words 'you're her father' had made sense in his head. His clear eyes burrowed into me as though waiting for me to recant it. No air came in or out of his mouth or nose, so I knew he wasn't breathing. All of a sudden, his upper body lurched and he was taking big gulping breaths, the breaths of a man who'd been flung, fully clothed, into the big wide ocean of parenthood, and had only now broken the surface of the water.

'Wha . . .? Huh . . .?' he began.

'Nate,' I reached out to touch him but he wrenched himself away.

'What are you telling me?' he said. 'What are you saying?'

'Nate, it's true. You're her father.'

Nate launched himself off the park bench, stood stock-still, jammed his hands into his hair, sat down again. His hands, the hands that had been erotically unbuttoning my coat minutes ago, went to his paled face. He rubbed his palms over his cheeks, then they went to his eyes.

'No kids,' Nate said. 'We always agreed, no kids. And now you're telling me, what? I've *got* one?'

I nodded.

'You're wrong. It has to be some kind of mistake.'

I shook my head.

'It has to be. I can't be her father. It's not possible.'

'Did you use contraception when you slept with Adele?' I asked.

Nate grimaced, closed his eyes, shook his head in shame.

'Well, then it is possible,' I replied, my voice clipped and icy.

'But she always said it was a married man she met through work. A one-night thing with a man who wasn't capable of

289

loving . . .' Nate's voice trailed away as it dawned on him that what she'd said pretty much described him. Even the work thing because they had run into each other a few times at media parties before I met him.

'It didn't occur to you that she had a baby nine months after you slept with her?'

'No. Why would it? She never let me know. Never gave me even the slightest hint . . .' He pushed his hands against his face again. 'How long have you known?' he eventually asked from behind his fingers.

I lowered my head, concentrated on my hands, which lay cold and motionless in my lap.

'How long?' Nate repeated a little louder, I cowered a little more, waiting for his explosion.

'That's why you left,' he said. 'I never understood why you wouldn't talk to me, why you wouldn't let me explain. You found out and you didn't bloody tell me, you just . . . What the fuck!' He was off the seat again.

'Adele didn't want you to know,' I stated.

He swung towards me. 'Adele didn't want me to know and you agreed with her?'

'She's Tegan's mother. She didn't want Tegan's life disrupted. She said not to tell you.'

'That's all right then,' he said. 'WHAT THE HELL ARE YOU TALKING ABOUT?' he shouted. 'YOU WERE WITH *ME*, NOT HER, *ME!* YOU SHOULD HAVE TOLD ME!'

I was off the seat as well, marched up to him until our bodies were angrily butted together. 'LIKE YOU TOLD ME YOU'D FUCKED MY BEST FRIEND, YOU MEAN?' I shouted back.

He glared at me, then his top lip curled back in a sneer as he hissed, 'Fuck off.' Then he stalked away, the dark night greedily gobbling him up as he went.

My instinct was to leave him to it because he needed time to get used to things. And, well, no one talks to me like that. Not even him. Then sanity returned: I was alone, in a dark park, with trees and hedges, behind which could be lurking attackers, or even social workers who were gagging to take away my child. I propelled myself after my ex-fiancé.

It didn't take long to catch up with him, he was striding away on the path, each step angry and determined. 'Nate,' I called. 'Please! Stop! Please!'

Nate had changed in the years since we parted – he didn't stop. Being a few years older than me, and of even temperament, he would always rather talk things out than storm off in a rage. He thought it added to our problems if we didn't talk straight away. Clearly, that had changed.

'Nate,' I called again. Was it my imagination or was he . . .? Yes, yes he was – he was speeding up. 'Nate! Just let—' I was cut short by my heel skidding on a patch of ice, taking my legs from under me and depositing me unceremoniously on the ground.

I sat in a heap on the stony ground, the cold instantly seeping in through my clothing. After a few seconds I shifted off my legs and pulled up my throbbing left ankle, cradling it in my hands. My right knee, which had somehow hit the ground first, despite my left leg being the one that gave way first, smarted enough to make my eyes water. The black nylon tights were in shreds around my knee, stained with blood from where the cold ground had split my skin. More tears sprang to my eyes as arrows of pain tore up my legs. I wasn't a crier, normally, not even when I was in this amount of agony, but what was normal about my life now? What had been normal about my life in the past six months?

This was the perfect ending to a traumatising evening: I was stranded in a park with no way of getting home. The person who had been seeing me home, hated me and had stormed off. And I was in an extraordinary amount of pain for such a small fall.

I allowed the ridiculousness of my situation to sink in for a few more minutes, and allowed myself a wallow in self-pity before I accepted I had to call Luke to come and collect me. I picked up my black leather bag, rooted through it until I found my mobile. As I pulled it out, a picture fluttered to the ground. Tegan had drawn it while she was waiting for me to take her to school last Tuesday morning. It was a picture of a house with a yellow sun in the sky and red flowers in the garden. In the bottom window, stick versions of me and her were waving out. I'd been impressed by it, she'd got my hairstyle – longer at the back, shorter at the front with a fringe that swept across my face – almost perfect. She'd drawn herself with yellow bunches and we were both wearing red dresses. Tegan had given it to me as we walked to school, saying, 'You can put it in your work.' It was a way for her to connect herself to the life I had away from her. She was fascinated by this thing called 'work'. Wanted to find out all she could about what I did when she couldn't see me. She'd often ask if I'd had a good day at 'your work' when I went to pick her up, questioned me on who I spoke to and what I did that day, how many calls I made and emails I sent. It was a world she wanted access to by any means.

I shoved the picture back into my bag, went back to the mobile. I pressed a button to get my house number up, paused before I dialled. Luke would come out, of course, but he'd have to wake up Tegan, put her in the car, drive—

'Are you OK?' Nate asked, stopping in front of me.

I lowered my head so he wouldn't see the tears in my eyes as I nodded at him. I didn't want him to know that I was crying not only because I'd hurt myself but because he'd upset me. I put away my mobile as he helped me to my feet. Holding onto Nate, I limped over to a nearby bench which, like the ground, was slick with frost. We sat beside each other in silence for a while until he moved towards me. His fingers closed around my lower thighs and he gently lifted my legs up onto his lap. He rolled up my dress and stared down at my gashed knee and swelling ankle.

'Look at you,' he said with a regretful sigh.

'I'd rather not if it's all the same to you.' I surreptitiously wiped at my eyes.

From his pocket he pulled out a tissue. 'Don't worry, it's clean,' he said as he wiped grit and blood from the wound.

We sat in silence: me staring at the dark, rolling hills of the park and the spikes of the trees piercing the black sky; him tending to my knee.

'She was my friend, too,' he said quietly, his voice loaded with sadness. 'She was one of my closest friends and she's gone. And no one told me. I had to read about it in some trade magazine. She was such a big part of our lives, of my life, and then she died.' He stopped dabbing at my knee. 'Why didn't you tell me?' He stared at me until I looked up at him. 'Do you hate me that much?'

'I don't hate you. Nate, I didn't think. It was hard enough getting through every day after she died, and there were lots of things that didn't occur to me. Telling you was one of them. It all happened so suddenly. I know she had a terminal illness, but I didn't think she'd die. She told me she would but I didn't quite believe it. Still don't to some extent.'

Nate nodded. 'The last thing I ever said to her was that she'd ruined my life. And I'd hate her for it as long as she lived. How's that for not thinking someone would die?' Nate closed his eyes. 'After you'd gone, I rang her and asked why she'd told you. She said it was an accident but I didn't listen. I shouted at her. Told her . . . Told her she was a jealous bitch; that I hated her. That she'd ruined everyone's life.' He shook his head, his eyes still closed. 'She's the first person I've known who's died.

293

Even my grandparents are still alive. I . . .' His voice cracked with emotion. I took his hand. His fingers closed around mine and clung to me. 'I want you to know it wasn't planned.'

I lifted my face to the night sky and the cold wind rushed over my features, the sharpness chilled my skin. 'Nate, I don't want to talk about it.' His fingers tightened around mine as I lowered my head to him. 'I feel sick every time I think about it. When I first moved up here, I used to throw up every time I thought about you and Adele . . . I still do sometimes. Occasionally I look at Tegan and it'll come to me who she really is, what her existence means, and I have to turn away because I'm so overwhelmed by how she came about. Not her − *I love her* − the circumstance. It hurts. I don't mean it makes me cry. It doesn't. It actually rips away at me inside . . . And I can't talk about it. I thought I could, but I can't. So, not now, OK?'

'Why tell me about Tegan, then?'

'Because you deserve to know.'

'You could have told me on the phone.'

'No I couldn't. And, there's something else.'

'What?'

'I . . . I need to ask you something. Adele wanted me to adopt Tegan. And I'm trying to. But, if the adoptee has one living parent whose whereabouts you know, then the prospective adopter has to get permission. I need you to sign over all rights to being Tegan's parent to me so I can adopt her.'

Nate shook his head. 'I only just found out that I've got a child and you're asking me to give her up?'

'You don't want kids, you said it yourself not five minutes ago.'

'Neither did you but you're doing it.'

'I had to. I was always the other person in Tegan's life, you know that. But you don't have to. You can just . . .'

'No,' Nate cut in. 'We can't talk about this here. It's cold and

294

we're tired. We need to discuss this properly. And you need to get your knee cleaned up and your ankle strapped up.'

'Yeah, shall we see if we can hail a taxi out on the street?'

Nate leaned forward, put his hand on my face and stared straight into my eyes. 'Come home with me,' he said. 'Please.'

'Mummy Ryn,' Tegan's voice insisted as she tugged at my arm.

I wanted to cry even before I'd opened my eyes. I hadn't slept in so long, and now I was being roused from the depths of a lovely sleep.

'Mummy Ryn,' Tegan said again.

'Yeah?' I mumbled.

'Why have you got your clothes on? Did you sleep in them again?'

I groaned. Had I fallen asleep during sex again? That'd be bloody stupid, especially when I hadn't had sex with Nate in years. NATE! My eyes flew open and I found that I wasn't looking at my bedroom window, I was looking at the television and the red beanbag because my body was hunched up on the sofa.

Images of the night before flashed through my mind: going back to Nate's; him cleaning up my knee and tacking on a plaster; his strong fingers massaging Deep Heat on my ankle which wasn't bad enough to require a bandage; us drinking tea as we sat side by side, watching television but not talking; him calling me a taxi. I remember, too, he'd tried to get me to stay the night, saying he'd drive me home in the morning when he was less tired, but I'd insisted on going home. For both our sakes. After checking on Tegan when I'd come in, I'd stood in the corridor, unsure whether to climb into bed with Luke or not. It'd wake him up and we'd either talk or make love, neither of which was appealing. I'd ended up curling up on the sofa and falling asleep, using my coat as a blanket.

295

Luke was at the stove, cooking – from the smell of it – bacon and eggs. There was toast on the go as well. From the way he stood, his tall body rigid, his back perfectly straight, he was avoiding looking at me.

'See, you've got your clothes on,' Tegan confirmed.

'Oh, yeah,' I said absently.

'Leave Ryn alone,' Luke said to Tegan. 'She must be knackered. Come sit down, eat your breakfast.'

Tegan, who would fly to the moon if Luke asked her to, went skipping over to him and took the plate of food he'd prepared for her.

'Why don't you go to bed for a little while?' Luke said to me as he busied himself putting out eggs and bacon for himself. 'I'll bring you a cuppa and some breakfast in an hour.' He still wasn't looking at me. I stood up, I had to make this right with him; he had to understand I hadn't been unfaithful.

'Your orangey dress is all creasy up,' Tegan commented.

'Yeah, it is,' I said, glancing down at the red and orange silk present from Luke. 'I'll have to iron it.'

'Yes, you will,' Tegan admonished.

Luke's eyes dared to stray to me, taking in my crumpled appearance, then flinched with pain when he spotted my tights shoved in my coat pocket. His eyes darted away as though scorched by the thought of why my tights would be in my coat pocket, what it inferred. 'Go on, get to bed,' Luke ordered. 'I'll bring you a bacon sarnie, Tommie K on the bread not the bacon.'

'Thanks,' I mumbled. The moment to reassure him had passed. And I might not get another one, he might go on believing I had betrayed him.

'The toast is a T!' Tegan squealed in delight when she saw her plate.

'Yes, it's T for Time to eat your breakfast.'

'No!' Tegan giggled. 'It's T for Tegan!'

'It might be,' Luke laughed back, 'but I think it's for Time to eat your breakfast.'

He gets on better with her than I do sometimes, I thought as I slunk away to bed.

I woke up again when I was being gently shaken. I opened my eyes and found Luke perched on the edge of the bed. On the bedside table was a mug of tea and a plate with a toasted bacon sandwich. Had I been asleep for only an hour? It felt like days.

'Thought I'd better wake you up before I go,' Luke said, avoiding my eyes.

'Go?' I said with a yawn, pushing myself upright.

'Yeah, I've got stuff to do. T's playing in her room, so she's fine. But I thought I'd better tell you before I go because you know how much mischief she can get into.'

'What stuff do you have to do?' I asked.

'Just work, back at my flat. I'll see you later.' Luke lifted himself off the bed but I reached out, grabbed his arm, held him back.

'What's going on?'

He sat heavily on the bed, finally turned his gaze on me. 'You tell me.'

I said nothing, unsure what to say. How much would he want to know? Not all of it, that was for certain. And how would I explain it, anyway? He didn't know the complexities of my relationship with Nate. That Mr Turner wasn't simply an ex or even The Ex, he was . . . Nate, as simple and complicated as that.

'Look, Ryn,' he said after my long silence, 'I'll be honest, I don't know how to handle this. I've never been in this situation before. You know how I feel about you and Tegan, the pair of you have become my life. But he's her real father and there's obviously something going on between the two of you.'

'There isn't!' I protested.

'No? Then why won't you make eye contact for more than two seconds? Why didn't you come to bed last night? Why were you walking funny? I'm hoping you didn't fuck him but I wouldn't be surprised if you did because I know you still love him.'

'I told you, I don't any more.'

Luke ploughed over my correction. 'I can't deal with this. It's best I go and we talk about it when I'm less angry. Yes, that's it, that's what I'm feeling, I'm angry. It's not fair.' He stopped. 'I don't want to do this now. Not when Tegan's around and not when I haven't thought things through.'

'OK,' I mumbled, there was no getting through to him that I hadn't been unfaithful.

Instead of leaving, he sat stock-still, stared at the door as he asked, 'Did you?'

'No,' I replied. Some people would have been offended to be asked, but I'd ask if I was in his situation. It wasn't a lack of trust, it was a need to know. A need to not drive yourself crazy by wondering what if . . .? Could they . . .? Did they . . .? It was also a way of telling that person you trusted them. Trusted them to tell you the truth. 'I didn't even kiss him, Luke.'

'Did you want to sleep with him?' he asked, then braced himself.

Without hesitation, I replied, 'No.'

'Really?'

'Yes, really. I told him about Tegan and we had a row in the street, then I fell over, hurt my legs – that's why I'm limping, not because of some sex marathon. I went back to his place to get cleaned up – that's all, nothing happened. Then I got a taxi home. I didn't come to bed because it was 4 a.m. when I got back and I didn't want to disturb you. That's it. That's all that happened.'

'Is he going to sign?'

'I don't know. He was so freaked out by what I told him, he couldn't deal with anything else.'

'And you seriously didn't want to sleep with him?'

'Seriously.'

'OK. OK. Budge up,' he said, and lay down beside me. I wrapped my arms around him, snuggled up against his solid body, resting my face against his back. I closed my eyes and let myself drift away into sleep.

I'd been telling him the truth. I didn't want to sleep with Nate. Not in the slightest. I wanted to kiss him. I wanted to hold him. I wanted to make love to him. And afterwards, I wanted to go back to watching him as he floated in dreamland, but at no point did I actually want to sleep with him.

I couldn't tell Luke that. Luke wouldn't understand that last night was like stepping into a memory, stepping back into an old Kamryn suit that I'd never been given the chance to grow out of. The events surrounding Adele's confession had wrenched me out of a life and personality that I'd liked. Loved, even. Everything I felt for Nate last night had been about that. Had been about a time when I was with a man I adored absolutely, when I knew what it was like to be unequivocally desired and cared for by someone. It was also about being with someone who reminded me of a time when my best friend was alive and my Tiga was unmarked by abuse and bereavement. Wanting Nate last night had nothing to do with longing for another man at Luke's expense it was about wanting another me at this me's expense; wanting another time and being willing to sacrifice this time to get it.

Luke wouldn't understand that. I wouldn't if he tried to tell me the same thing about his ex-fiancée, Nicole. I'd see it as betrayal no matter how honest he was being. And anyway, I wasn't going to see Nate again – I was going to send him the papers and that would be it. So it didn't matter what I'd felt last night, now was the important thing.

299

chapter thirty-three

Rat-a-tat-tat!

I glanced at the front door to my flat, wondering who was knocking. Luke, who was out with Tegan, had a key, and Betsy, my office partner, never visited me at home any more for fear of encountering Tegan – small children were not her thing. And there ended the list of people who would drop by without calling first.

I slipped on the thick security chain I'd had fitted since my flat became Tegan's home too, cautiously opened the door and peeked out.

Nate.

I hadn't heard from him nor seen him in the week since our dinner, I'd simply told myself I'd send him the papers another day. Another day hadn't dawned yet. I slammed the door and with trembling hands undid the security chain then opened the door again. 'What are you doing here?' I asked, the shaking of my hands also present in my voice.

'I wanted to see you.'

'You can't just turn up unannounced like this.'

'I can because I have,' he replied.

'How did you know where I live?'

'I heard when you gave the taxi driver your address.' He tapped his temple. 'Mind like a steel trap.'

'What do you want?' Hostility and fear tainted my voice. This was not going to end well. Luke was gagging for a reason to kick seven types of hell out of Nate. And Nate, the jealous man I'd dated for six years, would probably welcome the chance to batter the man I was sleeping with.

'Like I said, to see you. And to see Tegan.'

My body contracted in terror. 'What? Why?'

'She's . . . Look, do we have to do this on the doorstep?'

'No, no.' I stepped aside to let him in and indicated straight ahead to the living room/kitchen.

Nate, dressed in blue jeans and a black polo neck jumper, didn't sit, he surveyed my living area, taking in the bookcase, the cream sofa that had been scuffed a multitude of colours over the past few months, the big red beanbag that lived beside the television, the red rug that ended where the small dining table sat, marking the kitchen area from the living space. He looked on, to white kitchen cabinets, topped with wood-effect worktops, which were covered in breakfast and lunch things that I was going to be washing up the second I could peel my tired body off the sofa.

'Where is she?' Nate shortened the distance between us so I had to look up his six-foot-two frame to his face.

'She's . . . Luke's taken her to the park to feed the ducks or rather she's taken Luke – she decided last night that the ducks were going to starve without her intervention, and wouldn't stop going on about it until we agreed to take her, after her karate class. Luke volunteered to get out of the washing-up.'

My ex-fiancé's face twisted with resentment. 'Take her out a lot, does he?' he snarled. I'd never heard that low, accusing vicious tone to his voice, it scared me slightly. 'Quite the family man, isn't he?'

'Nate, stop it, please.' I touched his arm. 'This isn't you.'

His whole body relaxed with a deep exhalation. 'No, no it's

301

not, is it?' He shook his head. 'I'm all over the place right now, most of the time I don't know what I'm doing or feeling.' He moved back from me, parked himself on the sofa. I sat beside him.

'What are you doing here?' I asked again.

'I wasn't lying, I want to see Tegan.'

The panic rose again. 'But why?'

'No matter how she came about, she's my daughter. I have to accept responsibility for her.'

Oh, no. No. I might not have wanted her initially but that didn't mean I could live without her now. She was my only link to Adele. I promised to take care of her, adopt her. And I loved her, needed her. What if Nate fell in love with her and wanted her too?

'Why? You don't want kids. Are you going to try and get custody of her?'

Nate drew away in horror, his features stricken. 'God, no!'

'So why do you want to see her?'

'Kamryn, she's my daughter.'

'But you don't want kids.'

'That's a moot point, isn't it? I've got a child and I have to deal with it.'

'If you don't want custody of her, why do you want to see her?'

'What sort of person would I be if I didn't even try to get to know her before I gave her up?'

'You don't understand, they won't let me adopt her if you're still around. That could be seen as you being capable of looking after her, which would mean I won't be allowed to properly adopt her.'

His eyes studied me for a few seconds. 'Were you expecting me to sign away my parental rights then walk away like it was nothing?'

When he put it like that, what I asked of him sounded

302

callous — something he wasn't. 'No, course not . . . I don't know.'

'Kam . . . *Ryn*, we haven't even started to talk about what happened between us, I'm not going away until we have.'

That thought filled me with terror. He was a stranger; he'd become a stranger the day I found out what he'd done. He wasn't Nate, my rock, he was a man capable of betrayal. And whilst I didn't know why he'd done it, I suspected I knew. My suspicions haunted me, night and day, they plagued me just like not letting Adele say all she wanted to before she died haunted me. They were part of those grooves of guilt and loss in my mind. I didn't want those thoughts confirmed. Didn't want any of those grooves to become a permanent fixture of my personality.

'This isn't about us, this is about Tegan,' I said. 'I need to give her the stability that her mother would have given her and to do that I need to be able to adopt her.'

'And you haven't thought about the possibility of us getting back together and bringing up Tegan as her parents? Us being a family?'

Terror punched the air out of my body in one vicious blow and I turned away from Nate, clutching my stomach.

'Kam?'

'Don't take her away from me,' I begged. 'She's all I've got left. Please don't take her away.'

His arms slipped around me. 'Why would I take her away?' he asked. 'I was only saying that if we gave it another go we could be a family.'

'But you won't sign unless I say yes,' I replied.

'I never said that. And I didn't mean for it to sound like I was putting pressure on you. I wouldn't . . . Not ever. I just want us to talk properly. The other night wasn't proper talking, was it? We need to sort things out.'

I shook my head. 'I don't want to.'

'We can't leave things like they are.' Nate ran his fingers through my hair, pouring comfort into my veins with every stroke. He knew that would calm me, would sometimes send me to sleep. My two favourite things were having my hair stroked and my neck kissed. Nate knew that, Luke didn't. 'I want to make things right between us. And, unexpected as it is, I need to accept this new responsibility . . . How are you doing for money? Because I should start paying for her.'

This wasn't what I wanted to hear. I needed him to be uninterested because they wouldn't let me adopt her if he was on the scene. This was what Nate was like, though: honest and noble. A good guy.

'I could manage about two hundred and fifty pounds a month. Is that all right?'

I crumpled again. That money would be a godsend. Even though Luke tried to help out, I resisted his attempts to pay for Tegan – she was my responsibility, not his, and I didn't want to rely on something that could be taken away at some point. I wasn't living in cloud-cuckoo-land, Luke and I might not be for ever.

Nate slid off the sofa, knelt in front of me, engulfed me in a hug. 'Is that enough? Maybe if I give you a lump sum from my savings, then the two hundred and fifty would go a bit further. About three thousand? Don't worry, I'm not going to ask for it back – it comes with no ties. It's for ever, no matter what happens between us. I'll set up an account for her that you look after until she's eighteen and I'll see if I can give more as she gets older. Well, actually, I have to pay more as she gets older there's no two ways about it, is there?'

'Nate, I . . . thank you.'

He lifted my head and gazed into my eyes, used his thumbs to wipe away my tears. 'Ryn . . .' he began but was silenced by the sound of the key in the lock. We both instinctively jumped up, faced the door. I quickly wiped tears from my eyes.

'We're back!' Tegan chorused as she and Luke bustled in the door and came into the living room. Tegan, swaddled in her red winter coat, her furry black hat on her head, a black fleece scarf at her throat and furry black mittens on her hands, paused in the doorway when she saw a tall white man standing beside me. Luke, who was two steps behind her, stopped short too.

'Did you have a nice time?' I asked, sniffing away the rest of my tears.

'Yes,' Tegan grinned, her inquisitive blue eyes darted from me to Nate. 'Who's that?' she asked when the suspense became too much for her.

'This is Nate. Remember I told you he was an old friend of mine?'

'You had a pretty dress,' she said to Nate.

Nate frowned comically. 'No, I've seen some lovely dresses in my time but I've never worn one. Promise.'

Tegan laughed although she took a step back and pushed herself against Luke's leg, needing his reassuring, familiar presence. 'Not you!' she giggled. 'Mummy Ryn. She had a pretty dress cos she was going to be married.' She raised her mittened hand and pointed. 'To you.'

Shock stumbled into the room; staggering and reeling into each adult, rendering us mute. The fact that Nate and I had been engaged was a subject none of us would have raised if not for Tegan saying this.

'That's right,' I said, recovering first. 'I didn't know you remembered that.'

Tegan grinned. 'I did.' She looked up at Luke, seeking his praise. He grinned at her then dropped to his knees and reached for her feet. 'You're a clever girl,' Luke said as he unstrapped her trainers and slipped them off.

When he stood, Luke glared questioningly at me. 'Luke, this is Nate. Nate, this is my boyfriend, Luke.' Nate came around from the sofa and reached out his hand. Luke begrudgingly shook it.

'Pleased to meet you,' Nate said.

'Yeah,' Luke replied. I knew that expression and tone of voice well – from the moment we met.

'Are you Mummy Ryn's boyfriend?' Tegan asked, in case she hadn't unsettled us enough already.

'A long time ago I was,' Nate replied. 'But I'm not any more, Luke is now.'

Tegan seemed pleased with that, she scrunched up her nose and mouth and nodded her head in agreement. Luke looked like he might punch Nate just for the hell of it.

'We fed the ducks, didn't we, Luke?' Tegan said.

'We surely did,' Luke said.

Nate's face softened and he focused completely on Tegan, a soppy smile taking over his face. 'Oh, wow,' Nate said. 'What colour were they?'

'Duck colour,' Tegan giggled.

'Oh, were they bright yellow?'

'No!' Tegan squealed.

'Well, that's the colour the duck in my bath is.'

Where had Nate's ability to talk to a child come from? He used to run a mile when asked to stay with Tegan while I went to the loo if we were babysitting.

'There wasn't that many. They were brown. And green and purple with yellow around the neck. Luke said they fly away for winter.'

'Right, I'd better go,' Luke said.

Nate glanced away from Tegan, made uneasy eye contact with Luke for a moment, then he swung to me. 'I'd better get off. Got a work thing tonight.' He leant over, pressed his warm lips against my cheek. My heart quickened at the touch of him. 'Bye,' he said to me. 'Luke.' He held out his hand and Luke shook it. 'And Tegan,' he bent to Tegan height, 'it was a pleasure meeting you again. I'll see you soon, OK?' He held out his hand and she shook it, the joy at being treated like a grown-up showed on her face.

Luke gritted his teeth, a heartbeat away from smacking Nate as he came towards the door. I held my breath, scared he'd follow through with the venomous look in his eye, but then he stepped aside. Nate's leaving was marked with a click of the lock as the door shut behind him.

'He was nice,' Tegan said, coming into the room and jumping on the sofa. She was still in her coat, scarf, hat and mittens. 'But not as nice as Luke.' She tugged off a mitten, picked up the remote and flicked channels on the television, uninterested in this world now the excitement of a visitor was over.

Luke's eyes flicked from me to the corridor, accompanied by a small jerk of his head. I followed him to my bedroom and he shut the door behind me.

'I don't like him being here,' Luke hissed.

'I didn't ask him to come, he came of his own accord.'

'Did he?'

'No, Luke, I waited until you went out for an unspecified amount of time to ask him around here for sex.'

'I don't like him being here,' he repeated.

'It's my flat.'

'Did he try it on with you?'

'At last, you get to the point. No, he didn't and even if he did – which he didn't – nothing would have happened. I'm with you.'

'What did he want?'

'To see Tegan.'

Luke quailed. 'He wants her?' He sounded as panicked as I felt.

'I don't know. That's why I was crying when you came in. You did notice that, didn't you? We weren't all lovey-dovey, I was terrified because he wants to take responsibility for her and that could mean all sorts for my adoption application.'

'Shit.' Luke sat on the bed.

'I've never seen him like that with a child, not even Tegan. But I've never seen him with his daughter before. I'm scared, Luke.' I sat beside him and he put his arms around me. 'I'm scared that he's going to fall in love with her and then he's going to want her and I'll lose her and I'll let Adele down.' I pushed the palm of my hand against my forehead. 'I'm scared, Luke.'

'It'll be all right,' he said without conviction. 'I promise, everything's going to be all right.'

He didn't understand, I wasn't only scared about losing Tegan, I was scared about Nate. Seeing him with Tegan, how he'd made an effort with her, had made me wonder if we could make it work as a family – Nate, Tegan and I. I was scared because, for the first time, I was having doubts about Luke's place in our lives.

chapter thirty-four

The after-work crowd, people who stumbled out of offices, shops, train stations, other places of employment and into the nearest bar, was something I used to be a part of. Betsy, Ruby, me, and a few other people from Angeles would often head to a bar near the store and drink our hard-earned wages. Since I'd inherited Tegan the circle of friends who I saw outside of work had been whittled away to . . . Luke.

Friends rarely saw me away from work. The simple reason was I didn't like going out and leaving Tegan. She might not mind, but I did. When I was at home I was very rarely completely there with her anyway. I was thinking about the work I had to do. The shopping. The washing. Ironing the washing. Cleaning up. How I'd afford things on the wages that now had to stretch to two people. The fact was, I didn't give her enough attention, but she'd get none if I wasn't home at all. Also, the thought of leaving Tegan with a stranger was too scary. Which was why I was so lucky to have Luke at times like tonight, my first after-work drink in months. They were at home now, probably making dinner – wrecking the flat in the process. It was always an all-pan, all-utensil effort when they cooked. And they usually made a 'Bung It'. Adele and I had come up with the recipe for 'Bung It' when we were in college. We'd literally take all the odds and ends in the fridge, 'bung it' in one pot and hope for the best. Sometimes it'd be great, sometimes disgusting. But we always had fun doing it. Tegan had resurrected it the first time she and Luke had made me dinner, and I was most likely going to be getting a combination of onion, tomato and sweetcorn when I got in – of course, I'd then spend the best part of the evening cleaning up after them. But it was OK because they always had fun when they cooked, and that was the main thing.

I pushed my way through the huddle of bodies standing in trendy bar Paragon, in central Leeds. Some of the people I sidled past still had their winter coats on, most stood protectively over their bags, and everyone had some kind of drink in their hands. I'd forgotten how packed these places got, how the air hummed with conversation and the atmosphere was tinted blue by smoke. I searched through the gaps in the bodies for Nate. We were having a quick drink because he was meeting friends in Leeds that evening. I spotted him, sitting at a table in a corner, staring into a half-drunk pint, a glass of white wine for me opposite him. It took me back to the times we used to meet after work. He'd get there first, buy me a drink and then I would show up, buy Adele a drink, and then she, who finished work last, would arrive.

I'd barely swallowed the first mouthful of the first glass of wine I'd had in ages when Nate asked, 'Are you going to tell Tegan I'm her father?'

His question reminded me why I liked being around Luke. Luke was normality. There were no big swooping loops of emotion with Luke. Normality didn't carry a kick of excitement, but when your life was a constant plunging spiral of emotion, where one minute you were in a side-clutching fit of laughter and the next you were digging your fingernails into your palms to stop yourself sobbing, there was a lot to be said for normality. Ordinariness was a sought-after commodity. One that Nate and I didn't trade in any more. With us, it was something big and dramatic, like this.

'I don't know,' I replied. I set down my glass on the table, traced the grain of the knotted wood with my finger. 'Tegan's a smart girl, she's knows you're hanging around for a reason.' Twice Nate had dropped round to our place since his unexpected visit last Saturday – first of all to give me the details of the bank account he'd set up for Tegan. He'd deposited three thousand pounds in it as promised. Two nights later he'd brought round the cash card that came with the account. Tegan had been cautious around him, stared at him with guarded eyes as she asked him tentative questions about his job, warily answered his inquiries about school. Luke hadn't been happy about Nate's visits, but he hadn't complained because he was desperate for Nate to sign himself out of our lives.

'Is that how you see it, me hanging around?' Nate asked. 'Like a bad smell?'

'Don't be like that, Nate. I just don't know if she's ready to hear that you're her father.'

Nate drained his pint, but made no move to get a refill. One drink always meant one with him.

'For Tegan, "Daddy" is something she didn't have for the first years of her life and now . . .'

He didn't raise his eyes from staring at his pint glass. 'Go on, say it.'

'And now, "Daddy" is Luke. Not that she's ever said that, he's just stepped into that role in her life. She's completely devoted to him.'

Nate raised his head, pinned me to the spot with his navy-blue gaze. He was going to ask me about Luke; he was going to ask if I was devoted to Luke, too. If I loved him. But instead of saying anything, Nate sat back suddenly, stretching out his muscular frame. His mouth was a line, his face a blank, the only part of him that did anything were his eyes, which bored into me. I swallowed, felt my heart rate skip up a couple of notches. It was unnerving how he was able to do that to me. Very few people could unsettle me like Nate did. 'I'm seeing someone,' he said.

I'd been bringing my wine glass to my mouth and this revelation caused me to accidentally bash it against my teeth. I wasn't expecting that. In my mind, I'd always hoped he'd never go near another woman, in the vain hope that I would return. I lowered my glass, unable to put any kind of spin on my distress that he'd moved on. I had moved on – I had a boyfriend and a child – you couldn't move on any further than that, could you? 'Oh,' I uttered.

'I've only been seeing her a couple of weeks,' Nate revealed.

Since he saw me again. Oh God. Did that mean seeing me must have reminded him that reality doesn't match fantasy; that I wasn't 'everything' as he used to believe?

'She's one of the producers at the radio station.' She saw him every day. They probably flirted over the kettle while making coffee, snogged when they went to lunch, shagged after evening drinks. 'She's nice, you'd like her.'

'Let's not play this game, Nate, it makes us both look pathetic,' I snapped.

'All right,' he agreed, dropping his gaze.

We sat in silence, the buzz of our fellow drinkers vibrating over us. I hadn't asked Nate what he'd gotten up to in the preceding years, I'd assumed he was single because he'd tried to kiss me the night we went to dinner, but what had he done in the years since we'd parted? Had he shagged around, or settled down with someone else? I had no right to ask. It wasn't my business. I was seeing him for one reason only – to get him to sign away his rights to Tegan. Not to torture myself about who he slept with. 'Why are you doing this, Nate?' I asked, nudging the conversation in a safer direction. 'Why are you so interested in Tegan?'

'Well, it's not for the reason that you and no doubt everyone else thinks.'

'And what's that?'

'That I'm using her to get to you.'

'I don't think that.'

'Right, and that never crossed your mind, did it?'

I lowered my gaze as shame burnt up my face. He was right, of course. That thought had occurred to me – more than once – because Nate was usually so uninterested in children. A few times I'd wondered if he was taking an interest in Tegan as a way to get back into my life, my bed. I thought it but knew deep down it wasn't true. It was a way of making life simpler. Thinking that classified Nate as a calculating bastard who would never be as good as Luke because he was using his own child. The reality was, I knew Nate wasn't like that. He wasn't devious by nature. That was why I had been destroyed by what he'd done. I couldn't comprehend, couldn't compute how Nate – solid, dependable, adoring Nate – had cheated on me. It just wasn't him.

'I'm doing this because she's my responsibility,' Nate enlightened. 'You know I take my responsibilities seriously. I even take responsibility for that night with Adele. She tried to blame herself but I was there too. I . . .' Nate stopped talking, probably because I was trembling. The thought of Adele had set me off. I was lurching into grief, teetering on the edge of falling into the abyss of pain. I hadn't realised until this moment that today was a bad day. A pain day. A day when even the slightest thing would dismantle me. Days like this were rare; most of the time I could put that debt to grief to one side and carry on, but on days like today, even thinking about Adele could paralyse me. The memory of her lying still and cold would crowd out all other thoughts and I would start to shake, while my stomach was crushed with nausea and my eyes would moisten.

'Sorry,' Nate whispered. 'I didn't mean to upset you.'

'Did you talk about it a lot then?' I asked, calming myself.

'No, it wasn't like that. I was going to . . .' He stopped again but his expression – shocked by what had come out of his mouth – revealed all I needed to know.

'You were going to leave me.'

'We have to put this into context, Kam. Ryn. Emotions were way off the scale; my head was all over the place. Me and you were . . .'

'You were going to finish with me? For Adele? You wanted to be with Adele?' My voice rose with every word, people around us glanced over but I didn't care. She never told me this. When she asked me to take on her child, *his* child, she never said that Nate wanted to be with her instead of me.

'Kamryn, stop it,' Nate commanded, his voice stern with barely restrained anger. 'I was going to finish it because you were in love with someone else. Or have you forgotten that?'

I was like a rabbit caught in headlights: unable to move, unable to believe what he'd said. 'This is why we need to talk about this properly,' Nate said gently. 'You don't want to right now, which is fine, but we can't discuss things out of context. There were so many things going on, and I was so low at that time.'

'But . . .' I began, then realised I couldn't deny it without lying.

It was a stupid flirtation with someone from work. He (I can't even remember his name now he was so insignificant) was someone who came from our Edinburgh branch to work with us for six months. We clicked almost instantly, had the same sense of humour and shared a lot of views, and so we became friends. We went to lunch together, had drinks after

314

work and flirted with each other, but nothing more. When he returned to Scotland we didn't even keep in touch. It meant nothing and I hadn't realised that Nate had picked up on it. That he had any clue I'd had feelings for someone else. 'I didn't do anything,' I reassured him. 'I never cheated on you.'

'I know you didn't,' Nate replied. 'It was never about that. I thought I'd lost you and I wanted to cut my losses and get out. Adele convinced me not to.'

What, by sleeping with you?

'And no, not by sleeping with me, I know that's what you were thinking. She said some simple but truthful things. And that made me decide to keep trying with you, to not give up. She's so wise . . . She *was* so wise. *Was* . . . I keep forgetting she's gone. That she's . . .'

Dead. That cold, heavy word that was so brutal and final. 'Passed away', 'gone' were all transitional words. They said that she'd done something to not be here any more, she didn't just stop. End. Become 'dead'.

'So do I. Not when I'm at home, but you know, at work and stuff. I'll be carrying on as normal, and then I'll get a call from Tegan and I'll remember and I'll want to stop. It doesn't seem right sometimes to be carrying on life as normal. To laugh, to enjoy myself. Even to be able to go to work when she can't. I don't know how to describe it . . . I don't get to speak to her ever again. And you don't realise how long for ever is until you can't do something. Especially when it's . . .'

When it's my fault, I should have added. When I caused so much heartache by not speaking to her, when I got my wish and didn't have to speak to her ever again.

I had right on my side when I cut her out of my life. She'd hurt me and I couldn't speak to her. Adele had no one else, though. And I knew that. I had my family who, for their sins, loved me, would support me if it came down to it. But Adele didn't. I'd robbed her of the one person she relied upon. Adele's last few months were empty and lonely when they shouldn't have been. That was my fault.

Anguish settled on Nate's face. 'I have to tell you something . . .' he said gravely. He sat forwards, rested his elbows on the table, hiding his face in his hands momentarily. 'Adele texted me six months before she died, asked me to come and see her. I wouldn't, I was settled up here, and even if I wasn't there was no way I was going to see her after everything. She rang me then, and I avoided her calls. She ended up blocking her number and ringing me. She asked if I could look after Tegan for a while because she was going into hospital. She said Tegan would stay with me because she knew me and there was no one else. She was begging me and I wouldn't.' He paused, swallowed a mouthful of emotion. 'I said there was no way on earth I'd do anything for her, especially not look after her child. Even while I was doing it I could hear how horrible I was being but I wouldn't stop. I couldn't. She kept saying she was sorry and that if I'd give her a chance she'd make it up to me, she just needed me to do this one thing. That's when I told her I'd hate her till the day she died.'

I couldn't imagine Nate being so nasty. He had the capacity for it, obviously. We all had the capacity for it. When he and I had rowed he'd said evil things, but he'd never meant them. He and I were nasty to each other because we were certain it wouldn't break us up. But to be so vicious to someone and mean it . . . I couldn't imagine that from Nate.

'That's the other reason I'm doing this. I don't know what I would have done if Adele had told me she was dying, but I want to make up for how much I let her down. We were like a family once, the four of us, and now I'll do anything I can do to make her daughter's life easier.'

316

'You're not doing this because she's your flesh and blood?'

Nate cast his eyes to the table. 'I'd love to say it was,' he admitted. 'And, you'd think that having seen her again and spoken to her and knowing we're related, I'd feel something, but no. I do like her, she's a good kid, but there's no genetic pull. I don't look at her and feel the miracle of life has moved from me to her . . . But that might change, the more time I spend with her.'

'So you're sticking around?'

He nodded slowly. 'For now.'

I drained the last of my wine, put the glass down and Nate pushed his chair out. 'Hadn't you better be getting back? Tegan and Luke will be wondering where you are.'

As I watched Nate shrug on his coat and wind his black scarf around his neck, *inamorato* flashed into my mind. I was jolted. The thought of the word was followed by the memory of the first time we'd slept together; how he'd looked all those years ago. His bruised lips, mussed up hair, flushed skin as he sat in bed staring at me. He'd been delicious then. He was delicious now, too, in a different, more settled way. The slide of his lips, the shape of his blue eyes, his slight ski jump nose all still gave me a kick deep inside, and even though he wasn't, he still felt like *inamorato*. Lover. I bet his new woman felt this too. I bet she got that jump of excitement every time he walked in a room. Every time she thought about their first kiss, I knew her knees turned to mush. When they made love, I was sure she felt deep in her soul that he was The One.

Was it the same for him? Was he in love with her, too? Actually, I realised, that's probably why he wanted to meet me for a drink, he was killing time before a date. Before he scuttled off to make love and a new set of memories with his new woman.

'So, you've got a hot date tonight then?' I asked with a

laugh. I managed to make it sound genuine, that I didn't mind being a space filler.

'I wouldn't exactly call it "hot", we're going to dinner.'

'Oh.'

'Just dinner. Not all dates end back at my place, you know.'

'OK, have a nice time.'

'Nice isn't the word I'd use. I've got to tell her that it's not going to work out between us.'

'Why not?' I replied, failing to keep that note of hope out of my voice.

'You know why,' Nate replied, staring straight at me. 'There's someone else.'

chapter thirty-five

I don't love him.
 I do love him.
 I don't.
 I do.
The world was still. Subdued. It was the middle of the night and everything was resting. Apart from me. I couldn't sleep. I hadn't been able to sleep for days. Not since the night I met Nate for a drink. Not since I bumped into him in John Lewis, if I was honest. Or was it before that? Had I slept properly since Adele died? I couldn't remember it, if I had.

Recently the problem had moved from bad to chronic. It'd take me hours to drop off and then after an hour or so I'd wake up again, lie in the still of the night, staring at the off-white ceiling, trying to sort out my thoughts from my feelings. Trying to decipher what I was thinking and not feeling; feeling not thinking. Trying to work out if I loved Luke or not.

Luke's gentle breathing beside me cut into my thoughts. It was him being here that made thinking difficult. He was either breathing or moving around in bed, unintentionally mocking me with his undisturbed slumber. If he wasn't here, if I didn't feel envious of his ability to sleep, maybe I wouldn't feel all this resentment towards him. Maybe, but maybe not. We'd been going through a rocky patch of late. Nothing was said, it lay under the surface of every conversation, look and touch – all was not well with us. And that was because neither of us knew where we stood with each other – I knew he was suspicious of my feelings for Nate, and I was just as suspicious of Luke's feelings for me.

Things for me had changed since I said 'I love you' and he waited a week – until I was going to dinner with my ex – to say it back. I'd said it because it was what he'd needed to hear at the time, but I had said it. First. I had made myself vulnerable, had opened myself up and he couldn't even utter two words. Two words – 'me too' – was all it would have taken to show I meant something to him. And he couldn't do it. And it had made me doubt everything I thought he felt for me.

I don't love him.

I do.

I don't.

My tired eyes were fixed on the ceiling as I lay flat on my back, arms heavy, legs heavy, torso heavy. I was trying to leave my body. Trying to remove myself from this reality, trying to float away. Was that how Adele had felt when she'd died? Had she felt herself being removed, molecule by molecule, from her body? Or was it quick? Was she unaware that she'd gone? Or for the second before it happened did she know that the next moment she wouldn't be there?

Luke made a sound with his breathing, and turned in bed, butting me gently as he moved. His arms reached out for me, pulled me towards him. I held my breath, hoping he wouldn't wake up. He might, as usual, want to have sex if he did. And I couldn't think of anything worse at that moment. I didn't want to be in my body and I certainly didn't want anyone else to be in it either. I didn't want him to touch me. I didn't want anyone to touch me. But especially not him.

I do love him.

I don't love him.

I do.

I don't.

Luke snuggled into me, nuzzled his face into the crook of my neck, moulded his body against mine. 'Hmmm,' he said against my neck. I wanted to push him off.

I just want to be alone.

Soon he was deeply ensconced in dreamland again, so I moved his arm off me and slipped out of his hold, then slipped out of the bedroom. Halfway down the corridor I stopped and opened one of the cupboard doors. My corridor was narrow because along one side were floor to ceiling length cupboards with white, spring-loaded doors. I'd shoved Adele's boxes in them after we'd come back to Leeds and hadn't looked at them since.

I pulled out one box Adele had labelled clothes and carried it to the sofa. After I'd turned on the side lights, I shut the door and sat down beside the box. *I should go through all the boxes, especially when there aren't that many of them.* And I would eventually, but I'd start with this one. I opened this brown cardboard box, peered in.

The item on top was made from black velvet and instantly I knew what it was. I pulled it out, the cloth soft and furry under my fingers. It was mine, my black velvet jacket. I'd leant it to Del for a work do years ago, it'd been quite big on her but she'd been coveting it since the day I'd bought it, so hadn't cared. She'd worn it over a satin burgundy bra and the tightest pair of shiny burgundy trousers I'd ever seen. It'd flashed the white gold bodybar in her pierced stomach.

A snapshot of how she looked – blonde hair falling in waves around her face and onto her shoulders, make-up that brought out her long lashes and emphasised her eyes, my shiny black evening bag clutched in one hand – came back to me. I ached suddenly at how beautiful she'd been. That night and every night. A snapshot of how she'd looked when she came in five hours later flashed across my mind as well – shoes in one hand, make-up rubbed off one eye, lipstick kissed off her mouth, hair streaked with the scents of different brands of cigarette smoke. She had stumbled into her living room and ended up in a heap on the floor. She'd been dishevelled but still pretty. Still beautiful.

I buried my face into the material, expecting it to smell of Del. Smell of how she did that night, maybe a few notes of her heady perfume mixed with her skin. Of course it didn't. The party had been over four years ago, so the jacket smelt of soap powder, like it should.

As I moved the jacket it crackled. I moved it again, and again it emitted a dry, papery sound. I shoved my hands into the jacket's pockets, and in the left one there was a folded-up envelope. I unfolded the white envelope and on the front, in clear letters, it said,

Kamryn Matika.

With a rapidly increasing heartbeat I stared at the thick white envelope in my hand for a few seconds, unsure how this was possible. And then scared of what it meant. What it would say. Because it was Adele. It was like all the other letters she'd sent me, the ones that sat unread and mostly forgotten at the bottom of my underwear drawer.

My finger was shaking as I slipped it under the flap of the envelope and opened the letter.

I unfolded the fifteen sheets of paper, all written in Adele's neat, considered handwriting. For someone as scatty as she was, Adele was very neat when it came to certain things.

Hey, Beautiful,

the letter began. I could almost hear her voice. Almost feel her lying beside me on the floor, propped up on one elbow, her legs curled under her.

Let me start by saying, I love you. I'm sure I never got the chance to say that to you before I died. Yes, this is weird. I'm sitting here in my father's house, writing this knowing I'm going to be gone when you read this. I know I'm dead because you wouldn't have this if I wasn't, would you?

I love you, Kam. I've only ever been loved by two people in my life - you and Tegan - and I love the pair of you more than anything.

But I know what you're like, Kamryn Matika - you're a stubborn bitch who shuts down whenever the going gets tough. So I know you won't have let me explain what happened with Nate. And you need to know, Kam, you really do. It wasn't what you thought, it wasn't an affair, it wasn't like we ever thought about the other person in that way . . .

323

chapter thirty-six

It wasn't what Kamryn thought, it wasn't an affair, it wasn't like we ever thought about the other person in that way. I never longed for Nate romantically or sexually, he was such a dear, precious friend, almost as close to me as Kam, it was just, when it happened, it was a time when everything was so mixed up. So many things were going on. It was messy when it started and the end was just, what's a word more extreme than messy? I can't think, but that's what it was.

Kamryn never understood how much Nate loved her. She loved him back, of course, but he'd do anything for her, his love for her was limitless, I think. Unconditional. She could have done virtually anything to him and he would've forgiven her. I'm not sure that's very healthy but that's how it was.

I was always a little in awe of how much Nathaniel loved her. And it must have been love from the outset because she was awful to him. Even when they got together properly. The shit I went through to become her friend was nothing compared to how she treated him. How sarky she was, offish, snappish and downright rude. But, he stuck it out. Cut through all her bullshit and proved every single day how much he cared. She often said that I didn't know him, didn't know what he could be like, that he often needed her to prop him up, but she didn't say that resentfully, I think it was her way of showing that it was a two-way thing. That whilst he loved her unconditionally, she cared for him in ways that weren't immediately obvious. I thought

I was going to die with happiness the day she said they'd decided to get married.

Even then, though, Kamryn didn't quite believe that Nate was for real. I could see it sometimes, in the way she'd get a concerned look across her face when he left the table. She'd always wonder if he was taking the mick, if he'd mutate into one of the controlling bastards who'd plagued her past. She worried, constantly and unnecessarily, that he'd find someone else. She'd start conversations about whether love really lasted for ever. 'What happens to love when you've been together so long that you can't remember the reasons why you got together in the first place?' she said once. 'When you're together and it's fine but it's not the be all and end all.' When she saw my face she covered by saying, 'I'm just wondering. I'm allowed to wonder.'

The time it happened, Nathaniel was so torn up. He'd just come back from driving Kam to Leeds, where she was going for business. He often did that, would drive her up there, then drive back again that day because he got to spend all that time with her. And when she was ready to leave, he'd drive up there to get her again. She never asked him to, he simply wanted to do it. Anyway, he drove her there and then dropped by my flat on the way back because Kamryn had told him to. She worried, you see, about me being on my own if she wasn't around, so she'd told him to go check on me when he got back to London. He was knackered, exhaustion showed on every line of his face, his clothes crumpled, his skin pale, but there was something else. He was troubled, hurting. I could see it the second I opened the door.

He flopped onto one of my sofas and refused the drink I offered him. He said he wouldn't stay long, just wanted to make sure I was all right.

'I'm fine, but you're obviously not – what's the matter, Nathaniel?' I asked.

'Nothing.'

'Ah, right, that's why you look like death then, is it?'

He rubbed his hand across his eyes, stared into space for a moment.

325

Then he exhaled. 'I think Kamryn's going to leave me. She's found someone else.'

'Don't be silly,' I said, trying to be honest.

'She has. I can tell. I know my fiancée, I know how she gets when she's in love, and she's definitely met someone else. She can hardly look me in the eye nowadays and she won't talk to me – not even to snipe at me. This drive up North was hell – five hours of virtual silence.'

'Nathaniel, if there's one thing I know for sure, it's that Kamryn would never jeopardise your relationship. She wouldn't even look at another man.'

He shook his head. 'You're terrible at lying, Adele. But thanks for trying. I need to work out what to do for the best. But I can't seem to think.'

'She really hasn't done anything,' I reassured him. 'And she wouldn't. Kam's not the cheating kind.'

'No, she's not. My ex was, she did it for years and I put up with it. I couldn't bear it with Kam. Not after . . . I know she wouldn't physically cheat but I reckon I should end it before she leaves me.'

I was horrified. By the hopelessness in his voice, by the fact he was going to end their relationship. I had to make him understand that it was a glitch. 'Look, Nate, she's not going to leave you. Now, say, hypothetically, she's met someone. Maybe at work. This is all just hypothetical, remember. And, say she clicked with this person and they started to spend lunchtimes together, had a laugh. That is all it would be. A laugh. Maybe she'd start to question certain aspects of her life, but Kamryn would never give you up. Not for anyone. We both know she's never loved anyone but you.'

'Yeah,' Nate breathed. He raked his fingers through his hair. 'I'm so confused . . . Do you mind if I lie down for a second before I go home?'

'Course. You lie down, get some rest.'

Nathaniel went to lie down in Kamryn's old room, while I watched telly. Hours later, I went in to check on him. He was sound asleep when I crouched down by the bed and, bless him, he looked so peaceful. Angelic. I jumped a little when his eyes flew open and he was *suddenly wide awake and staring at me. I don't know if it was because he'd looked so beautiful in his sleep, if I'd forgotten who he was, or if I'd just taken leave of my senses, but I did it. It was all my fault.*

I kissed him.

Nathaniel looked surprised, then jerked his head away. That shocked me back to reality and I remembered who he was, that I didn't fancy him, that I'd done a stupid, terrible thing. I turned to run away, horrified that I'd kissed my best friend's fiancé, but he grabbed my arm, stopped me. I was scared as I turned back because I knew he wasn't going to shout at me, I knew what was going to happen. We kissed again, and then it happened. It wasn't frantic and lust-fuelled. It was slow. Loving, gentle, beautiful. I'm sorry, it's not what Kamryn would want to hear but I want to make it clear that it wasn't about us fancying each other, about feelings building up over time that we couldn't ignore. It was about two people who had different reasons for doing what they did. No man had been nice to me like that in a long time. And for that little while, I could pretend that the person I was with cared about me, was making love to me rather than just fucking me. That's what most of the sex I'd experienced up until then was — fucking, sex without emotion. I know Kamryn could do that without it hurting too much, but that was because Kam had got used to compartmentalising her life so early on. She had to shut off bits of herself so she wouldn't hurt from the bullying and the ill treatment from men. I'd never got the hang of it. I was always too much, as I once told Kam. I'm too much. Too everything all the time. I couldn't put bits of myself away no matter how much hurt I'd been through. So each time I had sex without love I could barely convince myself that it was OK, that I didn't feel worthless and lonely afterwards. With Nate, for those few moments, I could pretend he cared about me. It wasn't real but it felt real, for a little while.

When I woke up, Nathaniel was fully clothed and sat on the edge of the bed. 'I'm really sorry,' he whispered. 'So, so sorry.'

Even in the dark I could see how ashamed he was. I was too. 'What have I done? How am I going to make this right? I've done the worst thing possible,' he said. I knew how bad he was feeling because I felt that same anguish. Only, I'd been far worse than him. I'd known Kam for longer, I'd been there when all those other men had treated her like dirt and I'd just done something far worse, first by kissing him, then by making love to him. *'When she gets back,'* he was saying, *'I'll finish with her and move out. She doesn't want to be with me anyway, so I'll tell her what I've done. But I won't say it's you. I'll say it's some girl I met in a bar, and then I'll go. She doesn't need to know about you, this doesn't have to ruin your friendship.'*

I couldn't let him take the rap for this. We'd both done it. And he was so decent that in his mortification all he could think about was making things better for me. We talked and talked until we agreed we'd put it behind us. We'd forget all about it. And it worked. We didn't fancy each other, neither of us had any wish to repeat it, so it didn't become an issue.

Then I found out I was pregnant. I knew straight away he was the father and I knew I couldn't tell anyone. Not Kamryn. And definitely not Nathaniel. He would have confessed and Kam would have left me.

It's selfish, I know, but I couldn't bear that thought – Kam leaving. When she did go, it broke my heart. I knew what she was like, she'd never stop to listen. She'd only think of it as betrayal, which it was. But it wasn't like Nathaniel and I loved each other in that way. We'd simply done something unbelievably stupid. And I can't even say I wish it hadn't happened because that would be wishing away Tegan. Would she be Tegan without her nose, her talent for drawing, that unusual royal blue of her eyes if she wasn't Nate's child? Of course she wouldn't. After everything I went through with my family, having a blood relative who loved me as much as I loved her was the most important thing in the world. I hadn't planned on getting pregnant, but I didn't regret it once it had happened.

That sounds awful and I don't blame Kamryn for being so angry. I just want to apologise. I wish I had the time to explain it to her. I wish I had enough time to try, in the smallest way, to put it right.

328

chapter thirty-seven

When it was over, I sat on my sofa staring into the mid distance. I couldn't move.

Adele was there with me. I could feel her. As though she was sitting beside me, and now, having relayed her story, was waiting for my reaction. Waiting to hear what I had to say, feel what I had to express.

I turned my head and she wasn't there. She wasn't sitting beside me on the floor, her hair wild around her face, her vest top stretched tight over her toned body. She wasn't looking at me with fear and anticipation in her steel blue eyes. Slowly the feel of her faded, evaporated into the ether, and I was sitting alone in my living room.

Why? Why had Nate done it? I now knew it was an impulse for her. That was what she was like, impulsive, spontaneous. Act first, think later. But Nate thought everything through. Even if it seemed to be an instant thought, it would have been one of the many things he spent time brooding on. He said the other day he was feeling low at the time it happened, was that one of the ways he made himself feel better? Imagining making love to Adele? Had he been waiting for the chance, which eventually presented itself?

I had to know. I picked up the phone, which was sitting in a cradle by the sofa and stared at the buttons. I couldn't call him, not with Tegan and Luke in the house. I launched myself off the sofa, moving like a mad woman, I went to the coat rack and grabbed my coat, I crushed the letter into one of the pockets, then shoved my bare feet into Luke's trainers, not caring that they were too big for me. I opened the door, slipping my keys into my pockets. Shutting the door quietly, I crept down the stairs and outside into the bleak midwinter night.

Standing outside in the navy-black night outside my flat, I dialled his number, and after its fifth ring his sleep-musty voice croaked, 'Hello?'

'Why did you do it?' I asked, louder than I intended.

'What?' he replied. There were muffled sounds as he moved in bed.

'Why did you do it?' I repeated. 'Why?'

'Kam?' He coughed to clear his throat. 'It's 4 a.m., what are you doing?'

'I have to know. She told me. She told me what happened; I know why she did it. But I don't know why you did. Why?'

'Jesus, Kam, what are you doing? Where are you?'

'In the street.'

'What?' I could hear him wake up, sit up suddenly. 'The street where?'

I sniffed back cold-induced snot. 'I had to come outside because they're asleep . . . Why? Was I that terrible? I was, wasn't I?' Suddenly it felt as though my internal organs were being crushed, compressed by a vice. I gripped the phone tighter, as the pain intensified. 'I'm sorry,' I gasped. 'I was such a bitch. I knew you'd leave me one day because I was such a bitch.'

'Kam, I'm coming over. Stay where you are. I'll be there soon, OK?'

I nodded.

'Kam?'

I sniffed. 'Yes,' I said in a small voice.

'OK.' His voice was clearer, stronger, he was obviously standing up. 'I'll be there soon.'

Nearly thirty-five minutes later the silver Audi driven by my ex drew up outside my building, and I straightened up from my position huddled against the brick archway entrance. I'd had my arms wrapped around myself the whole time, trying to keep warm.

He'd obviously dressed in a hurry: black jogging bottoms, a heavily creased black T-shirt and a navy-blue fleece. There were no socks with his trainers, he hadn't even had time to spike up his hair into its usual style so it was partially sleep-crushed. He crossed the pavement towards my flat as I came down the path to meet him. We met at my gate, his face a mix of confusion and worry and sleep. Unbidden, wild uncontrollable anger spiked through me. Before I knew what I was doing, my arm was raised and I'd slapped him across the face.

There was a lack of surprise on his face as his head moved slightly at the blow, he just cast his eyes down to the ground. Nothing was said for a few seconds, then Nate raised his hand to his slapped left cheek. 'That's been a long time coming,' he said.

I shoved him, he stumbled backwards. 'So has that.'

I pushed him again and he stumbled backwards again, this time against his car. I wanted to hit him, but was scared of actually hurting him. Because it was in me. The rage in me was enough to cause him permanent damage. 'Why?' I asked. 'Why did you pull her back? I know what she's like. I know she's impulsive. I know she would have kissed you and not meant it. But why did you pull her back? How could you do that? Why did you do that?'

Nate stayed huddled in his silence.

'Why Nate? What did I do? Was I that awful? I didn't mean to be. I just . . . I was a bitch.'

Nate looked up then, took me in his arms. 'Shhhh,' he hushed against my ear. 'Shhhh.' He continued hushing me until I stopped speaking.

'I always thought you didn't care that much,' Nate said, still holding me. 'You never reacted like this at the time and I thought you'd gone because of the betrayal. I never thought it had hurt you that much. It's hard to fathom you sometimes.'

'Of course I cared. I just couldn't speak about it. For more than two years I couldn't speak about it because it'd make me fall apart. And I knew it was me. I'd done it. I'd pushed you two together.'

'We were never like that, Kam. Adele and I were just friends.'

'So why did you pull her back? Kiss her? Make love to her? She told me, you know? She told me that she kissed you and was going to run away but you pulled her back. Why?'

'Because . . .'

I tensed in his arms, knowing he was going to say it was because I was rubbish. In bed and out of bed. That I was so rotten to him that he had to pay me back somehow. This had always been my terror, my fear, why I couldn't talk about it: what happened confirmed that I was different. Broken. Adele and Nate had come together because I was so awful.

'Because right after she kissed me and I pulled away from her, she looked so terrified. She bit her lower lip, her eyes all wide, and that simple action reminded me of you. That time when we first had sex. Afterwards you got dressed and were about to go home and I asked if I'd see you again, remember? You turned around, kissed your palm, blew me a kiss, said, "We'll see," and left. Just before you blew me the kiss you had that same expression on your face. You looked so scared, so surprised and I don't know whose mannerism it was first, but you bit your lower lip. It was only a fleeting thing, but it was so honest that I fell for you. And, that night with Adele, I was so confused about us, I knew we were almost over, and I saw

332

that look again. It reminded me of that moment I fell for you. I wanted it back. I wanted to make love to the you I fell for, not the one I'd been existing with for the past six months.

'I know it was wrong, but I did it. That's why I told you the other day I took responsibility for it. What I did was selfish, it was all about me and trying to get back what I couldn't. I hate myself, but the whole time I was thinking about you. I'm not just saying that, I was. She had a different body to yours so it almost felt like that first time with you. I did that to Adele. I used her to make myself feel better. And then I was a complete bastard to her when she told you what we'd done. She didn't realise that I was blaming her for something that was my fault. Do you have any idea how much I hate myself for not making things right with her before she died?'

'Yes,' I replied. 'Because I hate myself more.'

Nate pulled away from me slightly. 'You didn't sort things out with her? But you took Tegan . . . How did you know what happened that night?'

I pulled the balled-up letter from my pocket. 'I just found it,' I explained. 'I thought you knew that I didn't know. Why do you think I called you now? I just found out.'

'You never talked to her?'

I shook my head.

'Oh God, Kam . . .' He pulled me close. 'Why not?'

'I couldn't think about it, let alone talk about it. And then there was Tegan. You made her together. You two had something that I could never be a part of. I hated you both for that. You had a baby. I never wanted a baby but if I did want one, it would have been yours. You're the only person on earth I'd want to have a child with and you did it with someone else. Someone I loved. That's why I had to leave. I couldn't stay when you'd made a baby, a new life, with someone else.' I was incoherent. Every thought in my head rushing to come out at once. 'And I thought I had more time. I thought I had a few months to get used to the idea of having her back in my life, and then one day we'd have that conversation. But she died. She died so suddenly. I knew it was going to happen but when it did . . .' I pressed the palms of my hands onto my eyes. 'I wasn't ready . . . I didn't get to say goodbye. I didn't tell her that I was sorry. That I didn't hate her. I didn't tell her I loved her. I walked away not knowing that was the last time I'd ever see her.' Nate held me up as what little strength that had been holding me together, holding back my grief, disintegrated. 'I'm such a horrible person. She was dying and I didn't let her talk. I was too scared to hear it. But I wanted to say goodbye. I just wanted to say goodbye.'

Nate didn't say anything as he held me together. He'd never had to do this with me before. I was the strong one with Nate and me. He looked after me, sorted my life out, made the most amazing love to me – and I wasn't just talking sex. He gave me the kind of confidence I never thought I'd have. But when a crisis hit, it was me who sorted it out. Me who found a practical solution. Nate and I balanced each other out, and although he got to parts of me no one else had, he'd never had to deal with Kamryn in tears. Kamryn in breakdown.

'Babe,' he whispered in my ear as I cried, as everything I'd been feeling for weeks came gushing out in a tidal wave of emotion. I couldn't hold it back any longer and all of it came out. 'It's OK,' Nate reassured. 'It's OK.'

Eventually the tears stopped and I was dry crying, my body the only thing quivering. Then, my body stopped shaking and I stood empty, drained, in Nate's strong arms.

'I'm sorry,' I whispered, so tired I could hardly form words. 'I didn't mean to do that.' I mustered enough strength to push him away and rubbed at my red eyes, embarrassed at myself. I did know why I'd broken down like that. It'd been a long time coming but I didn't know why it'd been with him. If it'd been with anyone it should have been with Luke.

'It's all right,' Nate said, concern on his face and in his voice. 'You can talk to me any time.' He came towards me, as though to hold me again but I stepped out of reach, put my hands up to stop him. To halt this.

'Nate, this is so fucked up. I can't be breaking down in front of you. I've got a boyfriend, who I love. He's the one I should be crying with, not you. I just wanted to know why, that's all. I didn't mean to do this. I don't know why I did. You were there, I suppose.'

'Don't push me away,' he pleaded.

'You are away, Nate. The sooner we both get used to that, the better.' Even I lurched inside at the coldness in my voice.

He nodded slightly, abject misery on his face as he turned away.

'I'm sorry,' I blurted at him. I couldn't let him go like that. What if it was the last time I saw him? What if it was like Adele all over again? 'I didn't mean to say that. I'm sorry, OK? I'm sorry for saying that. I'm sorry for hitting you. And for shoving you. I'm sorry for all of it. I'm sorry.'

He stopped opening his car door, rotated on the spot towards me. 'I'm sorry too. I never said that but I am. I'm sorry for what I did. For breaking up our relationship. For wrecking your friendship with Adele. For hurting you so badly. I'm truly sorry.'

I nodded. Nate had aged since the last time I saw him. Time had become ingrained in his face. He was weary. His eyes were bloodshot, his mouth, the beautiful mouth with which he'd asked me to repeat my marriage proposal, was pressed into a grim line.

'I'll talk to you soon,' I said.

'Yeah,' he replied. His car started as I opened the main front door.

Upstairs, I quietly opened the front door to my flat. I didn't even notice that the lounge light was off. I hung my coat up on the rack and kicked off Luke's shoes. Barefoot, I crept into the bedroom.

I jumped when I found Luke, fully dressed in jeans and his thick-knit blue jumper, sat on the bed. The room was dark but he looked as though he'd been waiting for me to return so he could leave. I noticed his feet were covered in his socks but no shoes, he'd been unable to go because I'd been wearing his trainers.

'I saw Nate outside,' Luke stated quietly. 'What's going on?' His face was angry but also afraid, if he'd been watching from the window then he'd probably seen Nate holding me, stroking my hair as he comforted me. Luke probably thought Nate and I were about to get back together. Nothing could be further from the truth. I moved slowly towards my bed and climbed onto it, lay down, curled up in the foetal position.

'Give us a cuddle,' I asked.

Luke hesitated, then did as I asked, curled up around me. I relaxed against him, he was warm and comforting after the cold and brutalness of the outside. I covered his hands with mine and my fingers began to thaw.

'What's going on?' he murmured, anxiety in his voice.

In short bursts, I told him.

'i'm not precious,
i'm tegan'

chapter thirty-eight

'Mummy Ryn,' Tegan said quietly. So quietly that I wouldn't have heard it if I hadn't been waiting for it.

I knew what she was going to say because over the past couple of weeks Tegan had changed. She had become restless. It took her nearly an hour to settle at night; she'd often come into my room in the middle of the night, and would only go back to her bed if I sat with her until she fell asleep again. Her appetite had halved, she'd retreated into quietness, and she'd taken to drawing pictures of a woman who could only have been her mother, but if I asked who was in the picture she'd shrug and whisper, 'Don't know.' I knew what she was thinking because I was thinking it too. I too had become edgy and restless – my insomnia had gone from chronic to critical, I got at most four hours of sleep a night – during the day I could barely summon the energy to open my emails and I didn't return any of Nate's emails and calls.

'Yes, Tiga?' I replied.

She lay stretched out on the floor in front of the television, colouring in a picture of Luke at work. She put down her blue felt-tip pencil, with which she was filling in the body of Luke's shirt, and regarded me with caution. Her pink lips were twisted in thought and her eyes slightly narrowed, she tucked a lock of blonde hair behind her ear. She didn't say anything, just looked at me. I patted my lap to get her to clamber up.

'You know it's Christmas?' she said cautiously as she settled in my lap. I linked my arms around her body and nodded. Christmas was in just under three weeks, she'd finish school in five days and would go to the Kayes' house during the day. It was Christmas outside and in the flat – we had a small tree that lived next to the TV where the beanbag had once been, decorations were up, lights were in the window, cards sat on every flat surface, every day Tegan opened the chocolate advent calendar that Luke had bought – but inside us the festive spirit was absent. Where Christmas excitement should be was an ache. Memories. We hadn't discussed what we were doing on the big day yet, and every time Luke tried to bring it up, I changed the subject, or said I hadn't had time to think about whether we were going to London to be with my folks or not. Christmas in London wasn't an option – I was simply putting him off until Tegan and I could talk properly. We hadn't been able to do that until now, when Luke was in New York for a week on business (Angeles were thinking of opening up a store or a franchise over there and his experience of that market meant he was off playing with the big boys). I'd decided to leave the start of the conversation to Tegan, to wait and see if she'd properly remembered or if I was worrying about nothing.

'Yes, sweetheart, I know it's Christmas soon,' I replied.

'It's . . .' Her voice died in her dry throat.

'It's your mummy's birthday,' I finished for her.

She nodded.

'I know,' I said. Adele's birthday was Christmas Day. When Tegan was very young we'd have a double celebration – Adele's birthday in the morning, then lunch would be Christmas, and then after Tegan had gone to bed it'd be

Adele's birthday again, and me, Nate and Adele would drink ourselves stupid.

'Do they have birthdays in heaven?' she asked.

'Erm . . .' I didn't know. I never knew the answer to these questions. I didn't think about it. I was religious, but I'd never thought about the physicality of the afterlife. If I thought about heaven, it was to think that I might one day end up there. But not if time passed. Not if birthdays happened. And because I didn't think about it, I wasn't able to answer these questions. Was heaven a place with big white clouds, or was it a place like this, only better? Was it a Technicolor world where everything was fantastic and everyone was happy or was it whatever you needed it to be? 'Erm . . . Maybe,' I replied carefully. 'I don't see why not.'

'If I sent her a card, would she get it?'

'I don't think so,' I replied gently.

Tegan curled up against my torso, buried her head against my chest. Her shoulders started to shake, and then her whole body. Her sobs slowly became audible. She hadn't cried in front of me since her mum died, since that day in the hotel. I didn't know this would be the thing that would set her off, that revealed the rivers of pain that flowed through her.

'I'm sorry, sweetie, but we'll think of another way to let her know that we're thinking of her, OK?'

Tegan slipped off my lap, ran out of the room, her feet pounded the corridor carpet to her bedroom, but she didn't slam the door. After a few minutes of controlling myself, I got up, followed Tegan to her room.

On her blue and white duvet, Tegan was a pink and purple crescent shape that shook with long, keening cries. Tears streamed down her face, and her little hands kept wiping them away. Beside her on her pillow she'd placed the picture of her and Adele that usually sat on top of her television.

'Tiga . . .' I began, then realised I didn't know what to say.

I sat on the bed beside her, rubbed her back. I stared at the picture of Adele, at the woman who grinned happily beside her daughter. I'd almost forgotten that's what she looked like. Now, when I thought of Adele, she was that grey shadow from the hospital morgue.

'Why isn't my mummy coming back?' Tegan asked through her hiccuppy sobs. 'Was I a bad girl?'

'No, sweetheart,' I said. 'Your mummy was just ill.'

'You were ill,' she said.

'I know, but I was a different kind of ill. Your mummy was very, very ill and she couldn't get better. She wanted to be here, but she was too sick.'

'I want her to come back,' she insisted.

'So do I.' A thought blossomed in my mind. 'Tiga, have you been thinking that your mummy is coming back?'

'Yes,' she whispered. She nodded her head, hiccupped a few more tears. 'She might not like heaven and come back. She might like Leeds more.'

Adele and I did a great job of explaining death to her, didn't we? 'I'm sorry, baby, your mummy isn't coming back. Not ever.'

The gulps and their accompanying wail increased in volume and distress. It tore through me because I knew how she felt. I knew how that realisation, the final acceptance that you weren't going to see that person again, was like a sword through your heart. I scooped Tegan into my arms, held her warm body close to me, trying to envelope her in comfort. A memory began to glint in my mind then slowly solidified, became a hard shaft of light amongst my memories: Tegan was a month old. Adele had asked me to watch her daughter while she took a shower. I perched on the bed, in Adele's bedroom, staring at the blue and white carry cot. Tegan was still pink and wrinkly with the finest covering of fair hair on her blotchy head. Adele had dressed her in a blue Babygro and she was

342

sleeping under a couple of white blankets. She'd stirred the second her mother shut the bathroom door, almost as though she knew Mummy was more than a foot away. The shower came on and Tegan woke up and let forth the loudest cry I'd ever heard. I'd frozen for a moment, convinced she would stop, but no, the gaping hole of her mouth showed no sign of abating, her eyes were squeezed shut and her face was filling with red from the wailing. I reached into the crib, pulled back the blankets and picked her up. She was incredibly light. I'd held her in the month since she'd been born but I kept forgetting how light she was. I rearranged the squalling bundle in my arms and rocked her, hushing her, willing her to understand that her mum would be back soon and she could get fed some more if she wanted. By the time a wet-haired Adele returned, Tegan had stopped her howling and was moving her lips at me, her unfocused eyes staring up at me as though I was about to reveal the secrets of the universe to her. 'Tell me again how you don't want kids,' Adele whispered as she came back to the bed, lay down and tried to get a little sleep.

'I rocked you like this when you were born,' I said into Tegan's hair. 'You were so funny looking when you were born, when you were a little baby. I thought, Gosh, have they given us the right baby at the hospital? She's real funny looking. But then you smiled, and you looked just like your mummy, just as pretty as your mummy, and I knew you had to be hers. Ours. Because you were mine too, you know? You were my little Tiga. Even when I was away for all that time I thought of you. I had your picture in my purse and when people said, "Who's that?" I'd say, "That's my little Tiga."

'I'm sorry your mummy's not here, Tiga. I wish she was. Every day I wish she was and I know it's going to be hard to get used to. Why don't we call Christmas Day, Adele Day? Adele was your mummy's name, you know that, don't you?'

'Yes,' she whispered.

'OK, we'll have Adele Day. We'll make special Adele Day cards and send them to everyone we know. And we can draw pictures of her and I'll show you some of the pictures in my photo albums. We can even make a special Bung It for our tea. Hmmm? What do you say?'

'Is Luke going to come?' She'd stopped crying, that was something.

'No. It'll just be me and you. No boys allowed!'

'What about Mr Nate?' she asked.

'Yeuck! No! He's a boy! No boys allowed! And, just so we don't miss out on Christmas, we can have it the next day. And open our presents then.'

'Luke can come to that one, can't he?' Tegan asked.

'If you want him to,' I said.

'I do. And Mr Nate.'

'Really? Why?' That was something I never thought I'd hear her say. He was nice to her, the three or four times she'd seen him since their first meeting, but he wasn't Luke. And each time he'd dropped by, it'd been for ten minutes at the most, why would she want to spend such an important day with him?

'You like him,' she said simply, sniffling back tears.

'But he doesn't have to come to our Christmas Day if you don't like him.' There was a note of panic in my voice. I hadn't seen him since our confrontation in the street a fortnight ago. I hadn't spoken to him or returned his emails – I'd been actively avoiding him. Luke sure as hell wouldn't want him around, either.

'I do like him. He's funny.' That surprised me even more. What had he done to make her say he was funny?

'All right, I'll see if he can come. He might not be free, though, so we mustn't be upset if he can't make it.'

I cuddled her closer. Inhaling her smell of cinnamon and cherries from the bubble bath Luke had bought her. I didn't like to see Tegan upset. I didn't like to know she was hurting. Of course she was hurting, but life was easier if I pretended that Tegan didn't understand what was going on.

'It's all right to cry, you know,' I said. I'd stopped her doing that. Not intentionally, but I'd felt better when she did stop. It might not be pleasant for the listener, it might disempower and unsettle the witness to a breakdown, but crying was good. Crying was an acceptable outlet, even if it made you feel raw and empty inside, it was still better than that build up of resentment that grew from not letting your emotions out. I didn't want Tegan to grow up angry and bitter because she'd been denied the opportunity to express her grief. 'If you feel sad about your mummy or you miss her, you can cry any time you want. You can talk about her any time you want to as well.' I stroked the long, fine waves of her hair. 'It's all right to miss your mummy, you know, I do understand, and anything you want to say, I will listen.'

'I'm going to sleep now,' she mumbled.

'OK, precious.'

She shook her head, and gave a glum giggle. 'I'm not Precious, I'm Tegan.'

A joke she and her mother had. 'Are you sure now? I could have sworn you were called Precious.'

'No, my name's Tegan.'

'OK, *Tegan,* you go to sleep. I'll sit here for a while, if you don't mind, and then I'll go make us some lunch.'

'OK.' She crawled out of my lap and under her covers, lay facing away from me. I went to the window and pulled her blue curtains across to darken the room from the midday light. I sat on the floor by the bed, watching her sleep, like I did sometimes in the middle of the night. She took karate lessons, she'd joined the football team, she spoke to Luke and me like she was an adult, but I kept forgetting she was fragile. I resisted the urge to stroke her hair away from her pale, tight face, just watched her

345

features relax as her breathing slowed and she slipped away into sleep. Poor fragile Tegan. My poor, poor baby.

'What and what?' was Luke's reply when I told him the plan for Christmas Day and Boxing Day. We hadn't seen him in the two days since he'd returned from America because he'd been to London for meetings about New York. I'd been dreading telling him and decided away from Tegan was the best plan, which meant doing the deed at work.

He stood over my desk, arms folded, imposing in his charcoal grey suit, white shirt and blue tie. I was always amazed that despite the hours he worked and despite spending time at our place, he still managed to maintain his gym-made body. My head moved up slowly to Luke's face, and when I met his eyes my fears of visual contact were realised – the unusual hazel colour of his eyes added a flint-like quality to the stare that burned accusation and displeasure at me. He wasn't simply upset he was deeply aggrieved – his jaw began a slow grinding motion.

'I don't get to spend Christmas Day with you two, but I do get to spend Boxing Day with your ex?' Luke said when I didn't reply. He looked over his shoulder at the glass walls of my office, then up at the ceiling, before sweeping his unimpressed gaze back to me. 'Am I on a hidden camera show? Because that's the only way this can be happening.'

'I have to do this for Tegan. It has to be just us on Christmas Day. And she's the one who suggested Nate come on Boxing Day, not me.'

'What if I come over in the evening?' he asked with an American twang – a week in New York brought out the shades of his Stateside accent again.

'Luke, no. This is for Tegan. It's her mum's birthday, the first big event since Adele . . . since Adele . . . *died*. I can't believe you can't see how important that is.'

'I do. It's just . . . I don't have a family, either, remember? I

346

usually spend Christmas in New York with friends but this year, I turned them down because I thought I had a family to spend it with.'

'And you have, just not on the twenty-fifth.'

Luke's face crunched into a frown as his mouth flattened into a line of anger.

'What do you want me to do, Luke? Put you before my child?'

For a moment, he was going to say yes. I could see it on his face, in his eyes, in the way his lips twitched.

'Is that the sort of person you want me to be? The sort of woman you want to date?' I added to stop him saying something he didn't mean. 'I don't need this, you know? It's going to be a hard enough day without worrying if you're going to dump me because you can't be there. I'm sorry, Luke, but Tegan comes first. It's only dawning on her now that her mum isn't coming back, I'm not going to let her down by going back on what I promised. And I don't regret promising it.'

The black phone on my desk rang, and I glanced at the LCD display to get the number. I didn't recognise it, so picked it up, put it to my ear. 'Kamryn Matika, how can I help you?' Luke stood and watched me.

'It's me,' Nate said.

'Oh, hi,' I said. The temperature in the room rose suddenly. I pressed my phone closer to my ear so that Luke wouldn't hear his voice or what he was saying.

'I know you're at work so you can't talk for long, but you don't return my calls to your mobile or reply to my emails,' he said. He spoke without accusation, in fact, the only thing I detected in his tone was understanding. 'I wanted to talk to you about Christmas.'

'Oh,' I replied.

'I know it's Adele's birthday, well, would have been Adele's birthday and I was wondering what you were doing? It's going to be hard on you and Tegan, I was wondering if you wanted to spend the day together like we used to?'

'I was going to call you about that actually,' I eyed up Luke, who was the model of disinterest, perched on the end of my desk, leafing through pages for the new issue of the magazine that were languishing in my in-tray.

'Really?' Nate's voice lifted.

'Yeah, Tegan and I are spending the twenty-fifth alone but she was wondering if you were free on the twenty-sixth, when we're having Christmas Day.'

Luke stopped at a particularly interesting proof page of a list of the concessions we had in various Angeles stores and read it, several times, as he waited for Nate's answer.

'Is Luke going to be there?' Nate asked.

'Of course.'

'Then I don't think it's a good idea, do you? Much as I'd love to, I don't think the four of us would have a good time. How about I come over on Christmas Eve and give you your presents then?'

'OK,' I said, relieved. Greatly relieved. Not only because Luke would spend the whole day – and probably the following month – in a foul mood, but because I didn't want to spend time with Nate. The elements of our relationship – our deceased relationship – had altered with the knowledge of why he'd slept with someone else. He hadn't done it out of malice, he'd been driven to it by loneliness. I could understand those feelings. I'd had them so many times in my life, and for him to have had them when he was with me . . . That meant a lot of things about me. My constant fear that I'd driven him to do it was right, but I was wrong about how I'd driven him to it. I hadn't bitched him into it, I'd withdrawn from him. I'd abandoned him, left him lonely. Of course, he didn't have to sleep with someone else, but he was only human. We'd all done stupid things in moments of weakness: I'd flirted with the guy from Scotland I'd got close to at work; I'd almost slept with Ted that time in the hotel room. I understood a little more about Nate now, and that modicum of knowledge was dangerous.

'Christmas Eve, then,' he said. 'Can I see you before then?'

'Erm, I don't know if that's a good idea,' I replied, after a sideways look at Luke who was still reading Angeles's concession list.

'What about Tegan? Do I get to see her before then?'

'If you want. I can drop her off at your place for an hour or so.' There was no way in hell I would do it but this was a test – did he really want to see Tegan or to see me?

'Or I could come over and you could go out for an hour?' he replied. 'Less disruptive for her?'

'You know that's not going to happen, don't you?'

'Not now, maybe, but in time, it might. I do genuinely want to see her. And you, of course.'

'Nate, I'm busy.'

'He's there, isn't he?'

I sighed. 'OK, I'll call you, maybe you can come over at the weekend, I'll see if Tegan's up for it.'

'OK. I'll see you soon.'

'Bye, Nate.'

'OK, babe, love you, bye.' Click went the phone as he hung up. BOOM! went my mind as I repeated what he said in my head. With a trembling hand I put down the receiver.

'Is he coming for Christmas?' Luke asked.

I shook my head, afraid to look at him in case my face betrayed what was going on in my mind. Nate had said it so easily. No big deal. Two words dropped into a conversation. It's what he always said when we were together, how he'd always ended our conversations. 'He's, erm, busy, probably going to his parents' place. He's going to come over on Christmas Eve instead, just to drop off Tegan's presents.'

'Ryn?' Luke began. I turned to look at him, hoping my face

349

wouldn't betray what Nate had done to me. My boyfriend's face creased in a shy smile, the anger gone. 'I'm sorry for being such an ass earlier. I do understand, I'm just disappointed is all.'

'I know.'

'No, you don't know. For the first time in my life I've got a family, I've got you and a kid, I never had a child I could spoil at Christmas. Do you know how excited I was? Christmas is a time for families, so I wanted to be with you both. But the twenty-sixth will be OK. It'll be great, in fact.'

I nodded.

After checking no one had returned early from lunch and could see into mine and Betsy's glass-walled office, Luke leant forwards, kissed me quick. 'See you tonight, babe.'

'Yeah, see you tonight.'

He left my office. And when he left, the thumping of my heart at what Nate said increased. I could replay it, hold it up to the light like a precious jewel, examine its perfect facets. 'Love you, babe, bye.' Nate's smooth voice telling me he still felt how he did before, was something I hadn't expected to happen. I suspected he still had feelings for me, but he'd said he loved me. Did I love him? If I did, what would it mean for our lives? And it would be *our* lives. Who I chose to be with wasn't only about who I wanted to be with, Tegan's feelings counted as much as mine. If she wasn't around, I know who I'd choose. I'd make my choice in a heartbeat.

My mobile bleeped on the desk beside my mouse. When I opened the message from Luke, it said:

Forgot to say, I love you :)

I cleared the message, almost threw the phone down onto the desk.

Do I really know who I'd choose? Do I?

chapter thirty-nine

Adele Day dawned and Tegan was out of bed before light managed to break cover and peek through the night sky.

The sound of her footsteps padding down the corridor had stirred me from the light sleep I'd spent most of the night drifting in and out of. And as her head popped round the door, I struggled upright and blinked awakeness onto my face.

'Am I allowed to come in?' Tegan asked.

In all the time we'd lived together she'd never asked if it was all right to come into a room, I didn't understand where her sudden reticence came from. 'Course,' I replied. She walked slowly in, climbed up on the bed and under my covers.

'Do you want breakfast first or your present?' I encircled her with my arm as I spoke, pulling her into the nook that she fitted so neatly in.

'I'm allowed a present?' she asked.

'Yes, of course, Madam. This is Adele Day, which of course means a present. Afterwards we can have breakfast and you can ring Nana Faith. It's up to you.'

Tegan's eyes widened as she thought about what to do. All the possibilities. 'Present,' she whispered after much rumination and lip screwing.

'OK,' I said. I shifted in bed, opened the drawer at the top of my bedside table and pulled out her present, a gold box with a red ribbon around it. 'Here you go.'

Tegan's eyes widened some more as she took the box with two hands. She sat staring at it, slight apprehension on her heart-shaped face. 'What is it?' she asked.

Any other chid would have ripped the box open by now, but not Tegan, she had to think it through, find out all she could before diving in head first. I was like that, always a bit cautious, Adele would've had the box open the second she saw it was for her. That's what came from having romance in your soul, I suppose. You believed in things like love at first sight and perfect presents.

'Open it and find out,' I advised.

Tegan didn't move for a couple of seconds before she started playing with the ribbon, trying to untie it, until she realised that, like the white laces on her favourite pair of trainers, if she tugged on one end, the whole thing would come apart. She cautiously lifted the lid of the box and gazed inside.

'Is it really for me?' she gasped, her head snapping up to search my face for any hint that I might take it back. I nodded.

Carefully, like she did most things, she reached into the box and from its bed of blue silk padding she picked up the gold necklace with a disc hanging from it. She stared hard at the disc, brought it right up to her face and scrutinised the dark, holographic picture on it.

'It's me and my mummy,' she said eventually.

'It sure is,' I replied. I'd had a photo of Tegan and Adele copied onto the disc.

'Can I wear it all the time?' she asked, staring at the neck-lace in her hands.

'If you want to. It's up to you.'

She held it out to me to put on. I took the chain from her, and instructed her, 'Lift up your hair so I can hook it up at the back,' before I slipped the chain around her slender neck.

'There,' I said, when I'd finished. She let her hair fall back into place, and I wondered as her blonde locks touched her shoulders if I should get her hair cut.

I hadn't done so in the past few months because it hadn't, if I was honest, occurred to me. I got my hair straightened and cut every eight weeks, but I hadn't noticed that Tegan might need the same thing. She didn't have split ends, as far as I noticed, and it was always conditioned when we washed it of a night. Hair that flowed down to touch the middle of her back suited her, though. When she played sports I put her hair into a ponytail then wrapped it around in a bun, secured in place with pins. When she wore it loose it complemented the shape of her face and the slight slant of her eyes, making her prettier, if that was possible. Sometimes she asked me for corno's (I'd eventually worked out she meant cornrows, which I used to put in her hair when she was young). I reserved them for special occasions because plaiting her hair in neat rows away from her face took time. She suited them better than Bo Derek in *10*, and she loved it when I took them out and her hair was all wavy.

I stroked her hair, smiled at her gazing down at her medallion. I liked Tegan with long hair, but what would Adele have wanted? What would Adele think of Tegan having longer than shoulder-length hair? Her daughter's hair had always been cut when it reached chin-length. Tegan hadn't complained about that, and she didn't complain about it being long, but what would Adele say?

Does it matter? I thought, mutinously. *In the grand scheme of things, does it matter what Adele would have wanted? She's not here.* Guilt skipped close behind those rebellious thoughts. Luke had planted those seeds of mutiny in my mind a few days ago.

I'd been pondering aloud if I should send Tegan to middle school, or if I should wait and send her to a comprehensive, and if I'd have to move to get into a good catchment area and would I have to do that now? But wasn't Horsforth a good part of Leeds? I explained to Luke that I hadn't ever had that discussion with Adele, I didn't know if Adele would want her daughter to go to an all-girls' school where the pupils were said to perform better than they did when they were in a mixed school, or a mixed school where she'd learn that she had to compete with males in the real world anyway.

Luke had listened to all I had to say on the matter before replying, 'You're not Adele.'

I'd been offended. Did he really think I was stupid enough to believe I could replace her in Tegan's life? Had I not explained to him on many an occasion that my biggest worry was that I couldn't be an Adele substitute? 'I know that,' I replied.

'Well then stop trying to be her,' he'd said, from my bed. He was working on his laptop while I was working on the computer. 'You call Tegan your daughter, so act like she is. Stop trying to second guess what Adele would have wanted and do what you want. She's your responsibility not Adele's.'

I'd frowned at him, and he'd set aside his laptop, raised an eyebrow as he waited for a reply. 'I know she's my responsibility,' I eventually said.

'I'm not saying you're not taking responsibility for her, babe, it's just that it's very easy to become frozen. You could worry so much about what Adele would want that you do nothing. And, I hate to say this, but it's the ultimate fallback, isn't it? If things go wrong, you don't have to accept you made a bum decision because you can say it was what Adele would have wanted and not you that messed up.'

I bit my lower lip as I dropped my eyes away. 'I don't do that.'

'I would, if I was in your position,' he admitted. He stretched and scratched his hairless chest. 'It's a get out of jail free card. Who the hell wouldn't use it if they had someone they could pass the buck to every time something went south?'

'I'm doing the best I can,' I replied, feeling chastised and caught out, even though I seriously hadn't ever thought like that. Tegan was Adele's daughter so of course I was going to do whatever it took to make sure that she was brought up how Adele would have wanted. But he had a point – she was my baby now. My burden. My hope. My love. Everything, good or bad, was down to me. From now on, the personality traits that she developed, the habits, the foibles, the way she did things would be a result of what came next. Of what life was like with me.

I looked down at Tegan again and fear kicked up a fuss in my head and chest. If I thought too closely about this, I had an urge to hide. To scramble under the covers and hide until it'd all passed me by. I'd never had the urge to be defined like this. To be someone's mum. I never had an urge or need to procreate; to have someone dependent upon me. Yes, I'd taken care of Nate, but only because he took care of himself back. If I forgot him one night to go out on the lash, he wouldn't starve. I knew all this when I'd agreed to take on Tegan, but it was at moments like this, moments when she was so completely reliant upon me for not only her physical well-being but also her emotional well-being that it hit me again. I was in charge. Of it all. All the time. For ever.

'Come on then, missus, we've got a whole lot of things to do, we can't be lying around in bed all day.'

Tegan's face disappeared behind her grin. I flung back the covers and Tegan slid out of bed, me following her. 'Let's make some calls and have breakfast.'

'OK,' she replied.

In the living room, I handed Tegan the phone and she hit the speed-dial button with 'M&D' beside it. It was only just six o'clock but my mum was obviously waiting for her call because almost instantly Tegan said, 'Hello, Nana Faith . . . Fine . . .' She laughed a little tinkly Tegan laugh and replied, 'You said Happy Adele Day.' Her grin got even wider as I heard the soft tones of my mother talking to her down the phone.

When I'd told my mum about Adele Day, she'd been a lot more supportive than Luke had been. She'd said she'd make us a cake if we wanted, but I'd declined the offer, it was nice but not necessary. Just as I'd said goodbye Mum had said, 'You know, Kamryn, your father and I are very proud of you.'

'Pardon?' I replied, shocked that my mum had said that about me. Our relationship had been defined by my non-wedding. By me embarrassing them in front of their friends and our wider family by not getting married and not really explaining why.

'Tegan is a big responsibility,' Mum continued. 'I was very surprised when you told us you were going to look after her. You are doing very well, though. Very well.' Mum often rang to speak to Tegan, and Tegan often called my parents. During the summer my parents had driven to Manchester to see my sister and came via Leeds to pick up Tegan so she could spend the day with them and my sister's family. They loved Tiga. Everyone loved Tiga.

'Thanks,' I mumbled.

'Ever since you didn't get married –' We'd never talked about it and when either of my parents tried, I changed the subject – 'we were worried about you. What you would do. And we didn't understand why you moved so far away so suddenly, but now, we're not so worried. You have someone.'

'You mean Luke?' I asked.

'Tegan. You've got a family now. That makes me very happy.'

'Thanks,' I mumbled again, not sure what to say. My parents had never let on that they worried about me being alone.

Even if they wanted to, when would they have got the chance? I wasn't known for staying on the phone long enough for them to reveal anything earth-shattering. In fact, in the time since I'd inherited Tegan I spoke to them more than I had in all my life.

Tegan finished talking to my mum, then spoke to Grandpa Hector. Then she asked if she could call my sister, Sheridan, and her kids. By the time she'd spoken to all our family, I'd made us toast and scrambled egg for breakfast.

Adele lay on her back, one arm supporting her head, the other lying on her bare stomach. Sunglasses hid her eyes, her skin shinny with sunblock. She was pouting up at the camera, her long hair that fuzzed around her head in curls the only thing, she thought, that distinguished her from Marilyn Monroe. 'Imagine if she was my mother,' Adele had said when she saw that photo I took of her that summer when it was so hot all we could do was lie on towels in my parents' garden, reading magazines and drinking ice water, pretending we didn't mind not having much money to start next term with. 'Imagine if Marilyn Monroe was my mother, how different my life would be.' And we did imagine, and then it'd occurred to us both at the same time that Marilyn would have had to have had sex with Adele's father, which was too gross a thought to take any further.

Tegan flipped over the page in one of my college photo albums. There was a picture of me slumped over my desk, my head literally in a book, waist-length plaits hiding my face. I was wearing a big, shapeless white jumper and black knee-length shorts. I'd been cramming for my finals and Adele had caught me asleep on the job. Also on the page, Adele and I were being a hieroglyphics in front of the pyramids in Egypt at sunset, my plaits were hidden under a burgundy scarf, my body in a white T-shirt and blue trousers. Adele had on a strappy pink jersey dress that came down to her thighs over floaty white trousers. Her hair was crammed up on her head in pins and she had sunglasses on too.

The opposite page, Adele and I were graduating. We were in our green and black gowns with mortarboards and matching smiles. In the background my parents were uneasily talking to Adele's father and his wife. When Tegan spotted her grandfather and Muriel, she snapped over the page quickly, and over the next three pages that had our graduation pictures. We moved on to another album, later pictures of Adele and me and Nate. I'd kept those pictures even though I hadn't looked at them in an age. There was Nate and I sitting on the sofa in Adele's and my flat. We were kissing and Adele had taken the picture. There was another of me and Adele playing Twister, taken by Nate. She'd bent herself backwards to keep her feet and hands on opposite circles, then managed to move her right hand to another blob on the left side of her body. Her head was thrown back, her hair trailing along the mat. I was on all fours because I wasn't a show off. There was me and Nate, showing off my ruby engagement ring. There was Adele, two months pregnant, pointing to her stomach, Nate in the background watching telly. Adele, nine months pregnant. Tegan in Adele's arms, minutes after she was born – Adele looking as bedraggled as if she'd run a marathon. Me holding Tegan. Nate holding Tegan, having been threatened with no sex for a week by me if he didn't.

Tegan was the one who aged most noticeably in the photos, lines appeared on the adult faces but it was Tegan who evolved from lying to sitting to crawling to walking to running to dancing. All the while laughing, giggling, smiling. Happy.

We looked through all the pictures, had a Bung It for our tea, then an exhausted Tegan asked to go to bed at six o'clock. She didn't need a bath, a story or a chat, she just changed into her PJs, got under her covers and closed her eyes.

'Goodnight, Tiga,' I said after I'd switched off the light beside her bed.

'I want my mummy,' she whispered.

I'd decided not to read Tegan the card Adele had left her for Christmas Day, nor any of the other letters she'd left just yet. It'd only confuse her, make her think there was a chance Adele would return. Maybe the day had, too. Maybe it'd been too much for her.

A small sob escaped her lips, 'I want my mummy,' she said again, quieter.

I didn't know what to say so ran a hand over her bescarved hair. Had I done the wrong thing today? Had I screwed up and thereby screwed Tegan up? 'I want my mummy,' was her last whisper as she slid into sleep.

Switching off all the lights apart from the corridor one, I trailed to bed dragging my conscience with me. I'd hurt Tegan instead of helping her. I should go back to what I was doing before – not talking about Adele. It didn't do this to her when we didn't talk about Adele. I slipped into bed, even though it wasn't even seven o'clock.

I woke up again when I was being nudged aside in bed. I opened my eyes a fraction: Tegan. She put a foot on the base of my bed, hoisted herself up onto the bed. She moved aside the covers, and snuggled against me. I wrapped my arm around her and she moved slightly to get closer to me. Within minutes she was breathing gently and slowly, asleep.

At least she knew she had me. I wasn't her mum, but I was there.

'you can call me tiga
if you want'

chapter forty

One of my favourite parts of the day was the time right before Tegan went to bed, when she had her bath.

We'd often have a random chat as I sat on the floor beside the bath, handing her flannels and waiting to shampoo her hair. Luke never gave her a bath, and never offered to, either, he didn't want me to get the wrong impression about him and why he spent so much time in our company, I suppose. Even if he did offer, I would have turned him down because bath time was Kamryn and Tegan time, the most precious twenty minutes of our day.

Two months after Adele Day, Tegan and I had settled into a routine. We were used to each other. It'd been seven months since she'd died and Adele Day had cemented in both our minds that she wasn't coming back. Beautifully written letters, her scent in her clothes, funny pictures, all of them lovely, all of them precious keepsakes of this person called Adele Brannon, but not her. Just fragments of the impression she'd left upon the earth. Tegan and I could look at those things as much as we wanted, but she wasn't coming back, we had to get on with life and with each other.

Normality had settled on our lives. Luke spent more time with us with each passing week, he'd had a key quite early on, but now he spent almost every week day here and even at weekends he didn't go to his place in Alwoodley. Nate also came around a bit – despite the drive from his place to ours, he would drop by for half an hour or so, have a cup of tea, chat to Tegan, ignore Luke's seething in the corner. Luke asked me a few times if Nate was going to sign the papers, which in my boyfriend's mind meant Nate would then disappear. I'd always reply that I had no idea. I hadn't asked Nate what his plans were because I didn't want to push him and, since our confrontation in the street, we didn't talk about those sort of things.

We had a good routine worked out, even if my heart did skip every time Nate walked in, but I knew that would stop as time went on and I got used to seeing him again. There was only one fly in our ointment. Or rather a huge elephant sitting on the table that every adult pretended they couldn't see, especially since it tripled in size every time Nate dropped by.

Tegan scooped up a handful of white bubble bath foam and dumped it on my outstretched hand. I'd lowered my head to blow the bubbles at her when she decided to point out the elephant by asking, 'Is Luke my daddy?'

I struggled to keep my voice steady while panic streaked through me. In all this time I hadn't worked out what to say to her. The truth? Unveil Nate as the sperm donor who had brought her to life? Or lie and say I didn't know him? That had been true until a few weeks ago. I hadn't known the Nate who slept with Adele. He'd explained, now. I did know him and I did know why. 'Why do you ask that?'

'Regina Matheson said that everyone has a mummy and a daddy. And I said I only had a Mummy Ryn and a mummy who was in heaven and she said I had a daddy too. And then she said maybe Luke was my daddy. And I said no because he's my friend. But then she said he might be. Is he?'

I am going to hurt this Regina Matheson, if I ever meet her. Or, as is most likely, give her parents a mouthful. She has been the bane of my life, bringing up subjects I don't want to think about let alone talk about with Tegan.

'Luke isn't your daddy.'

'But I do have a daddy, don't I? My teacher, Miss Lewis, said everyone has a daddy.'

'Yes. Yes, you do, Tiga.' My mouth dried, my heart buffeted itself against my ribcage.

Tegan stopped chasing bubbles with her hands and splashing with her feet, she sat very still as the bubbles disintegrated, pooling into oily patches on the cooling water. My shaky voice had alerted her that something was wrong and she asked, cautiously, 'What's his name?' Tegan's face was flushed from being in the hot bath, while clumps of wet, blonde-brown hair hung in tendrils around her cheeks as she waited for my reply.

I sighed, feeling my body tremble down into the breath as I bit my lower lip. 'Nate,' I said quickly.

Tegan's little hands came up and she wiped them across her eyes in surprise. 'Mr Nate?' she asked, blinking at me.

I nodded. 'Yes, Mr— I mean, Nate is your daddy.'

'Not Luke? Luke isn't my daddy?'

I shook my head. 'No, sweetie.'

'Really and truly?' She was disappointed.

I nodded again.

'Do I have to live at Mr Nate's house?' she asked after a tense silence.

'God, NO!' I screeched. 'You're with me for ever, Tegan. Never forget that. It's always going to be me and you.'

'And Luke.'

'Erm, yeah.' Not as convincing as I would have liked.

'Are you going to marry Luke?'

'I don't know, I haven't thought about it.'

'If you married Luke, would he be my daddy? Would he be Daddy Luke?' She didn't hide her happiness at that prospect.

'I suppose so,' I replied.

'Are you going to marry Mr Nate?'

'No.' I was sure about that. Nate and I were not getting married. Or back together. It wasn't even a possibility, no matter how much my heart skipped when he was around. Or how my stomach flipped when we accidentally made eye contact. It was over with Nate, really and truly, as Tegan would say.

'Why not?'

'Because Luke's my boyfriend.'

'But you had the pretty dress.'

'I know.'

'Why is Mr Nate my daddy?'

Did I really have to do the birds and the bees? Shouldn't she be allowed a few more years innocence? Shouldn't I? That's what I paid my taxes for, so someone else could go through the embarrassment of explaining the physicality of sex. I didn't even know how birds and bees came into the whole reproduction thing.

Tegan blinked her wet eyelashes while she waited for an answer.

'Erm . . .' I began. I had to do the only other thing I did in these situations. 'Do you mind Nate being your daddy?' Ask a diversionary question.

Tegan twisted her lips into a thinking pout and looked down at her bubbly water. She shrugged her shoulders. 'I don't know. Mr Nate is funny.' She scrunched up her nose and shook her head. 'Luke doesn't like him.'

'Did he say that?' I asked, ready to bawl him out for pushing Tegan into something she wasn't involved in.

She shook her head. 'No. He talks funny to Mr Nate.' Tegan lowered her chin to her neck and deepened her voice.

'Nate, you're here again. How nice.' She started talking like Tegan again. 'That's what he says to Mr Nate, all the time. That's not very nice, is it?'

'Men are silly sometimes,' I replied.

'Mr Nate looks at you. Sometimes, he smiles at you. You don't see him or nothing. He likes you more than he likes me.'

'Nate likes us both.'

'Do you like Mr Nate or Luke more?'

Now if I knew the answer to that question, I'd be sleeping better at night. I wouldn't have this constant guilt at wanting them both. Luke for being here now, for having not known Adele so not being a constant reminder of her. Nate for being a reminder of the person I used to be. The Kamryn who was sometimes nice and who often laughed. I'd always known that Nate loved me, Luke had yet to prove that he did in fact love me because we were still dancing around the 'I love yous', neither of us willing to put ourselves completely on the line first. But then, unlike Nate, Luke had never cheated on me . . . On and on in my head it went, this never-ending loop of who did I prefer? Who should I be with? 'I like them both,' I informed Tegan. I put my hand under her chin, lifted her face, turned it left and then right. 'But I like Tegan the most.'

She broke into a smile. She had such beautiful features, that cute little ski-jump nose, the big royal blue eyes and the exquisitely curved mouth that made her the image of Adele when she grinned. She took her head back, and scooped up some bubbles, blew them at me, covering my red jumper in bubbly white spots.

'Mummy Ryn, I'll think about this,' she said, as serious as a judge at sentencing time.

'OK,' I agreed. If it wasn't Tegan talking I would have scoffed at the gravity of her tone, at her precociousness. But I didn't laugh because all she was doing was reminding me that she was a thought-filled child and she needed to examine this new information properly.

'I don't know if I want Mr Nate to be my daddy,' she explained. 'I'll think about this.'

I nodded my agreement. And I would have to think about how to tell her, that, like it or not, want it or not, Nate was her daddy. That was something neither of us could change.

chapter forty-one

Nate was hunched over a cup of coffee in the Horsforth Coffee House on Town Street, his head resting on one hand, his eyes staring into the depths of the white coffee cup. When I'd rung to arrange this meeting, I'd suggested we meet in central Leeds but he'd said he didn't mind driving over to my neck of the woods. When I walked in and found him sitting with his coffee as though he'd been there for hours, I was reminded of our first date.

I arrived at his table and he raised his head. My stomach flipped in horror. He looked like a ghoul, a hideous shadow version of himself. The dark scores under his eyes told me he wasn't sleeping, his cheekbones starting to poke through his skin meant he probably wasn't eating. The dark stubble on his chin revealed he hadn't bothered to shave in days. His finger-nails were picked into a ragged state. And his slow, lethargic movements showed that just sitting up was an effort.

He wasn't taking care of himself and that hurt me. He was precious to me. He was Tegan's father after all. I was getting used to that. Starting to accept that what happened, happened. I couldn't change it. I wasn't sure I would change it if I could. Like Adele said in her letter, Tegan wouldn't be Tegan if Nate hadn't fathered her. But he was also precious to me because he was Nate.

'I'm not late, am I?' I asked.

'No, I was just excited about seeing you, even though you did sound very serious on the phone, so I got here early.'

I sat down, close up the devastation was more marked, more ingrained into him. This wasn't an overnight occurrence, this had been building up for some time, it was only now it was visible.

'Are you OK?' I asked.

He nodded, dismissively. 'I'm fine, gorgeous. So, what was the serious tone on the phone about?'

I hesitated, wanting to question him further about his health instead of starting this conversation. The state he was in, this was the last thing he needed to hear, but I had to do this. He was important, but Tegan was number one. Everything I did had to be for her benefit. 'Nate,' I moistened my lips, scared of how much this would hurt him, 'it's been nice having you around, seeing you, but I want you to sign the papers to allow me to proceed with adopting Tegan.'

Nate sagged in his seat, staring at the table in misery.

'I know you like her, but not enough to be her full-time dad. And she needs the stability that will come from me adopting her. She's six years old in a few weeks and in this past year she's lost her mum, moved to another city, discovered what having a dad is like, discovered who her real dad is, and that's on top of all the daily things she has to contend with . . . I just want to give Tegan the sort of stability where she knows that I'm not going to leave her. You understand, don't you?'

Mr Turner nodded his tired head, stared into the depths of his cup as though he might find solace there.

'So you'll sign?'

Another tired, dejected nod.

'Can I still come and see her?' he asked tentatively.

'Of course,' I said. 'You have to stick around, you're part of her life now. It'd traumatise her if you disappeared. I mean, she's still freaked out that you're her father, that's why she looks at you a bit funny, but she constantly talks about you. She likes you, Mr Nate. A lot. I don't blame her.'

'Don't,' he muttered with a shake of his head. 'Please don't be nice to me. It just reminds me how much I screwed things up.'

'I never thought I'd see the day when you asked me not to be nice to you. Phrases you never thought you'd hear, or what?'

'Ryn, do you really think I'd have stuck around if you were as nasty as you seem to think you were?'

I shrugged at him. Who knew how the male mind worked?

'You were so incredible to me. You were always looking after me – making sure I ate properly, you did my washing, came to every one of my work functions even though you hate those things. I remember how many times you'd stay up until I got home from work when I was on the late shift. You were always encouraging me, I believed I could do anything when I was with you. I sometimes used to wonder why you didn't want children when you were so good at taking care of people, not just me, Adele too . . .' He closed his eyes, dug his hands into his hair. 'Even when you wanted someone else you weren't horrible to me. You just stopped relating to me in the same way. That's how I knew. Every day was just flatness.'

'Nate, let's not . . . What you described was this perfect relationship and it wasn't. I drove you into someone else's bed. I made you—'

BAM! Nate slammed his hand onto the table top, making me jump. 'Stop it!' he snapped. 'Stop being so hard on yourself. That was what drove me crazy about you. You were so hard on yourself. Always blaming yourself for things you had no control over, thinking anything bad was down to you. You didn't make me do anything – I cheated on you. It wasn't your fault.' He calmed himself with a few deep breaths, softened his voice. 'It wasn't your fault. I did it, I screwed things up. Not just with you, with Adele too.'

'Anyway, I'm meeting Tegan and Luke down at the park,' I said, injecting sunshine into my voice while I changed the subject. I wasn't talking about this now. I couldn't. If I carried on thinking about these things, I'd start to crack up again. Before Christmas I'd been on the verge of a breakdown, crying in Nate's arms had been a part of it. Thankfully I'd been able to shut the door on my emotions again before they took over, before the deep scores of grief on my mind were allowed to overwhelm me. I wasn't going to risk opening myself up to all that hurt by talking with Nate about it. 'So I'd better be off.'

'OK,' Nate replied. 'Do you want me to drive you?'

'Sure.'

We left the café, and walked under a grey sky mottled with rain-swollen clouds towards Morrisons car park where Nate had left his car. This probably wasn't the best time to be going to the park, but Luke and Tegan were convinced they'd have at least an hour to run around before the heavens opened. As we reached his silver Audi, Nate's footsteps slowed to a halt, then he spun to me. 'I . . .' he began, then stopped. His arms reached out, pulled me into a hug. His hands stroked down my back, then slowly caressed their way up again. 'Do you ever think about us being together?' he murmured against my ear.

I more than thought about it, I fantasised, I hoped, I wanted . . . Nate's mouth grazed against my neck as he snaked a hand around my waist. His lips against my cold skin increased in pressure. More neck kisses. He knew I had no resistance to kisses on my neck. My knees weakened and he pressed my body closer to his. I lost my mental footing and suddenly I was tumbling into an emotional time machine. Back to the days when we'd stand at train stations, in the street, sometimes even in supermarket queues, necking and not caring what anyone thought. Kissing and snogging like we'd only just met.

Laughing when people shouted 'Get a room!' at us. Nate's free hand went into my hair as he kissed my neck harder. 'I won't leave a love bite,' he murmured and reality and the present slammed itself against my head.

'Stop, stop,' I said, pushing him away until he stepped back, creating a safe distance between us. We stared at each other, both of our chests heaving as we gulped down air. 'No more. This can't happen,' I announced breathlessly. 'Not ever.'

'I know this can't happen,' he closed his eyes, his face scrunched up. He pressed the heels of his hands on his eyes. 'I know. It's all going wrong . . . Everything . . . It's going wrong . . . I've been forced to take two weeks off work because I was stuffing up. Not concentrating.' My heart lurched for him. He was always professional, no matter what was going on in his life, nothing stopped him working, so for him to have been signed off . . . I hadn't realised how fragile he was. 'I don't know what I'm doing most of the time,' he blundered on. 'Instead of sleeping I lie awake at night thinking about us.' He kneaded his face with his knuckles, leaving white marks on his sallow skin. 'Wanting us to be together again . . . I know you're with him. And that's the worst part. I like him. He hates me, I know, but I like how much he cares about Tegan . . .' Nate collapsed into a crouch, his hands still pressed onto his eyes. 'Do you remember our first huge row? You went storming round to Adele's. Remember? I came round after you but she was having none of it. Do you remember? She went, "If you two split up, neither of you will get custody of me – I'll go live with Kam's parents." Do you remember?' I nodded to his bent head, I remembered. 'It doesn't seem right that you're back in my life and she's not around.'

Nate was grieving. I hadn't even thought how Adele's death would effect him. If I did give it one second's thought, I'd have known that there was no way he could be over it because he had been bereaved too. She was like a member of his family

373

and she had died. Of course he'd be mourning. I was still blaming myself for what happened before her death, and we'd made the first tentative step towards peace before it happened. The last words Nate had said to Adele was that he hated her. That he'd never forgive her. The whole conversation was full of bitterness, anger and recriminations. The guilt of that must have been consuming him; burning him up from the inside out.

How had I missed that? Especially when he'd been trying to tell me he was suffering. He'd told me the night we went to dinner; he'd told me when he offered to pay for Tegan; he'd told me when I asked him why he was making an effort with Tegan; he'd told me the night we had our confrontation in the street. Nate had been asking me for help, begging me to see his pain, and I hadn't heard him. I was meant to know him and I hadn't seen he was falling apart. My baby was falling apart.

'Tegan is so like Adele. I look at her and I see Adele, staring at me. But she's like you too. She says things like you do. And she has your mannerisms. Have you seen, she plays with the lock of hair by her ear if she's tired, like you do? Have you noticed that?'

To be honest, I hadn't. It wasn't important right now, though. He was. I bobbed down beside him, slipped an arm around his shoulders. 'Why didn't you tell me you were feeling this bad, Nate?'

He shrugged. 'Don't know,' he said, with the same intonation as Tegan when she was upset.

'Come on, let's go to the park, have some fun and take our minds off all this.'

'OK,' he whispered.

'What's he doing here?' Luke demanded in a low angry whisper.

His eyes had doubled in size when he saw me arrive at the

park with Nate and once he'd helped Tegan off the swing he'd glared at me until I went over to him, leaving Nate and Tegan together. Nate sat on the red swing Tegan had vacated, staring at the ground.

'Nate's in a bad way. He's had a bit of a breakdown,' I explained.

'This is meant to be our time, I can't believe you've brought him,' Luke hissed.

'He's suffering! He's not coping with Adele's death very well.' At that, Luke's glower softened a fraction. 'I didn't realise how much pain he was in until earlier – he's not eating or sleeping. He's been signed off at work. He's falling apart, I'm really worried about him.'

Luke sighed, seemingly moved by Nate's hurt, then reached out, pulled me into his arms. 'I've got you to support me,' I muttered into Luke's chest. 'Nate hasn't got anyone. So I have to be there for him. He was one of my best mates once, I can't let him down.'

'I know,' Luke conceded. 'I don't like it but I do under-stand.' He kissed the top of my head then kissed my mouth. As we returned to the swings, we both halted when we saw Tegan staring at Nate with big earnest eyes, as though viewing an exhibit in a zoo. She often found adults curious objects of study because they were so different to her. Other children were intrigued by other children, Tegan was always staring at big people, trying to uncover their secrets by observing their behaviour.

Eventually, she reached out and patted Nate on the knee until he turned his head to look at her. 'What's the matter, Mr Nate?' she asked quietly. 'Are you ill?'

Nate smiled at her and shook his head. 'No, I'm just tired.'

'Oh. Do you want to sleep in my bed? It's very pretty.'

'Thanks, but I've got a bed at my house.'

Tegan twisted her mouth together and chewed the inside of

her lower lip, then her forehead crinkled into a frown, she was thinking very hard. 'You can stay at my house, Mr Nate,' she eventually declared. 'You can wear Luke's pyjamas and sleep in my bed. I'll sleep in Mummy Ryn's bed. Mummy Ryn won't get cross. She never gets cross.'

Nate smiled at her. 'Thanks, Tegan, but I think it's better I sleep at my house.'

The weather started to break, a few spots of rain falling down on us, which gave me an excuse to interrupt. That moment, sweet as it was, was probably wrenching for Luke because she was relating to Nate how she related to him; and making Nate feel guilty for the fact that she was like Adele. 'All right, I think it's time we went home, boys and girls. It's going to start raining,' I said.

'O-OK,' Tegan said, rolling her eyes theatrically at Nate. 'Are you going to come to my house for your dinner, Mr Nate?' she asked. Nate looked up at Luke, who was standing beside me. Luke shrugged and glanced away, that was as close to 'Come over' as he'd get.

'OK, Tegan, I'll come.'

She grinned. 'Come on then.' She held out her hand to him. He took it and stood up. 'You can call me Tiga, if you want,' she informed him, nodding to emphasise her point. 'Not T, Luke calls me T. But you can call me Tiga.'

'OK, Tiga, thanks.'

Tegan grinned another wide grin at him and then started off down the path, pulling Nate along with her. I slipped my hand into Luke's, our fingers interlacing closely, as we followed Nate and Tegan home.

Things could work out between us four, I thought as we headed home. They really could. If I didn't keep touching my neck, running my fingers over the echo of Nate's kisses. If I didn't have the distinct feeling that I was falling for him again.

376

chapter forty-two

Luke got used to seeing Nate a few times a week.

'Used to' might be overstretching the case, he simply limited his (cue Tegan's deep voice) 'Nate, you're here again, how nice,' to once a week because Nate started spending a lot of time at our place. At least four times a week he would show up, almost always at Tegan's request. She hadn't elevated him to Luke status, but he had become like the ducks in the park she was always wanting to feed – she decided without her intervention he would starve. Almost every other night we had to call Mr Nate to ask if he would come round for his dinner. If he couldn't make it she'd want to know what he was going to eat. Sometimes she'd ring him to find out what he'd done at work that day and if he had any new friends. When he came over she would ask me if it was OK if he took her to the shop to buy sweets. Luke wasn't forgotten in this. Whenever she returned from a trip with Nate she would always go straight to Luke, climb onto his lap and tell him the details of their mini-trip and then ask him if he'd take her to the shop next time. She didn't ever forget to let Luke know that whilst Nate was fun, Luke was number one.

As a result of the time he spent with us – the realisation that he wasn't hated by me or Tegan, Nate slowly got back to normal. As normal as he could. He moved into the phase where it hurts but you can function. He started to sleep, eat properly, look better, and we even had conversations about Adele. 'Remember that night Adele came to my house and threatened me?' Nate asked once when the four of us were in the park.

I smiled as the memory returned to me.

'She told me she'd kill me if I ever hurt you. "Proper kill you," she said.'

'She was funny.'

'No, she was serious. I remember when I first met you I quickly realised that Adele was a part of our lives. And then when she had Tegan the three of you came as a package.' I turned to look at him. 'Not complaining. It was nice, actually, to have a ready-made family. I was just waiting for that day when you would say, "Why don't we buy a house so they can live with us?".' I grinned because the thought had crossed my mind. 'Yeah,' Nate said, 'I knew it!'

'I know you fell out, but she did love you,' I admitted.

'Only as a friend, though. You realise that, now, don't you? I was just like your brothers were to her.'

'She slept with my brothers as well?' I asked.

His eyes widened in horror. 'What? No! I never said that— Ah, you're joking. Very funny. Very funny.'

'Del would have thought so.'

'Yeah, she would have.'

The fact that I could talk about Adele without breaking down, also meant that I was getting better. I was dealing with what had happened. In tiny increments, but I was doing it. I'd had to force myself to. Since the day of Nate's breakdown I'd been jolted to my core. The realisation that I was falling for Nate again had scared me. It meant I wasn't paying enough attention to Luke. If I wasn't careful, I was in danger of driving Luke away just as I had done briefly with Nate all those years ago. I'd started saying 'I love you' every day to Luke,

378

because I did. He was the one I was with, the one I'd chosen to be with and I was going to prove that to both of us. I'd decided upon the perfect way to do that.

'This is like being proper boyfriend and girlfriend,' Luke said. We'd snuck out of work separately to meet up for lunch down by the river. We'd gone away from the main drag so we wouldn't be seen by anyone from Angeles. Although most people suspected we were together – Betsy was waiting for the day when she'd be allowed to gossip about it with the girls on the shop floor – we liked to keep it quiet. Separate our work persona from the dating one. Neither of us could have worked effectively if we were constantly worrying that everyone was watching to see how we reacted to each other vetoing an idea or pointing out a mistake. 'It's like we're on a proper date.'

'I know,' I smiled. I'd asked him to come out to lunch because I wanted to talk to him, wanted to do the thing that would prove beyond a shadow of a doubt that it was him I wanted to be with.

My boss checked around for any Angeles staff before kissing me, his lips were salty from his beef and horseradish sandwich.

'We should do this more often,' he said, stopping in front of me. 'We don't spend enough time together, you know. Just you and me. Do you reckon your parents would come up and stay with Tegan one weekend whilst we went out for the night?'

'Probably. Or Nate could do it.'

'Yeah,' Luke mumbled and looked away. 'He might even sign those papers.'

When it came to this subject my boyfriend was like a person hanging onto a cliff edge – no matter how weary he got, he wouldn't let it go, because he thought it'd kill him. 'Do you really mind him being around?' I asked. 'Really and truly?'

'Don't Teganise me, Ryn. It's not easy having your ex

379

practically living with us. T is the image of him, I look at her, I see his face. And if that's not bad enough, I know that he spent years fucking you.' Luke said 'fucking' deliberately. He was trying to diminish what Nate and I had by making it sound sordid and emotionless – the only way he could cope with regularly seeing the man I almost married. 'I can't get away from him. Show me any other bloke who has to spend time with his girlfriend's ex. If you were me, would you be able to do it?'

'I understand it's not easy, but he's so much better now and you must have noticed he's started coming over less as a result?'

'Here's to a speedy recovery, so he can disappear completely.'

'Don't be an idiot, Luke, you know you're a good person. And if you don't remember how good you are, I won't tell you why I asked you to lunch.'

He glowered like the dying embers of a coal fire for a few seconds, then curiosity doused his fume. 'Yeah, I have noticed that he's been coming round less.'

'OK, Mr L, I was wondering if you fancied moving in with us? I know you live with us anyway but what if we make it official? Then you can give up your other place and if you're up for it, we could start saving together and buy a bigger place. Maybe even a house? With a garden for Tegan.'

Luke's reply was to glance away and retreat into silence. A quiet that deepened into a hush that promised to haunt our relationship for years to come. I'd messed up, I realized, as his silence continued and my heartbeat slowed and slowed, threatening to stop at any moment. I'd messed up by bringing this up. 'This is a big step,' Luke finally said. 'I'll have to think about it.'

That's it? I thought. *After asking something so important, after all my recent efforts, that's all I get?* It was the whole, 'I love you'/'That's good to know' scenario all over again; another slap in the face when I showed him my heart. 'OK,' I mumbled. How many times was I going to let Luke do this before

I accepted that I wasn't meant to be opening up to him? That maybe he wasn't thinking we'd last the distance.

'That's not a no,' he added, 'it's just, well, it's a big step.'

'You said.'

'Ryn, there are lots of things to consider.'

'I know.'

'I do see my future with you and T.'

'So what's the issue?'

'We've been together less than a year.'

'But when you know, you know,' I blurted out. Did I really say that? Me? Adele said that sort of thing, not me.

Had I had changed that much since Adele's death? Had I become a swoony woman with a sense of destined romance? No, I realised. I was as romantic as I had always been. What I said could only mean one thing: I was begging. I shuddered. Luke was making me beg for his affection.

'I do know,' Luke began. 'I just need to—'

'It's OK,' I interjected. 'You don't have to give me an answer straight away. Take as long as you want.'

'Sure?' he replied.

'Positive.'

As far as I could see, this meant one thing: Luke wasn't in love with me. He adored Tegan, he'd die for her, there was no doubt about that, so it was me, wasn't it? He wasn't in love with me. There was no way he would have reacted like this if he did. And even though I'd had my doubts when Nate had reappeared, and I'd had more doubts since the day in the car park, that hadn't changed the fact that Luke was who I'd chosen to be with. I loved him enough to ask him to take this big step with me. After the hurt I'd gone through with Nate, I hadn't thought I'd ever take such a risk on a man ever again; I hadn't expected to meet someone who would become such a part of my life that I'd want to do this. It just seemed that Luke didn't feel the same way. When we first kissed I suspected that he would sleep with me but wouldn't want anything else. And it seemed every so often he'd revert to that mode: one minute he was telling me about his childhood, the next he seemed to be dismissing how I felt; one minute he was madly jealous about my ex, the next he didn't want to move in. I never knew where I stood with Luke. He was so transparent in his affection for Tegan, but I never knew what he truly felt about me. That scared me. I had invested a lot of emotion in him and it wasn't even a sure thing.

'You're very quiet,' Luke stated.

'Just thinking,' I replied.

Luke sighed, dropped his half-eaten sandwich in a nearby trash can, then rested his hands on my shoulders as he pinned me to the spot with the weight of his gaze.

An expression crossed his face and his hazel eyes clouded over for a moment. 'You wouldn't want me to agree to something I wasn't sure of just because it's what you want to hear, would you?' Luke asked.

I shook my head. ''Course not. But I am allowed to be disappointed and hurt that you've not jumped at the chance to make things permanent,' I pointed out.

'I . . .' he began, stopped. The expression crossed his face again. I couldn't read it. Didn't understand what he was thinking but not saying. 'Ryn, I'll be honest. I've been thinking about asking you to marry me. Every time I pass a jewellery shop I go in to look at rings, but then . . . We've been together less than a year. We can't be getting married after less than a year. It's not the sort of thing I do, I'm not that impulsive. So you springing this on me . . . I need to think about it. Us buying a house together would be a halfway step but I don't know if I want to do things in half measures. Which brings me back to getting married . . . Which is impulsive. Do you understand why I need to think about this? It's not that I don't love you, it's not that I don't see my future with you, I've just

382

got to work out what's best. I've done this before, remember, and it didn't exactly work out.'

'Yes, Luke, I remember you've done this before. And so have I. I almost got to the altar so I'd have thought you'd at least have thought to talk to me about marriage if you were thinking about it.'

'You didn't talk to me about buying a house.'

'What do you think I was just doing? I haven't been looking at houses, or planning where we should live, I brought it up so we could talk. Do you realise what marriage will mean for adopting Tegan? Who does she change her name to? What will it look like for the social workers and judge who decide these things? It'll make me look impulsive and flighty when I need to come across as steady and stable and suitable to bring up a bereaved child. If you'd mentioned marriage to me at an earlier stage I could have told you these were the things we need to think about. Buying a house together was some way down the line, like I said, we'd save up. And, let's be honest, it's no different to how things are now. All it'd be is that you'd be with us all the time and that's what Tegan and I both want. And the fact you're there ninety-nine per cent of the time suggests that's what you want as well.'

'If I had proposed, you would have said no?'

I nodded. 'I'd have thought you'd know by now that I'm someone who needs to talk about these things. It's my future too and you being ready for marriage, doesn't mean I am. Especially when I've got a child to consider.'

'I see what you mean . . . We're not doing a very good job of planning a future together, are we?'

'I guess not.'

'But I do want us to have a future, though,' Luke said. 'Really and truly.'

'Don't Teganise me,' I replied, with a thin smile.

He laughed, then his features fell into seriousness. 'I want us to be together for . . . for the rest of our lives. And I'll think carefully about moving in, OK?'

'OK.'

Luke grinned at me, kissed me full on the mouth without checking if there were any Angeles staff around first. As he held me close and kissed me deep, a small treacherous inkling began in my mind. It started growing at an alarming rate until it was a full-blown thought that eclipsed everything else: that whole conversation would have gone so differently if I'd had it with Nate.

'And we found the response we had to the vouchers had increased five per cent on the last issue of *Living Angeles*,' Betsy was saying to the assembled members of the advertising, merchandising and marketing teams for our weekly round-up meeting. 'We're investigating why this is the case, although Kamryn thinks it's because we used a picture of people instead of the usual still lives to push them.' *She's impressive*, I thought as I listened to her. *And she's glowing.* Glowing because she was madly in love with the man she'd met back in the days when Luke and I hated each other. She'd been right, he was The One.

I glanced down at my notepad and instead of notes, it was covered in drawings of houses. Houses that my 'The One' had told me a couple of hours ago he had to 'think carefully' about moving into with us. That still stung. Betsy stopped talking and, because I wouldn't be called upon now to participate, I tuned out as Luke's PA, Carla, started the diary check where she listed all the meetings the three departments had in the coming month to ensure there were no clashes. 'And I've just had confirmation that the Edinburgh direct marketing campaign roll-out meeting will take place on the fourteenth, Luke. Shall I go ahead and confirm your attendance?' Carla asked.

My pen froze in doodling on the page. *The fourteenth? Hang on,* I glanced up at Luke who had paled as he looked at Carla. His eyes slid across the room to me, then moved away as he seemed to immerse himself in thought. I didn't know what he was thinking about. What there was to consider. Of course he couldn't go. Of course he couldn't.

'Luke?' Carla asked when he'd been silent for a full minute and the quiet had caused all eyes in the room to fall upon him. 'Shall I confirm your attendance and book the hotel?'

'Erm,' Luke's eyes moved back to her, via me. 'Erm, sorry, Carla. Yes. Please confirm my attendance.'

My fingers closed in a death grip around my pen, tight enough to crush the plastic case as the heat of anger burnt through my veins.

'If there's no other business then let's end there,' Luke said. 'Thanks, guys.' Everyone picked up their pads and pens, cups of tea and coffee, and glasses of water and filed out of the boardroom. I remained in my seat, rage stampeding through me. Luke stayed in his seat as well until the last person to leave shut the door behind them.

'I can't believe you're going away on the fourteenth,' I said, my voice quiet and measured, a far cry from the bile I wanted to scream at him.

'I was never meant to,' he said, trying to placate me. 'I was hoping it would get cancelled, we've been dancing around with dates for weeks now and I was hoping that this wouldn't turn out to be the only time in May we were all available.'

'But you're not available, it's Tegan's birthday. You've known about it for months. We've been planning her party for months. You're not available.'

'Ryn, you remember what it was like to have a career, what extra you have to put in. I can't say that I've got a child's birthday party so I can't make the meeting.'

Remember what it was like to have a career? I still had a career,

I was still in charge of the magazines and they were bloody good even if I did say so myself. *The extra you have to put in?* I was always putting in extra. The only other people who worked as many extra hours as I did without the glory, without the recognition and chance of promotion were other mothers who had to do it to keep their head above water. Wouldn't I love to be working all those hours during the day, stopping to do another type of work, and then picking up all over again a few hours later because I'd get a promotion at the end of it. Or even recognition. No one went on about the magazines being a success but I'm sure there'd have been trouble if my work slipped. The board of directors would notice the quality of my work then.

Of all the things Luke said that made me want to swing for him, though, it was 'a child's birthday party'.

'A child?' I said, venomously. 'Since when has Tegan been "a child"?'

'That came out wrong.'

'Really. Well, this certainly won't come out wrong – I'm taking back asking you to move in,' I said.

'What?'

'You called Tiga a child. We can't live with someone who can put his job before the girl he's been treating like his daughter for the best part of a year, then dismiss her as "a child". She thinks of you as her dad. Even though she knows Nate's her father, you're the one she wants to be her dad. And you see her as "a child".'

'I didn't mean it like that.'

'Don't care.'

'I'll see if I can change it.'

'Don't do us any favours, Mr Wiseman. I can vaguely remember what it was like to have a *career*, and I remember that if you cancel meetings you don't look professional. I wouldn't want you to have to look uncommitted in front of your colleagues, what with you having a *career* and everything.'

He glared at me, not willing to concede he was wrong in this. 'Fine!' he spat, throwing his pen across the long meeting table.

'Fine,' I stated.

I got to my feet, picked up my notepad, pen and mug of cold tea. My heart was beating at triple speed in my chest and my limbs were trembling as I walked the length of the room.

'I'll see you tonight,' he said as I fumbled with the door handle.

'Not at my flat you won't,' I replied without looking round. 'Why don't you go back to that flat you were so desperate to hang onto earlier and plan some more meetings.'

His reply was a heavy sigh.

I stomped down the corridor, rage pulsing in my temples. I was as angry with myself as I was with Luke. Because I understood why he'd chosen to go to the meeting. There was a time when nothing would have stopped me working. He'd always been über-ambitious. And, much as he loved Tegan, she wasn't his daughter, wasn't his responsibility, so he was allowed to put his career before her, before us, because, in the grand scheme of things, he only had to look after number one. That was all true, but it didn't mean I had to like it.

chapter forty-three

Tegan turning six meant she was going to be an official grown up, at least that's what she kept telling people. 'I can do lots of things when I'm six,' she'd remind me on a daily basis in the run-up to her party.

I couldn't think of anything she couldn't do at five that she could do at six, although my answer was always, 'I know,' so as not to put a dampener on her enthusiasm. The day her birthday dawned Luke wasn't there. He was at work before he left for the meeting that I had asked him not to change on our account. The rough patch we went through before Christmas was a walk in the park compared with the preceeding three weeks. We'd been silently rowing about the Scotland trip since that meeting. Three weeks of not getting on, of him going back to his Alwoodley flat after Tegan had gone to bed, of us making love only three times because I'd discovered this huge reason to believe we weren't Plan A with Luke. 'When you get to the end of your life, I'm sure you'll be grateful that on the day Tegan turned six you were off at a meeting,' I said to him the night before he left.

'Please . . . I feel bad enough as it is, Ryn. I didn't think and there's nothing I can do now. I'm sorry.'

'Tell it to your kid. Oh, I mean, my kid. The "child".'

Luke drew back and looked away, furrowing his brow and

grinding his teeth together, his face pinched as though he might cry, and I knew I'd gone too far. I'd seriously wounded him. 'I'm sorry,' I said, taking his hand, kissing it, 'that was an awful thing to say. I know you don't think that. Let's call a truce, OK?'

'You're right to be angry, I was out of order. I do think of Tegan as my kid. You know that, don't you?'

I nodded. 'Course I do.'

We kissed and made up.

Tegan took the news better than I had done. 'But are you coming back the tomorrow of my birthday?' was all she asked.

'Yup, first thing.'

'OK,' she shrugged happily. 'I'm going to have balloons, you know.'

We had hired the community hall down the road for the party and were having a red and yellow bouncy castle out the back. We'd invited thirty children, most of them from Tegan's class at school and a couple from her holiday playgroup.

I'd had considerable help from Mrs Kaye when it came to organising the party and, where Luke would have been, Nate stepped in. He took me to the supermarket the day before and we'd spent nearly two hundred pounds on party food: sausage rolls, mini sausages, mini pizza, burgers, crisps, cakes, fizzy drinks and more white bread than I'd ever seen in my life. As a concession to healthiness, I'd bought strawberries, pears and apples to make a fruit salad. Nate had then stayed most of the night hand-making beef patties, and cutting round shapes out of the white bread to make them into burgers. The fridge was crammed with food, and he'd said he'd arrive early to help make the sandwiches.

I'd been up since five o'clock buttering bread for sandwiches by the time Tegan ran into the kitchen at seven o'clock, holding onto Meg, screaming, 'It's my party day!'

'I know!' I said and scooped her up into my arms. She felt real now. A proper human being, not the shell of a girl who'd been too scared to breathe when I'd taken her from Guildford. Her royal blue eyes looked keenly into my face and I couldn't help but smile.

'Does Tegan want her present now or would she rather wait for her party?'

'Now!' she squealed.

We moved to the sofa and I put her down beside me. I reached down the side of the sofa and pulled out the parcel that I'd hidden there last night when Tegan had gone to bed. It was wrapped in gold paper and tied with a red bow. Ever cautious, she put down Meg and took the parcel in her little hands and stared at it in wonderment. 'Is it really for me?' she asked.

'Read the tag and find out.'

'For my dar-ling Tiga. Happy sixth birthday, love Mummy Ryn,' she read dutifully. 'It is for me!' she laughed. She held onto the present as though it was a doll.

'Open it then,' I coaxed.

'Oh yeah,' she giggled. She examined the parcel, looking for somewhere she could open it without tearing the paper, when she didn't find it, she bit her lower lip and looked up at me in bewilderment.

'Do you want me to help you?' I asked.

She nodded.

I found where I'd taped down the thick gold paper, and peeled it back carefully so as not to distress my obsessively neat child. 'There you go.'

With glee, Tegan opened up the parcel and her mouth fell open, her eyes wide. 'Wow,' she said and reached into the paper's folds and pulled out a white dress with red spots. It had a full skirt, long sleeves and a red ribbon around the middle. 'It's a dress!' she exclaimed. 'It's very pretty.'

'I thought you might want to wear it to your party.'

'Am I 'lowed? Really and truly?'

'Well, yeah. Although, I think you should see Luke's present as well.'

I reached down and found the package Luke had wrapped and left the night before. To save time, I untaped the box-shaped parcel and gave it to her. She pulled off the paper and revealed a shoebox. She opened it and found white shoes with red spots on them. 'It's the same as my dress!' she said.

'So you can wear them today.'

'Thank you!' she said and threw her arms around my neck. 'I love it, Mummy Ryn.'

'There's one more pressie for you to open right now.' I pulled another parcel, smaller than our other packages from the side of the sofa, and repeated the opening procedure. 'To Tiga, with love from Nate.' She gasped with delight. 'Mr Nate brought me a present!' She eagerly opened it and then squinted at the contents in a confused manner. He'd brought her a small silk bag that matched her dress and shoes.

'It's a bag, so you can carry things in it today.'

'It's very pretty,' she decided.

'Yes, and you'll look very pretty with it.'

'I wish my mummy could see me.' She scrunched up her face and nodded at me. But, instead of looking sad, she seemed fine. As though she'd resigned herself to the fact her mother wasn't going to be at the party, had come to accept the reality of the situation.

'So do I. But, I do have something from your mummy.'

Tegan's already wide eyes, widened even more. 'She sent it from heaven?' she gasped.

'No, sweetpea, she gave it to me before she went to heaven.'

I'd known she was ready to get this, she seemed so much more settled than when we'd arrived in Leeds, but still I had toyed with the idea of opening it and reading it first. I just wanted to check it wasn't anything upsetting, then realised that Adele wouldn't put anything that would hurt her daughter. And anyway, the white envelope wasn't for me, it was for Tegan. I took the card from my dressing gown pocket and handed it over. Her little fingers received the envelope and, biting her lower lip, she stared at the white square before she sought my guidance.

'Shall I open it?' she asked.

'If you want to, baby.'

She opened it carefully and just as cautiously pulled out the card. On the front was a blonde princess with a pink crown and a huge number six on her pink dress. 'Happy Sixth Birthday' the front declared. Tegan opened it.

My darling Tegan,
Happy Birthday.
I'm sorry I can't be there with you today
but I'll always love you.
Never forget that, OK? Mummy loves you.
I'm sure you'll have a fabulous time today.
Have a dance for me.
I hope you're being good for Kamryn.
Love, Mummy.

A smile lit up her face as she turned to me. 'My mummy loves me,' she stated. 'She said so. In my birthday card.'

'I know.'

Her smile grew. 'You are Kamryn, aren't you, Mummy Ryn?'

'Yes, I am.'

'Am I being good for you?'

'You're being more than good for me, you're being perfect for me.'

'So my mummy will be pleased.' Again, the kind of logic I

never expected from a six-year-old. I leant forwards and took her in my arms. I frequently had a need to hug Tegan these days. She'd be minding her own business, watching television or drawing or reading, and she would find herself swamped by one of my hugs. Unexpected and unsolicited. I couldn't help myself, I just needed to remind myself that she existed, that she was touchable. Our roles had been reversed these past few weeks. After Adele died, Tegan always needed to have me around, so I could ground her with a touch or a look. Now I needed to know she was always going to be there. I needed to be reassured that she was real and that she wasn't going to do what Adele had done and leave me. There was a limited time, too, before she'd squirm out of my hold, too grown up and cool to be hugged by me. Right now she accepted my cuddles without question or resistance.

'Right, baby,' I said releasing her, 'we've got a lot to do before your party. Let's have your bath, and then you can have breakfast before Mr Nate, I mean Nate, arrives to make sandwiches? Does that sound OK to you?'

She nodded and, still holding the card in one hand she scooped up Meg. Tegan was going carry the card around with her all day, as it turned out. She would only forget about it much, much later in the day.

chapter forty-four

Tegan beamed at her princess cake.

She'd been grinning for most of the day and she showed no signs of stopping the smiling. With every present, she grinned, with every kind word, she grinned, with every game, she grinned. But her biggest smile of the party so far was reserved for the cake. The six candles reflected in her royal blue eyes as I set down in front of her the large square pink-covered chocolate cake with a picture of a princess on top. Everyone crowded round and sang 'Happy Birthday' to her. She paused to make a wish before blowing out the candles in one huge puff. After the candles, she opened her mountain of presents. My parents had bought her a digital camera, my sister's children had sent her the complete set of Roald Dahl books. My younger brother's two children had both sent her Disney DVDs and my older brother's children had bought her a karate suit. We were having a family party in London in two weeks when my older brother's family were flying in from Japan, so none of Tegan's cousins had come to this party. The other children's gifts varied from DVDs to books, from dolls to jigsaws.

After the cake most of the children ran back to the bouncy castle and swings outside, Tegan went with them while I took the cake into the hall's kitchenette to cut it up for the goodie bags. This party was going well – during the last two hours only a couple of children had cried, a lot of the food sat in uneaten heaps on paper plates rather than being stamped into the parquet floors inside or the neatly cut grass outside. And no one had wounded themselves. That was a perfect party as far as I was concerned. The two parents who had stayed for the party followed the children outside leaving only me in the kitchenette, while Nate, the fourth adult, sat in the hall, talking to a young lad who hadn't really joined in with the others.

Nate had made himself indispensable. He had been on bouncy castle duty when we'd first arrived, overseeing its inflation, then making sure that no kids ended up on it with their shoes on. When one of the other mums took over, he went round picking up rubbish and dumping it into black bin liners. He'd whizzed back to the flat a few times to grab things I'd forgotten, like the camera and some of Tegan's birthday presents. He'd then made a mercy dash back for the candles for the cake. No one who saw how useful he had been would guess that he didn't like being around children, didn't understand them and didn't know how to relate to them.

In the kitchenette, I paused in cutting up the cake and, through the serving hatch, watched Nate. He was dressed in a V-neck blue T-shirt and dark green combats, he'd recently cut his hair, and he was looking handsome. Healthier, stronger, *delicious*. I'd had no *inamorato* moments with him, didn't think 'lover' when I looked at him but I did . . . I quashed that thought before it became even partially formed. It would do no one any good to start thinking like that.

The thin boy Nate was talking to listened avidly to whatever it was Nate was saying. Nate was using lots of hand gestures and smiling lots, and the boy's shy little face slowly unwound as he immersed himself in Nate's tale. I wondered what he was saying. If he was telling him some adventure story that would stay with the boy into adulthood. If he knew that what he said today could, potentially, permanently influence the boy's life. Whether—

Nate glanced up suddenly, spearing me to the spot as our gazes collided. I wasn't swift enough, couldn't tear my eyes away and pretend I hadn't been studying him. I continued to stare. Nate's lips slid up into a smile and his eyes twinkled – in response, a treacherous streak of excitement tore through me. I tried to quash that too as I smiled back.

'Mrs Brannon,' a girl's voice said beside me. When I saw who had spoken, I stifled the urge to roll my eyes.

'I've told you before, Regina, I'm not Mrs Brannon. You can call me Ryn or Tegan's mum, not Mrs Brannon.'

This child, this Regina Matheson, with her short, bobbed mousy-brown hair and stripe of freckles across her pig-shaped nose was everything I'd expected her to be: bossy, overbearing and arrogant. I hadn't been surprised that her parents had ditched her at the party, running off into the afternoon, knowing they wouldn't have her for at least three hours. Regina's freckled nose wrinkled up as she considered what I had told her about my name. Eventually she shrugged. 'There is rather a lot of junk food at this party,' she stated.

I frowned theatrically at her. 'You're right, Regina, I hadn't thought of that.'

She sighed smugly. 'My mum says too much junk food is bad for you.'

'Does she? Right, well, I'm sure just this once won't hurt.'

'I'm sure it won't,' she stated with another smug sigh. From Tegan that would have sounded cute, from Regina . . . I didn't want to finish that train of thought.

'There is some fruit, though, Regina. Strawberries or a fruit salad. Why don't you have a strawberry?'

'I suppose.'

396

'Go rejoin the party, Regina, I'm sure there are lots of people who want to talk to you.'

'OK, Mrs Brannon,' she said and skipped off to harass someone else.

I returned to cutting up the chocolate cake for the goodie bags and had just finished when Nate entered the kitchenette. He came to me and stood so close I felt the warmth from his body before I'd even turned to him. 'Can I help you with anything?' he asked. I moved to look at him and found we were almost face to face because he'd dipped his head to my height. His navy-blue eyes stared straight into mine, making the breath catch in my throat.

'See them bags?' I said.

He nodded, not looking at the expensive, red foil party bags lined up on the big table in front of us. I'd already stuffed them with a noisy blow toy (which every parent would hate me for), a bag of sweets, a thank you note I'd helped Tegan to write, and a bendy straw. Now they were awaiting their cake. 'These pieces of cake, cake, in those bags would be very helpful. Helpful. You need to wrap them in napkins first, though. Though.' I couldn't speak properly, he was doing that to me. 'Napkins. Cake. Bags.'

His eyes travelled from my eyes to my lips, lingered there then moved up to my eyes again. What he was thinking was clear on his face. He moved a fraction closer. He was going to kiss me, I realised. At our daughter's birthday party he was going to cross the line and kiss me. Would I kiss him back? Would I slip my arms around his neck and kiss him back? Or would I push him off, remind him of my boyfriend? Nate moved slightly closer, parted his lips. 'OK,' he whispered. Suddenly he pulled away, robbing me of his lust. He'd done that on purpose, I knew. He'd wanted to get me stirred up and then push me into making the next move by stepping back. It was a game he'd played a couple of times after a row,

397

when he needed me to prove that I desired him as much as he did me.

He took half the cake on its chopping board with him to the other side of the table. He washed his hands before starting to wrap up the chocolate squares in the white napkins. 'This is weird,' he said in a normal tone of voice, as though he hadn't been about to seduce me. 'Me and you, kids, not going crazy.'

'They've started to grow on me,' I replied, matching his normal tone. I wasn't going to let him know how much his game had affected me.

'Me too.'

'I saw. You and that boy seemed to be getting on pretty well.'

'He reminded me of me when I was that age: shy, terrified of the other kids – especially the girls.'

'It's nice to see you relaxed again, Nate. You seem a lot better.'

'I am. Thanks to you and Tegan and Luke. The past few weeks have really helped . . . I'm not so . . . You know, about Adele. I feel guilty though.'

'About?'

'You're the one I was meant to be looking after, you lost your best mate and all I did was fall apart on you.'

'We helped each other. And you know I'd do almost anything for you, Mate.'

'Do you think this is what it would have been like if we had decided to have children?'

'No, Nate. If we'd had kids they'd have been evil and the church would assign a special hit squad to rid the earth of them.'

'They'd be cute,' Nate protested. 'Big eyes, shiny black hair, mocha skin, big smile . . .'

'Are you broody?' I asked. He'd obviously thought about this. 'There's no shame in it if you are.'

He thought about it. 'No.' He shuddered. 'No, not at all. It's something that crosses my mind nowadays. I wouldn't actually want one. I mean, any more.'

'Me neither. I love Tegan, couldn't live without her, but I'm not wanting to do it again.'

'What about Luke?' Nate asked, he paused in folding a napkin around a piece of cake and watched me in that unnerving way of his. 'Is he all right with that? I get the impression he wants lots of kids.'

'Maybe he does,' I said. Of course he did. That was our elephant in the corner. We hadn't talked about it directly, but I knew he wanted to be a dad; he knew that I'd finished with all that when I acquired Tegan. It was a fundamental issue that we'd never broached because once you started that conversation, where would it go? We both had set ideas and neither of us were going to change. It'd been difficult and complicated enough trying to agree to live in the same house. A discussion about more children would end with . . . It would end. Everything.

'Do you love him, Kam?'

I glanced up. No one had called me Kam in so long, I'd actually forgotten that I'd once been called it. I nodded. 'I do.'

'More than you love me?'

'My feelings for you are past tense, Nate.'

'You're lying, to me and yourself.'

'We're getting married, Luke and I. We talked about it a few weeks ago.'

Nate shrugged, unmoved and unbothered. 'Don't care. You're still lying to me and yourself.'

'You don't know what you're talking about,' I said.

'I'm not saying you don't love him, I think you're torn – you want us both. You're not very good at hiding your feelings, so he knows as well. I'm surprised he hasn't said something. Or has he? Is that why he proposed, because he suspects you're not sure of your feelings?'

I went back to wrapping the cake pieces in their neat, napkin envelopes, ignoring what he was saying.

'I love you, Kam.'

My hands started to shake as I moved a piece of cake to the napkin in front of me. I hated this about Nate, his freedom with emotions – mine and his. His ability to simply say what he felt without thought for what it might do to me.

'I'm not going to put pressure on you. I just want you to know that. And I want you to be honest with yourself.'

I stared at the table top. What I felt was my business. If I was lying to myself that was my business too. I didn't have to admit to anything. And what was there to admit to? That I fancied him? Well, obviously, he was gorgeous. That when Luke pissed me off Nate was who I wanted? Every woman did that – before Nate walked back into my life I would fantasise about being with Jamie Foxx or Keanu Reeves. It wasn't fair for Nate to accuse me of this. Especially since I knew Luke thought the same. The pair of them assumed they knew what I felt and when I corrected them, they never truly accepted what I said. I searched for a way to tell Nate he was wrong. To let him know that yes, I fancied him, but Luke was my lover.

'Mrs Brannon,' Regina Matheson began, tugging at my skirt.

I ignored her. And decided to keep ignoring her until she got it right. 'Mrs Brannon.' She tugged harder.

I continued to bag up cake pieces without acknowledging her existence.

'Mrs Brannon,' Regina said again.

'What is it?' I snapped, finally turning to her. I was about to say, 'And I'm not Mrs anything,' when I noticed the anxiety on her face.

'Tegan's turning blue,' she stated.

'What—' I threw aside the cake in my hand and ran out of

the kitchenette across the hall and towards the doors that opened out to the back of the hall. I ran, but felt I wasn't moving. That everything was in slow motion. When I was younger, I used to have a recurring dream where I would be running away from danger and my legs would be moving fast, my arms would be pumping at my sides and I'd hear my breath in my ears, but still I was moving slowly. Running through tar. This is how I felt as I raced out towards the bouncy castle. I was running but it didn't seem fast enough. Beside the bouncy castle, all the children, silent and solemn, stood in a circle, staring at a spot on the ground. As I got nearer I saw at the centre of the circle was a parent who was crouched down beside Tegan and was calling, 'Tegan, can you hear me?'

Tegan lay on her back on the ground. Still. Still and perfect. Her pretty white and red spotted dress was crease-free, her legs stretching out from the hem of her big skirts ending with her red and white spotted shoes. Her bunches with their red ribbons were in perfect symmetry on either side of her head. Her eyes were closed and her mouth was gently parted, but she was indeed turning blue. Bluer by the second. She was so still. Adele. The memory of the last time I saw her settled like a vulture in my mind. Adele had been this still the last time I saw her. Still and cold and dead.

I shoved aside the woman by Tegan as I dropped to my knees. I pressed my ear to her chest, listening. *Thud*. Soft, faint, but confirmation her heart was still beating. But she wasn't breathing.

'Nate! Get an ambulance!' I screeched.

'It's on its way,' he replied from somewhere near me.

'Did she choke?' I asked the assembled group of children as I gently tipped Tegan's head back and opened her mouth.

'She put a strawberry in her mouth,' Regina said, pointing. I glanced to the side and there was a strawberry, perfect, untouched. She hadn't taken a bite, hadn't choked, that meant

401

she was allergic. When you had an allergic reaction you needed antihistamines and adrenaline to keep your heart beating. I knew that much. I had to keep her heart beating and get her breathing.

I blew into her mouth, then moved to her chest and pushed carefully, didn't want to break her ribs. Five counts, five gentle pushes. Then back to her mouth, blow. Nate dropped beside me to her chest, he was going to start chest compressions but I shook my head at him. I had to do this. I had the rhythm going. I had to bring her back to life. I went back to her chest. Five counts. Back to her mouth. No movement and she wasn't breathing. Back to her mouth, blow. Back to her chest. After the final push, I put my head to her chest. *Thud*. Again, small and gentle. Her heart was still beating. Back to her mouth, back to her chest.

The sound of children crying, asking what was going on cut into my thoughts. Then I heard them being rounded up, being ushered away. I blew into Tegan's mouth again, not daring to notice how cold her lips were. How the blue of her skin was deepening with every passing second. I just had to keep going. To keep trying to bring her back. I heard Nate's voice, he was talking.

I breathed into her mouth again and then Nate's strong arms hooked around my chest and hoisted me away from her. I almost fought him, almost screamed that I wasn't going to stop, when two green-clad paramedics took my place. The first paramedic, a wiry man in his late forties, placed an oxygen mask over Tegan's face, covering her pretty visage with the ugly plastic. The other, a plump woman in her thirties, measured clear liquid into a syringe.

'Don't hurt her!' I shouted. 'She's only little, don't hurt her!'

Nate's arms clamped around me, held me back to stop me interfering. He held me close, whispering something into my ear. I knew it was comfort, reassurance, but none of it sunk in. I was fixated on the needle, and I flinched as the woman injected the contents of the syringe into Tegan's thigh. Nothing happened. She didn't suddenly sit up, fighting for air. She didn't move a fraction to let us know she was OK. She didn't even flinch when the paramedic injected her. She lay motionless on the ground. As though horrified by Tegan's lack of reaction, Nate's arms slackened around me and his reassurance faltered. My knees buckled and I landed in a heap on the ground.

It's over, I realised as the paramedics exchanged concerned looks. *She's gone.*

chapter forty-five

I wandered blindly along the hospital corridors, aware of nothing, feeling nothing. I was numb. Physically and mentally numb. I stopped and rested against a wall, trying to hold myself together until Nate's denim-jacketed arms slipped around me and pulled me towards his body. I allowed myself to be swallowed up by him, for him to engulf me in his arms, hold me against his chest and shush me. Without realizing it I'd been quietly whimpering as I wandered the corridors.

'Babe,' Nate whispered in my ear.

'Sh . . . I . . . I thought, I thought she was going—' My voice dissolved. I put my arms around Nate and clung to him. He was solid, dependable, the rock I needed at a time like this.

'Shhhh,' he hushed, 'it's OK. She's OK. It'll all be OK.'

'But it nearly wasn't,' I whispered. She almost died. Tegan, my baby, almost died. A few more minutes and they wouldn't have been able to get her lungs working nor her heart beating properly. My body and mind quailed every time I thought how close I came to losing her. That she had been at death's door. She was sleeping now, and breathing on her own. But her fragile little body lying in that bed, hooked up to a heart monitor, reminded me of Adele's final days of lying in a hospital bed, connected to machines.

Nate gently pulled me away from him and looked down at my face. 'It's OK,' he reiterated.

'Thank God you were here,' I said. 'I couldn't have handled this on my own.'

'Yes you could,' he replied. 'I don't think you give yourself enough credit for what you do. She's a lovely girl because of you. You know, even me, the person who doesn't like kids knows that.'

'Flatterer,' I said with a small laugh.

He smiled at me, stroked a lock of my hair away from my face.

'I hate to say it, but if ever there was a case for eating junk food, this is it – you've never heard of anyone being allergic to a burger, have you?' Nate said, succeeding in making me laugh a little more. The beam on his face deepened into a look of affection and concern. 'Hey,' he said, 'how about tomorrow I sign those papers, so you can start the adoption process for real? I know you asked me to do it weeks ago but I kind of put it out of my mind. I'll do it tomorrow. Or even tonight, when I drop you home from the hospital.'

'Really?'

'Yes. I don't know why I've been delaying for so long. Guilt, I suppose, because I shouldn't really give her up, but she's more your child than mine. Even from the day she was born you were like her second parent.'

'Oi, are you saying I'm butch?'

He stroked away the lock of hair that had fallen back onto my forehead again. 'Course not, gorgeous. I'm saying that you're going to get Tegan like you wanted.'

'Thank you,' I said and pressed my lips against his, in gratitude. There were better ways to say thank you, I knew that, but I didn't care. I had an abundance of emotion – relief, fear, love, lust, anger – surging through my veins. They swirled together, creating a dangerous cocktail of recklessness that made me kiss Nate. I didn't care about anything at that moment. I just wanted to kiss him because he'd supported me in one of the scariest chapters of my life. Because he was going to give me what I wanted by signing the papers. Because the one person who should have been there wasn't.

As our lips touched, another emotion overrode all the others: shame. It wasn't Luke's fault he wasn't here. He had to work and he didn't know what was going on. If he did, he would be here. Of course he would. I pulled away from Nate, wishing I hadn't started this.

Nate stared at me for a few seconds, confused as to why I'd kissed him then pulled away almost immediately. Slowly he raised his hand and stroked his thumb across my cheek. All resistance to him faded with that touch and when Nate pushed his lips onto mine, I let myself glide into it. I allowed his tongue to part my lips and slip inside me. I let his hand caress the small of my back and the other hand bury itself in my hair. Kissing him was so familiar. Easy. Simple. It opened up my memories to a time when I was happy. When I was a different woman. I loved this man once upon a time. I loved him now. But not like I loved Luke. *Luke.* His face elbowed its way into my head and I pushed Nate away. I really couldn't do this to him.

'I can't do this, I'm with Luke.'

Instead of replying, Nate rubbed his thumb over my mouth, caressing in the impression his lips had made – it was the erotic move he'd used on me the first time we'd slept together. I jerked my head away before I fell for it and kissed him again.

'I'm with Luke,' I repeated.

'Really?' he murmured, lowering his head until our lips were millimetres apart. 'Why are you kissing me, then, *Kamryn*?' He said my name as though it had been dipped in desire, and it had the intended effect of making passion explode in my stomach. I was desperate to kiss him again, to feel all those sensations and memories again.

I glanced away, desperate not to be seduced by Nate. I refocused my attention down the corridor, searching for something to look at that would cool me off, bring me back to reality. Something banal and everyday that would calm my mind. I stared at the coffee machine. At the plastic chairs. At an empty hospital trolley. At Luke.

Luke was standing in the corridor, staring at me. At us. At what we were doing.

His face was expressionless, as though all emotion had been blasted off with the shock of seeing me kissing my ex. Me doing the one thing he feared most.

'Oh, fuck,' Nate breathed before I had the good sense to step out of his hold.

I took a step towards my boyfriend, 'Luke,' on my lips, but he cut in with, 'Is she all right?'

'Luke it's not—'

'IS SHE ALL RIGHT?' He raised his voice to drown out my explanation.

I nodded. 'She's asleep. The antihistamine and the adrenalin knocked her out. She's going to be fine.'

Luke said nothing as he assimilated this information. Nate stepped forward. 'Look, it's . . .'

Luke shot Nate a look so deadly it could have been fired from a gun, a look that said if he didn't shut up, blood would be shed. 'Can I see her?' Luke asked me.

I nodded. 'She's got a private room, this way.'

We walked in silence down the corridor and turned the corner, our footsteps out of sync because Luke was a couple of paces behind me. He didn't speed up to catch up with me and if I slowed, he slowed. He couldn't have been clearer if he said it: 'I don't want to walk with you.'

Tiga was lying on her side in a bed with side rails. Her hair was pale against the white pillow and her face was ashen. Luke perched himself on to the chair on the left side of her bed. He stared down at her with a wounded expression on his face. I knew it wasn't because of what he'd seen in the corridor, it was because she was hurt. She'd been hurt and he hadn't been there to protect her. Luke tilted his head to one side, pressed his lips together as though stopping himself from crying as he stared down at Tiga.

'How did you know?' I asked in a low voice from my place at the door.

'I, erm, cancelled the meeting,' he whispered, never taking his eyes off Tiga. 'I got up there and turned around and drove back. I couldn't stand the thought of missing T's birthday, so I came back. I went to the community hall and Mrs Kaye told me what happened . . . What did the doctors say? Will she be all right? Will there be any side effects?'

'She's going to be fine,' I whispered back. 'She's staying in overnight just in case of complications, but she should be fine. She'll be knackered for the next couple of days, until the antihistamines wear off, but there should be no lasting side effects.'

Luke took her little hand in his, bent his head and touched his lips against the back of her pale hand. 'See you tomorrow, Gorgeous,' he murmured. 'Sleep well.' He got up from his seat, still staring at her, then turned and stopped short for a second, as though he'd forgotten I was there. He composed himself and stalked out of the room as though I didn't exist. Checking Tiga was still asleep, I turned and left the room to follow him.

He marched down the corridor at a breakneck pace. 'Luke,' I called, trying not to raise my voice too much in the hospital, I didn't want to disturb other people.

He didn't ignore me in the purest sense, he didn't reply, but he speeded up as he heard my voice call his name. I increased my pace, trying to catch up with him, our footsteps making a flat squelching sound on the rubberised floors.

I followed him out of the hospital and into the car park.

Out there I could raise my voice and I did, bellowing, 'LUKE!' with a ferocity that scared me.

He stopped, then spun to meet me which caused us to collide because I was closer to him than he realised. He caught me in his hands, then shoved me away as though touching me had burnt him. I stumbled back and he stood watching me. His burnt-orange hazel eyes that had been gazing tenderly at Tiga not five minutes ago, raged with something close to hatred.

'What do you want?' he asked, his voice flat but frighteningly aggressive.

'Let me explain,' I said, not daring to move any nearer to him.

He shook his head. 'No.'

'But . . .'

'But what? I don't need an explanation. It's quite clear what's been going on. You've been playing me for a fool since day one. I was the stand-in; someone to play happy families with until he came back.'

'You know that's not true,' I said, hurt that he would think such a thing.

Luke nodded, reluctantly. 'Yeah,' he conceded, 'I know that's not true.' He took a step closer and I could see how exhausted he was, having spent most of the day driving. 'But you know what is true? What is true is that *I* − ' he poked himself in the chest − 'love her. *I* − ' another chest poke − 'would do anything for her. I'd die for her if I have to. I WANT TO BE HER FATHER! And *he* − ' Luke pointed an angry forefinger in the direction of the hospital building − '*he* doesn't. He doesn't give a crap about her. He'll never love her.' Luke brought his finger back and jabbed it angrily at the hospital again. '*He'll* never care for her like I do.'

Luke was right about that one thing. Nate would never care about Tegan like Luke did. He may have tried but it was always that – trying. *Trying* to love Tegan. *Trying* to understand her. And if he thought there was some chance of it ever becoming easier, of him caring enough about her like a father should, he wouldn't be willing to sign away all parental rights.

'He's only around because of you. Because he wants you. And you're so fucking stupid, you've fallen for it.'

'Don't call me stupid,' I replied. 'I haven't fallen for anything. Nate isn't that calculating.'

'You're pathetic,' he spat. 'Sticking up for that man. That man who couldn't even pretend to give a crap when his daughter was rushed to hospital. Actually, no, he must have thought it was Christmas, the perfect way to put the moves on you.'

'He gave a crap enough to be there at his daughter's birthday party though,' I snapped back at him. 'And where were you? Working. At least Nate didn't put work before his daughter.'

'You really can't see that everything he does is to get into your knickers, can you?'

'At least he fancies me.'

Luke's face twisted in confusion. 'What?'

'At least I know that Nate fancies me. Always has done. From the moment he saw me, in fact, he thought I was attractive. Sexy. Gorgeous. He never thought I was ugly or needed to lose weight.'

Luke's eyes darkened, and he lowered his head. 'I can't believe you've brought that up. That was a long time ago. Things were different then.'

'Do you think it doesn't hurt, still? That I could forget how you used to look at me, the things you said?'

'No, I guess not. But I suppose if I slept with your best friend and fathered a child with her you'd forget that, wouldn't you? You'd be willing to jump into bed with me the first chance you got.'

410

It was my turn to lower my head, I put my hands on my face. This was wrong. I was meant to be apologising, explaining that it was a one-off, that I wouldn't be kissing anyone except Luke ever again.

'Ryn, I love you,' he said, his voice quiet and measured. I looked up at him, his face had softened. 'And I always knew that you and Tegan came as a package deal – you can't have one without the other. And, to be honest, that was fine. I love you, even though I liked Tegan first. But I— I can't understand why you would want a man who doesn't love your daughter as much as you do.'

'I don't want Nate.'

Luke sighed, rolled his eyes a little and shook his head. 'I don't think that's true,' he said. 'And I'm not going to stick around to find out if it is or isn't.'

'You're leaving me?' I was so shocked I nearly fell over.

'Ryn, you don't get to kiss someone else and still be with me.'

'But it wasn't like that. I didn't . . . I was so scared about Tegan and he was there and you weren't. And I wanted you. And he said that he was going to let me adopt Tegan for real. And I was—'

'Ryn,' he cut in. 'Tell it to someone who gives a fuck.'

He turned on his heels and marched away. His car was sitting a couple of parking bays away but he didn't acknowledge it.

I stood and watched him walk out of the car park onto the street, disappearing into the Saturday afternoon throng that passed the hospital.

chapter forty-six

'I'm glad you're better,' Luke said to Tegan. 'I was very worried but you're all better.'

I stood by the doorway of the small hospital room, watching them. The adventures of the day before showed on Tegan's heart-shaped face: her skin had been bleached white by the drugs, dark shadows lurked under her eyes and a greyish tinge coloured her lips.

Luke had brought her another birthday present – a photo album that had a maroon leather cover and a gold embossed 'T' in the bottom right-hand corner. He'd already stuck in a photo of the two of them at the beach when we went to Whitby for the day. Tegan held the album in her arms, watching Luke with suspicion and apprehension – she could tell something was wrong. He wasn't the best at hiding his feelings and his distress was radiating from him in waves. I'd called him last night, left a long rambling message on his phone asking him to call me so we could talk but he hadn't. Nate, who couldn't apologise enough, who genuinely hadn't wanted to damage my relationship (I wasn't fooling myself, he wanted me and Luke to split up but not like that) had offered to drive me to Luke's place but I'd turned him down. Luke obviously didn't want to speak to me and I didn't blame him – I'd messed up, I'd hurt him, why would he want to talk to me?

'What's the matter, Luke?' Tegan asked.

'Nothing,' he replied, avoiding her eyes.

'Mummy Ryn says that when there is something wrong,' she admonished. He should know by now that she was an expert on picking up the feelings of those close to her.

'OK, there is something wrong,' he admitted. My heart stopped, was he going to tell Tegan what I'd done? 'I have to go away.'

'Go away where?' Tegan asked, her eyes wide at the very idea. My eyes doubled in size too.

'Remember I went to New York last year?' She nodded. 'Well, I'm going back there, to live. I have to go to London first, to finish this job,' he said. Tegan's face became a mask of horror. 'I went for the interview when I was in New York,' he replied to all the unasked questions circling my brain. 'They offered it to me a few weeks ago. I accepted it yesterday.'

'But why?' Tegan asked.

'Because it's my job,' he said.

'Are you really going to heaven to be with Jesus and the angels and my mummy?' she asked suspiciously.

Luke shook his head, 'No. Not at all, T. I'm going to America. Remember, I showed you it on the globe?'

'Is it because I was ill?' she asked. 'I won't be ill no more, promise. Double promise for ever and ever.'

Anguish flew across Luke's face at her pleading tone. 'Of course not,' he reached out and took her hand in his. 'Of course not. Baby, even if you were well, I'd have to leave. It's something I have to do. I have to go.'

'Don't you like me no more?' she asked.

'Tegan, I don't just like you, I love you. You're the best thing that's ever happened to me. I wish I could stay but I can't. I'm sorry.'

Tegan's face fell even further into misery. 'Aren't we friends, no more?' she asked.

'Of course we are,' he replied. 'We'll always be friends.'

'Are you still Mummy Ryn's boyfriend?' she asked.

I held my breath.

'I can't be her boyfriend if I'm in America.'

'I don't want you to go,' she said, her voice without hope.

'I don't want to go either,' he replied. 'But I have to.'

The corners of her mouth turned down and she stared at her hands. She was trying not to cry, I guessed. She was brave like that.

'OK, baby,' he eventually said, moved towards her. 'I have to go.'

'And you're never coming back?' she asked.

'No,' he replied. 'But I'll call you. And I'll write to you.'

'OK,' she replied sadly, clearly not believing a word of it.

Luke closed his eyes as he hugged her. She moved her arms as far around his torso as she could get. She hadn't looked so sad in months. Untangling himself from Tegan, I saw his eyes were glistening. He kissed her on the forehead and then forcing a smile, said, 'Bye, T. Tegan. Bye. I love you.'

'Bye, Luke,' she whispered.

'I'll be back in a minute,' I said to Tegan as Luke shut the door behind him. I opened the door to go after him. This would be the last time I got to speak to him, I had to stop him leaving us.

I expected to have to run to catch up with him but he was a little way down the corridor. From the look of him, the way he leaned against the wall, his face in his hand, his body shaking, I guessed he was crying. I walked up to him and placed a hand on his shoulder. When he didn't shrug it off, I slid my arm around both his shoulders. 'Let's talk?' I asked.

We sat in the canteen, without drinks, hunched over in our seats, staring down at the Formica tabletop in silence. I'd been surprised but pleased when he agreed to talk. It was a glimmer of hope. I had one eye on the clock, though, because I had to get back to Tegan. She couldn't be on her own for long, not if he was still going to leave.

'Luke, I'm sorry for kissing Nate,' I began. This was where I should have started yesterday, with an apology. 'And I'm sorry that you saw me, I can imagine that hurt a lot, but it was the first time. The only time. I was just terrified about Tegan and all my emotions were mixed up. I would have told you, you know. Because I want to be honest with you. I know that you never understood this, but, Luke, you're the one I want to be with. I love you. It's not been easy because you and I had to work to even start liking each other, but you turned up in my life just when I needed you. You've helped me grow up. And yes, that's mostly to do with Tegan being around but it's to do with you, too. You've helped me and you've helped Tegan, I don't want you to go.'

Luke's reddened eyes watched me talk.

'It was only a kiss you know, just that one time. Nothing more. I haven't slept with him. I wouldn't do that to you. I know how that feels and I wouldn't do that to you. The kiss shouldn't have happened but it did and I'm sorry. I'm terribly, terribly sorry. But please don't leave us because of that.'

He watched me until I stopped speaking. 'Ryn, if Tegan loved Nate like she loves me, would we be even having this conversation? Would you be back with him?'

I paused before answering. I was sick of this. I'd had enough of being the imperfect one with suspect motives and impure thoughts. Why was it always me who got in trouble for not being clear and single-minded about my reasons for doing things? There was no one on earth who knew, without a single sliver of doubt, what they wanted 100 per cent of the time, who wasn't tempted and swayed even momentarily. I wasn't the only person on earth – in this relationship – to have doubts, but I was the one who was constantly having to defend myself. Defend my thoughts – even though I didn't express them. If we

415

were going to play the 'what if' game then we had to play it properly. Not just with me in the defendant's seat.

'I don't know, Luke,' I replied. 'But she doesn't and she does love you so I can't answer that question. Not even in abstract because even if you do leave now you'll still have been around, how she feels about you will always be that barometer. But if we're going to go down that route, let me ask you something, if it wasn't for Tegan, would you have even thought about having a decent conversation with me, let alone kissing me or going out with me?'

It was his turn to pause. His pause elongated into one of his noisy silences. He couldn't even lie. Did he understand now that 'what if?' wasn't fair when, under a different set of circumstances, you were asked to polarise things into one moment of time, when you had to defend what you wanted at a completely different moment?

'And, whilst we're here, I have to know something else – why didn't you tell me you'd been for an interview when you were in New York? And that you were offered the job?'

'Because I wasn't going to take it.'

'But that's why you were so hesitant about moving in with us, wasn't it? You were still wondering if you should take that job.' And go back to Nicole.

Another silence when he couldn't deny the truth.

'OK, maybe you'll have an answer to this question. When I said I didn't want any more children, you didn't think I meant it, did you?'

'But you'd be such a good mother . . .' He stopped as he realised what he said. Even after all this time, all our conversations, all his reassurances, he still said it.

'You don't think of me as Tegan's mother, do you?' I said, tiredly. 'And if you of all people don't, how is anyone else going to?'

'I do. That came out wrong. I do think of you as her

416

mother and I saw how brilliant you were with her, and I wanted you to have more kids. With me.'

'But I told you, I don't want any more. Didn't you believe me? Did you think I'd change my mind or something?'

He reverted to silence.

'I told you I've never wanted children, I haven't changed my mind, I never will. I suspected you didn't understand that but I ignored it, thinking it'd be all right . . .'

'It doesn't matter now, does it?' Luke interjected. 'I'm leaving.' He didn't want to play this game any more. Not now he found out that 'what if?' wasn't fun when you're not the wronged party.

'Yes, you are,' I replied calmly. He was going, there was nothing more I could do to stop him. I'd apologised, I'd explained, I'd told him how I felt. All of it no good. Nothing would do any good, he'd made up his mind to go and that was it. That day in the hotel when Nate tried to get me to come home with him, nothing he could have said would have made me come back. Nothing, except, 'It's not true.' Luke was going. I had to deal with it.

'I hope you and Nate are very happy together,' he spat.

'Thank you,' I replied, not rising to the bait. I got to my feet and as I did so, I decided I was finished with defending myself when it came to this. I did a bad thing in kissing Nate but not as bad as not forgiving Adele before she died. Nothing I did could be that bad. 'Keep in touch with Tegan, please. She's going to miss you.'

'I'll miss her. Bye.'

'Bye.'

'Did you say bye-bye to Luke?' Tegan asked, clutching her photo album to her chest.

I nodded, trying to smile at her. I sat in the seat he'd sat in by her bed and put my head on her lap. 'I'll miss him,' I said.

417

And I would. In less than a year I'd lost three people I loved. First Adele, then Ted, now Luke. It was too much. Too much loss in a lifetime let alone a year.

'Mummy Ryn, is Luke really going to 'Merica?'

'Yes.'

'Are you sure? Because I think he might go to heaven.'

I turned my head to look at her. She squeezed her mouth and nose up in that way she did to emphasise something as she nodded her suspicions at me.

'He's not, Tiga, I promise you. He's going to America. And it's not your fault, I promise you that too. He had to go.'

'OK,' she said, and patted my head. She started to stroke my hair like I was the cat she'd desperately wanted at one point.

'It won't be so bad with just me and you,' I said. 'We'll be all right.'

'We'll have fun,' she agreed.

'We can go on holiday. Maybe to Italy where my friend Ted lives.'

'Really?' she said excitedly. 'On a plane and everything?'

'Yeah. In the summer holidays maybe? Just the two of us.'

'Mummy Ryn, that would be fun. And I could take lots of pictures with my new camera. And then put them in the 'bulm.'

'Yeah.'

She smiled to herself for a minute then sighed. 'I wish Luke was coming.'

'I do too,' I replied.

Rat-a-tat-tat! Sounded at the door. Tegan and I exchanged puzzled looks. 'Come in,' I called.

The door opened and Meg appeared in the doorway. Tegan's face lit up.

'Look who I found in my car,' Nate said, his face appearing in the doorway, too. 'I thought you might want her, Tegan. Was I right?'

'Yes,' she laughed.

'Good, cos I don't think she liked it in my car.' He entered the room and handed Tegan her rag doll.

'Mr Nate, Luke's gone to 'Merica and he's not coming back,' Tegan said as Nate perched on the edge of her bed. Nate's navy-blue eyes darted to me for confirmation. I nodded that it was true. He frowned slightly, asking with his eyes if it was because of the kiss. I nodded again and regret flew across his face. 'Oh, that's sad, I'll miss him,' Nate said to Tegan. He may not have meant it but he had the good sense to sound convincing.

'You're not going to 'Merica, are you, Mr Nate?'

'No, I'm not,' he said. 'I'm not going anywhere.'

Nate turned his eyes on me, fixed me to the spot with a steady, intimate gaze and my mouth curled up into a smile because I knew he meant it. I knew that out of everyone in our lives, he'd never leave us.

chapter forty-seven

Dearest Kamryn,

I've asked Nancy to send you this a year after I die. I'm not trying to spook you out or anything, I just wanted to make contact with you, if that makes sense? And to remind you that you're doing a wonderful job bringing up Tegan. How do I know? Because you couldn't fail to do anything else. You may not have wanted children, but I've never seen you back down from a challenge yet. And this is one you'll excel at, of that I'm certain.

I know Tegan's in good hands with you and that you're in good hands with her – I'm sure you know what I mean.

I hope that you will have found my other letter by now. If not, then I am disgusted, lady! You haven't been through my things? Didn't you even want to see if I had anything of yours?! Well, I did. I had that black velvet jacket I wanted from the day you bought it – and that's where I put the other letter which explained about me and Nate and why I did what I did.

If you have found it, then now you know and I hope you don't still hate me. I was wrong and I'm sorry. I have learnt though, that life is short, too short to bear a grudge. Too short to shut people out without listening to what they have to say first. Beautiful, sort it out with Nate before it's too late. I never saw two people who were more suited to each other, please talk to him, let him explain. Give him the chance to make things right – I know that's all I ever wanted.

Remember that first day we met? You were so instantly nice to me. Yeah, you were prickly and acted like you didn't give a crap about anything but you'd betrayed yourself, Ms Matika. I knew we were going to be friends because rather than follow-through with not wanting to come for a drink with me, you did. And you were just lovely — although not in the traditional sense. You just, I don't know, it was like you couldn't help yourself. No one has ever treated me like that before or since. No one has ever taken to me instantly and stuck with me. Thank you for that. I never said it, but thanks for being my friend. Thanks for being you.

Oh, I'm rambling . . . I'm sorry. I miss that most of all with you. We used to talk for hours about nothing, didn't we? I never had that with anyone else after you moved to Leeds. No one would tolerate it apart from Tegan and, well, she had no clue what I was on about most of the time.

I'll go now, beautiful. I just wanted to say goodbye properly, I suppose.

I'm pretty sure we won't have had the chance and I wanted to say it. Good. Bye. Not bitter bye, or unhappy bye. Goodbye.

All my love, for ever.

Adele x

'are you going to be
mummy ryn's
boyfriend?'

chapter forty-eight

'Luke!' Tegan exclaims with delight in her voice and, no doubt, on her face.

I don't look up from the newspaper I'm reading, instead I reach out and pick up my mug of tea and take a sip. We're in a café about ten minutes from our flat. It's a haven for parents at the weekend because you come here, have a coffee, read papers, have a meal, and the owners of the place, for a small fee, will take your child downstairs and teach them to cook. Pizza, fairy cake, trifles, chocolate mousse, all sorts of easy things that give you a couple of hours' quiet time. They're making pizza today – in about five minutes the supervisors will come up and get the children and right about then you'll see parents' shoulders relax and tension fly off their faces, and we'll smile conspiratorially at each other like prisoners let out on day release. We love our kids but time apart is good, too.

I don't look up after Tegan's exclamation because she's always doing it. It's been sixteen months since Luke left and in the early days I did it too. I thought I'd see him, and would go to call out to him, but then I'd realise it wasn't him, and feel stupid. It'd been like that when Adele died too. Even though in my head I'd know it couldn't be her, I'd get a flash of her walking down the street, standing at a bus stop, queuing in a supermarket, and would then have to stop myself calling out to her.

Tegan is still doing it with Luke. She swears blind she's seen him. And I believe she believes she's seen him so I agree with her, just so she knows I'll always believe in her. So, despite the excitement in her voice, I don't look up.

'All right, T.'

His voice is deep and smooth, and my heart flits over a couple of beats in response. I keep my head lowered even though I hear Tegan scramble up onto her feet on the chair, then scuffle sounds as, I presume, she wraps herself around him. It's Sunday, I've no make-up on, my hair is barely combed, my skin is still sleep saggy. *Oh well, he's seen me looking worse*, I decide. I sit back in the chair and then raise my head. I have to smile because Tegan has wrapped her arms around his neck, and her long legs are curled around his torso.

'All right, Ryn,' Luke says.

'All right, Luke,' I reply.

He hasn't changed much. He's still tall and muscular, no spare pounds on his frame. His head is almost shaved, his eyes are still that striking orange-hazel in his golden brown skin. The only difference from the last time I saw him and now is that he's regrown his ridiculous line beard around his lips and along his jawline.

'I don't like your beard,' Tegan informs him.

'Why thank you, Madam.' He's talking to Tegan but staring at me, probably thinking I haven't changed much. My hair is still layered with a sweeping fringe, the dark circles under my eyes have faded a little since I've become used to surviving on less sleep. I haven't lost weight or put any on. I'm virtually the same.

Tegan lifts herself away from him so she can have a better look at his beard then raises her hand to her face, rubs her cheek. 'It's itchy. That's not very nice, is it, to make Tegan's face itchy?'

Luke draws his eyes away from me back to Tegan. 'It's gone.' He has that American twang to his voice again. 'The second I get the chance I'll shave it off.'

'OK,' she says. 'Are you going to be Mummy Ryn's boyfriend again?'

'All right, Tiga, it's pizza time, isn't it?' I stand, move around the table to take Tegan out of Luke's arms.

'O-OK,' she says reluctantly. 'But it's not fair.' Standing on the chair she stares me in the eye as she makes this declaration. 'I want to talk to Luke as well. He's my friend too.'

Tegan is unrecognisable from the girl I moved up to Leeds with over two years ago, this lass has no worries about telling me what she thinks, or protesting over some perceived injustice. We often have involved disagreements over when she's going to bed and what she can and can't wear. (The infamous pink bikini top row had raged for two days and isn't resolved – she still wants one and I still won't let her have one.)

'You can talk to Luke,' I say, keeping eye contact. 'You just have to go make pizza first. Afterwards, you can come back and talk to him. OK?'

'O-OK,' she replies, realising that she's not winning this round. 'Don't even like pizza,' she adds at a mutter.

'What did you say?' I ask as I help her down onto the floor.

She looks at me, knowing that if she repeats that untruth she'll never get to eat pizza in my presence again. No more making it downstairs here or ordering it in. Tegan has worked out that I rarely shout, I'd never hit her but I will take her at her word – and there'd be no reasoning with me if she lies about something just to win an argument. 'Nothing,' she replies.

'Do you want to go down on your own or shall I come with you?'

'Come with me,' she says, slipping her hand in mine. 'See you later, Luke.' Holding hands we descend the wooden stairs into the huge basement kitchen. Tegan goes to the hooks where they've hung out small aprons and picks out a red one.

'I like red,' she reminds me as I tie the strings around her middle.

'I know,' I say, and kiss her forehead.

As I'm about to stand she throws her arms around me, not caring that it's not cool. 'Thank you, Mummy Ryn,' she says and kisses my cheek. I don't know what for. She often does that, randomly kisses and thanks me, and because I like it, I don't question it. 'You're my bestest friend,' she whispers in my ear. 'Apart from Matilda and Crystal and Ingrid. And Luke.'

'You're my bestest friend too,' I reply. She kisses my cheek again.

I climb the steps, my heart somewhere near my throat. I thought I'd never see Luke again. I'd resigned myself to a life of hearing what he was up to through his letters and emails to Tegan. I never dared hope I'd get to sit opposite him again.

When I return to the café area he is sitting in Tegan's chair, his long legs stretched out under the table. That's how Nate sits, too. It was only when Luke had gone that I noticed how similar they are. Mannerisms, ways of speaking, sense of humour.

'Well, she's grown up,' he says as I take my seat opposite him.

'But she's also become a little girl again, not having so much to worry about that isn't seven-year-old stuff, which is nice to see.'

The waiter approaches, sets down a large mug of coffee in front of Luke. 'Café mocha, easy on the coffee, heavy on the chocolate, right?' the guy says.

'That's right, mate,' Luke says with a laugh. 'Glad you remember.'

When the waiter has retreated, I ask. 'Have you been here before?'

'Erm, a few times . . . I, erm, come here most weekends. I used to come hoping to get a glimpse of you and T whilst I got up the courage to talk to you. Sometimes she saw me.'

So, she wasn't losing the plot because, it turns out, Luke has been stalking us. 'When did you get back from the States?' I ask, ignoring how unsettling that is.

His eyes dart to my left hand then dart away again, frowning at what he sees.

'About three months ago. The job didn't work out . . .' He leaves the sentence unfinished because I know something he knows I know. He made sure I knew, in an attempt at revenge, I guess.

'Did your wife come back with you?' I ask.

Luke married Nicole six months after he left Leeds. We got the news and photos in the office a few days after the wedding. I'd walked into the office I shared with Betsy and saw the picture open on her computer screen. She'd slapped her hands on the screen to try to hide it, but it was too late. The image of Luke's handsome face, grinning with happiness as he held his bride, his Nicole, in his arms, was scorched into my memory. I'd made the right noises to Betsy about being pleased for him and brazened it out the whole day. I threw up in the staff loos before I left and cried into a pillow in the middle of the night when I was alone.

'No, she's still in New York,' he reveals. 'She's staying there too. My marriage didn't exactly work out either.'

'I was surprised at how quickly you got married, but then it was to Nicole. I suppose it was easy to pick up where you left off.'

'Not that easy as it turns out, she wasn't . . . How's Nate?'

Our eyes meet, he searches mine for a hint of what I'm about to say. 'He's fine. Better than fine, actually, he's great. He moved to Leeds, to be nearer to . . . Well, to be nearer. Him and Tegan are good mates, too, she even lets him pick her up from school a couple of times a week so I can work a little later.' I'm still not Marketing Director of Angeles and I never will be, I've accepted that now. For as long as Tegan needs me around I have to put my career second. 'It's funny how she bosses him around and they cook like you two used to – creating a huge mess as they go.'

Luke inhales, stiffens his upper lip as he asks in a tight voice, 'Does she call him "Daddy" now, then?'

I reach out, cover his hand with mine. 'As far as Tegan's concerned, her only "daddy" is you.'

'Really? Still?'

'Just cos you left, doesn't mean she stopped talking or thinking about you. She's asked me more than once why you didn't want to be her daddy.'

'What did you say?'

'That if you were around, you probably would do. Nate knows that too. He wouldn't try to take your place.'

'He's her father.'

'Yeah, but that doesn't mean he wants to be her dad. He likes Tegan, he cares for her, he just doesn't love her like you did. But, he'll always take responsibility for her. Luke, he's a good guy. You and him could be . . . Could have been friends if you'd given him a chance. He always liked you for how much you cared about Tegan, you know. He's always wanted what's best for her, and if that means letting someone else be her parent, then that's what he'll do. He signed away all rights to her.'

'Really and truly?'

'That day I kissed him, he said that's what he'd do and he did it. You wouldn't believe the amount of grief he went through when his parents found out, but he didn't back down, he just wants what's best for Tegan. And he's sticking around for ever – as her father, not her daddy. He'll do anything for her. Luke, take it from me, Nate's a good person.'

'Are you and him . . .?'

'No.'

'Why not? I'd have thought you'd have . . .'

'Been engaged and married before your plane took off? No, me and Nate couldn't get back together, too much has happened, we've changed too much.'

'So you didn't even . . .?'

'I'm not a saint, Luke,' I reply. 'Much as I pretend I am.'

It was two months after Luke's departure that Nate and I made love. And, on and off, for a year, we carried on doing so, always stopping before we started a full-blown relationship. Then we'd be tempted again and fall back into it. Recently we'd stopped altogether, had gone cold turkey because we admitted that we were actually in a relationship. And we weren't free to be boyfriend and girlfriend. Boy had 'cheat' hanging over his head and Girl came with a child. Nate liked, possibly even loved, Tegan but didn't want her full time, I'd forgiven and understood about Adele, but I hadn't forgotten. Those things would always keep us apart. Besides, 'Nate's got a girlfriend now. They've been together three months and it's looking long-term.'

'Do you mind?'

'Not as much as I used to, believe me.' I'd broken down in tears in front of Nate when he told me, but managed to stop myself asking him to finish with her. I had to let him go, I accepted. We both had to move on, and he'd been brave enough to take the first step towards that. It still hurts that he's with someone else, but every day it's easier. I accept it's for the best. 'It's good to see him happy.'

'I mind that you mind,' Luke states.

I'll ignore the fact that you got married, shall I? 'Nate and I could never get back together. I mean, I hold my hands up, I fancied him, I still felt stuff for him but I had this amazing boyfriend.'

The old me loved Nate more than anything, he was everything to me; the me who'd been bringing up Tegan loved Luke, and the life – the family – we'd created, more. That had shocked me when I realised that. I loved Nate, but I loved the weekends of Luke, Tegan and I cleaning the flat, of trips to the park, of tickle-fighting Luke while Tegan kept score, of sitting in front of the TV and listening to Luke and Tegan discuss the finer points of drawing with felt-tip, more. More than anything else in my life, I loved my hotchpotch little family. 'I had this amazing boyfriend who I adored. And even though I was tempted by this other guy, the only man for me was my boyfriend. And despite the fact he went off and married someone else, I didn't stop loving him.'

'You mean that?'

'Wouldn't say it if I didn't mean it.'

He sits forwards, takes both my hands in his and strokes his thumbs along the back of my thumbs. 'You know, it was only months after I'd left that I realised what you were asking me when we were sitting in the hospital canteen,' he says. 'I thought you were accusing me again of not loving you like Nate did. Then I worked out that you were asking me if I loved you at all. Independently of Tegan.

'Because you never thought I did, did you? You didn't realise that yes, Tegan brought us together but I would never have dated you if I didn't genuinely feel something for you.

'I fell for you the day you had your migraine. When I found out who T was to you, it was as though a curtain was lifted and I saw how incredible you were. Then I thought I had no chance because of how vile I'd been to you but I kept hoping . . . That day I first kissed you, I was so nervous. The whole drive back from London I kept thinking about your eyes, your smile, the smell of your skin mixed with Emporio

Armani Day. When I was in New York I used to go stand in the perfume section of Bloomingdale's and smell it because it was you. And that's why it didn't work with Nicole – she wasn't you. Ryn, I did fancy you. I did think you were beautiful. You're the most beautiful woman on earth. That was after everything else I felt for you. I love the way you answer questions with a question so you can stall for time; the way you go out of your way to look after people but pretend you don't care; the way you—'

'I've told you before, if you keep saying things like that, I'll think you're flirting with me,' I cut in.

The expression on Luke's face hardens. 'That's why I never said them, though. You wouldn't have believed me, you told me that, good or bad, you don't believe what others say, so I stopped saying them. I tried to show you how I felt in what I did, not simply what I said. That worked, didn't it?'

'I'm sorry, Luke,' I say. 'I've only ever had one person say those things and mean it. I didn't quite believe there'd be two people who could think them ... But, let's be honest, you always seemed to back off whenever I tried to take a step forwards and then I find out you had your escape plan worked out all along. I've never seen someone disentangle himself from a life so fast. Are you surprised I didn't believe you loved me?'

'Yeah, but I'm an ass. Things go wrong and I take to the road, that's what I do, that's what I've always done. And for me, Nate reappearing was the ultimate worst-case scenario. He had more claim on you and Tegan than me, I was preparing for what I saw as the inevitable. Although I have to say, you're an ass if you didn't believe I cared for you independently of Tegan.'

'I'm glad you're back, Luke.' I grin at him, then recall he hasn't actually said as much. 'You are back, aren't you? Back to be a part of our lives?'

'Yes, but things have to change.'

'Yeah, I know. And the first change is that you've got to be honest with me. Tell me everything, job interviews, plans to get married to me or someone else. Everything. And I'll do the same.'

'OK, I can live with that.'

'The second change is that you've got to accept that Nate is a part of our lives, for better or worse.'

Luke scrunches up his lips, gives a short nod.

'I mean it, Luke. It's over between me and him but he's here for ever.'

'OK. But I don't have to like him, do I?'

I sighed. 'I suppose not. But it'd be easier for you if you did. I don't want Tegan feeling caught between you two. She's very clever and as she's got older she picks up on everything, so no nastiness, OK?'

'OK, my condition is that we talk about having more children.'

My heart sinks. 'I don't know . . .'

'We just talk about it. It's not fair on Tegan that she's got no brothers and sisters, you had them, so why can't she?'

'Erm . . .'

'We just talk, Ryn. And if we decide no, then we decide no. It's not fair that we've never talked about it properly; that you've made up your mind and I've got no say in it. That's not what a relationship is about. I mean, it could be adoption, but we talk.'

'OK, we talk, but I'm warning you, Luke, Tegan's more than enough for me.'

'I think she might be for me, but I want us to talk about it.'

'Cool, we'll talk.'

He grins.

'Of course, you do realise that if we do get back together, there'll be lots of gossip – you're a married man and I'm a single mother . . . My reputation will be in tatters: "Single mother in sordid sex shocker with mucky married man" . . .'

434

Luke leans out of his seat and pushes a languid kiss onto my mouth. I can't help but sigh into it, I'd forgotten how good he was at that. As he sits back, Tegan comes into view. She's standing by our table, a grin so wide, you can hardly see her face. This is what she wanted – me and Luke back together, her and Luke friends again. Behind her stands a less than happy cooking supervisor.

'Ms Matika, I really must talk to you about Tegan's behaviour!' she says with barely restrained anger. Tegan climbs onto my lap, snuggles into my torso as she looks reproachfully at the cooking supervisor. It's all an act, she's not really worried or feeling vulnerable, she simply knows I'm less likely to get cross if she's playing at being my little girl.

'What's she done?' I ask.

'In the middle of cooking she decided to come back up here. When I said she had to finish making her pizza, she told me to "stuff it!"'

This girl is a nightmare sometimes. Luke swivels in his seat to hide his face while his broad shoulders shake with silent laughter. Obviously he thinks it's funny – it's not him getting told off. 'Maybe she meant the pizza?' I offer hopefully. 'She might have seen those stuffed varieties on television.'

The supervisor fires me a look of disdain and snottily adds, 'I'm sure she's been picking up lots from television, but not that, Ms Matika.'

No, that excuse wouldn't have washed with me either. 'Tegan, say sorry to . . .' I glance at her name badge. *Adele.* My heart skips a beat and a lump forms in my throat like it always does when I think of her or hear her name. 'Tegan, say sorry to Adele.'

'Sorry, Miss Adele,' Tegan says, looking and sounding suitably sorrowful. 'I didn't mean to be horrible, I won't do it again.' She didn't have to add that bit but I'm glad she does.

Mollified, Adele crouches down in front of Tegan. 'That's OK, precious. I'll see you next week.'

Tegan nods and manages to keep her sorrowful look until Adele has returned downstairs. When she's gone, Tegan turns to face me, her big eyes beseeching me not to shout at her. 'I'm sorry for being naughty, Mummy Ryn. I wanted to see Luke. I thought he might go. I don't want him to go.'

'Luke's going to stick around for a while,' I reply. 'Aren't you?'

'Sure am, gorgeous. I'll be around so much you'll both get sick of me.'

She grins, showing all her perfect white teeth. 'Mummy Ryn, can I tell Luke?' she asks.

'Of course, baby.'

'I've got a new name,' she proclaims to her returned best friend. 'My name is Tegan Brannon Matika. I've got the same name as Mummy Ryn. We are family, now. Proper, proper family.'

'That's fantastic!' Luke exclaims. 'T, I'm so pleased for you! And you, Ryn. When did you find out you were finally allowed to adopt her?'

'We got the final certificate two weeks ago. It's been a long road, two long years, with social workers, counsellors and courts but we got there, didn't we, baby?'

Tegan gives a short, decisive nod. 'Mr Nate bought us 'hampain but only Mummy Ryn was allowed to drink it. I had fizzy pop. It was OK. And Mr Nate took us to the cinema and to pizza.'

It was only as I looked at the adoption certificate that would replace Tegan's birth certificate that I realised what it signified, what it truly meant. It meant I didn't need to worry about how I said goodbye to Adele, I could stop fretting that I hadn't told her I forgave her, because she knew. My best friend knew that I'd love her no matter what because she had left me her most precious keepsake. She had trusted me with her one true love. And adopting Tegan, turning my best friend's girl into my girl, was all the forgiveness Adele would have needed. She hadn't screwed me like I thought she had all that time ago, she'd simply changed my life like I knew she would that first time I met her.

'Guess what, Luke?' Tegan says.

'What, sweetheart?' he asks, smiling at how I cradle my daughter in my arms.

'I think Mummy Ryn is going to let me get a cat.'